CU00970940

Alun Lewis

COLLECTED STORIES

Alun Lewis

COLLECTED STORIES

Edited by Cary Archard

SEREN BOOKS

SEREN BOOKS is the book imprint of
Poetry Wales Press Ltd
Andmar House, Tondu Road, Bridgend,
Mid Glamorgan

© The Estate of Alun Lewis
ISBN 1-85411-012-8

All rights reserved. No part of this publication may be
reproduced, stored in a retrieval system, or transmitted
in any way or by any means, electronic, mechanical,
photocopying or otherwise, without the prior
permission of the copyright holder.

Cover illustration by permission of
the Estate of Alun Lewis

The stories in Part 1 of this book were
first published by Allen & Unwin Ltd in
The Last Inspection (1942) and
In The Green Tree (1948).

Typeset in 10½ point Plantin by Megaron, Cardiff

Printed by Billings & Sons, Worcester

CONTENTS

Part II

from *THE BOVIAN*

from *THE DRAGON*

from *THE SERPENT*

from *THE MANCHESTER GUARDIAN*

MISCELLANEOUS

UNPUBLISHED STORIES

INTRODUCTION

Alun Lewis (1915-1944) was the finest short story writer of the Second World War. This recognition should have come sooner but until recently critical attention has been largely concentrated on the *poetry* of war. The prose, for some reason, has been largely neglected.

Born and brought up in South Wales, Lewis was only twenty-four when war broke out, yet within three years he had published a book of poems, *Raiders' Dawn* (1942), and a collection of short stories, *The Last Inspection* (1942). After his death in Burma in March 1944, on the very edge of action, two more books appeared, a collection of poems, *Ha! Ha! Among The Trumpets* (1945), and *In The Green Tree* (1948) which contained a selection of his letters from India and six more short stories. Nearly all of Lewis's published work was written following his enlistment in the Royal Engineers in May 1940 while he was training to be a soldier and an officer, first in England and later, at the end of 1942, in India.

Although Lewis wrote short stories from an early age, he has been regarded primarily, and sometimes totally, as a poet. Two of the most influential books about him emphasize his poetry. Ian Hamilton in his *Alun Lewis: Selected Poetry and Prose* (1966), which re-awoke interest in Lewis's writings, refers to him as "the outstanding poetic talent to be wasted by the Second World War" and makes available just six of his stories. In his introduction to *Alun Lewis: A Life* (1984), John Pikoulis calls Lewis "The first poet of his generation". Most books about Lewis have implied that he is pre-eminently a poet and the tendency has been to play down his achievement as a short story writer. Until now it has been impossible to challenge this emphasis: whereas a selection of the poetry has been in print since 1981, the short stories have been unavailable since the nineteen forties.

This Collected edition aims to show that Lewis's short stories have been unjustly neglected. Part I includes all the stories he published in his two books — his mature work. Part II contains a selection from the stories Lewis contributed to magazines as he grew up — his apprentice work, as it were. Although not his finest work, they are all worth reading. The final six stories have been chosen from the dozens of unpublished stories he wrote in the period 1936-1940. These were difficult years but very important for Alun Lewis's development as a writer: a time when he was finishing college and couldn't decide what direction he should take as he tried journalism and teaching, when the war broke upon him with all its moral choices and creative force.

Lewis's writing career began when, in 1926, he won a scholarship to Cowbridge Grammar School in the Vale of Glamorgan, a boarding school twenty miles to the rural south of Cwmaman, the mining town where he had been brought up by his school teacher parents. At Cowbridge his precocious talent was encouraged by his enthusiastic English teacher, Eric Reid, and his stories appeared regularly in *The Bovian*, the school magazine. John Pikoulis has commented about the six remarkable stories written between the age of thirteen and sixteen:

These are his earliest writings and constitute what I take to be one of the most remarkable sets of juvenilia any great writer can have produced.

From 1932-1938 Lewis was a student. For four of these years he attended University College Aberystwyth, where, in 1935, he obtained a first class honours degree in History, and to which he returned in 1937 to complete a year's teacher training. While he was at Aberystwyth, Lewis contributed no fewer than eleven stories to the university magazine *The Dragon*. *Y Ddraig*, as it was also entitled, was one of the most prestigious student magazines in Britain. Founded in 1878, it has been associated with the earliest work of many of the better known Welsh and Anglo-Welsh writers. The magazine's encouragement was crucial to Lewis's development as he tried out different styles and increased his range of subject matter. This process culminated in the ambitious story 'Attitude' (1938), which, in its contemporaneity and mature treatment of complex relationships, stands out from the other *Dragon* pieces.

In between these periods on the West Wales coast, Lewis spent two unhappy years at Manchester University, writing a thesis on a thirteenth century Papal Legate for his Master's degree. *The Serpent*, Manchester University's magazine, was a much slighter periodical than *The Dragon*. Lewis contributed several stories to it, not all under his own name. (He signed one 'A.A.M.' — Assistant Advertising Manager.) Generally, these stories were much shorter and less ambitious than those he had written in Aberystwyth.

Lewis's valuable association with institutional magazines continued when he taught at Lewis School, Pengam, to whose splendidly named *The Ludovican*, he contributed the only story he wrote actually set at a university. 'The Testimonial' illustrates the destructive effects of dry, academic life, through the character of a history professor who, having lost touch with reality, realizes with dread in his final dessicated days that he cannot remember the names of the real people, the students, he has taught. During his year of teaching in 1939, before the outbreak of war, Lewis was writing furiously, and a great number of the forty-odd unpublished stories, which he left in manuscript, date from this period. Some, however, were published and in a publication not now known for fiction. Three very short stories appeared in *The Manchester Guardian* (in November 1938, in February and June 1939). Although they are brief — they show extremely well his powers of condensation — two of these pieces are important in illustrating Lewis's movement towards representing political and topical events in fiction. 'Cardinali Crisis' is about the effect of Italian Fascism on a local Welsh-Italian cafe owner in the valleys town of Glanamman. 'The Poetry Lesson' is a delightful, if idealistic story, based on Lewis's recent experience of teaching English.

'The Poetry Lesson' ends with a question about the English teacher:

'What's he like?' — 'I dunno,' Pedloe answered. 'He's a funny chap. You can't tell — yet.'

It could be said that the war gave Lewis ample time to find out what sort of 'chap' he was. During his training he was forced immediately to think about the major questions of life and death, under extreme conditions. There is no doubt that Lewis's stories about soldier life, the class-ridden army, loss in war, and about the terrible strains put on love and family relationships are his finest work. Publishing circumstances seemed to help his fictional explorations of the war. Julian Maclaren-Ross, writing about short story outlets during the war, said: "There were in that peak year of 1942 — no less than sixteen markets for a short story writer to choose from." The war brought about a remarkable demand for the short story, unparalleled before or since in this century. In Wales, home encouragement came from

The Welsh Review, edited by Gwyn Jones, in 1939. Lewis contributed reviews in its first year and his famous Lawrentian gypsy story 'The Wanderers'. 'The Renunion' appeared in June 1944, shortly after his death. Between November 1939 and December 1943, Lewis contributed short stories to five different London magazines: *Life and Letters Today* published 'Lance-Jack' and 'Night Journey'; *Horizon*, itself founded in 1939, took 'The Last Inspection' and 'The Orange Grove'; *Penguin New Writing*, another magazine which the war brought into existence in 1940 as a monthly paperback, took 'The Farewell Binge' and 'Ward 'O'3(b)'; *Lilliput* published a photo of Lewis, included him in an article on the English Poets, and took his story 'Manuel'; finally, *Tribune*, the left-wing weekly, published 'It's a Long Way to Go' and 'Flick'. Lewis's outlets were not confined to magazines. Anthologies also flourished as the publishers attempted to satisfy the insatiable appetite for war literature. Lewis contributed to six of these between 1941 and 1943: his work appeared in *English Story* (series 1,2,& 4), *Bugle Blast* (1 & 2) and *Modern Reading Six*.

   The Last Inspection, Lewis's only complete book of short stories, was put together and published in a hurry. Although the book carries the date 1942, it did not appear until 1943 when it was widely reviewed in England and America. By the end of the year, it had sold three and a half thousand copies. It was at least as popular as his book of poems, *Raiders' Dawn*, which had appeared the previous year. Lewis's 'Author's Note' conveyed both the urgency of the writing and the book's publication:

> Eighteen of the twenty-three stories in this collection are concerned with the Army in England during the two years' attente since the disaster of June 1940. They are, if you like, studies of a 'hang-over'. Death in battle, death on a large scale, and all the attendant finalities and terrors — these are outside. They are the bread and water of our comrades overseas; we have the cakes and ale. The only deaths in these stories are from air raids and accidents; the main motif is the rootless life of soldiers having no enemy, and always, somehow, under a shadow.
>
> Written out of immediate experience, typed up on leave, impelled by a perpetual sense of urgency, they are rather personal observations than detached compositions; and, *faute de mieux* I leave them to say what should be said: — that in England it was thus and thus, in a time that — God be thanked — is past.

   In fact the book included 19 stories not 23 as the author claimed. At least two other stories had been considered, 'The Paying Guest' and 'Duration'; the latter is published for the first time in the last section of this volume.

The Last Inspection was arranged in three parts: the first and third contain stories directly linked to the war, the middle section's five stories are specifically Welsh. The tendency has been to underestimate the Welshness of Lewis's writing, especially when the argument has been based on his poetry. Although his 'Author's Note' does not mention Wales, and although most of the short stories do clearly deal with the 'phoney war' period, almost half of the collection's stories contain significant Welsh characters and at least six of them are actually set in Wales. Of the Welsh stories in the middle section, 'The Housekeeper' is the most important. Lewis wrote many stories (most unpublished) exploring the life of a mining town like his own Cwmaman in a style that was both documentary and emotional, attempting to portray the desperation of the struggle against poverty without lapsing into political sloganizing. 'The Housekeeper' contains enough material for a novel: there is the fairly common figure in Anglo-Welsh fiction of the clever boy Jackie hoping to escape poverty through education; there's the miner father whose reliance on his allotment to provide food for the family suffers a catastrophic blow when his one and only sow dies giving birth; and there is the mother, Myfanwy, whose courage and perseverance keep the family afloat. The story is rooted in details like "his legs were so thin; his knees were little bony lumps like the stalk of the seed cabbage" and ends appropriately with the family escaping from the unpalatable realities of their life to the threepenny seats of the local picture-house: "The big picture was just ending. The faces of the characters seemed to stretch for miles, like faces in the convex mirror of a spoon."

The first half of *In The Green Tree* (1948) contains a small selection of Lewis's letters to his parents and wife written after he had left England for India in October 1942. Although the book contains six short stories completed after *The Last Inspection*, it was the letters which attracted most attention at the time. Walter Allen, reviewing the book in *The New Statesman* praised Lewis's prose above his poetry and singled out the letters as the finest writing:

"It may be that these letters will ultimately take a higher place than either the poetry or the stories for, like Keats's, they point to a maturity beyond anything their author had been able to express in his works . . ."

Nevertheless these 1943 stories, all, bar one, set in India and Burma, are remarkably assured and represent Lewis's finest achievement in the short story. The one exception to the Eastern settting, 'Night Journey', would have been perfectly at home in *The Last Inspection*. Lewis said more than once that the war had created a world of chance meetings and journeys. 'Night Journey' is set on a train journey from Paddington to Wales and examines in Mansfield-like detail the interactions among travelling soldiers in a single compartment. Such is Lewis's skill in the form that almost through dialogue alone the reader learns of the war's profound effects on these soldiers' lives. Lewis's own journey to the East added another dimension to his writing. The five Indian stories exhibit a new density of meaning, an interplay of surface description and psychological depth rarely found in earlier stories. Whereas the war stories set in England rarely go beyond the character and his immediate problems or treat army life on the satirical level, a story such as 'The Raid' achieves its power by questioning the whole point of the British in India. Through the central character, Selden, Lewis exposed the superficiality of the British understanding of India. Selden's 'heroic' capture of the pathetic Indian terrorist questions not just the purpose of the British presence in India but also underlines the meaninglessness of all war.

'The Orange Grove' is surely Lewis's masterpiece. It is much more than a story *about* the British in India. No brief analysis can do justice to its power and suggestiveness, its layers of meaning. Beales, the officer on reconnaissance, attempting to find his way back to camp loses his way and is gradually stripped of all his civilised supports. After the murder of his driver in stormy darkness and the abandonment of his truck in an unnamed river, "naked man" as he is, he struggles to survive in a world he no longer understands and is forced to rely on a group of wandering gipsies. The story ends:

Stumbling up the track in the half-light among the ragged garish gipsies he gradually left the stiff self-consciousness with which he had first approached them. . . . He wished, though, that he knew where they were going. They only smiled and nodded when he asked. Maybe they weren't going anywhere much, except perhaps to some pasture, to some well.

All that matters in the end is one's own place, the orange grove, the pasture or well — Beale puts his trust in a simple humanity whose life has an instinctive integrity which was unavailable to the British Officer.

The six unpublished stories which complete this *Collected Stories* have been selected from the forty or more kept among Lewis's manuscripts. These stories are interesting in their own right but they also reveal how Lewis was developing during the two or three years immediately before he joined up in May 1940. 'Duration' was written after this period and, on the evidence of the girl's name Gracie, was worked on about the same time as 'Cold Spell' (whose heroine has the same name). It was probably excluded from *The Last Inspection* because it handles the theme of sexual desire between the departing soldier and his girl in such a direct and uncompromising way. Certainly the treatment of the same theme in 'Cold Spell' is more subtle and oblique. The other five stories have been selected to give the reader some idea of the extraordinary range of Lewis's styles and themes in a period when he was still learning the craft of the short story. For instance, he adopts a wide, almost bizarre, range of narrators, from monks and tramps to elderly women and young girls.

'And at my Departing' (a line from a popular prayer) is narrated by an elderly spinster on holiday in St. Malo. Many of the details are based on Lewis's own walking tour of Normandy in August 1938. This story blurs the line between dream and reality (Lewis was very interested in dreams) — the reader begins to realize, before the narrator herself, that her sudden illness and strange dream are the harbingers of death. The untitled story beginning "Enid didn't know what to do" is seen through the eyes of a young girl on her fourteenth birthday who feels she has to mark the day in some way she has never experienced before. It is a story of the change from innocence to experience as in the space of a short mystery bus ride Enid sees for herself the terrifying force of sexual desire. The story fills us with a sense of the ugliness of this force and of its uncontrollable energy. Both of these stories are interesting for their obvious experimentation with symbolism. In the former, the narrator dreams of a child buried up to its neck in the sand calling out for help as the tide comes in. In the latter Enid, having left the bus for a short stroll, comes across a pool of eels:

They were wriggling all over each other, all over each other. It made her wriggle inside. She could feel them trying to get up the rock, wriggling against each other and against the dribble of water that washed them back. Their eyes were too small for her to see them, and they had such funny bodies, so thin and with no features, no hand or anything. They didn't seem real at all. They were the same all over. And yet, they were alive, terribly alive, and they *wanted* to get up that slimy rock!

'Impasse' is typical of the many heavily allegorical stories Lewis wrote in college and during this period. The inability of beauty to survive in a hostile world, the corruption that lies behind the beautiful appearance, is the most common theme of Lewis's adolescent stories. In 'Impasse', Beauty, the greyhound, experiences an end some readers might find both shocking and melodramatic.

The longest of the stories included in this section is just one of his attempts to write about Morlais, the miner's son growing up in a small town like Cwmaman in the 1920's. It bears comparison with 'The Housekeeper' from *The Last Inspection*, indeed in its authentic dialogue, realistic detail and unvarnished portrayal of working class family life it surpasses the story which Lewis chose for publication. It could easily be an extract (perhaps re-written) from the unpublished novel *Morlais* which he worked on throughout 1939. In a typical passage Morlais seeks solace outside his home:

Morlais wandered out into the backyard. The darkness settled his disquiet, dissipated his apprehension. He knelt down by the rabbit hutch. There was no sound. He made hissing noises with his lips: there was a scutter in the straw of the inner compartment. He smiled and pushed his fingers through the netting, feeling for and finding the warm deep nostrils that trembled against the pads of his fingertips!

In its faith in life, in the trembling yet nevertheless direct way it touches and explores both the dangerous outside world and the inner world of caged darkness, the story of Morlais is typical of all the stories collected in this remarkable volume.

Cary Archard, August 1990

(The editor wishes to acknowledge the invaluable assistance and warm hospitality of Gweno Lewis and her brother Hywel.)

I

THE LAST INSPECTION

The Last Inspection

Everything was O.K. in the loco sheds. A couple of sappers were running the shed doors up, the grey rainy half-light swirled into the dusk of the sheds, lapping against the glittering green engines and the braziers of burning coal where the fitters were working on a broken down shunter, everything was O.K. Old Baden-Powell, an L.N.E.R. 1910 box engine detailed for the day's special job, hissed and screamed fierce clouds of steam while the driver and fireman just touched her up with big swabs of cotton waste and a fitter with a flare lamp squeezed a last drop of oil into her nipples.

December 31st, 1940, and the Brigadier ready to start his last tour of inspection before retiring with the old year. He had retired once before, but when war began he came forward in the same spirit of service as the rest of us to help the nation in her war effort. He was very fat indeed, with a red apoplectic face, and he walked slowly just to be on the safe side. He was going to see everything today, for himself. It's only natural when you're retiring, you want to see for yourself whether any work has been done during your tenure of office, how things have been getting along, sort of thing; because when you're at the helm you haven't any time to go dashing into the stokehold to supervise the trimmers, have you? You even have to rely on the word of your mate that the anchor has actually been raised.

The sergeants in the sheds were arguing about beagles. One said beagles only hunted hares. Another said that was wrong because there was a pack of beagles at Woolwich Arsenal and they didn't hunt hares because there weren't any hares left in London. Another one said beagles didn't hunt hares anyway; down his way they used "lurchers" for hares, mostly on a Thursday. There were a lot of sergeants in the shed. Nobody knew what half of them were doing.

Fred Tube was driving old B.P. He was a driver on the London to Brighton line in civvy street, cool as a cucumber at seventy an hour.

Morgan Evans was firing her. He had a boil on his neck and he was browned off. He chucked his cotton waste away and sat on a packing case and yawned.

"Have a fag, Mogg?" Freddy said, finishing wiping the oil off the scrubbed footplate.

"No thanks," Mogg said, yawning again. "I've chucked smoking. Somebody's got to lead a clean life, even if the missus won't."

"It's cold these mornings," said Fred. "I'm wearing my long pants."

"Too thick for me," Mogg said. "I've sent mine to my old man. He's warm, even if the old lady isn't."

"What are they? Pensioneers?"

Mogg nodded.

The R.S.M. came out of the loco office, resplendent in Sam Browne and brown shoes, looking most important.

"Get her out of the sheds, Tube," he said. "Come on, Evans. What are you lounging about for? None of your Bolshie ways here. Get cracking. Waken your ideas up. And remember both of you, don't jar her when you brake. Brake her gradually. There's a dining car on her to-day. If you tip any of the dishes you'll be on a charge for careless driving. And I'll see to it you get no mercy. Get cracking."

"Yes, miss," Mogg muttered, swinging himself onto the footplate.

They pulled out of the sheds, picked up the two posh carriages that had been waiting for fifteen years in the carriage sheds for this supreme occasion, the diner and the saloon, comfortable as upstairs in the pictures, smelling of carbolic and Jeyes and the simmerings of lunch, and rolled along to the regulating station to pick up the party.

They were all waiting, the colonels and captains turned out like new pins by their batmen, the women in sables and astrakhan with little veils on their hats and silk stockings showing right up to their knees. And in the middle of them a mountain of flesh and khaki in a brass hat with a lovely red band round it, the Brigadier. Beside him his daughter, a blonde whom the boys called Unity, and beside her, at a decent interval, her fiancee, a dark thick moustache and a cap pulled down over his nose. He was only a second lieutenant and he wouldn't have been allowed to come if he hadn't got engaged to Miss Unity, so he got engaged. He was due for a couple more pips now, no doubt. Leave it to Unity, as the boys said; it was a kind of slogan in the camp — when the latrines wanted cleaning out and that.

And off they all went.

There were a lot of things to inspect. The camp area was several miles square and the military line wound about like an undecided snake from barracks to barracks, from construction yards to stores depots, from ordnance dump to M.T. park. And at every station a guard of honour stood on the cinders that made the platform and slapped their rifles when the sergeant yelled Pree-zent — AMMS and the whole party piled out and the Brigadier saluted and inspected the guards' buttons and the whole party piled back again and Freddy Tube said "Up, Nelly," and off they went.

During the last twenty years they had been trying to make the two ends of the railway meet by constructing a loop at each end which was to meet in the middle at a point among the gorse and scrub which was marked X on the big chart in the Brigadier's office. But one thing and another had prevented the completion of the task during peace time. There was no real urgency in peace time. Now things were different. National emergency, supreme effort. When the Brigadier came out of retirement to answer the call he said "The line *must* be completed. Immediately." It would show he realised the gravity of the situation. But the line hadn't been completed although he had spent many week-ends in London — before the Blitz — in trying to get the War Office to allocate him sufficient construction stores. Meantime the work gangs went out to the job every day and did what they could. In winter it was rough on them because they couldn't keep warm without working, but in summer it was O.K. Anyway the Brigadier was looking forward to seeing how much they had done. It was *his* line, his monument.

But first lunch.

Freddy drew her into the siding and he and Mogg sat on a lump of coal each and ate the huge bully beef sandwich they'd drawn from the cookhouse before coming to work.

The diner was next to the engine. Mogg went for a stroll along the line to hear what they were eating.

Lunch was scheduled to take an hour and a quarter. Then the party was to transfer to a little open internal-combustion car which would run them along the new loop line as far as it went. But it was cold and morbid out, and — damn it all — it began to drizzle a bit; the windows of the diner were wet with drizzle outside and with condensing heat inside; and lunch took longer than they expected. You can't knock such good red wine and old scotch back in a hurry, it's a crime, and when a fellow is retiring like that, well, it's a shame to gabble the speeches off and hurry off and get wet and catch a cold as like as not. So they cancelled the inspection of the new line. With regret.

Mogg and Freddy were sorry, too, for one of their mates was waiting on the party and he'd promised to save them a bottle of scotch and some

fowl which they'd be able to eat when the party was off down the line.
And the sergeant in charge of the work gangs was sorry, too, for he'd
gone to the trouble of indenting for 80 pairs of gum boots for the men
and getting the men to wear them for the day. And now he'd have all
the trouble of collecting them at evening and returning them to
Brigade Stores without the compensating pleasure of the Brigadier
remarking on how well equipped the men were.

But there you are. An order is an order.

Mogg enjoyed listening under the windows in a hungry sort of way.
There were four speeches, three by colonels about the Brigadier and one
by the Brigadier about the three colonels. And then there were four
toasts. The Brigadier. The Ladies. The Army. And of course The King.

Then the Brigadier said he had one last toast to propose.

Silence in the diner.

"To Victory!" he said.

"To Victory!" they all replied.

Mogg strolled back to the footplate where Freddy was dozing by the
fire. "The war's nearly over, Fred," said Mogg, grinning sulkily. "We've
dug for Victory and saved for Victory. And now they're drinking for it."

"D'you think there'll be any left for us?" Fred said.

Then a waiter came along with two glasses of whiskey on a tray
marked Players Please.

"From the old man," he said.

"Hacha!" said Fred, grabbing a glass. "Come on, Mogg, this'll
warm you up."

Mogg took his glass.

"To the old man," said Freddy.

"To his successor," said Mogg. "Let's hope he knows there's a war on."

"Now then, none of that Bolshie talk," said Freddy, savouring the
drink on his tongue. "You don't know no more about it than the old
man. So drink his whiskey in a Christian spirit."

"Who said it's his whiskey?" said Mogg, sticking to his guns.

Then the R.S.M. came along and told them to get cracking.

And did old Baden-Powell make a dash for home?

He was in the sheds, cooling down, before you could look round.

"*And* I didn't jar the brakes, neither," said Freddy, the master
craftsman, patting the antedeluvian tank.

"There's a telegram in the office for you, Fred," somebody said.

"Oh Christ," said Fred, turning grey at the thought of his wife and
kids in Shoreditch. "Oh Christ. Oh Christ."

Mogg took his arm, gently.

Flick

When he joined our battalion in January '41 I was a soft-foot subaltern fresh from O.C.T.U. with no experience of actual fighting. He came to my platoon. I remember looking at his dirty book, then at his strong travel-tired face and square body loaded with equipment. F.L.C. Wilson was his name.

"Lot of initials, Wilson," I said, rather fatuously. "Call me Flick, sir," he said, a little grin in his close-set blue eyes. An unusual way for a private to address an officer; but it was so natural I scarcely noticed it was strictly — shall I say? — improper. I glanced through his paybook. Payment in French and Belgian francs from March to June 1940, then no entry until January 1941. Odd I thought.

"Why this gap in your pay?" I asked.

"The paymaster'd done a bunk, sir," he said. I liked the little grin he had in his eyes. "I stayed in Belgium till I got browned off. Then I did a bit of hitch-hiking through France and Spain. Home again, now."

"Christ!" I said, looking at him with awed respect. "Do you smoke?"

He didn't tell me much then; he was tired and had to draw some blankets from the stores and get a snack in the Naffy before it closed. But I got most of the story out of him bit by bit during the next week. He didn't want to talk about it; he waited to see what I was like first. He could be a mule, I discovered.

He'd been in three prison camps. In occupied France he'd killed two sentries with a knife in getting away. In Marseilles he'd drained 100 Czech lorries of petrol, filled the tanks of a pleasure launch anchored off the island where he was jailed, and with two others sailed three days for Gib. before being picked up by a French destroyer and yanked back to solitary confinement and trial for theft. A brave French barrister defended him, arguing successfully that the Czechs were British allies and that theft was therefore inadmissible. He got away again and made for the Spanish frontier. Two Scotties went with him; both died of exposure in the Pyrenees. (He lived for three weeks on a bottle of whiskey and wild plants and snow). It took him from October to December to reach Madrid. The Embassy smuggled him home.

He'd discovered several petrol and munition dumps during his wanderings and had blown them up. The War Office checked up on this at an interview they gave him. A general thanked him and recommended him for seven days leave and a commission. He didn't get the seven days because the battalion was expecting embarkation; he refused the commission; so he was, as he said, just about where he'd started. I asked him why he wouldn't take a commission. He shrugged his shoulders.

"It isn't what I'm looking for," he said; his eyes I noticed could become very reflective, despite their laugh.

I got to see his way of looking at things after a time. It was so simple that it baffled me for a month or two. In such men you look for cross motives. His impulse was basically direct. He didn't want rank; swagger cane and Sam Browne didn't concern him. Similarly, before the war, he didn't want to be top of the form in school, or a know-all in College. His old man wasted a lot of money on him by the time he reached Greats at Oxford. Then he gave it up and went into business through his father's connections and insistence. He didn't want that, either, but he wanted to be independent of his father, who was fed up with him, so he got his elbows shiny and mooched along on the theory of diminishing returns. What you might call a failure; or the aimless youth which is the raw material of Fascism, etc., etc. Only you see he had a constant underlying seriousness, a touchstone of good sense; also a purpose in living, though its unfulfilment meant perpetual restlessness. You wouldn't ask a man what he wanted to become; you only ask children that, and you feel an old fool even with children. I never asked Flick what he had in his mind; I knew he was serious though.

Anyway he didn't want a commission. He was nearer what he wanted in the ranks, kipping down in dirty blankets, eating off boards, drinking in any old boozer, knocking off for a smoke during a day's digging or wiring, yarning quietly with the colliers and labourers who were his mates. He wasn't the submissive type and I knew a lot of things riled him. The way the R.S.M., immaculate and peremptory and arid, snarled at the men when he was inspecting them on guard mounting; or the retarded coarse little C.S.M. keeping them on parade for twenty minutes after a route march out of sheer bloody-mindedness; or the O.C.'s fussy and not over-competent interference in their daily ritual of weapon training and gas training á la pamphlet —

all this angered him. Only he didn't see that he'd be any less involved as an officer. What he wanted to do was to get out of it. He wasn't a peace-time soldier, he said, and as soon as it became clear that the Battalion was not going overseas he put in for a transfer to Commando. The O.C. was relieved, I believe; he didn't understand a man of Wilson's experience and 'social qualifications' (*quelle phrase!*) refusing even so much advancement as a stripe; he felt uneasy with him — the little grin in the blue eyes — and strongly recommended his application.

I managed to sneak a fair bit of time in Flick's company. It was taboo in the battalion for an officer and private to consort; so we got out of the place as much as possible, or he came round to my bunk in the nights and we argued about life and friends and motives till the small hours. I grew to think that my chief duty was to waken his imagination; he'd become very like a Hemingway man, taking what came, selecting his friends by trial, valuing nothing higher than independence, mistrusting all ideologies. I argued Socialism at him, got him to read again — it didn't matter what; his taste was the better for its neglect — and we had a good time together. We talked more and drank less during the three months he was with us. And his spirits became more spontaneous, more responsive. He was worth a lot on route marches or the dull hours of the big invasion exercises. He'd get a rabbit or a pheasant for supper; he'd find and chat with the wise and eccentric old people of farms and pubs; he carried the anti-tank rifle on his strong shoulders when the march got over-long for the rest — he called it his next-of-kin; and he never let the hypnosis of footslogging and subservience subdue him. When he left us at the end of May every man-jack in the platoon, from me to 28 Smith who carried the mortar and always had a moan, regretted his going. We all had a drink with him the night before, even the teetees; and afterwards I strolled under the pines with him till God knows when in the dusky glow of the moon. It was as if he had something he wanted to tell me, I guessed; later I found I was right; but he didn't manage to break the long silences with it. Going to turn in at last he said, "Well, good-night, chum. I think this war is worth winning after all. Thanks for straightening it out for me. I didn't understand there was so much in the balance." And off he strolled without a handshake.

He wrote one or two letters during the summer, but not much. He liked the Commando better than the battalion; less blanco and bluster about it, more chance of action; otherwise not much difference; they didn't seem to bother about the war, he said, and wished I was near enough to argue about Lenin and Lilburne and Milton and Franklin

D. I wrote back and said I didn't know why I wasn't.

Well, in the autumn I got a third letter from him. One about as long as the other two — that is, short enough to quote in full. I'll copy it out when I've finished this last thing that happened.

News doesn't travel fast in the Army; your pals may be killed or sent overseas, dropped in France or thrown into Madagascar before you find out by chance when you're on leave, or meet someone in a pub. So it wasn't till January, just a year from the time I met him first, that I heard what had been Flick's particular luck. He was in the Commando which raided Vaagso; and he was one of the unlucky ones. Actually it was an H.E. bomb from our own planes that got him; perhaps he was at fault, perhaps the pilot misjudged it a bit. Not that it matters; the thing is, Flick is dead. I was told that in a pub. I did a sloppy thing in a way; ordered a pint and left it on the counter for him.

This is his letter. "Dear Nicky, — I'm told there's something big in the air, and for once I've got a hunch I'd better tidy my affairs up — not that it's possible to tidy them much. Look, will you do me a very great honour? If I don't come back, keep in touch with Mrs.... of ...(an address). She's the mother of a girl I was engaged to before I went to France. When I was missing after Dunkirk, Mary (my fiancée) had a baby boy. She was a nurse and she went back to nursing. She was killed in November, when I was in the Pyrenees. Her hospital had a bomb, dead-plumb. Her mother is a brick and is looking after the child. I haven't seen him. Couldn't, somehow. Please help them when you can, Nick. Sorry to bother you. Cheers. Flick."

Private Jones

Dafis the post came down the lane to Siencyn's cottage earlier to-day than usual. He walked his bicycle through the stony muddy ruts, ringing his bell to call them out. Siencyn was still in bed, but Marged, his wife, had been up a couple of hours, feeding the wild chickens that nested in the apple trees and gorse bushes and mixing some swill for Granny the sow.

"It's come, Marged fach, it's come," Dafis shouted, his excitement at a gleeful pitch. "Siencyn's notice is come."

He brandished a small brown envelope.

Marged straightened her heavy body, wiped her wet hands in her sack apron, showed nothing.

"Diw mawr," she said to herself, thinking that something important was happening inside her.

"Siencyn!" Dafis called, leaning his bicycle with its tied-on parcels against the crumbled wall of the cottage. "Your calling-up notice I got for you. Look alive, boy."

Siencyn poked his long head out of the tiny bedroom window, his hair the colour of swedes. He was in his flannel nightshirt.

"Coming now, Dafis," he said cheerily and withdrew. He pulled his trousers and clogs on, and came downstairs buckling his leather belt across a handful of trousers, very excited.

Dafis opened the letter, Marged looking over his shoulder. She was twice his size.

"Printed matter," Dafis said. "There for you. Instructions, look. Railway travel voucher. Free trip, see?"

"In the train?" Siencyn asked.

"Third class," Dafis said. "From Cardigan station, Great Western Railway, to Talcen station, ditto. East Wales Fusiliers it is for you, Siencyn bach, poor dab. Plenty of V.C.'s they got already. Watch out, you."

"East Wales Fusiliers, is it?" Siencyn repeated. "Well, well. Third class?"

"When is it?" Marged asked.

"Friday next, 21st inst.," Dafis said. "Take your identity card, Siencyn bach, don't forget that, now. Or it's C.B. you'll be right from the word go."

"Jawch," said Siencyn, "there's a lot to remember, Dafis. Where's my identity card Marged? In the poe in the spare room, is it?"

"And your birth certificate is there," she said, knowing where to put her hands on things. "You'll have to find somewhere else to keep your things from now on, Siencyn bach."

"Aye, that's true," he said, rubbing his tangled hair. "Well, I better go round and tell everybody."

"Don't trouble," Dafis said. "I'll tell them on my round. Stay you, my boy. I'll come down to-night and give you a bit of wisdom, see? Four years of it in the last war I had, and no more for me thank you." He looked at his right hand, from which three fingers were missing. "German sniper did that," he said proudly, and then screwed up his red bunioned face into a wink. "Held it up above the parapet, see, Siencyn, and got a nice little blighty. But there, you don't know what a parapet is yet, I don't doubt."

"I'll learn," Siencyn said, with all the good will in the world.

"You will," Dafis said, speaking with the sardonic finality of experience. "Solong both."

"Solong Dafis, thank you," Siencyn said.

Dafis pushed his bicycle off, the cycle clips pulling his small trousers up nearly to his knees. He wore a straw boater all the year round, Dafis did.

The third winter of the war was just relaxing its grip on this closed corner of Cardiganshire; six weeks of frost had held up the winter ploughing and the spring sowing, and Siencyn had been having a soft time of it, lying in bed in the mornings, chopping a bit of firewood, mending a few broken scythes and shafts, patching up the cowsheds of his employer, cutting enough hay for the drayhorses, and a pint or two some nights. He had been medically examined and registered a whole year back, but his call-up was deferred for the summer harvest and the autumn trapping, — Siencyn was the offical trapper of the parish and sent four hundred and thirty-seven rabbits to Cardigan station, Great Western, in five weeks, — and then the winter ploughing. He had got tired of waiting, restless and unable to merge himself in his work and the weather and the requirements of the horses and of Marged. He was a good-natured man, but out of patience with things. He had quarrelled with Marged a lot this winter, beating her once, leaping out of bed on a Sunday morning when the cracked church bell was tolling, and beating her for calling him an idle heathen. And she used her tongue on him for that. Said that people were saying things about them. What things? She shrugged her shoulders. Once he'd cleared out of the way, they were saying, perhaps they'd discover before a year was out whose fault it was there were no babies coming in their house. Well, that wasn't a nice thing to say, and it says a lot for Siencyn's good nature that he only shrugged his shoulders and said pity they hadn't got more important things to think about than that. She didn't use the rough edge of her tongue on him again, but she was very secretive and moody all the winter. He didn't worry about her; he'd go and she'd stay behind; she was his wife; there you are; nobody is indispensable; she wouldn't want to leave the place she'd been born in, whether he went or not. It was different with him. He wanted to see the world. Lots of the boys from round about went into the merchant navy; either the sea or the land it was with all the boys. And he held it a grudge that his widowed mother had kept him home to work at odd jobs instead of letting him go to sea. His father must have been an old soft, too; he wasn't wounded and he wasn't ill in the last war. He just died. Ran home three times from the army, and then died in detention barracks. Heart-broken, his mother said. Well, what a complaint for a man!

Nobody had a bad word for Siencyn, except that he was idle and fond of his drink and irregular as a christian and not reliable for doing a job or fetching you something from market or being prompt at the chapel concert rehearsals. So, when he went round to say solong, everybody was sorry to see him go and genuinely hoped the army would make a man of him before it got him killed. Old Mari Siop, who had a soft spot for anybody in trousers, said she thought strong men like him ought to stay at home in case the Irish attacked us. And he had a real good walk-round, ending up at the Ship hotel, saying good-bye and drinking basin after basin of tea in the cottages and then a pint all round on the house. This was on his last night, and you wouldn't believe the offers he had to knit comforts for him, and old drovers and flannel vests fetched out of the cupboards where they had lain since their wearers had died. He took them all, and all that he didn't drop on the way down from the pub he carried into the kitchen where Marged was sitting doing nothing by the wood fire. She was cross with him for taking them; they'd be saying how she couldn't look after her husband's pants even. She was always seeing the worst side of everything these days. She was almost fit to cry with desperation over a little thing like that.

So they had a bit of bread and milk for supper, not saying anything at all. Then he fetched the money from under the bed upstairs and counted it out, five pounds thirteen and four, and divided it into two piles, three pounds thirteen for her and two pounds for himself. And then he got up and very clumsily and hesitantly smoothed her hair back. She was vexed, and said what a mess she was, all untidy and fat-getting, and she bent her head forward as if she was feeling bad; and she was all white and her eyes were yellow and suffused with watery blood. He was shifting from one foot to the other, uneasy about what to do, and she wouldn't say a thing one way or the other. Dumb she was.

And he was thinking how happy everything and everybody had been when he went round the farms this afternoon, and now Marged spoiling it all. But when she looked up at him, raised her head to him slowly as if there was a millstone round her neck, and then stood up with her arms raised a little, and said that Welsh word to him that she hadn't said since they were courting, then he knew it was a million times better to feel black and torn in pieces like this than to be laughing and drinking tea and saying the Germans wouldn't last long now he was in too. He picked her up, and she wasn't heavy any more; and carried her up the creaking stairs as if she was a young virgin. Only she was better than a virgin, her fine big body which his big shivering hands slowly divested of the red jersey and thick skirt and woollen stocking and flannel vests that she wore on it winter and summer. The moon was out and the river ringing on the stones and the old jollyboy owls crying goodywhoo in the wood, and he knew he'd been waiting for this for a whole year, to say good-bye to Marged like this. And she lay warm and silken and trembling under his huge hands and she heard neither the river nor the owls but only him grunting and breathing in her mouth and in her ears and something gentle at last opening inside her, like a baby begging her to receive it in.

Onions she boiled for his breakfast the next morning, and two hard-boiled eggs and a whole small loaf uncut for his pocket, and off he set, six miles to walk to Cardigan station. Dafis the postman had forgotten to bring him some stamped addressed envelopes, but he had found a letter in the grandfather clock with their address on it. He didn't know how to write the address himself, but somebody would copy it off this old letter for him when he got there, no doubt. So everything was alright. Plenty of wood left for the fire and Marged walking to the crossroads with him, and the weather crisp and young, the cockerels crowing all the way in to Cardigan station, and Dai Pencwm passing him on the road giving him the benediction of the big pew. His heart was like a feather, walking like this through his own countryside, seeing the sea through gates in the sandy hedges, and singing Dr. Parry's *Jerusalem* to himself which was this year's test piece at the Eisteddfod, and feeling a free man, as if he owned the place and no need to pick up a shovel nor a scythe nor the handles of the plough....

There were other men like him on the train the last part of the journey, from Swansea. But they were different to him, smoking cigarettes and wearing posh navy suits and pointy shoes, with white silk scarves and grease in their hair. He sat a long way from them and he felt hot and uneasy. But when they got there it was all in together and fags out and form up in threes with a soldier showing you how with a silver-knobbed cane, and march through the streets into the barracks. Then he lost direction and control, there were so many things and people. He knew how to sign his name, S. Jones, where they told him, but they wouldn't give him enough time to do it in, and he had to keep on signing in every room they went into, whereas he had never signed his name more than twice a week before, on the dole that was. But he was doing pretty well out of it; same as last night everybody was giving him things — mug, knife, fork, spoon, blankets, bag for straw, khaki suit, leggings, boots, cap, and lots of straps that he didn't know what for. And then a rifle and a bayonet. You didn't take long to become a soldier, for a fact. Then they had a good meal in the cookhouse, with girls in khaki doing for them, and then the most of them went out for a booze, and cursing everything they were when there were no corporals about. But Siencyn didn't open his mouth, and he was frightened a bit because he'd lost count of what was happening, and he wanted to lie down and sleep, being suddenly very weak and shaky and yawning all the time. As for Marged and all them at home, they didn't exist any more. It was all up with them, there was no doubt.

"You're looking buggered, Jack," a dark man said, sitting on the floor cleaning his rifle in the empty barrack room.

Siencyn, like a frightened animal, watched him suspiciously.

"Yes," he said. "Yes."

"It isn't worth worrying about this lot here," the man said. "They don't count in this war. They're all peace-time soldiers. They don't know what the war's about, they only want to stay here and shout on the square and take the tarts out. You keep your head up. Don't pay any attention to them."

"Yes," said Siencyn not understanding much except that the man was friendly, "that is so for a fact."

The man began cleaning his buttons with a button stick and silvo.

"I'll learn you how to do things," he said. "They don't mean anything, all the things they do here, but you might as well do them properly, just to show them there's nothing in it, and then get on out somewhere where there *is* a war."

"You been a soldier before, is it?" Siencyn asked, friendly with him now, like a dog that barks first, then growls, then wags its tail and sidles up.

"Not in this army, mate. I fought two years in Spain, though. Seen a bit of it then, like."

"For a living, is it?" Siencyn asked, shifting up, willing to listen.

"No, not for a living," the man laughed. "A collier I am for a living, when the pits are open. Collier, stay-in striker, party member, anything's better than keeping a greyhound, chum."

"Spanish they speak in Spain?" Siencyn asked.

"No, not much now. German and Italian they speak there now. But it doesn't matter much there now."

"*This* war will do for me alright," Siencyn said. "Farm labourer I am, see, and trapper."

"That's right. You keep to the plough, mate. It's only a knife in your back or a few years in jail or no work and no friends you'll get if you start doing what you believe in. I've never had time to marry a wife, and yet I've never done nothing I can show."

"I'm married," Siencyn said. "It isn't very much of a thing; only down our way you got to get married if you want any peace, see." The man smiled, and Siencyn smiled back, and then sat thinking of the thing he'd just said.

"No girl in the valleys would take me on," the man said. "They want a steady man, see. I'm an anarchist. I won't go and live in two rooms and feed my kids on bread and dripping and make them sell the *Football Echo* and read the race results in the paper and shout hooray in the park on Labour Day."

Well, well, thought Siencyn, this is a different life to mine, and what it all is I don't know. But I wouldn't like to be on the wrong side of this man, because he is like the prophet Ezekiel, and he can kill people by seizing their wickedness in his hands and squeezing it till they choke.

And Siencyn became devoted to this man, and he wasn't afraid of all the things that happened to him in the next few weeks.

Well, Siencyn became 283749551 Private Jones, S., before you could look round, and the nickname he went by was Timoshenko, which was something like Shenkin, his own name. And the first morning he wore his battledress he had to take it all off and lift his shirt and cough and bare his arm and have a needle in it, all in a whirl, walking round the room with all the others because there was no time to sit down and no furniture, not like waiting for the doctor at home. And then they all walked past a man in a white apron standing on a stool and they had to open their mouths for him and when he looked in Siencyn's mouth, he said "Christ! Take the lot out. Top and bottom plate for this man. Ever used a toothbrush?" Siencyn said yes, because he'd used one in the infants' school, but he wasn't a kid any more so of course he hadn't used one since. He was a married man now. Jawch!

He was very bad after that, with a big swelling under his arm, and he crawled into his bunk like a sick animal and lay there till he was better, which was a day later. And then he had all his top teeth out, and his new boots were hurting something wicked, and he didn't have a handkerchief to wipe his bleeding mouth which was dripping into the tin of potatoes he was scraping, and the sergeant called him a dirty something and the next morning he was marched into a room and the officer looked fierce at him and said "283749551 Jones, S. Is that your name?" And he was told by the officer to get a shake on and wake his ideas up and not to come back to him again or look out. And Siencyn said he didn't want to come back to him again, not likely, and then he saluted the way he'd seen them do it, and he'd have smiled just to show there was no ill feeling, only his mouth was full of blood. And when he got back to his bunk and they asked him how he got on, he grinned — because he'd spat the blood out on the way back — and said "The bastard!" And that made everyone laugh and slap his back and say he was a bloody good soldier already, calling the O.C. a bastard like that. And he always called everybody a bastard after that if they said anything rough to him, which was nearly always, and he felt better straight away then.

After he'd been there a fortnight and getting on famous with the boys and not too bad with the sergeants, and knowing how to slope and present, and halt and start up again, and fix bayonets and standing load, and unload, and two weeks wages, ten shillings a time, a telegram came for him, and that made him hot and excited and the centre of every eye, as you might say. But it was only Marged wanting to know if he was alright, because on account of forgetting to bring Dafis's stamped addressed envelopes he hadn't written home, not liking to ask any of the boys to copy the old address out for him; and no news is good news, isn't it? But the O.C. sent for him again and asked him if he had quarrelled with his wife or what, and told him it was bad for civilian morale not to write regularly and tell them you was getting on fine. So he confided to Daniel Evans from Spain and Dan wrote a letter for him in two shakes and addressed it and they posted it together on the way to the Naffy, and Dan said why hadn't he asked him before, it was nothing to him and he'd write Siencyn's letters regular for him. If he wasn't such a good man and a good scholar and knew everything about fighting and mining and unemployed and capitalists, Siencyn would have grabbed him by the waist and wrestled with him the same as they used to do in the country when they was boys in school and big friends.

And at the end of three weeks the whole issue of them was sent off by train to the east coast of England to finish their training in a battalion that was short of men and wanted them handy in case of invasion. And in this new place it was the same as before only worse if anything. They had a new sergeant-major who shouted like a bull and you could smell his breath when he shouted. He came up close and shouted in your face, so you could only *think* he was a bastard, he was too near for you to mutter it. But their sergeant didn't like the sergeant-major and told the boys that he was separated from his wife for stripping her and thinking out dirty things to do to her, and he was only shouting like that because he wanted to keep in with the colonel. So Siencyn didn't bother about the sergeant-major shouting, now he knew there was no religion in him. But some of the boys that you'd have thought wouldn't care a bit — boys always boasting about what they'd done, big breaks in billiards, supper in married women's houses and that — they became like shivering wet rats after a bit and the sergeant-major used to pick on them all the time and shout at them till they shivered all over, only with Siencyn and Spain he never bothered at all. And as for the sergeant, well, he couldn't keep a straight face on parade with Siencyn. And when Siencyn caught a rabbit one day out on an exercise by putting his hand in a hole where he knew a rabbit was, and gave it to the sergeant to give to the grass widow he was always telling them about, the sergeant was always kind to him after that. Siencyn couldn't remember all the names on the Bren gun and the mortar and the 36-grenade and the anti-tank rifle and war gases and all that. So the sergeant never asked him the names when they were being tested.

The only fly in the ointment was the officer in charge of them. Not the young one, he was alright, nobody bothered about him; but the one with the three pips that walked around all day looking at everybody; and when he stopped in front of you on parade he grunted and muttered to himself and then told you what a bloody army you were to be sure. Siencyn didn't like the smell of him, and he didn't feel strong in front of him the same as with the other sergeants and officers.

Everybody was frightened of him, yet they all said he didn't know his job and ought to be sacked. And there were lots of stories about what he did in the nights with his spare time, but still Siencyn couldn't stand up to him. Not even when he found out that the colonel could make the captain shiver like a rat the way the captain did to those under him. And one day, when their training was over and they were taking part in brigade schemes and defending aerodromes and building dannert fences and laughing at the Home Guard like hardened regulars, the captain sent for Siencyn and said "I hear you're a country bumpkin, Jones." And Siencyn said "I live in Penyrheol, Cards, sir." And the Captain said, "I hear you were a poacher, Jones?" And Siencyn said "Trapper, sir." And the Captain said, "I'm putting you to work in the Officers' Mess, to catch rabbits and partridges for dinner, and you will be my batman; and if there's any silvo on my uniform or you get caught with a dead partridge trespassing, I'll break your bloody spine, do you understand?" And Siencyn wasn't brave enough to say no, so he said "Yes, sir."

So he became a batman for a change, and it was as bad as he feared, because when he woke the captain in the mornings it was like shaking a nest of adders; he always had a liver and a white tongue and never pleased with anything. But sometimes Siencyn got away on his own, three times a week, after rabbits and pheasants, and then he was as happy as could be. When the captain was shouting for him to clean his Sam Browne or fetch some hot water because the hot water had gone luke warm on account of him not getting up when he was called, Siencyn felt as bitter and cynical as Dan Evans Spain, who was always sneering at the talk in the papers about fighting for freedom and decency and our children's futures. But when he was lying in the ferns watching the way the pheasants went for grubs, or setting a snare in a rabbit's run, then Siencyn really felt as if he were fighting for freedom and the right of a man to live his own life. Anyway, it was no good looking at things the way Dan Evans did. No doubt it was true all he said about the coal owners taking all the profits and the children without a decent pair of boots or a warm coat, and about the men in London exploiting the natives in Africa and India, and about the *Daily Worker* being banned like in a Nazi country; and when he put it to you you did find it queer to wonder why the poor women and babies suffered themselves to be bombed in the slums in Swansea and London when they wasn't getting anything out of it that you could see. Siencyn didn't have anything against the Russians, but all the same he didn't think it much sense wishing you could be one; and it was easy to see that nothing was the way it ought to be these days if you went by what it says in the Bible. But Dan was only making it hard for himself, refusing a stripe and barely civil to the captain and the sergeant-major and both of them with their knives in him, and it was a pity he was always getting daunted by what he read in the papers, or by what he said about the army being unprepared and untrained and unarmed to fight a war with tanks and divebombers like they'll have to. But all the same, if it came to a fight, Siencyn wouldn't think twice whose side he was on. Dan's side he was on. Dan Spain was a man and he'd like anyone to deny it.

Every now and again he got a letter from Penyrheol, written in Dafis the postman's copperplate hand, with bits dictated by Marged in it and grandiloquent flourishes of Dafis's invention embossed on it, giving him the news as it left them at present and hoping he was in the pink. The first two or three letters had nothing abnormal, except that the sow had been up to the boar and was expecting, and the latch had fallen off the back door and she had tied it with string till he came home, and her marriage book had come and she had to walk to the post office every week to draw her twenty-eight shillings, and she was putting some of it by to buy blackout curtains so she could have a light in the house after dark for a change. Then came a different letter, very brief, and not written in Dafis's hand at all, but in pencil by Marged, and it said: "Siencyn bach, wen coming back are you i am being sick in the mornings and the doctor jest been an sed i am in for a baby hopping you are not angry yewer loving Marged."

Siencyn sat with this for a long time, and then he began laughing to himself, and got up feeling like the lord of creation, and went to look for Dan Spain to tell him and see what he said. And he didn't want to tell anybody except Dan, although he was just bursting with the news. So he went out of the guard room where he was on guard and across the farmyard and through the sheds looking for Dan. But Dan was out on the cliffs the other side of the wood laying some mines, so Siencyn went after him, forgetting he was supposed to be on guard. And just as he came out of the woods and could see the grey North Sea and the black stubby shapes of a convoy jinking southwards in the middle seas, zoom-woof-scream, down came a big two-engined Dornier 215 for you, straight for the soldiers working in the minefield, straight out of the clouds over the sea. Somebody shouted and a couple made a run for it, and a few more fell on their faces, but most of them just looked up at it. And Siencyn looked at it with great interest, not having seen a Swastika before, and then it opened fire and swept past him only just above his head. One of the boys who was running staggered and clutched his guts and went sprawling, and Siencyn said "Diw Mawr, too bad," and ran out of the woods to pick him up. The plane had zoomed up over the trees behind him and was climbing in a great ellipse, going seawards, but Siencyn was only concerned to fetch the boy who was hurted, because he was one of the rest of them, and he was hurted. It was Nick Powell Tonypandy as it happened, and he was a mate of Siencyn's, they'd been on a charge together for putting Naffy buns in their respirators and he was going to get married to a butcher's daughter next leave, so his prospects were too good to waste by a bit of bad luck. And Siencyn picked him up and carried him fireman's lift, like in P.T., to the shelter of the woods. Nick was groaning and cursing healthy enough, so Siencyn told him to be quiet, it wasn't a thing to blaspheme about. And he put Nick against a tree and Nick said "He's coming again," only he didn't say it as polite as that. And Siencyn saw the Jerry diving in from the sea again like second house at the pictures and he saw the Bren gun the working party had brought out with them ready loaded by a gorse bush just in front of him in the open; so he said "Look out, boys bach," and made a dash for the Bren gun and grabbed hold of it, kneeling, with the butt against his hip. And the Jerry was coming straight for him with spurts of flame coming from the wings and bullets like a little shower of hail sweeping towards Siencyn. And a silvery bomb fell out of the plane as it came to the bottom of its gradual dive and was showing its nose to the climb, just at the sea edge of the minefield. And Siencyn said "Now!" and pressed the trigger as cool as you like. And nothing happened. Oh Jawch, there's a pity for you, Siencyn thought, what is the matter with the old thing? And the explosion of the bomb knocked him over before he could see whether the safety catch was on Automatic or Safe. And when they brought him round with plenty of cold water and his arm in a sling, Spain was kneeling by him and the captain fidgeting and muttering same as usual, and he remembered he had something to tell Spain about, but for the life of him he couldn't think what it was. And Spain said "Well done, Siencyn boy. You're a chip off the old block, you are." And Siencyn said "Is Nick Powell alright?" And Spain said "Aye, it was only a flesh wound; he's O.K. for the butchery business, don't worry." And Siencyn said, "The gun wouldn't go." And the captain said "No wonder, you bloody fool. It was on Safe. What the hell's the good of wasting khaki and food and training on a cretin like you?" And Siencyn, although he was on his back with his arm in a sling, suddenly felt immensely stronger than the captain for the first time in his life, and he looked at him and grinned and said "You bastard!"

Well, the captain's face was a sight to behold. He pulled at his sagging cheek and opened his mouth and stood on his toes and didn't say a word. Then he said to Spain, "You're a witness, Evans." And Spain said "I didn't hear a thing, sir." And he looked at the captain with a funny look in his eyes; he'd killed a tidy few men in Spain, Dan Evans had, and Siencyn got the wind up and he said, "Don't do it, Dan bach. Leave him be now. We're all in the war together so make friends, the two of you." And the captain said "Consider yourselves under arrest, both of you." And off he went to fetch the sergeant-major. So Dan sat on his heels like the colliers do in the back lanes and waited for somebody to come back, and kept on spitting and spitting and saying he'd give him what for if he dared to court martial them. He knew very well the colonel would dismiss the case if he heard what the captain had said to Siencyn when he was knocked half daft by the bomb; and Dan said he'd get it brought up in Parliament if they did anything to them; and Siencyn lay against a tree as idle and as happy as ever he'd been in his life, because he'd called the captain a bastard and Dan had said "Well done."

Siencyn didn't take long to mend; his collar bone wasn't broken, only bruised; and the colonel praised him in the court of enquiry that sat on Nick Powell's wound; and nothing was heard of the little difference they'd had with the captain, and everybody was buying him drinks in the Naffy for what he'd said. So he had a very placid fortnight on light duties because of his arm. And then, at the end of the fortnight, two things happened that demanded a good bit of thinking out.

First there came a letter for him, and it was a very short one, and it wasn't from Marged and it wasn't signed. Dan read it and said it was an anonymous letter. And it said that Marged was having a baby in case he was interested, and who was responsible, this person would like to know? Funny there'd been no baby in four years when he was living with her, and now as soon as he'd gone to serve his country she goes and gets in the family way. And then several names of likely men from the neighbouring farms and a hint that Marged had been seen coming out of the wood by Twm Gors's cottage late one night. And this person anonymous said it was a shameful sin if nobody could respect a soldier serving his country in her hour of need, and was pleased to sign at the bottom, Sincere Patriot.

Well, whether to ask for compassionate leave or not was the question, but Siencyn wouldn't go and tell the captain all these terrible stories about Marged fooling him, so Dan said why didn't he do a break and hitch-hike home. And he thought yes, he'd do that; but he had no idea at all where Penyrheol was from where they were then, and he'd never find it in a month of Sundays. So he made up a story with Dan that his mother was dead — which was true enough — and Dan wrote it out for him in case the captain asked to see the letter, which he would. And Siencyn was just off to see the sergeant-major to ask for an interview, when the runner came down and said they were both wanted in the company office. So up they went and the sergeant-major had a cunning look in his eyes as if he had them on toast at last, and he showed them into the office, quick march, right wheel, halt, left turn, salute, "Privates 32 Evans and 51 Jones, Sir." And the captain looked up after a minute as if he was busy, and said, "You two are on draft for overseas service. Hand in your A.B.64 to the C.Q.M.S. (Siencyn never knew what all the initials meant, but Dan would tell him afterwards), and take your blankets to the stores. Seven days' leave. Any questions?" "No sir." "March them out, sergeant-major." About turn, quick march, halt, dismiss.

"That's what comes of calling him a bastard, Siencyn," Dan said, philosophically tracing the effect to its cause. "You'll be able to see your missus, anyway, chum."

They had their pay and ration cards and passes and off to the station, six miles of it, full kit, enjoying every inch of it. Dan said anonymous letters wasn't worth noticing, he'd had plenty in his time; and the best thing to do was to find the sod who wrote it, and not say a word to Marged. Siencyn said he wouldn't put it above Twm Gors, but he would put it above Marged, who was a good wife if trying at times. And so they parted at Paddington the best of friends, with Dan seeing Siencyn was on the right train and telling him to mind he came back and didn't shirk it, because Dan didn't want to go abroad by himself. So Siencyn told him not to worry, solong.

And nothing more to do except stand all the way to Cardiff, and then a seat the rest of the journey, change at Carmarthen and Pencader like Dan told him, and then safe and sound in Cardigan, having had sandwiches from an old lady before they got to Cardiff and cake and biscuits from another younger lady between Swansea and Carmarthen. He wasn't going to spend his pay himself. And he didn't tell anybody he was going overseas because it was information likely to aid the enemy, so he pretended he was nobody special. And so he started walking home along the old roads he knew inside out, singing *Jerusalem* and wondering if the chapel would be holding its Eisteddfod

this week, and if so he'd sing *Jerusalem* in his battledress and walk away
with the first prize over them in civvies.

And soon enough he was turning down the lane to the sea by the
black wood and heard his employer's horses shuffling in the stalls; he
stopped to listen to the good sound, and then went into the stable to
take their heads in his arm and put his palm against their hot wet
nostrils. It was fine, that was, pushing old Deri aside to say good night
and welcome-home to Nansi, and their hooves clashing on the cobbles.
It was only round the corner then to his own cottage and he felt as if
he'd never been away.

There was a blackout up in the kitchen now, very posh, and when he
opened the door slowly Marged was sitting on a sack of meal by the
stick fire on the flagstone in the corner. But never such a face did she
have before he went away. No red in her cheeks at all, but like a funeral
in her black shawl and drooping shoulders. And she looked at him like
he was a ghost, never a word, but frightened of him, and then again as if
she was finished with him for good. It gave him a bit of a turn; and
before he could say "Well, nghariad, it's Siencyn turned up again," she
began to whimper to herself. Siencyn knew there was a scene going to
be, so he took his kit off and knelt down by her with a sack under his
knees not to spoil the trousers he'd creased under his bed every night,
and then he asked her what was up with her. How they straightened it
all out isn't anybody's business except their own. Marged wasn't
willing to believe he'd forgotten about her letter owing to being
knocked daft by a German plane, but in the end believe it she did, and
slowly she began to think differently about him and not with despair
and hatred the way she had been since he hadn't replied. And then
there was all the old gossip, and a letter in the local paper about it too by
someone signed Sincere Patriot; and she knew who it was, it was a
certain black-marketing grocer keeping a shop on the top road. And
Siencyn said thank God it was a man, anyway, thinking what a pity if it
had been a woman he couldn't give a good lamping to. And, to cut a
long story short, Marged said she wanted it to be a boy and Siencyn to
be his name, and Siencyn showed her his new false teeth and she
wouldn't believe he took them out at night, so he said "Wait and see."
And she rubbed her cheek on his battledress and looked at the shine on
his boots and wouldn't believe they were his working boots. And if
eveything wasn't as smooth as their words made it sound, the rest was
only a question of time, for a woman will mend herself with time if so
be the man means what he says when he speaks kind to her. So she
patched up alright with a bit of praise from Siencyn which was as rare

as Cadbury's chocolate to her and every bit as sweet. And Siencyn felt worried and exhausted with pulling her round to his way of seeing it all, and it was worse than driving the old sow up the lane or helping to shoe a young colt, but Jawch, it made all the difference. And next day he went without any malice to the certain grocer's just mentioned and after he'd pasted him good and proper he bore no ill feeling at all. And when they asked him how's the army he said it was alright and nothing to worry about, although his mate Dan Evans said it wasn't much of a concern.

And then, the night before he went back, the chapel held its annual Eisteddfod, which was right in Siencyn's line having a rich tenor a bit loud for volume but very good for tone. And he went in his battledress as clean and straight as a new pin with vaseline on his hair the colour of swedes, and they all cheered when he came up to sing his version of *Jerusalem*. And he never let on to a soul that he was down as a C. of E. in the Army through no fault of his own, having told the clerk when asked his religion "Christian, sir." Not that there was any need to say sir to a clerk, but he was new to the game then. And it was fine to be standing there in the whitewashed old chapel with Marged sitting in the pew where he'd carved his initials fifteen years ago, and everybody quiet as the grave except old Twm Morris Cobbler at the harmonium, saying "One Two Three Four — *Now*." And off he went with old Twm creaking along just level with him and the faces of the congregation uplifted and swaying slowly as if there was a little breeze going across the pews. And he'd sung it so often in the back of a lorry on exercises in the Army, and in the latrines, and peeling potatoes on jankers, that it came now with all the intimacy and rejoicing of all that had happened to him and not harmed or beaten him. And when he'd finished there was a great silence on them all, and then the men wiped the sweat from under their celluloid collars, and the women sniffed at their hankies and wouldn't look up. And Siencyn walked down and sat by Marged. And then they began to clap, and Siencyn didn't think they were ever going to stop. And although the adjudicator was a conshie in the last war he didn't have any option about giving Siencyn the prize. No money in it, of course, not with singing sacred music; it was a different matter from money.

And Siencyn walked home with Marged arm in arm, and he said Dan Spain would write to her regular, but he didn't have the heart to tell her where he was going to, meaning abroad; not yet, because he could only just imagine himself going abroad, and as for coming back again, he couldn't see that at all. But there was nothing to be done about it, only go to bed early and poke his head out of the window to listen to the river and tell the cockerel mind to crow at five thirty to catch the train. And that made Marged laugh for the first time, and Siencyn thought well, it's not so bad so far and no blame attached to me. And Marged promised she'd call the baby Dan as well as Siencyn. And they slept so sound that Jawch if he didn't miss the train. But never mind about that now.

Almost a Gentleman

The last evening of our O.C.T.U. course we decided to go to the music hall for first house and then have a farewell round of beers at the end of the night. A modest leavetaking; we were good friends, we didn't need to get drunk in order to enjoy each other's company; and we were pretty washed-out with the last fortnight's series of route marches and exercises both by day and by night. We saw a lot of acrobats and crooners and patter merchants; and Billy Bennett, whom the programme described as 'Almost a Gentleman.'

"Reminds you of poor old Burton," David whispered to me.

And I laughed.

I can't tell you why I laughed; I felt ashamed of myself for laughing; but I can tell you about Burton, the little that I know.

He was a beefy six-footer with black curly hair, huge arms and feet, hooked nose, twinkly sharp eyes and a skin that was blue with shaving in the morning and stubbly by night. He'd come to the O.C.T.U. from an infantry division and he looked a good soldier. The first few casual chats I had with him sufficed to show that he had an active critical faculty and a roving surface intelligence. He resented the inaugural homilies we received about developing the officer mentality, and, sitting next to me in the lecture hut, made facetious remarks *sotto voce* on the theme of democracy and the forward march of the peoples. He evidently knew his Churchill. He had an oblique way of making his cracks, an ambiguous irony, as though he were always covering himself against a possible accusation of being Red. For instance, we were talking in the canteen one evening about imperialism. I was suggesting that a century ago Britain was bored with her colonies and only the Nonconformists and Evangelicals at the Colonial Office felt any interest in the Empire, and they only because they wanted to spread the Christian gospel to the natives.

"And we're still utterly disinterested," Burton said. "I think we're wonderfully lucky to be born under the Union Jack. I think the British are awfully decent. Still, don't let's talk about it. It's unEnglish to talk about things like that."

Only the sly grin on his red little mouth showed his real meaning. Somebody took him seriously and felt unusual pride; "We've been jolly good to the Jews, too," this chap said.

I felt something grow hot and awkward in our little coffee group then, and for the first time it dawned on me, in that momentary silence, that Burton was a Jew. Of course, the hooked nose; and perhaps the voice, too. He had a weak voice for a big chap; insinuating and a bit plaintive, with a double entendre instead of emphasis. His word of command in front of a squad was boring and devoid of personality. Two other obvious qualities in his character were laziness, or rather unpunctuality, and greed, or perhaps a huge appetite. He was invariably last on parade; and also last to enter the mess. People said he was late at meals because the last table usually only had a few stragglers to eat the twelve men's rations placed on each table. And one or two of the more arrogant Britisher type taunted and insulted him about it. They would put a plate of scrag-ends and cheese-rind salvaged from their own table in front of him as they passed out after the meal; and — here is a third characteristic — he endured their insults with as patient a shrug as Shylock on the Rialto. This submissiveness riled me; I asked him why he didn't use his fist — he was big enough.

"It's no use making things unpleasant," he said. "It doesn't do your career any good."

He was deliberately prepared to swallow insults in the belief that his career would prosper thereby. I saw that his idea of careerism was affability all round. He selected the cadets who were important in any way — Grenadier Guardsmen, Military Medallists, M.A.'s — and cultivated conversation with them. He analysed the instructors and officers to the same end, deciding which were straight, which were snobs, which were bluffers or bookworms; and he knew what each one wanted to see. He altered his mode for each instructor. At the same time he always talked democracy. He had a pile of dog-eared Left booklets in his kitbag. He pasted little Help Russia handbills in the latrines; and he never ceased jibing at the pukka cadets — not that there were many of them — with public school ways and B.B.C. accents, private cars, money, women, and levity.

He hitched himself onto our crowd after a month, evidently considering us worth supporting, and we liked him quite a lot. He was very racy, and really not at all vicious. He had a handsome young wife and a two-year-old daughter, of whom he talked a lot. He saw them every week-end he was free and he was very happy talking about them. "I travelled 200 miles by road this week-end just to spend one night with my wife," he told me one Monday. "I don't suppose you chaps would think it worth while. I suppose you think me silly. But we think it's worth it. She and I."

"Alright," I said. "Don't boast about it."

He flushed, thinking he'd made some breach of etiquette.

"Beg your pardon," he said silkily. "It's that ass Burton, doesn't know what's correct."

And he switched the talk over to his favourite theme, the pamphlet mentality of the Army. "What we want is to get blitz-conscious. We're not panzer-minded enough. Still resting on our Waterloo laurels and studying Wellington's letters." And similar catch-phrases.

And then he got scared. It was within a month of the end of the course, we had begun negotiations with the tailors who flocked round the gates, we could see the end of our incubation period in what some of us called the O.C.T.U., others the O.G.P.U. Burton was asked to present himself at the Company Commander's Office one morning. When we saw him at the mid-morning break his rather flabby face had an ashy debauched look.

"I've been warned," he said, dramatically.

We were taken aback.

"If I don't improve in my leadership during the next month I won't be commissioned," he said. "D'you know what he told me? He said I lacked decision." He paused, looking at us beseechingly. "I ask you. Have any of you ever seen me lack decision?"

David, my mate, who is impulsive and frank to an unusual degree, blurted out — "Decision? I've never seen you show any."

"Aw, Christ." Burton complained. "I've never made a mistake in the field since I joined up. What d'you mean?"

"Well, you asked me; and that's what I think," David said.

"What about a cigarette?" I said.

The last month of the course played the devil with Burton. Failure ravaged his mind, his voice became sly and apprehensive, he developed a persecution mania, avoided the officers and instructors, and used every break in manoeuvres and lectures, every evening in the reading room or the canteen or the local to gain the sympathy and approval of his fellow cadets. He talked incessantly, moving restlessly from one group or table to another, talking politics, tactics, strategy, religion, uniforms, films, and most of all the shortcomings of cadets who had not been warned to improve. It was pathetic, the way he tried to woo public opinion; and of course it gained him nothing.

We had two written tests during the month and he swotted like hell for them, then got into a panic, and finally cribbed his answers from me. The tests weren't marked, so nobody was any the worse. But it showed me how terrified his mind was, like a rabbit's in front of the weasel.

And on the last Saturday of the course the weasel got him. He was told to take the white band off his cap, hand in his equipment and get out. I saw him before he went. He was surprisingly calm and dignified.

"I knew they were determined to get me," he said. "I didn't say anything. It wasn't any use. They've got the power. What can I do? Nothing at all."

"Never mind," I said, feeling rotten about it all. "You can do as much for the world in black boots as in brown, Burton. Don't let it get you down."

"Thanks a lot," he said, his eyes moist. "It's nothing unusual for me. Well. It's been nice to see the inside of an officer factory. They can't take my memories away, can they?"

His little blue eyes were already roving vaguely round, as though exploring his new environment and considering the likely direction of hostility and of advancement.

"I think it's rotten luck," I said, acutely embarrassed. "Solong, and keep your heart whole."

"Solong," he said, giving me the clenched fist. "Salud. Or is it Heil?" And he went off to catch his train.

What perplexes me is how they found him out. He was so plausible in public, and he looked a useful bloke to have in a scrap. The officers couldn't know that he cringed under an insult or ate more than his fair share or was scared to death by the fear of disfavour. They didn't see him as often or as intimately as I did. On an outward showing he was much more intelligent than lots of the men who got their commissions without mischance. But whatever the reason, they got him alright. I felt that they'd made a good soldier into a bad one in five minutes; still, that was their pigeon.

The thing that touched me most deeply, and which made me regret laughing at David's remark about Billy Bennett's "Almost a Gentleman" turn, is that he assumed the mantle of persecution with such a quiet fatalism, as if it were his customary wear. He deserved it in a way. But how did they know that he had the soul of an underdog? this mute inglorious Dreyfus?

The Farewell Binge

The soldiers had been drinking pints for an hour when the three A.T.S. girls came into the bar. There was a blue fug, and a noise. Everybody was talking and smoking. The yellowing piano was doing its best, considering its age, the row of pint glasses that weighed it down, and the maudlin, heavy-handed crooner who was thumping it.

'If I should fall in lerve agen,
I'd fall in lerve with you agen,
The same old moon aberve....'

"I'm sweating," said Dick, undoing the neck fastener of his khaki tunic. "Hurry up, Tony. Empty that pint. Four pints, missus, and one Worthington."

"Here's to those who are going East," said Tony, waving his glass over his head. "Good lads all as I well do know. And to hell with the Wops! Cheers!"

He smacked his empty glass on the counter, startling a young officer who was leaning over the counter talking to the fat little platinum barmaid.

"How about those A.T.S. dames?" said Mack in a stage whisper.

"Forget them," said Dick, long and serious, and stooping slightly. "Why waste time?"

Tony remembered a wet morning, months back in June, when he and Dick were sitting together in a tin lean-to peeling potatoes. They were somehow very browned-off, and for ages didn't want to speak, but were content to peel potatoes, simply. Their hands got cramped and wrinkled. They didn't know each other much. Then they got talking. Dick told about his girl. Tony listened. Dick spoke so quietly.

She'd jilted him; he saw her one night in a pub in Brum, with a snake. He began to get queer. Everybody seemed to be laughing at him. When he entered the office they changed the conversation. When he left it they began talking and laughing about him again. He broke with his pals. One day he hit the chief clerk in the office. Then he lost the guts to go out of his digs at all. He hadn't touched a girl since.

'I'll never smile again
Until I smile at you;
I'll never lerve agen....'

Mack and Ted asked the A.T.S. girls what they were drinking. Rouge and lipstick looked silly in khaki.

"Get us two gins and lime and a gin and orange, Tony," Mack called out. He had taken a chair by the fire with the girls.

"Get them yourself," said Tony.

There was too much row in the bar for him to be heard.

"All right," said Dick, shouldering the young officer to one side. "I'll get them."

"Fool," said Tony, shrugging his shoulders.

Dick took the shorts over.

"This is Dick," said Mack, beaming all over his English face, his blue eyes, big lips and receding chin lapping them all in joviality. "Dick's my pal. He stops the floor from rolling when we come in on Saturdays, don't you, Dick?"

Dick grinned sourly. The A.T.S. tried to look full of "it."

It was a special night for Mack. His first binge, in fact. Naturally moderate and innocent, his suburban upbringing and his long years as insuranced clerk, together with his fiancée and his truss had combined to lead him decorously through life. He was very good-natured and had been in the same Company as Ted and Tony and Dick since they joined up. Route marches, squad drill, fatigues, church parades, manoeuvres, dances, innumerable cups of tea in the Naffy, countless gossipings on the worn grass outside the tent — all this they had shared. But not much more. Anyway, he and Dick and Ted were going East to-morrow. Houris, dates, topees, deserts, and Wops running away. And a vague feeling of great danger that he wouldn't summon into the light and analyse; instead he let it brood in him, and darken the brilliant colours of his idea of the East — a sunburnt land on a classroom wall-map — and give a certain solemnity to this their farewell binge.

"Two double whiskies," said Dick, leaning over the bar.

"Take it easy, Richie," said Tony. "You know I'll be sick if we mix them. And I'm on demolition work to-morrow."

"Who cares about to-morrow?" said Dick gloomily. "You'll probably blow yourself to pieces and get discharged for inefficiency. Why worry?"

He was tighter than he'd thought. Thoughts were whirling through his mind; he looked at the fat, indulgent barmaid, puffy and powdered a dead white, the amorous lieutenant, the shelves arrayed with gay bottles, the mirrors all over the show, the walls plastered with autographed photos of music-hall starlets, the A.T.S. girls laughing and smoking Turks, Ted and Mack on top of their form, a sergeant talking to a nice-looking girl in the corner, out of the way (she wouldn't look anywhere; their knees were touching); conventions whirled past his mind's eye like telegraph poles outside an express carriage window, all slants and angles, falling, falling.

"Here's a fine show," Tony was saying, looking at a big photograph in a cheap frame. "Smithfield cattle mart."

Dick stretched his long neck to look. It was a flashlight photograph of the annual dinner of the Licensed Victuallers' Association. Rows of boiled shirts and boiled faces and bottles and women.

"Now then, no politics allowed," Dick said. "Have another?"

"I often wonder what the vintner buys, one-half so precious as the wares he sells," Tony replied. "Like that, Dick?"

"Sure," said Dick. "Poetry, isn't it? Say some more."

He certainly was drunk. The words Tony was saying filled his mind with colours and sounds, expansions and contractions and undulations of loveliness. He certainly was drunk.

'Here in this battered caravanserai
Whose doorways are alternate night and day....'

"Have another, Dick?"

Tony had stopped.

"O.K." Dick replied. "I'm going outside first, though."

It was freezing outside. The stars were like hard incandescent jewels, poetic, tugging him as if he were a wave, a foaming up-rearing white wave. The dark was like velvet, ice-cold. Overhead a Jerry plane, turning round to make a down-wind attack on Southampton. Ack-ack in the distance, underlining the horizon with thunder. He turned back into the pub, feeling suddenly very sober and shabby. A bit sick, too.

His whisky was waiting for him. He knocked it back.

"What's the matter, Tony?" he asked — Tony looking so serious for

once, Tony who was always ready for a laugh, no matter how wretched
they might be — and they'd had a pretty lousy time, off and on, what
with dirty blankets and leaking tents, invasion scares, night guard, spit
and polish and fatigues, heath fires, orders, orders, orders. And the
home town being bombed every other night.

"I don't know," said Tony. "I feel as if I'm sitting up on my slab. I
don't know."

As if he'd paid the proper price for jollity and the goods weren't
being delivered. Was it the beer? Or mixing it? Or the cheap
commercial bric-a-brac of the saloon? The sham?

"I've just bought another three gin-and-limes," he said.

"Mack didn't pay you for them?"

"No."

"What a pal!" Dick said. "Sponging on his mates, eh?"

Dick joined the scrummage round the bar.

"Excuse me, gentlemen and other-ranks," he said. "Two double
scotches, please, missus."

The young officer flushed. Dick felt sorry at once. No politics
allowed, he'd told Tony. Damn himself!

"Let's sit down, Tony," he said, returning with the drinks.

They sat at the next table to Ted and Mack and the A.T.S. dames. It
was hot and noisy, a filthy heat.

They sat quietly, sipping their whiskies.

"Remember getting inoculated the first day?" Tony said suddenly.
"It made me home-sick as hell."

Dick looked into his glass as into a crystal.

"Remember that wet morning peeling potatoes, Tony?" he asked
quietly.

Tony's face lit up.

"You remember that, too?" he said.

"Of course," Dick replied.

They were silent again.

"I'll be glad when the war ends," Dick said. "Not that Civvy
Street's all that good. But the Army's no place. You're only a number
here; you've got no pals in the Army; a pal is someone you go with
wherever you are, someone you can *be* with."

"I wish I was going with you," Tony said thoughtfully. "I'd give my
life to have a real man's chance out there."

He picked up the empty glasses.

"Wait a minute," Dick said.

Tony watched him as he leaned forward, sour-faced, and touched

Mack on the shoulder. He was in the middle of telling the A.T.S. a risky joke. He shook Dick's hand off. After they'd had their laugh Dick tapped him again.

"Hallo, Dick. Still here?" said Mack, looking goofy with the light in his protruding eyes.

"Buy us two double whiskies, Mack," Dick said.

Mack laughed.

"I'm not that drunk," he jeered.

"I said two double whiskies," Dick repeated, like a gunman.

Tony felt something tense up in him. He could see now. In the middle of all this fug and booze Dick was doing something genuine, something vital to himself. He was testing the quality of a friend. He could see now just exactly what Dick wanted, what he sought, what he valued most, the thing by which he lived. It was his touchstone, his guide through the maze and the chance.

"Don't interrupt. I'm entertaining," Mack said, shaking free and beginning another joke. The lip-stick was running a bit. It was hot over the fire. The girls must be rolling tight.

"Sod him," said Dick, mostly to himself.

"Shall we have another, or go?" Tony asked.

"I don't care," Dick said.

"We'll drink then," said Tony. "Might as well help the management keep on its feet."

"Time, gentlemen, please," sang out the bushy-browed barman, wiping down the counter.

"When the gold in your hair meets the blue in your eyes," sang out the yellowing piano.

"Like a halo, tenderly," sang out Dick, tipping his glass on the floor.

"You've wasted a whole whisky, Dick," said Tony.

It's a Long Way to Go
(A Trilogy)
(i) Change for Dinner

"You'll have to put lance-corporal James on a charge, sir," the C.S.M. said with a sneer in his eyes; "it's the second magazine your platoon has lost. *I'll* help you write out the charge sheet, sir."

"Yes," 2nd-Lieut. Greening replied, shuffling and anxious. "Er — thank you, sergeant-major. Shall I do it now?"

"I've got to go now, sir. It's my supper-time. Leave it till to-morrow."

"Alright. Tomorrow. Goodnight."

"Good-night, sir."

A heel-click, a cut-away salute as sharp as a razor, still the gleam of contempt in the dark little Asiatic eyes, and the C.S.M marched out.

Cowan, the company clerk, stood smiling with obsequious superiority. Flat footed insurance clerk, he never left the office, never went on schemes, slept there, ate there, knew everything, typed everything; the C.S.M. and the O.C. were regular soldiers, and therefore glad of a clever civilian to run the administrative side. They disliked him, but gave him power. He scorned and feared them, but enjoyed his submissive authority.

"These N.C.O.'s, sir," he said, condescendingly, "you can't trust them to keep a pair of bootlaces. They're hopeless, sir."

Damn the fellow, he's sneering at me, too, Greening thought. Oh, damn them all, damn them all. He wanted to get to his room and lie on his bed and get a grip on himself. I'm losing my grip, he repeated in his mind for the hundredth time that day, and every day.

"But they're not bad," was all he said. "They're browned-off, that's all. Where did I leave my cane?" He looked round. "Not here, is it?" (I'm losing everything, he thought, everything. Oh Christ!) "Good-night, Cowan."

He wasn't going to listen to a lecture from Cowan tonight. He'd made the mistake of asking the fellow too many questions — on King's Regs. and postings and pamphlet amendments and even the characters of his own men. Cowan always replied with a Gladstonian oration, thumbs in his braces unless he was toasting the slice of bread he'd saved from his tea. (I find a slice of bread completely satisfying at night, sir. I never go to the canteen to guzzle cream buns like the rest of them, sir). Damn his frog's feet, and his conceit, and his white, horse's teeth.

He ran up to his bare little room, dropped his kit on the floor, rubbed water on his forehead and began biting his nails. His wife's photograph looked at him from the medley of pamphlets and files littering the trestle table. (Darling, I'm so sorry. I'm so useless, so worthless). He opened his diary and looked at the list of tasks he'd made out before breakfast. "Phone M.O. *re* 18 Harris's medical board. Check platoon ammo. Collect rangecards. Paint gas detectors. Toilet paper for billets. Write to factory for 27 Evans's wife to be released during his leave. Phone P.R.I. — can newspapers be bought for men's billets? Prepare A.B.C.A. lecture." He'd ticked off three of them. The others he hadn't done. What a marvellous achievement! Actually three things done!

God, how he bullied himself. Never left himself alone. If only he could get into action, he knew he'd be alright then. Even if he died. He knew he'd soldier alright. But this endless waiting, this normality in an abnormal life, letting things slide, lacking conversation in the Mess, knowing no dirty jokes, excusing himself from beer-crawls, never reading Jane in the *Mirror* or his horoscope on Sundays, eating more meat meals than his wife, doing less work than his collier-father — oh Christ, the weariness of it!

His wife smiled at him. (Darling, I'm sorry I can't write to you. I wish I was more of a husband to you, more of a man. Especially now the baby's coming. It used to be alright, didn't it, when I was teaching in the Settlement and taking evening classes in the Boys' clubs, and we had wild roses for our wedding, and there was the constant active fight for a better world, for the pits to be reorganised and money coming into the grimy streets, and books and playreadings and hiking for the pale boys?)

He stood up, suddenly realising he was an infantry officer. Time for dinner. What was Howells doing with his service dress? Arguing politics in the Naffy, most like. He laughed to himself. Good old Howells, Red as they make them, always getting manifestoes signed to send greetings from the boys to their Russian comrades, always saluting with mocking smartness, always joking, always in debt.

Howells came hurrying in, nipping his fag at the door. His blue-pocked collier hands, powerful and gentle, passed the S.D. with its shining buttons to his "boss." "Here's your tit suit, sir," he grinned.

They were both from the same mining village in South Wales.

"How's the missus, Howells? I saw a letter for you in the office."

"Doin' fine, sir. And the baby. Comin' out of 'ospital Tuesday. Joe I'm going to call 'im. Joe Stalin, see? Nice name, Joe, I've always thought. I won't mind takin' my turn at wipin' 'is little bottom, neither sir, when the British Army can spare me for a few days."

The O.C. had refused to give Howells a short leave when his wife was taken to hospital. (Christ, what if every soldier had leave each time a baby was born? Get out. GET OUT!) Howells had volunteered for paratroops the next day; not theatrically, but to find some loyalty which he could serve, some personal loyalty. (I'm finished here, sir. I only serve *men*).

"Look, Howells; send her this. I'm flush this week. Go on. Please send it. It isn't for you. It's for her, man."

"I can't pay you back, sir. I'm paying for the boots I let go beyond repair. I can't pay you back, sir."

"Take it, for the Lord's sake."

Howells took the pound note, and hid his embarrassment by picking up an A.B.C.A. pamphlet while his boss slipped his battle dress trousers off.

"They've gone into dinner, sir," he said. "America's resources this week, is it? Good old Wall Street."

"Pass me my braces, Howells. Never mind about the war."

"That's right, sir. First things first. You'll be saying 'Pass me my braces' when we're in the paratroops together, taking the jump." They both laughed.

2nd-Lieut. Greening apologised for being late. The O.C. lifted his ravaged angry young face and nodded.

"Nothing unusual for a civilian," he said, and laughed humourlessly.

Greening found with exhilaration that he didn't care. (Rats to you sir).

"Just had a message from Battalion about you, Greening." (Another dressing-down from the C.O. for failing to salute his car?)

"You're going on draft leave tomorrow. Get your tropical kit on the way home." He took another helping of cheese. "Indian servants are bloody good, next best to the Chinese. But I don't suppose India's worth living in now, since Cripps went grovelling there. Still — "

Greening put his spoon in his soup, tasted a slow mouthful.

She would have her baby without him.... Yet he was glad to be going.... In a daze he felt the soup burn his throat.... India.... It was a chance.

(ii) The Last Day

He had packed all his kit the night before, and when he woke up to see it all roped and piled ready for the P.U. to take him to the station he had a queer desolate feeling of being nobody, nowhere, an unknown man in the steerage or the railway waiting room, nameless. It cost him an effort to recover himself. He was leaving his company, going to India. Good. It was a relief to get away from them; the O.C. with his submerged dangerous power, sexual and symptomatic; the squat bull-shouldered C.S.M. who shouted into the men's faces, making them tremble in his bad breath; the lanky mournful second-in-command, querulous and absent-minded, always defensively quick to snub his juniors for knowing more than he; it was a relief to get away. He felt like a new loaf of bread, rising in the oven.

The Adjutant rang up from Battalion at breakfast postponing his embarkation leave until he'd been inoculated. He was bitterly disappointed for a moment, but showed nothing to the others. They went on eating and reading. He got up, fuming inwardly. Another day in their power. But only another day. Then home, even if he was sick after inoculation. Home... Yet he was glad to go. Even if India was as caste-ridden and 'regular' as the home forces, he was glad to go. It was a new field, a field in ferment. His will to serve would quicken there, like a worm climbing upwards in new earth. Here there was nothing to regret leaving. Withered boughs.

"As you're staying today you might as well be duty officer, Greening," the O.C. said, casual and malicious.

"Very good, sir." (Let him have his last stab if he wants it that way).

He began his tour of duty.

The company was defending a coastal radio-location station, patrolling the cliffs and the estuary day and night, manning the ack-ack guns along the beach, watching the sea and the grey eastern skies. He inspected the cookhouse, the barrack rooms with their neatly piled kits and folded blankets, the latrines, the stores. The men were parading in denims and balaclavas and scarves, mittens and gloves torn to bits with weeks of wiring, each man with a hunk of bread and margarine and cheese in his haversack for mid-day rations. They whispered and looked sideways at him as he passed. They seemed to know... They whispered like schoolboys.

He went up through the wood, under the interlacing pines, in the dark green aqueous shadows of the frozen wood, and out along the crawl trench across the last field in England. The wind beat at him, blowing with bared teeth from Europe, whipping the heavy grey seas through which a smudgy convoy slowly edged its way southwards. The radio masts, ten infant Eiffel towers, hummed like Jews' harps. Gulls hunched in the dead, blown grass, their necks ruffled, or were blown like newspapers over the cliffs, over the edge of the world, to scavenge among the rusted mines and scaffolding at the waves' tip. He felt a new and unexpected affection for these things; this was the way he would remember them.

The guard he wished to inspect was in the Martello tower where the cliffs fell down to the pea-green estuary whose flat black banks were littered with beached fishing craft and pleasure boats and tarred huts. He followed the frozen path along the hedge to the round sturdy Martello tower that for a century and a half had awaited the invader's armada; Christ, it was cold. He climbed the broken steps to the aperture on the first floor, entered the vaulted cellar with its thick central pier to which the guards' hammocks were slung, swaying slightly in the wind; then up the solid stone spiral to the roof. The guards were shivering and stamping their numb feet, greatcoats and groundsheets flapping round their shoulders. They were glad to see him.

They were all three in his platoon. Their rough white faces grinned a welcome. Little Brunter with his imp's face peering from his balaclava and his yellow pointed teeth. Rowdy Ginger Morgan with his long bent nose and invisibly fair eyebrows, the joker of the platoon. And Pat Baker, hugely shaped, manly, independent, the best soldier in the company, but unable to read or write.

"So you're going, sir?" little Brunter ventured, grinning; he knew he was permitted to take liberties.

"There's not much you don't know, you fly one," he replied, laughing.

"The telephone orderly told us, sir."

"Did he, be damned? Well, he's quite right. I'm off tonight."

"Want a batman to go with you, sir?" Ginger asked, like a friendly dog, rubbing his cold hands.

"You don't want to go to India, do you, Morgan? There won't be any rabbits for you to poach there, you know."

"Aye. No rabbits. But there'll be women, sir."

"Women? A married man like you?"

"Not much use being married if somebody else is sleeping with your missus, is it, sir?" — he still grinned amiably, ingenuously. "I know from my mates — there's a red-headed man same colour as me milking her every night. Never be able to tell whose baby it is, see, sir?"

"Gossip, that's all that is, Morgan." (God, say it's only gossip; but why does he grin so placidly, God alive?) "How's *your* wife now, Brunter?" Brunter had deserted three times to see his wife; tiny little bird-man that he was, it seemed funny he was so oversexed. The redcaps had caught him naked under the bed the last time; he'd gone to detention for 120 days and was now only getting 7d. a week wages. The rest of the platoon had a whip-round for him each pay-day. He never stopped grinning.

The buzzer on the D.5 field telephone interrupted them. Message to all units along coast. Hurricane fighter shot down at dawn five miles to sea. Pilot baled out. Keep watch. Time of origin 0855.

Christ, it was a cold sea, rising all the time, white and rough. Not much chance for a man in that.

"Poor bugger," Baker said quietly. He realised.

India was as vast as the sea; but it was land. One could walk on it, run, breathe, think. Not be sucked down, choked, filled, emptied, annihilated. Who was he? Who was he, sucked down into the trough of the sea?

"I'll be glad when dinner time comes," Ginger Morgan said, shivering. "A hot meal is something like it on a day like this. They didn't ought to have a bleeding war in this weather, did they, sir?" He shuddered, looking at the waves piling against the screaming shingle bank, and then turned to take his leave.

"Well, goodbye, lads," he said. "Look after yourselves. And keep a look-out for that poor devil at sea. He's just as important as you are, Morgan."

"We'll watch out for him, sir, don't worry," Morgan grinned cheerfully.

"It won't be our fault if he drowns, sir."

"No, it's not your fault, Morgan, for once in your life," he chivvied.

"Well, solong again, lads."

"All the best, sir."

Baker came down the spiral stairs after him.

"Excuse me, sir," he said, diffident yet not embarrassed.

"Yes, Baker?"

"I want to thank you special, sir, for learning me to read and write. I never thought I would, sir. But I can write to my missus myself now. It makes a lot of difference, sir."

"Good. Keep it up, won't you? And don't bother about thanks. Perhaps I'm more thankful than you. Anyway, good-bye, Baker."

He hurried because of the cold, through the rustling belt of withered sedge, along the frozen track to the wood, down through the trees. He knew they were watching him from the Martello, but he didn't look back. He didn't want to wave, and be sentimental, like a schoolboy leaving school after the headmaster's sententious farewell.

He went the round of the defence posts and wiring parties, was asked respectfully to estimate the age of a little field mouse one of the men was holding in his cracked red hands while the others argued and breathed over it; and took his farewell of them also.

Returning to the office he found the M.O. waiting to inoculate him. He rolled up his sleeve, thinking 'Now I can leave on the noon train.' The doctor offered to run him to the station. He asked the O.C. for permission. "O.K. Beat it." He loaded up, excited with new thoughts.

Away, away. Sorry and glad, sorry and glad. Away, away. Sorry and glad. The car revving, the train rocking, the telegraph posts falling past. Some vast thing, something universal, continuous, manifold, working tirelessly for good, moved in him, fortifying his uncertain impulses. He and the pilot who had baled out in the sea, and the three men in the tower, each in his way had a part in it, each in his way made manifest the mystery, each in his way.

(iii) The Moon

He began to grow anxious by the time his little train was well into the enfolding mountains of Mid-Glamorgan, panting and waiting aimlessly at each dirty station, crawling up the gradual gradients along the skirts of the bony hills, whistling like a policeman as it approached each grey terraced town and its clusters of sidings, pit shafts, coal tips and advertisements. He was nearly home.

He was anxious because he couldn't get himself to realise it. Ten minutes by his watch, that was all, and she would be standing under the dim lamp by the ticket collector, and he would be saying "Hallo, darling" and "How are you, sweet?" and she'd want to carry some of his kit, and he'd argue with her because of the steep hill. And he was frightened that it wouldn't be *real*. The journey had been so unreal: all the way through Suffolk and Essex and London and Bucks. and Wilts. and Gloucestershire and Monmouthshire, L.N.E.R., L.P.T.B., G.W.R., unreal all of it. Reading the *New Statesman*, thinking in big filmy ideas of the economic wastage and Indian nationalism and British Imperialism, of British capitalism and Russian Socialism, of second fronts and khaki fascism, democracy and the old vexed trouble of the miners, his father and cousins and Left Book Club friends — that was one part of the journey. Another part was the continuous projection of camp routine and preoccupations, persistent as the rhythm of the train — the Bren magazine that was missing and still not accounted for, the site of the new trenches which he'd forgotten to show to his platoon sergeant, Baker writing a slow scarcely-legible letter to his wife, the need to buy tropical kit (he should have stopped in London and ordered it at the regimental tailors — Mrs. Jones the dressmaker was the only tailor where he was going; it would mean two journeys to Cardiff, damn and blast it), and the question of money. He would be getting 11/- a day, she 4/-. How much could he allot her from his salary? How much did it cost to be pukka? Would she have enough money to pay the doctor and the nursing home, to buy Wincarnis and Ovaltine and a pram? Would she be able to have a holiday by the sea when the child was born? Would they send his kit allowance on in time?... It was a long crowded journey; he was tired and hungry. An inverted class-consciousness made him travel third despite his first-class travel voucher. He had sat in the corner all the time, reading, thinking, looking through the window without noticing much except houses, factories, fields, cattle, the Thames. Hungry and needing a wash; and now it was time to take his kit off the rack and buckle on his webbing. When would he tell her about India? His telegram had said simply "Coming on leave 8.30. Love. David." He wouldn't tell her till he'd had a meal anyway. He wanted a meal; something tasty.

He caught himself thinking of food again. How romantic, he sneered. Didn't he realise he'd never be meeting her at the station again? She'd never be just a minute away from him again? He reasoned with himself. He was hungry; therefore it was quite natural to think of supper. But he knew it shouldn't be important now, it should be trivial. Instead of which it was like a great bowl of water, and Death and Love were two dried peas soaking in the bowl, no more.

The train screamed and slowed down, slid along the platform, and stopped. Yes, she was under the dim lamp, in her loose tweed coat (the smart black one would be too tight now), and the lamp was on her hair like gold. He jumped out, right behind her, and he said "Hallo, darling." She turned and looked at him, and smiled; her hands were trembling. They crossed the black river by the footbridge. Oily black Cynon filthy with coal mines, fringed with scruffy trees. How beautiful it looked, black as ebony in the red and green lights of the railway and the hooded lamp of the bridge.

He put his arm gently round her waist and said "Are not Abana and Pharpar, rivers of Damascus, better than all the waters of Israel?"

And she said, "Are you going abroad?"

"Why do you ask that?" he hedged.

"You weren't due for leave for another three weeks," she said. "Please tell me," she said, stopping at the edge of the bridge, putting her palms on his chest, leaning to him.

"I can't talk with all this kit on me," he said.

"Where are you going?" she asked, holding his eyes in her insistent gaze.

"India," he said. It was a little word, wasn't it? Five letters.

"Darling," she said, resting against him, bowing her head on his trench coat between the shiny buttons. The weight and warmth of her. And in her nearness he felt her suffering quiver like heat on a sun-lashed road. He *knew* then; it smote him — an enormous tearing, a deep personal guilt. He had been so casual about it to himself, irresponsible, glad to go.

"Your supper'll be drying to a cinder," she said then. "Come on."

The kettle was boiling on the grid, the black kitten hiding under her fireside chair, the table laid in the kitchen for two. A clean snow-white towel in the scullery, which was also the bathroom. She had been knitting — white woolly things this time, not khaki. She put the news on for him while she dished up the cottage pie. She made everything so normal. The news was normal, too. The last imperial troops had crossed the Johore causeway from the mainland. One of our fighters shot down off the East coast, but the pilot was safe.

Good God! he started up, jubilant suddenly.

"He's safe," he said, very happy suddenly.

"Who?" she asked.

"We were watching for that pilot all the morning," he said. "It was such a rough sea, I didn't think he had a chance. Hooray!"

"Good omen," she said, half to herself.

They didn't sit up long after washing the supper plates. She put the kitten outside for five minutes, tidied the kitchen, put away her knitting, called the kitten in and put it in its bed in the duster box, and took his hand.

"Come and sleep, darling," she said.

He undressed quickly and lay on the pillow watching her slip her nightdress over her head and step out of her vest and comb her fair stubborn hair. She didn't comb the pucker out of her eyes, the nervous tension there. Her actions were very calm, though, controlled.

"I'm sorry for you, going out there *by yourself*," she said when he had put out the light.

He kissed her, hushing her, stroking her head.

"It's such a big country," she said. And then, after a long silence, "there's nothing I can do, absolutely nothing, darling. Is there?"

"But of course there is. You've got everything to do. You've got the little girl. And me, too," he whispered.

She was silent a little.

"She's an awful little girl," she said. "She makes me disgustingly sick. She's nearly as much trouble as you are."

They were both thinking of India in the darkness. He could only think of clichés, meaningless, unevocative. "Teeming millions," he murmured.

They laughed a little in the darkness.

"The moon comes up in about two hours," she said.

"Go to sleep now, " she said, putting her arm under his head, drawing his head down to her mouth.

When he woke the moon was a soft gold on the wall. The pattern of roses, the little Gauguin *Riders to the Sea* with its pink sands and the long shadow from its frame, the dark bars of the window frame. He lay quietly, knowing she was awake.

After a while he said "Can't you sleep much these days, darling?"

"I sleep in the afternoons sometimes," she said.

She kissed his hair.

"You're sweating," she said. "Your hair's quite damp. Please look after yourself for me."

When he had come on leave at other times they had acted like strangers, not understanding each other somehow. It was terrible, the coldness that wouldn't melt for days sometimes, and which they never mentioned, although they knew it was there. In his sleep he would give fire orders and tell men to take cover. And she lay awake, listening, holding a stranger in her arms, as if in charity.

This time there was no strangeness. It was good fortune. She had touched the life in him in that little pause on the bridge. And she was content if he were wholly hers, just for this little while.

"The moon will be out there, too, won't it?" she said.

"Yes, darling," he said, wanting to cry. "Yes, it's everywhere."

Lance-Jack

(i)

After the inflamed vulgarity and ugly tempers of the last hour, when the sergeant asked us whether we had any complaints, it is soothing and cool to talk things over intelligently to my *chance* companions at the mess table. One an insurance clerk, the other a private secretary to a biggish wig. I'd never met them before. They are both married; one of them says his wife is expectant. We chat together about the army, we think the same more or less — field manoeuvres which might do very well for the Roaring Forties and the Covered Wagon, even for the last two years of the Boer War, even for the Chinese *franc-tireurs* in Japanese-occupied territory. But not for a vast army in training for an encounter with Germany's tanks and air-supported infantry. We think perhaps things will improve as Morrison and Churchill get going. Anyway we are curiously impersonal, considering the imminent destruction of Fortinbras and all his braves. A soldier is always impersonal. That's the only way to preserve any privacy in conditions where one is never alone. Eight in a tent, lying on groundsheets, feet to the tentpole, kit piled high and in small space by one's side. Writing letters, looking at snaps, cutting toenails, sewing buttons, contemplating something distant, brooding over something immediate. It is all impersonal. The other seven don't notice, don't interfere. The soldier is non-political. He doesn't talk about Germany, but only about Jerry. When he becomes political, it is ugly. A primitive patriotism, refusing any quarter, burning eyes. We'll wipe them out , the *swine*. We can take it, and hit back, by Christ... But I haven't met many of that sort. The vast majority are kind and impersonal. The boys straight back from Dunkirk, bearded and dirty and slightly wounded and tired to death: I shall never forget how quiet their voices were, amenable as children, waiting for an hour and more till the bacon was found and cut and fried, or talking about it all as they lay in the sun outside the pub. "It's marvellous, seeing the houses all standing, and the milkman coming down the lane there," one of them said. He rubbed his forehead. "They're *all* mad over there," he said, pointing with his thumb towards the channel.

In the Army you begin again. All you were seems to have vanished. It was simply another mode of life, Civvy Street. I was a school-teacher in a big secondary school, a responsible and exacting job. Now I clean latrines, windows, barrack rooms, run errands for snooty little office clerks with a stripe on their arms, listen to filthy talk shouted from bed to bed, suffer a series of violent reactions; dismay that democracy has such a rough edge, bewilderment, sickness for two or three people whom I long for by my side, fatigue at having to begin again, to get to know people again, and again and again no doubt, feeling uprooted, unreal, dull and without conversation, reluctant to begin again. In some ways it is a good point from which to start, this sudden *levelling down*. Millions are facing it in Europe, in a much acuter form than I. I am not hungry, nor ill-clothed and shod. But the Poles, the Balts, the Germans in the Balkans and Russian Poland, and the refugees, they are bewildered by this nightmare of strangeness, of newness, broken homes, useless qualifications, forced labour, distance. They will have to wake and live this nightmare. It is incredibly, unforgivably cruel, inhumane, harsh — to the old, to the sick, to mothers and wives going alone. But to the young and the bold it is the loudest challenge ever sounded on the trumpets of the wind. Conventions go, respectability, narrowness, the suburban train and the Sunday best. Those who were trapped are forced to be free of the old routine. Those who were happy are forced to be unhappy, conscripted into a new way of life. Everyone will realise sooner or later that nothing is fixed, nothing inevitable. They will realise the possibility of change. Many long-standing abuses will no longer be able to conserve themselves.

But it is dangerous, too. The soldier doesn't bother. He is a migrant, an Arab taking his belongings with him, needing surprisingly little of the world's goods. He leaves his violin and his Cezanne and his garden behind. His wife, too, and his children, as time passes. Hitler's soldiers have been taught two simple things: Obey Commands; Forget Home. In the long run these two rules are easier to learn than to resist. That is the danger. That is why I say: to women, feel less; to men, feel more. I may be exaggerating this danger. Certainly the soldier's heart leaps for leave. But when I go home on leave I feel vaguely "out of it." The new carpet doesn't thrill me as it should; the troubles and little quarrels with neighbours are no longer my troubles; they are the preoccupations of strangers. I feel sympathetic, I listen and suggest. But I don't interfere, I don't trespass on them. And perhaps they think I don't talk much, don't open up, don't confide. Until one of them divines the reason and knows me as a stranger, and takes me in as a stranger, into her lonely arms. We talk quietly of strangenesses, night marches, bivouacs, odd and far-off incidents, Europe. Till our loneliness is complete, and we are united in loneliness, just the two of us, as it used to be when we first sought each other, losing and finding each other, never quite giving in, never quite defeated.

The soldier says "Life is a series of meetings with strangers. We are all strange, to ourselves as well."

That is true. But it is dangerous, like cynicism. For sometimes when he is utterly alone, utterly impersonal, on guard in the night at some outpost, somewhere, he can only envisage the human past, the great centrifugal force of the heart which draws into its orbit and unites in love all differences of people, mother and sweetheart, friend and pauper, employer and baby daughter, I say he can only envisage this great power of life as a swarming of bees on a bough, of flies on a fallen damson, a noisy, slightly indecent congress. A complex, if you prefer.

And if you ask why a man appears to prefer what is casual, rough, hazardous and incomplete to what is warm and personal and loving, I suggest you read Edward Thomas's poems again. It is, if you like, curious that the idealist should live casually with regard to himself and the preservation of himself, that he should find the haversack, the trench, the journeying, most suited to the pursuit of high ends. Christ had no home. Women dislike, even hate this quality in their men. It is the overturning of all that was so hard and slow to win, the gradual building up of friendship, love, mutual knowledge, home, children, the rooted beauty of flowers, budding and opening in petal and colour and curve *in one place*. But it is a fine quality, in the best men. And there is always, it seems, some suffering. There is Beethoven as well as the nine symphonies. Man or woman, each must discover the balance of forces. And now that the women are being bombed in their homes while the men are untouched in their trenches and tents, perhaps there will be less hatred among the women that their men should leave them to follow something else. It is a new way of *life*.

(ii)

These things I am going to write are about the imagination; I have
found them here and there in my scribblings. They are not poems.
The poems I have elsewhere. I don't want these to be poems, for
they are fragmentary, not all of me, as the dance-song says.

When I am walking back at night through the wet streets and the
darkness I hear the tramp of heavy boots. The tramp of heavy boots
drowns the sound of all other footsteps.

I wonder whose footsteps they are. I listen carefully.

I discover with surprise and a growing excitement that they are
mine. I grow slowly more and more pleased with the sound of my
hobnailed boots, drowning the bare and bleeding footfalls of the
beggars and the refugees who slink down the side streets as I
approach. Heil Hitler.

But now I am scared, now I am frightened, and now terrified of
the sound of my heavy boots. They silence all other sounds. I am
terrified they will start running.

Gott, Oh Gott.

In the middle of the city the Emperor had a great cemetery
planned, in the shape of a circle, with a circular paved road running
round it. At night, in the drizzle, I walk round and round the
cemetery, along the circular road, and I do not know when to stop
walking round and round the silent and eternal cemetery. I envy the
dogs barking and frisking and sleeping among the graves, rooting up
shinbones, gnawing contentedly and ignorant of all implications.

Where is my rightful place in which to sleep what is left of this
dark night?

Not in my sweetheart's bed, for she has locked her father's door in
my face, saying it is not proper for the unmarried to sleep together.

Nor in my lodgings, the garret where I have lain awake these last
five nights, tossing and feverish and foolish, for I do not want to
return there for a sixth time.

I will lie down and sleep among the rank grasses and the dripping
nettles of the common then, midway between my sweetheart's and
my lodgings.

It is cold and damp on the common. The ground is hard and
lumpy and my body wakes with stiffness and dampness. The mist
makes me cough.

My sweetheart does not love me; if she did she would come and
discover me, and lie beside me, warming my nostrils with her breath,

like new hay that steams a little in the sun.

My sweetheart has refused what I offered her. Yet I have lost what I offered her, somewhere. I have lost myself.

There is nothing left of me save my indestructibility, a small hard thing in my head, a stone the size of my fist. I can feel its hardness behind my eyes, aching.

There is no love.

I am cold and lost and hard among the dew-wet thistles and the rank dripping grasses and the useless weeds, God's forgotten ideas. God is cold and sullen, gloomy, unhuman.

And slowly he is fashioning man in his own image.

Every day it becomes easier for us to slay each other without cant, without feeling very much at all.

Their smiles are fixed and difficult to acquire; they do not alter their expression once it is made up, no matter how alarming are the headlines in the morning paper. And they die with white faces, saying nothing; only trembling a little, almost imperceptibly, with premonitions of the past.

They are the martyrs.

Your eyes are bright with anguish, bright as stones, and a network of veins stands out hard on your ravaged, still beautiful face. But the leaves blossom above you where you lie abject, and the sedge grows green around you, Europe. And out of the springing wood your tiny children running and tumbling, dragging their kites and singing the songs of the soldiers.

The trout do not hear the cruel violent speeches of the ambitious perverters. But in the deep water under the alder roots the trout taste the curious taint of blood in the river water.

The rooks scatter with the turbulence in the sky. The starlings and sparrows, and all animals are frightened at this new manifestation of hostility. But they also quickly forget.

When Virgil led Dante down into the darkness there were many who tore at his garments and begged him to help them get back, back home. They tore the hem of his garments to ribbons, and dirtied it with their filthy hands. Some who were humble lay at his feet and said nothing because they feared to be refused and dared not give their vast impossible longing the power of words over them. And others lay quietly, and with soft eyes seemed to say, "Hail and farewell; speed your troubles. We are of the darkness. Leave *us*. *Leave us*."

They were the exiles, like Dante.

The loafers at the street corner will tell you the places where you may forget; they are easy to find and there everyone is agreeable, out to please; and it is not too costly.

But there is no-one to go with you to the place of remembering.

You went there alone, didn't you, Judas Iscariot, my friend.

(iii)

The long-legged tough Aussie having a beer by the roadside with us:

"My wife said, 'I know you'll have a good time. I don't care anything but that you'll come home again the same as you went.' I said 'Let's change the talk to something about food'."

"Got a bit drunk last night, Joey, got in late. Duty officer there started giving me whatfor. I said to him, 'Don't sack me, boss. Jess gi'me good talking to'."

"You wouldn't believe what it was like. The voyage was so long, see? I felt I'd left my wife and kids for good, as if I'd got no line on them no more. But when I tried a woman in London it wasn't no good. I kept thinking of my wife when I was messing her about. It's funny. You wouldn't understand."

Sid has been in trouble. Got into a fight in a pub and was reported by the red-caps. "What was it all about, Sid?" I asked. "Oh, *he* said it was an Alarm and I said it was the All Clear. I thought he was right and he thought I was right. So we fought it out." He was tried by the Company O.C.

"What did you get, Sid?" I asked when he came out; marched out, rather, between the two escorting corporals.

"Read all abaht it in to-night's special," he said in a quavering old-vendor's voice.

Sid was on sentry duty when Jerry dive-bombed. He was the only one to get it. Shrapnel.

It seems so unfair. Such an infinitesimal gain for the enemy, such a terrible, absolute loss for his wife.

Khaki and discipline and angry imperatives are apt to over-awe and frighten — yes, frighten — the recruit. But it isn't so godalmighty, really. One of the corporals saw me reading a book of poetry the other day. He said "Do you like poetry?" I flushed and looked at him for a moment to see what he was playing at. Then I said "Yes. Why?"

"Oh, nothing," he said. Then he looked at me like a little boy confessing a longing for your apples. "I like it, too," he said. "I like writing it, at least. I never read any. I write a lot, though. Every letter I write to my girl I put a poem in it. Of course some of them are pretty soft, but now and again they're really good. She was proper nuts about one I wrote last week. Pretty intimate it was — about having a baby. She copies them up into a notebook. In INK. Tell me, can you have verses longer than four lines? Or have they got to be four lines?"

In any case, the Army is only an improvisation on a vast scale. There's bound to be some rough edging, and some pretty poor stuff, here and there. There are certainly plenty of friends. They come to you from Borstal and the Royal College of Music, from the Great War and the Spanish War, and anywhere else. It's a fine life in that way. There are a few snobs — crane drivers and navvies occasionally sneer at "bloody clerks, bloody school-teachers." But mostly it's democracy alright, mending the holes in its socks and sharing the parcel from home and showing photographs and being disconcertingly vulgar and humorous, ignorant and amazingly experienced, and calm, happy-go-lucky.

There are also Saturday afternoons and Sundays, if you're lucky not to get pinched for fatigues or guard duty. The mere in the valley of pine trees has a profound stillness. In the afternoon sometimes there are a few soldiers bathing there and lying in the sun. Young boys talking driftily about the A.T.S. girls, what they're like — "if they've got to have A.T.S. why don't they have them all smashers?" — and about the blue dragonflies which flicker on the still water, abrupt electric turns, vivid colour, then utter stillness settled suddenly on a thin blade of green, the long thin pipe of the body dipped in the water, the four transparent wings extended and still; sleeping on the flat heart-shaped sensuously-thick lily leaves or more fittingly on the wonderfully white spiked petals over the secretly open golden heart of the flower; or flying in pairs, tail to head fastened together; "Look at them dragonflies capitulating, the dirty dogs," says one of Seurat's bathers, tiring of the A.T.S.

I wish I could write a poem about dragon-flies. It would be like a schoolboy's face as he watched the mercury for the first time, in the great glass beaker of water.

At evening the mere is utterly still. The tangled rust-green underwater grasses cannot be seen from the top of the valley. Only the mirror of water, pure blue and magenta in the intense clearness of evening; the mere holds it all. And I think of Dick and Bill and

Gweno and home and watch the advent of the heron, its steady grey wing-sweep, its legs and neck out-stretched and calm, circling slowly the mere which it sees as I see it, a mirror of rest, a breast for the dark and silent visitant. But it is deterred by the laughter of soldiers and girls, and goes as I am going, elsewhere.

On the way back to camp I catch up with a hedgehog. He has thin, dragging hind legs covered with loose brownish-purple skin, four claws like tubercular roots, a little black snout, pointy, and beady intelligent eyes, hunched over a grub.

His nostrils blow little soap-bubbles of terror and his breath hisses when I prod him gently with a stick. Sacrilege.

It's only because I am alone that I touch him like this. I wouldn't have yielded to such a private intimate impulse had I been in company. But alone we are more primitive, more natural. We regard our faces in the mirror and examine the colour of our eyes, and touch the downy hair on our arms, ruffling it. Then I continue my way back over the downward sloping heather, and I am no longer alone. The forest is blue and hazy with warmth and distance, like lavender, and the sandy path runs forward to the cluster of tents on the open heath. I see only the distance, the forest, and I half forget my khaki and imagine myself an itinerant preacher, one of the old revivalists of the eighteenth century, of my own country, Wales. Hywel Harris perhaps, or Thomas Charles, crossing the mountains to the waiting hearth. Or a lover in a Hardy novel, fifty years ago, on this same path, Tess lonely and hurt, Jude instinctively seeking loneliness.

Do you know how quietly I sleep, on my groundsheet, between my three dirty blankets, in the crowded tent?

The Wanderers

The heat inside the caravan was too much for her. The wooden wallboards were warped and the blue paint bubbled and flaked by the burning high noon. She fell asleep in the middle of stitching a corner of the red quilt over a tear in the boy's trousers. Running up the steps in nothing but his rough green jersey, the boy found her lolling open-mouthed in the chair, beads of sweat on her pale face. He twined his grubby fingers in the fall of her black hair and pulled gently.

"Wake up, mam," he said, "Dad's coming across the fields."

She woke with a start, surprised to find herself sleeping.

"Jewks!" she muttered, rubbing her eyes. "I'm that sleepy. Where is he, Micah?"

"Just crossing the river," Micah replied. "He's got two rabbits."

"We'll have a change from bread and dripping, then," she said, yawning.

"Here, let's finish this patch. You've not been out like that, have you?"

"Only to the river," he answered. "I seen a dragon-fly an' followed him till he pitched. Look!" He opened his grimy fist to show the crumpled corpse of a yellow-barred dragon-fly. Grey-pink matter oozed from its long tail and congealed on his palm.

Revolted, she slapped his face.

"Oh! Micah, you cruel," she shouted, her face twisted up; "you mustn't — "

The boy was weeping passionately, hiding his face in her black frock.

"It's the gipsy blood you've got from your father," she said. She stood so still. And then, suddenly, she saw that he was weeping and hiding for shame in her body. Swiftly she stooped over him and lifted him into her arms.

"Micah, Micah," she murmured, kissing his hair and running her hands over his naked buttocks and down his almond brown legs.

"There, there, stop crying, my darling."

"Stop dandling the kid, for Christ's sake," the gipsy shouted. She shivered and almost dropped the boy. He had come in so quietly.

"He was nigh choking," she said, sullenly. Her voice was hard and reserved. Micah had stopped crying and stood in the corner, trying to stifle the sniffling sobs that broke from him.

"You'll make a woman out of him," the gipsy sneered. "Coddling the boy! Cover your arse up, boy, before I bruise it for you."

Micah hastily grabbed his trousers and, sitting on the floor, pulled them over his legs.

"Sell any pegs this morning?" the gipsy asked.

She pointed to the bed.

"There's one and six under the mattress," she said, almost scornfully.

He lifted up the mattress, took the money out and counted the coppers slowly. She watched his greasy brown hands fumbling over the coins.

"Good," he grunted. "I sold two bobs' worth myself. Christ it's hot."

He unlaced his boots and stretched his swollen red toes. His thick curly hair lay in a mat of sweat on his forehead. His beady brown eyes were brilliant with heat.

"There's an ironmonger selling out in the town," he said. "Promised to sell me sixty tin boilers for ten bob. I said I'd call back for them."

"We haven't got ten shillings," she answered, looking out from the caravan door at the blue haze on the hills.

"I can pawn something," he said.

"Pawn what?" she asked. Her back was towards him, her voice listless.

The corn was blue and still before her eyes. A slash of poppies burnt a red wound across the field.

"I was thinking it would be worth it, just for two days," he said cautiously. "We'd make a quid on the selling and then I'd recover them."

"What?" she said.

"Your ear rings," he ventured.

"Alright," she said, swinging her foot nonchalantly.

He had expected a quarrel. But instead of being relieved at her acquiescence, he was angered by her indifference.

"I'll take them now, then," he snapped. "And get them rabbits skinned and in the pot 'gainst I come back. Where the hell has that boy gone? Micah!" he shouted.

No reply. He ran down the steps, calling again.

"What're you doing under there, in Christ's name?" he snarled, pulling the trembling child from under the caravan. Micah cringed.

"What's two and two?" the gipsy asked, holding him by his hair. Micah did not reply.

"What's two and two?" the gipsy repeated, threateningly. Micah's lips quivered.

"Four," said the gipsy, "one — two — three — four," shaking the boy at each count. "You're a *fine* scholar. Get on and help your mother skin them rabbits."

Micah ran up the steps to his mother. He looked up at her, but she was looking fixedly across the fields. The gipsy turned away without a word and set off along the hedge.

It was a mile to the town, down Lovers' Walk by the river and across the common. The children stopped their cricket to watch the lean, dark stranger in the garish blue smock coat. They gathered fearfully together until he had passed. Gipsies steal little boys and take them away in their caravans, vanishing mysteriously into the wide other world. He passed the crowd of farmers outside the cattle market and climbed the steep shopping street. Ladies in white frocks stood under the window shades outside the milliners' and confectioners' shops. A podgy barman stood at the door of "The Wheatsheaf," sunning himself between hours. Children clustered round an ice-cream barrow. The tar melted on the road, burning the gipsy's feet. He turned down a side street and entered a tobacconist's. A shrivelled little Jew with scant, mousy hair and watery, peering eyes popped up ingratiatingly from behind the counter. His withered smile hardened as he looked at the gipsy.

"We-ell," he wheezed, rubbing his hands dubiously together.

"I want to pawn these ear rings," the gipsy said, fishing them out from his deep, poaching pocket and laying them on the counter.

The Jew bent over them, fondling them with his skinny fingers. The gipsy could only see the red tip of his pointed nose.

"Six shillings?" The Jew raised his puckered face.

"Ten," the gipsy said.

The Jew lowered his discoloured eyes to the ear rings. A dray rumbled past. The Jew looked out on to the sunlit street and saw a pile of steaming horse dung outside the door.

"One minute," he said, "excuse me, please." He fetched a bucket and spade from the kitchen at the back of the shop, shuffled hurriedly into the street, scooped the manure into the bucket, and returned into the shop, smiling.

He put the bucket in the kitchen and shuffled back to the counter, rubbing his hands on his trousers.

"Well then, eight," he said.

"Alright," the gipsy replied.

The Jew counted the silver into the gipsy's palm.

"I'll reclaim them in three days," the gipsy said, placing the receipt and the money in his trousers pocket.

"Very good, sir, very good," the Jew wheedled, "a nice day, isn't it?"

The gipsy spat on the doormat as he went out. He went straight to the ironmonger's, who promised to deliver sixty boilers at the caravan in the evening, and then, after a pint at "The Wheatsheaf," the gipsy made his way out of the town.

During the next four days the caravan covered twenty miles, the tin boilers and cans rattling like skeletons in corrugated iron coffins as the skinny piebald slipped and stumbled down the stony lanes. They were following the river to the coast, selling their ware at farms and cottages and villages. The gipsy was in a good mood, for they were selling well and he enjoyed walking at the horse's head even more than haggling. He let Micah sit on the mare's back when the road was flat, and he whipped the heads off the hedgerow dandelions and sang to himself. By the end of the fourth day there were only two boilers unsold. They decided to spend the night in a little pasture by the river, and after unharnessing the mare and tethering her to a hazel, the gipsy stripped and swam in the stream. The cold green water seemed to flow through him, dissolving his tired, sweaty body into energy and delight. He climbed onto the bank and lay in the long grass, biting off the leaves of sorrel with his teeth and tasting the bitter-sweet juice on his tongue. Micah was playing near him, yellow as a bee with rolling in the buttercups. His wife was sitting hunched up on the steps of the caravan.

"Hoah, hoah, hoah," a girl's clear voice made him sit up in surprise.

"Hoah, hoah, hoah," strong and bell-like and vibrant. Ah! there she was, two fields away, calling the cattle in. The reddening sun caught her obliquely so that one side of her was light, fleshy, quick, the other silhouetted darkly. Light and shadow moved over her as she walked. The gipsy pulled on his trousers and shirt, laced up his boots, and returned to the caravan. He tied a scarlet muffler round his neck, combed his hair back, and hooked the two remaining cans on to the crook of his arm.

"There's a farm over the fields," he said. "I'll try and sell these."

His wife nodded without lifting her bowed head.

With light springy steps he followed the girl. The cows were walking in a line before her, tossing their heads at the swarming flies, their full udders swinging against their hind legs. The gipsy caught her up as she was entering the cowshed. She looked at him boldly.

"Would your mistress need any cans?" the gipsy asked, his voice silken and lilting.

"Mistress is at market," she replied, pressing her full hips against the lower half of the cowshed door and stretching back a little. Her breasts pressed against her cotton blouse, strong and round, melting the gipsy's composure into an aching tumult of desire.

"Well, do *you* want anything?" he asked, the wild blood burning in his fingers and flushing into his neck.

"I've got no money for nothing," she laughed. Her teeth were white; Christ they were white, close against her lips; her full, laughing lips and her fresh cheeks and her bright dark-flecked eyes. The gipsy smiled. His face was devout and eager, even when he smiled.

"I'll milk your cows for nothing," he said.

"Are you a careful one?" she asked, tossing her head back.

"Yes, I'll be careful," he said.

She opened the cowshed door and he followed her in. The shed was low and warm with the fodder and the cows' breath and the sweat of their bodies. The darkness was rich and luminous, as though it were cloudy with purple, intangible grapes. The chains rattled as the haltered cattle turned restlessly in the mangers, waiting to be milked.

The gipsy's wife came up to the farm with three pennies and an empty jug, wanting a pint of milk. From the gate she saw the girl come out of the shed, picking the straw off her shoulders and pulling her dress into shape. The gipsy came out after her, brushing his hair back with his hand and caressing the girl with his eyes. He did not see his wife, and she turned back with the empty jug and made her way behind the hedge to the caravan. When she got back to the river she found Micah talking to a swarthy, dark-haired man. He wore a black flannel shirt and brown corduroy trousers; his chin was covered with a light stubble and his eyes were bright as blackberries. He looked up when he heard her step and smiled, looking swiftly at her body. She was breathing heavily, her bosom heaving.

"He's a Frenchman, mam," Micah said portentously. "Aren't you, mister?"

The man laughed, caught Micah by his leg and wrist and swung him up and down.

"Pas tout-à-fait, mon vieux," he said. "Je suis Breton — plus gallois que Français."

"Can you tell what he's saying, mam?" Micah asked.

She smiled. "I can't understand," she said.

Her face was dark and engrossed, her eyes filmy.

"You are dreaming of what?" asked the Breton.

"Eh?" she turned to him, her face suddenly aware and passionate.

"Your thought was absent," he said.

"Yes," she laughed breathlessly. Her eyes knotted again.

"You are a peddler like me?" the man asked.

She saw a smooth, rounded pole in the grass, notched at each end, with strings of onions lying beside it.

"Johnny Onions?" she asked.

"Yes," he laughed, "Johnny Onions. I leave my family in Brittany, I sail with my brother to Cardiff. I sell my onions across Wales, making friends with the little boys. This pullet — is he a gipsy?"

Micah tugged at her skirt, but she ignored him.

"Half and half," she said. "His father is a gipsy — he used to live with the Pembroke tribe. I'm Welsh — my father is a farmer."

"You speak nice," the Breton said.

"I went to school," she answered, and paused. "I didn't learn enough to keep me out of trouble, though." She laughed. He looked at her for a moment in silence.

"You like this life?" he asked.

She tugged nervously at the grass.

"Mam, look at this ladybird," Micah said, lifting his cupped hand. She did not hear.

"I do not like living in a house," she said.

The Breton stretched his sunburnt arms above his head.

"Well, I go before dark," he said.

"Stay and eat with us," she said suddenly.

He looked into her dark, brooding face. "Better I go," he said.

"No, stay," she begged. It was as though he caught a sudden glimpse of Hell. Her eyes and lips, the very look of her, were momentarily alive with a dark intense passion, as if night had broken into a wild, translucent dawn and still remained night. Her mood enveloped him like heat, filtering through his body, creeping through the roots of his hair. Micah put his arms around her neck, tightly, and bit into the white flesh at the nape of her neck. She screamed as his teeth cut through her skin and sprang to her feet, shaking the child off her back. Micah cowered on the grass, quivering like an animal. She stood over him, pale, her hand fingering the wound in her neck. For a second she stood, tense and trembling. Then she threw herself full length in the grass and her shoulders shivered with sobs. The Breton knelt over her, laid his hand on her hair, caressed her.

"It is alright, my darling," he said. "It is alright. Do not please — " Micah caught his hand.

"Don't touch her," he hissed.

"What's up?" The gipsy stood over them. He walked as silently as a fox.

"The little boy bite his mother," the Breton said.

The gipsy bent down, his fist clenched. Micah had turned limp and sallow. The gipsy hit him with his fist. The boy gasped. He was limp as jelly. The gipsy hit him again and again, ferociously. Then he straightened his back and looked down at the sprawling woman and the kneeling man.

"Johnny Onions?" he asked.

The Breton nodded. "Your wife ask me to stay to eat," he said; "eat my onions, eh?"

The gipsy laughed. Warmth flooded back into his body and he swung his arms.

"Sure, stay. We'll eat fried onions together." He touched his wife with his boot. "Come on," he said, "I'll light a fire."

The Breton put his hands under her armpits and lifted her to her knees. She got up lithely to her feet and entered the caravan, keeping her face averted. Micah slipped off, crouching, into the copse. The gipsy opened his clasp knife, cut three beech branches, tied the tops together with a length of wire, sharpened the other ends and stuck them into the ground to make a three-legged stand for the kettle. He worked dexterously, whistling between his teeth, engrossed and happy. The Breton watched the woman busying herself with cups and bread and frying pan. Micah returned with an armful of dry brushwood and gorse and laid it by his father. The gipsy looked up, smiled at him. Micah's face was white and serious.

"Little weasel," the gipsy mocked.

The gipsy talked and laughed a lot as they ate the fried onions. He did not grumble that there was no milk for the tea. He told the Breton tale after tale of his youth with the Pembroke tribe. He showed a blue weal down his side; the country folk called them Furies. His wife looked coldly at his animated face. Micah sat close to her side, his face shining in the firelight, his hand resting on her knee. Now and again he regarded the two men opposite him — his father and the strong, tawny

Johnny Onions — and edged nearer the soft warmth of his mother. She covered his small hand with her own and watched unobserved the fire flickering over the stranger's face.

When the meal was finished she put Micah to bed in the caravan, set a dry stump on the dying fire, and stayed listening to the talk of the two men. The Breton was working his way down the coast to Cardigan. There he would meet his brother and together they would return to Cardiff, selling in the coast towns of Pembroke and Carmarthen. It was not as pleasant as Brittany; at home there were friends in the evenings, "bons copains"; but better than starving, or working in a Paris factory. He choked in the city.

The gipsy lay back and yawned.

"I'll sleep out here to-night," he said drowsily. "It's too hot to sleep indoors. You sleep on the grass too, Johnny?"

"Hay after harvest dead and soft," the Breton laughed, "before the harvest sweet and hard. I sleep on my feet easy."

The gipsy yawned and turned comfortably onto his side.

"Goodni'," he said thickly.

They sat still by the fire, watching the flames dancing red and blue and yellow over the crackling wood. Occasionally a red ash leaped into the air with a small explosion and floated up into the purple dusk and lost its fire. The meadow was silent, washed with the scent of leaves and grasses, tremulous with the down-pressing night. The Breton looked up from the fire and caught her looking at him. He nodded with his head into the darkness and the fire sang out in his eyes. She stood up and softly walked across the gorse towards the river. The trees on the bank were masses of intenser dusk. She could hear the river swirling through the naked alder roots. The sound of it drowned the rustle of the grass against the Breton's boots but she was aware of his coming with all her body. When he put his hand on her shoulder she turned in to him and leaned against his body, her cheek tingling with the feel of his rough flannel shirt and the rise and fall of his breathing.

"You are not an easy woman," he whispered, "you do not do this before."

"Never," she replied, letting her hand move down his cheek and his neck until it rested on the warm flesh of his shoulder. "But he and I — we are nothing now."

"Why?" he asked.

She shrugged her shoulders.

"But that is not why I am with you," she said. Her voice was urgent.

"Why then?" he asked.

She did not reply. Then she said, "If my husband wakes, he will kill me."

He could feel how the tide had set in her. He laughed gutturally and it engulfed them both.

Afterwards, lying under the trees, listening to the water, she was silent.

"Best go back," he whispered.

She started. "I had forgotten," she said, and in a panic, starting up, "you won't leave me tomorrow, will you?"

He laughed. She heard him plucking the grass. It sounded callous, the sound of taking and not giving.

"Tomorrow, yes. I meet my brother in Cardigan after three days."

"No," she shuddered, holding him in a passion. He tilted her head back.

"Best to go," he said, kissing her lips. "If he finds us — "

There was a rustle in the long grass and he sprang back from her. She did not move, in terror. Then a plop in the water and a rat came swimming downstream. "Sainte Marie," he breathed, his voice quivering.

She went back by herself. The gipsy was lying by the dead fire as she had left him, and she slipped past him into the caravan. She stripped and climbed softly into bed. She put her hand out and touched Micah's naked little body. He wriggled close to her, put his arms round her bosom and his head in her breasts...

*****

The leaves were gold and dancing in the early sun when Micah woke her.

"Come on , mam," he said, shaking her head. "You be a cabbage and I'll be a caterpillar and you scream when I eat you — " she sat up.

"Look how fine it is," she said, her sleepy eyes dazzled with the tossing of light from the leaves onto the innumerable blue spear heads of the sky. Then she remembered the night and sat still. She threw the quilt off and dressed quickly, not wanting her husband to see her naked. Then she went to the door. He had lit the fire; the kettle was singing.

"I was just going to call you," he said. "Do some breakfast while I go for a swim."

"Where's Johnny Onions?" she asked.

He looked up shrewdly. "You sound excited," he said.

She was afraid he had gone. "I just wanted to know," she said.

"Well, he's over in the trees," he replied, smirking, "doing his business. Send Micah out. I'll take him swimming with me."

She went into the caravan and lifted Micah out of bed.

"Off with you, snake's body," she said. He ran out naked into the sunlight. The Breton had come back and he greeted Micah cheerily, holding his arms out, asking the boy to play pig-a-back. Micah shrank away, hanging his head and frowning. The Breton laughed.

"Sulker," he mocked, pulling his ear. Micah broke loose and ran after his father. The long grass reached to his thighs as he bobbed like a naked little cupid across the meadow.

"Why are you crying?" his father asked. "Afraid of the water?" Micah sniffled.

"What's up, boy?" The gipsy was gentle with him this morning. Micah sat on the bank and shivered. He would not enter the water. His father swam up to him, grasped a willow root and let the current break in a wave over his back.

"Say, boy, what's the matter?"

Micah's face puckered, angry and fearful.

"That Johnny Onions," he stammered.

"What's wrong with him?" the gipsy asked.

"He's going to steal Mam," Micah burst out.

The gipsy laughed contemptuously. "What for would he steal *her*?"

Micah was stung by his laughter. "He took her away last night," he said, his voice envenomed.

"Where to?" the gipsy asked.

"Into the meadow," the boy replied, frightened by his father's wild face. It was terribly ugly and cruel, and smiling, and his eyes all set. The water bubbled against his side and broke over his skin in a little rush of white foam.

"Don't say nothing to mam," the gipsy said. The tears were trickling down Micah's cheeks and dropping onto his belly and his thighs. The gipsy caught him by the ankle and jerked him into the water.

After breakfast the Breton put the strings of onions on each end of his pole, shouldered it, and stood up to take his leave.

"I remind me always of your goodness," he said, in his rich, curling voice, and added a few words of patois.

The gipsy got up lazily. "I'll come with you a bit," he said. "I'm going to town to get her ear rings out of pawn. Come with me?"

"Volontiers," the Breton said, clapping the gipsy's shoulder.

"Let's get some money from the bed first," the gipsy said.

He entered the caravan. His wife went to the Breton and stood in front of him, very near, rocking a little on her feet.

"You *must* come back," she said. She was nearly out of her body with longing. The Breton moved back.

"I must go selling to get money," he said. "I must get money for my own wife."

"Wife?" she gasped.

He nodded. "I have three children."

She blanched, and then her desire surged back.

"You must come back," she said, her eyes burning in her.

"Come on, Johnny," the gipsy called, "no time to talk."

"Tou'suite," the Breton answered. "Good-bye, missus, thank you." He turned away and walked through the copse with the gipsy. She could hear the twigs crackling under their feet long after they had gone from sight, and then there was an empty silence. She stood frozen. The tears welled up, turning her desolation to chaos. The day blurred in her sight.

Micah tugged at her skirt. "He's gone, Mam, he's gone," the boy's voice was jubilant. "We'll play all the morning, Mam, is it?"...

She could not stand it any longer. All the dead morning, all the parched afternoon, this tearing ache in her lungs, in her bowels. When her husband returned he would be bound to notice it. If she could be calm for a minute, perhaps she might muzzle her passion, drive it back to its lair. She must have respite from the aching for his hands, for the down on his arms, for the fire of his body and the swooning intimacy of his eyes. She had never burned like this before. Oh God! and the silly cows tugging at the grasses and chewing, chewing. And the standing trees all round. The life in her leaped in a frenzy to be mingled again with the other life. She stood up and walked dizzily along the path through the beeches. Micah was playing in the stream. He saw her go and ran after her frightened. She turned on him. "Go back," she flared, "go back. Tell your father I've gone to Cardigan."

Micah stood still. Her face wasn't like his mother's. It had no kindness. He watched her go between the trees. When he realised he was alone, he was afraid to move. He stood there, between the beeches, trembling, for a long time. Then he turned, his eyes blurred with tears, and ran in terror to the caravan, up the steps and into bed. He pulled the quilt over his head and lay in the hollow her body had made. In the dark he unlaced his boots and pushed them over the side of the bed. He pulled her pillow down beside him and stopped weeping....

He woke with a start. His father was bending over him, holding a

candle unsteadily in his hand. A fleck of hot grease fell on his body and
he cried aloud.

"Where's she gone?" the gipsy hiccoughed. His breath was sweet,
his face haggard. Micah was glad to see him — glad, yet frightened.

"To Cardigan," he said.

"Cardigan?" the gipsy laughed, rolling his head and laughing till his
voice cracked and he fell into a choking cough. "Cardigan?" he began
laughing again, spittle running from his mouth. Micah huddled in the
corner by the wall, the quilt drawn up to his chin. The gipsy began
singing drunkenly, waving the candle.

"The King of Spain's daughter
Came to visit me,
But I was as dead as dead could be."

"But it's a long way to Cardigan for a lady." He uncorked a bottle of
whisky. "Just a drop to keep my spirits up till she's back."

He took a long swig. The blood came into his face with the heat of it
and fled again. It seemed to sober him. He sat heavily on the bed. They
sat in silence, the two of them, for hours. The night grew threadbare
and grey; the pale gaunt day came lapping in through the open door.
The table, the two chairs and the cupboard turned from pitch black
pools to sharp silhouettes; as the darkness thinned they took body and
colour. The candle stump guttered to a feeble, sulphurous yellow and
spluttered out. And both of them sat waiting, saying nothing.

★★★★★

She knew every turn of the road to Cardigan. They worked that way
often in the caravan; before her fly-away marriage her father had driven
her in every week to shop and market. So she walked without looking at
the road, in a great haste. She walked for hours along the dusty white
lanes; only when the sun dazzled her eyes did she realise that it was near
sunset. She looked about her. There were fifteen odd miles between
her and Cardigan. She could never do it without a rest. Her feet were
sore and her legs like wet clay. She sat in the dusty hedge and idly
fingered a tangle of campion and speedwell. Her stomach was empty
and weak and the gnats gave her no rest. She got up, wearily brushing
them off her face and neck, and began walking again. Fifteen miles...it
wasn't much use. And no money for food. In any case he might not be
there for two days. What would she live on till then? And when he did

come, what then? He had no money, and he had had his fill of her. She
was like a common whore, a madhatter, looking for a man who didn't
want her. She took her shoes off and bathed her swollen feet in a little
brook. The water prattled like ice over her toes. She moved them up
and down and her body sighed with relief. She took a handful of cress,
broke off the roots, washed it and put it in her mouth. It was cool on her
tongue, and yet it burnt her like a remorse. Ever since she had seen the
gipsy come out of the cowshed, dusting his knees, she had been
helpless in the whirlpool of her mind and body. She saw it clearly,
looking down upon herself. She must go back to the caravan. If he had
stayed in town overnight, he would never know. And Micah there
alone — God! She pulled her sandals on, fingers trembling with haste,
and started back along the lane, walking swiftly with a new energy. The
night swirled round her, dew-wet, and a stripling moon moved with
her. Once she stopped for weariness, slept in the hedge for a little, woke
with a start, and went on. Then the road turned from grey to ghostly
white and the river gathered the first liquid radiance between its banks.
She stripped and slipped into the cold, gleaming water. If he was back,
it would be well to have her wits about her. She dressed again, tied her
dripping hair, and crossed the last few fields to the caravan. It was very
still. How she hoped he had not returned! She climbed softly up the
steps. She would slip into bed beside Micah. She screamed.

He stood up, confronting her, his arm upraised. He was chalk-white
and unkempt and his eyes were black. He rocked a little on his feet and
a filthy grin grew slowly on his face.

"You — whore," he grunted.

She saw the bottle clenched in his uplifted hand and she laughed.

"Whore!" she said shrilly, "you're a fine one to call me whore. You
creeping swine. Didn't I see you crawl out of the cowshed with that
farm girl yesterday? You — my — *husband!*"

She wasn't frightened now. She was mad with him. He had taken a
woman after refusing her. If he was going to fight, she was strong, too.

"I'll kill you," he screamed. She leaped at him. The bottle
splintered against the wall and they rolled over, fighting like cats. She
was strong, stronger than she had ever been, and his fists did not hurt
her. Micah climbed across the bed and ran in terror through the door.
He paused in the meadow. He could hear them scuffling and grunting
inside. He ran into the wood, out of earshot.

He pummelled her until his arms ached but she clung to him, her
hands locked round his neck, her ankles clasped behind his knees. He
was breathless; and suddenly, with a grunt, the fury left him and he

relaxed. She lay taut on his body for a minute, then slowly loosed him and lifted herself up on her elbows. His eyes were shut, his cheeks sunken. He had taken another woman. Well, *she* was mistress of him now. And she brushed his curly hair back from his forehead and wiped the sweat from his face. He opened his eyes and saw her face close bending over him.

"You are back, then?" — his voice sounded strangely young.

"Yes," she said, "yes. Do you want me?"

He took her head in his hands and drew her down to him.

"I always wanted you." He closed his eyes again. "I can't understand what happened — "

She covered his mouth with her hand.

"Never mind," she whispered, "never mind about that. Let's lie on the bed. It's alright now."

The gipsy pulled a paper envelope from his pocket, took her cupped hand and poured the ear rings into it. She bent naked before the mirror, screwing them into the lobes of her ears and brushing her black hair back.

After an hour lying in the deepest part of the wood, Micah came back slowly and fearfully to the clearing. Slowly he tiptoed up the steps of the caravan, apprehensive of the silence, and found them lying together under the red blanket, face to face and fast asleep.

The child did not wake them. Instead he sat quietly on the steps and carved a whistle out of a sycamore branch, knowing that when they woke everything would be the way he liked it.

Picnic

There were three of them sitting in the shelter of the sand dune. Auntie Flora with her thin hooked nose, her eyebrows that met in the middle like the drawing of a black gull and her gimlet eyes that bored into you when she asked you "personal" questions or told you that *somebody* had forgotten to pull the lavatory chain. Uncle Hubert, with his enormous tummy that looked as though a sack of barley had been propped up between his bandy little legs. And Marion, with the broad forehead and narrow shoulders of an early Flemish madonna, eating too many sandwiches because the silence embarrassed her.

"There's sand everywhere," fussed Auntie Flora, glaring accusingly at Marion, "you must have had sandy fingers when you buttered the bread."

Marion looked down and saw Auntie Flora wipe her false teeth in the hem of her voile frock as though they were a pair of spectacles. Prudently she turned to watch the sea, the flat, grey, monotonous sea.

Uncle Hubert coughed, sighed, breathed deeply and said "'Bout time our Leonard got here."

"Stop fussing about Len, for goodness sake," snapped Auntie Flora. "I dare say his boss needed him, or that precious Norah of his kept him waiting. If I had *half* our Leonard's gifts I wouldn't wait for any girl, *I* know."

Uncle Hubert wiped his perspiring hands in his indecently tight trousers and groaned as he tried to straighten his back.

"Why don't you go for a walk, Hubert," Auntie Flora snapped, "instead of wriggling like a worm. Take Marion for a paddle."

Uncle Hubert filled his pipe before replying.

"Walk?" he said ponderously, and lit a match. "What? In these boots? On this sand?" He cleared his throat. "I don't know why we came here in the first place. Oh damn!" The match burnt his finger and thumb and he thrust them straight into his round, fat mouth.

"Give it here" — Auntie Flora was exasperated — "You ought to know

better than to play about with lighted matches. Here's some butter."
Her false teeth clicked in vexation as she rubbed an opened sandwich
against the burnt skin.

"I can't see *anything* there," she said.

Marion was so relieved to think that Uncle Hubert had forgotten
about the paddle that she took another sandwich from the newspaper-
cloth and thereby exposed a Harrods' dance frock advertisement.
Quite suddenly she "saw" Auntie Flora trying to struggle into the
frock, and the sandwich went down the wrong way.

Auntie Flora slapped her back. "Eat slowly, for goodness sake," she
said.

And then Leonard yelled out from the top of the sand dune.

"Hallo, all of you," he shouted. "Mind us butting in?"

"Len!" cried Auntie Flora. "Mind? Oh ho, you *are* a one! Mind? I
should think not."

And Len, large as life in his new gaberdine grey bags and oxblood
sports jacket, came sliding down the sandy slope, gripping Norah by
the elbow. Auntie Flora's shining face wore her special smile, like a
smear of margarine.

They all stood up and shook hands. Marion was too embarrassed
either to see or hear. But when they all sat down again round the greasy
paper cloth, the awkwardness and the heat ebbed slowly back and she
looked up at Norah. Their eyes met and intuitively they smiled at each
other. She hadn't expected Norah to be like that.

Auntie Flora began saying how charming the beach was, and Marion
stopped listening. She scooped up a handful of dry sand and watched it
pour through a crack in her cupped hands and form a tiny, fluid
pyramid. God made the mountains like that.

She had heard Leonard tell Auntie Flora "all about" Norah — that
she was at college and had met him at tennis and was a jolly good sport.
And Marion was puzzled and distressed. What *could* Norah see in a
blusterer like Leonard? And then Auntie Flora's words broke through
her stockade of thoughts. Her body dissolved in the outflow of her
shame. "Of course Marion is only with us for a week or two," Auntie
Flora was saying. "She's had a thin time lately" — the usual suggestive
pause — "and we felt we'd like to help a little — you always *feel* for
people in trouble, somehow, don't you?"

Marion lifted her flushed and naked face and looked straight into
Norah's eyes. Norah knew that Daddy was in jail alright — Leonard
was so confiding — and her grey eyes were full of understanding, her
smile of healing.

"Ah well," Leonard sighed sententiously, "it's no use crying over spilt milk. Let's go and skim stones, Marion, shall we?"

Marion watched her toe scrape a furrow in the sand; a sand-hopper struggled against the landslide.

"Sulky," Leonard mocked.

"Come on, Marion," Norah whispered, touching her bowed head.

Marion climbed to her feet and began walking towards the sea.

"Off with you, Len," Auntie Flora directed, "Norah'll stay and tidy up with me. I *despise* leaving refuse, Norah, don't you?"

"You're not expecting me to leave Norah behind, mum, are you?" Leonard asked indignantly.

"Go on then," Auntie Flora melted into a beetroot colour, "the three of you. And take Dad with you."

"Pity to wake him," Leonard said.

When they reached the sea Marion and Norah wandered off and began picking shells, storing them in the skirt of Marion's frock, which she lifted up by the hem like a little hammock. She made tiny sounds of delight over the delicate whorled, subtly coloured shells. They were so *strange*. Quite different, somehow, from people or toys. New; a new, new thing; a whole new life. And she looked at the sea heaving, and the passionate green waves of curving glass. Oh! She danced light-footed into the water and the green turned white round her bare ankles. The shells laughed together in her rumpled skirt and she turned to look at Norah, laughing with joy.

Leonard was there, with his arm round Norah's shoulder.

"Watch that wave," he shouted. But the wave broke over her shoulders. He burst out laughing.

As they walked back across the beach Norah smoothed Marion's tousled hair.

"When do you return home, Marion?" she asked.

"Tuesday," Leonard said, when Marion did not reply. And then Marion shook the shells out of her lap, in a cascade over her bare, spindly legs.

"Don't you want to keep the shells?" Norah asked softly.

Marion shook her head mutely and would not look up.

"Come on, Norah," Leonard said. "She's sulking again. Let's run."

He grabbed Norah's hand and made her run with him.

And Marion followed behind, pale and shivering, though not with cold.

The Lapse

At 4.13 Henry showed his season ticket to the porter and climbed into the railway car. He nodded politely to Miss Burge, the teacher at the kindergarten, who sat in her corner seat knitting the green jumper she had started last month; and to the district nurse in her black pork-pie hat, her professional bag tucked warmly against her stomach. They both smiled back — nothing said, never anything said — and he went to his usual place at the far end of the car. He filled his pipe while waiting for the train to start, and then put it back into his pocket.

Back and fore, back and fore, like a shuttle, workwards each morning, homewards each night, ra-ta-ta, ra-ta-ta, the train's travelling beat — how many times have I done this journey, these last five years? If I put the journeys end to end it would stretch a long way — right into Tibet perhaps, along the Turk-Sib, among the moujiks... Oh dear! Henry yawned and gazed indifferently at the row of slatternly back gardens and flapping clothes lines past which the train ran. Twice a day for five years, Bank holidays excepted, those drab hotchpotch backs where the wives riddled yesterday's ashes and the children sat on the steps eating bread and jam. It was so depressing to see those streets every day, always the same, and the people always the same — how many of them knew they had been condemned to serve a lifer?

And then, with a rattle and a wrench, the open country; the hills swooping like swallows. Below the embankment the black river swirled, wandering down from the coal mines at the head of the valley. And the train rattled over the bridge that spanned the river; Henry felt the drop under the bridge, sheer and empty in the pit of his stomach, like a bird flashing through a hollow cave. And on, accelerando, through the cutting. What shall I do to-night, the tired voice asked in his head. Pictures? Or a nap and a stroll down to the billiard hall? I don't know what to do, I can never make up my mind. I know what'll happen — I'll stand by my bedroom window looking down into the empty street. And in the end I won't go out. I'll waste the night, as usual, as I waste everything. I ought to decide to *do* something, to get *on*... One day I *will* do something, to justify all this waste, something grand, careless... I *must*...

I wonder what's for dinner this evening. Mother will have it all ready, whatever it is, warmed up and waiting; and she'll sit opposite me while I eat it, watching me wolf it; and at the end she'll have a cup of tea with me... Doctor said she's alright. But often I dream she is dead, and I wake up sweating.

Halt number one. The schoolgirl comes in and sits where she always sits, and takes a book out of her satchel, a different book this week. She has grown a lot in the last five years. She used to be a scrimpy, flat-chested little thing, her head always poked out of the window; now she sits absorbed in her book and there is a difference about everything she does. She must be about sixteen; she hardly looks it, with her mouse-bitten fringe and her black stockings. She's got a strange face; those who don't know her would never call it pretty. They'd only see her prominent top teeth, her weak chin, her flat cheekbones. They'd miss the secret quality, the look she has when she turns from her book to look out through the window. She's pulling on her woollen gloves; she gets out at the next halt. I wish I knew where she lives — in the semi-detached red-roofed houses on the right, or the huddle of slums on the left? Not that it matters really; the train always starts off before she's left the platform. Sometimes, if she hasn't finished her chapter before the train stops, she walks along the platform with her book open....

The little woman who only travels on Thursdays is snoring; she always puts her feet up and snoozes. Her head hangs forward, her oak-apple nose nearly dropping into her shopping basket, her pink umbrella laid across her lap. Her shoes need soling. Oh, curse it and curse it. It's always, always the same, daunting you properly. Makes you want to smash the window, pull the communication cord, scream.... And instead you swallow the scream; you can hear it struggling inside you, battering at the door of your throat. And you sit still, and look at the old lady's brown hat, and Miss Burge knitting, and *her* reading. It's been lovely, really, watching her grow up, wondering about her, her name and what she thinks when she's reading and what Life will do to her, and feeling sorry for her, somehow...

The train stopped with a shudder that rattled all the windows. The red roofs and the biscuit facades of the new houses waited faithfully outside. The girl closed her book and obediently went out.

And then, all of a sudden, Henry got up and walked down the car, past Miss Burge and the district nurse, who stared at him in astonishment. The blood was beating like a steel hammer behind his eyes. He fumbled and tugged at the carriage door. But he got out, and was standing on the ash platform, for the first time, ever. She was a few yards ahead of him, finishing her chapter, walking slowly, unaware. He stepped forward. The porter shouted "O.K." to the guard. The engine-driver leaned over the footplate. Henry stood stock still, looking at the girl, at the railings, at the yellow advertisement of Duck, Son and Pinker's pianos. The guard shouted "What are you getting off here for?" The green flag and the engine's hoot... Henry scrambled back into the carriage, the guard shouted at him and a porter blasphemed. He shut the door with quivering hands and slouched back to his seat. Miss Burge and the nurse stared at him and at each other. He didn't notice anything. He just slumped into his seat and clenched his hands, squeezing them between his knees. After a couple of minutes he blew his nose hard and rubbed some smuts out of his eyes. The train crashed into the black mouth of the tunnel with a shriek. It woke the old lady. She opened her eyes and tidied her collar, as if it were the most natural thing in the world to open one's eyes, after they have been closed.

The train came out of the tunnel and stopped. The old lady picked up her basket and her pink umbrella, Miss Burge rolled up her knitting, the nurse fingered the silver hatpin that skewered her porkpie hat. Henry followed them out onto the platform and slunk past the guard like a criminal.

Interruption

The railway bridge was a good place from which to see. You could see the holes in the roofs where a winter wind blew away a slate or two. You could see the chimneys where the shiny starlings lived, where they croaked and preened. Or the back gardens — cabbage run to seed, ashes and flimsy fences of stolen pit timber and iron bedsteads — or the lavatories at the bottom of the gardens. But of course the real thing you could see was the railway line, passing right underneath the bridge, whew, right underneath. When the train came swinging out of the station, and raced towards the bridge, getting bigger and bigger, louder and fiercer and faster, whew, that was the time for you to be on the bridge.

"You're afraid to open your legs when the train comes, you are," said Dickie.

When Annie Mayhew didn't answer back he said it again, prodding her this time with his toe — the toe that stuck out of his toecap, his big toe.

"Oh, get off it and stop your messing," Annie said in a pet. She was squatting on her heels laying the table.

"Playing house." Dickie scoffed. "Pansy girl, paint your face next, won't play cowboys. You're *afraid* to open your legs." Yes, he was quite furious.

Annie picked up a stone from the house.

"I'll lamm you if you don't leave me be," she said viciously. "You know we been told to keep quiet to-day, till they've gone. *I* don't want a hiding when I get home even if you do."

"Pansy," muttered Dickie, cowed. "Wait till the next train comes. We'll see." He glowered darkly through the fencing at the empty line.

"It won't be long," he said, threateningly.

Then little Gwennie came up to the bridge, crying and snuffling and scratching her bottom. She had red hair and a patched blue coat pinned round her throat by a safety pin and her delicate face was dirty and stained with tears.

"Come on into the kitchen, Gwen," Annie said motheringly. "Been stung again?"

"No," Gwennie replied miserably hugging her trouble and staying outside the front door.

"What is it, my dear?" said Annie, stepping over the front wall with the careful grace of a princess of Brobdignag paying a state call on the duchess of Lilliput.

"Our Johnnie've gone up the mountain," Gwennie sobbed.

"Well, whassa matter, gal? 'E'll come down again when 'e's 'ungry?" Annie reassured her.

"'E won't," said Gwennie obstinately, beginning to cry again. "There's a stone up the mountain."

"'E'll climb over it, Johnnie will," Annie said with conviction.

Gwennie hesitated doubtfully, then stepped into the house.

"Is it washing day today?" she asked.

"Shift your old house, Annie Mayhew," Dickie said peremptorily. "They're coming now. The wheels will go over your house."

Annie looked down the road.

"Ooh!" she exclaimed, breathless with rapture. "Look, Gwennie; it's the coffin. Ooh, and all them white flowers. And the glass." She couldn't take her eyes off the little row of taxis and the gleaming hearse and the dark-suited bunch of men outside the dilapidated house.

"Ooh, there's lovely," Annie breathed, gazing and gazing. "Is it heavy, Dickie, for all them men to be carrying it?"

"Course it is," Dickie said scornfully. "You try and lift it."

"She didn't look heavy," Annie said thoughtfully; "she was in white and her hands folded, and white ribbons; she didn't look heavy."

"Shift your house out the way," Dickie insisted.

She cupped her tattered pinafore up and put the stones of the house into it. Dickie put a few into his jersey. Then they stood up. The hearse had started up the road towards the bridge.

"Come by here, Gwennie," Annie said suddenly, taking the child fiercely by the hand. They stood against the railings watching the hearse approach and the double row of mourners.

"I seen a dead rat, too," Annie said, mostly to herself.

And then, while they stood awed and silent, they heard a train rattle out of the station. They could see the white smoke, and then the train itself, very tiny, and then it grew bigger, swiftly, swiftly. Dickie shuffled his feet gauged the distance of the black crawling procession, shuffled his feet and frowned. Then he said:

"Come on, you baby. Come on by the railings. Open your legs, you baby." Before Annie could stop him he had dragged her by the skirt across the road. They were standing over the rail, looking down at the monstrous burnished engine, the screaming steam, the mad mechanical stampede, and she couldn't move her limbs or her tongue. She was petrified, rooted, like those nightmares when you're being eaten by wolves and you can't shout or anything. The train shrieked a warning.

"Open your legs,"Dickie shouted, deliriously.

She obeyed, and the train rushed through, whew, through her very legs, sucking her entrails out, emptying her, terribly. Her mouth was wide open but no sound came. Her lips quivered and her face was dead white.

The hearse went slowly past.

Even when the procession had gone out of sight she still stood shivering against the railings. Little Gwennie, crying again, tugged her skirt.

"Let's build the house again, Annie, is it?" she said.

"You're frightened," Dickie taunted, sticking his face in front of her's and then whooping off down the road, clicking his tongue like a broncho buster.

"What was in that box?" Gwennie said thoughtfully, "under them flowers?"

Between scorn and pity Annie gazed at the untidy red hair and the big soft eyes inarticulately.

"Why," she said, "don't you *know?*"

And then her eyes filled with tears, like Gwennie's. But not because of the train. Dickie could say what he liked. She wasn't crying because of the train. She'd shown him about *that* alright.

"Come on, Gwennie," she said thickly. "My mother said to bring you home to *our* house for tea to-day."

Clinging to Annie's skirt, skipping with delight, Gwennie went out to tea.

The Housekeeper

Mervyn walked sulkily into the kitchen, hanging his head and kicking the toe of his shoe against the passage skirting.

"Granny won't let me go out through the front door, Mam," he grumbled.

Myfanwy put down the floorcloth and straightened her back. She was kneeling on a piece of sacking and washing the kitchen floor. All the chairs were piled on the oilcloth table and the rag mat rolled back to the fender.

"Never mind, bach," she said. "Go out the back way instead."

"But I *want* to go out the front," he wailed, tears brimming into his eyes, "and she won't let me. She've put her chair right in the doorway and she said not to bother her."

"She's waiting for dad to come back," Myfanwy said. "She wants to see him coming up the street."

"Well, has she *got* to sit in the doorway for that? Oh Mam," — vexation made the child almost inarticulate — "why does she live with us?"

"Because she's your daddy's mother, that's why," Myfanwy said. "Now go on out the back like a good boy, and play with Jackie."

"Jackie won't play, he's reading," Mervyn pouted. And then, seeing that his mother had said her last word and was wringing the floorcloth in the bucket of black water, he trailed his feet towards the back door.

"I hope she dies," he muttered, "I hope she dies."

*****

"He's coming," Granny croaked in her ancient, broken voice. Myfanwy heard her mumbling excitedly to herself. A minute later she heard Penry's hacking cough outside the front door.

"Did you get the money alright?" Granny quavered.

"'Course I did, Mam," Penry answered. "They always pay the dole, gal, on the dot."

"And my pension? My five shillings?" the old woman pursued.

"Aye, and your five bob," he laughed.

"Let me see it, then," she said thirstily.

"Wait till I get into the kitchen, then," he said, good-humouredly. "You don't want everybody to know how rich we are, do you?"

"Alright then," Granny picked up her stick and pressing the end of it against the doorkerb tried to push herself onto her feet.

"Up you get," he said, putting his hands under her armpits. "You're nothing but an old bag of bones, Mam."

"Never mind about that," she replied, breathlessly. "I'll live longer than you now, my boy — the way she's feeding you."

★★★★★

"Haven't you finished scrubbing yet?" he asked, entering the kitchen and pushing his cloth cap onto the back.

"Not yet," Myfanwy replied. She did not look up.

"You're getting house-proud, that's what's the matter with you," he said.

She dropped the floorcloth into the pail and stood up. Her auburn hair had escaped from the ribbon with which she had pulled it back from her forehead, and fell in clusters over her face. She tossed it back with a shake of her head and tucked her stained calico blouse inside the waistband of her skirt. Her breasts pressed against the thin wet blouse; her face was flushed with bending, her hands puffed and red with immersion in the scrubbing water.

"Is a beggar proud of his rags?" she said, rocking on the balls of her feet and smiling in a way he didn't understand.

"Where's my pension?" Granny nagged. Spittle trickled down the runnels of withered skin at the corners of her sagged and toothless mouth. Myfanwy picked up the hem of her apron and wiped it off.

"Makes your mouth water, does it?" she said with a laugh.

"Get off me," Granny whined. "Where's my money?"

Penry took a brown envelope out of the back pocket of his frayed and dirty grey trousers, and spilt the contents onto the table. A bright silver shilling rolled between the chairlegs.

"There it is," he said. "Five shillings for you, Mam, twenty-six for Myfanwy and me, three for Jackie and two for Mervyn."

Granny's brown skinny talons closed over her portion.

"What are you doing?" Penry said. "Leave it be, gal."

"I'm going to keep it myself from now on," Granny said. She held the money against her flannel blouse, pressing it to her withered bosom.

"Well, you'll have to go and live somewhere else then," Myfanwy said, indifferently.

"No, I won't," Granny screamed. "I'm staying here, see? You've been taking my five shillings regular this last seven years, and making on me every week. I don't cost you five shillings the way you feed me, I know."

"Cool down a bit, Mam," Penry interposed, putting his hand on her shoulder. "You'll be having a stroke if you don't watch."

"I don't care," Granny shouted, her old face working and twitching, wet with tears and saliva, "I don't care. It's time somebody told her, she've robbed us all long enough. Tell the police, I would."

*****

Myfanwy laughed; her face was wild with scorn and anger. She untied her apron strings and pulled the soaking apron over her head.

"Well, manage for yourselves, then," She said. "I'm going."

She was just pulling her coat on when Mervyn came running in from the back, whooping like a redskin. He nearly knocked Granny over as he leaped to his mother and tugged at her skirt.

"There's fox and 'ounds on the mountain, Mam," he said, jumping up and down with excitement. "Can me and Jackie go and follow them?"

She ran her fingers through his hair.

"You *are* a dirty little thing," she said softly. "What have you been doing?" She wiped his running nose and tidied his red jersey.

"Digging for treasure," he said. "Can we follow the fox and 'ounds?"

"I'll take you up, now," Penry said. "I've got to go up to the allotment with the sow's food. Gi'me five minutes, that's all."

Jackie saw the money on the table.

"'Ad dole, dad, is it?" He gazed at the bright pile of silver and copper. "Can I 'ave a 'a'penny this week?"

Myfanwy picked two pennies up.

"You can have two this week," she said, "and give the other penny to Jackie, will you?"

"Oooh!" Mervyn was speechless.

"Now don't go spending it all," she said. "You've got to put some of it by for the Sunday school trip in the summer, mind."

"I'll only spend a 'a'penny,'" he said solemnly, and then shot out of the door, yelling the news to his brother.

Myfanwy took off her coat.

"There's hot water for the pig's food in the kettle," she said. "We're nearly out of coal, too."

"I'll go up the tip to-morrow all day," he said. "I can't leave the sow to-day, though. I think she'll be dropping to-day. She was lying on her side groaning this morning, before I went up for the dole, and swollen up so — she's bound to farrow before to-morrow."

He fetched a bucket full of potato peel from the back yard and tipped it into a round iron boiler. While he busied himself Granny quietly put the five shillings back on the table. She pulled her woollen shawl close round her scraggy neck and shuffled back to her chair by the front door.

Myfanwy watched her husband stir the boiler. He sat hunched over the fire, his eyes following the circling swirl of the brown liquid. As he stirred a warm dirty smell came from the boiler. Myfanwy shuddered.

"Well, why don't you say anything?" she asked.

"About what?" he said dully, avoiding her challenge.

"About the way she carries on," she said. "She pinches the children and tells them lies about me. She's always trying to turn you against me, and if I argue with her ever she starts snivelling and tells me I'm taking adavantage of her being a widow. I'm not going to stand it."

She was crying quietly. Penry kept on stirring the boiler.

"She can't help it," he said sullenly. "She's old."

"And I'm young," Myfanwy said. "Can't you see that? I'm not wasted yet. But I will be before long. She's sucking my blood. And it's bad blood, bad blood, all the time. And you don't think about it. You don't worry as long as you've got your allotment and the sow drops regular — "

"Don't carry on like this," he said, putting the boiler on the hearth and standing up slowly. All his actions were slow and careful; like his face, slowly losing its youth and settling down easily into middle age. "It's no use creating; you ought to know that by this time."

"Yes," she said, turning pale with the effort to stay her feelings, "I know it's no use. I wish to God I was dead."

He pulled his old working coat down from the hook in the passage. It had been boiled and worn until it was threadbare, but the blotches of oil and wagon grease that covered it kept the tattered cloth whole.

"Well, I got to go and see that sow," he said. "I may be up there all night — depends on how easily she farrows."

He hitched a Davy lamp to his coat pocket and picked up the boiler of bubbling pigs' wash.

"I'll bring your tea up if you don't come down before," she said.

"Solong, Myfanwy," he said.

As he passed her she looked into his eyes. He wasn't the weeping sort, but there was a wounded, helpless look in them, and she knew it had been bad for him, too.

"Go on," she said. "Go and coddle your old sow."

*****

When he had gone she finished tidying the kitchen, dusting the shiny black rexine of the chair seats and pushing the woollen stuffing back into the rips. When she had finished she looked at the room. It winked all over — the brass studs fastening the oilcloth to the table, the varnished legs of the chairs, the brassoed fender, the smooth knob of the poker. She breathed in deeply and smiled; then took a comb down from the mantelpiece and combed her hair back. She cleaned the comb when she had finished and threw the loose hairs onto the fire.

"Kitchen's ready, Granny," she shouted.

And as the old woman hobbled along the passage, she went out through the back door to play with the children.

The back garden was about four yards wide, and as the house was built against the side of the hill, the garden sloped up steeply to the shed at the top. It was fenced off from the gardens of the next door houses by a hotch-potch barrier of old zinc sheeting, rusted iron bedsteads, and tin advertisements of Colman's Mustard and Brooke Bond's Tea. There was no door to the shed, and the tarred felting which covered the thin wooden front hung over in flapping folds, like the crippled wing of a black vulture. The garden itself was a patch of rubble and ash, holding nothing but a few rows of rotting beansticks, a line of seed cabbage with knobbly whitening stems, a couple of purple pickling cabbage, and three bare currant bushes. Next door up had a line of washing out — long workmen's pants pegged up by the legs, the wind blowing through the holes where the darning had given way, a pair of patched sheets, three tiny frayed vests — flapping and beating in the gusty weather. Mervyn had climbed over the iron bedstead into next door and was standing alertly under the long prop which kept the clothes' line in the air.

"Come on back this minute," Myfanwy shouted. "You'll get your bottom tanned if Mrs. Williams finds you in her back."

"I'm playing ship," Mervyn remonstrated. "We'll 'ave to reef our sails if this wind don't go down."

"You come on back," she insisted, smiling inwardly.

Jackie was sitting in the shed, on the block Penry used for chopping sticks.

"You'll cetch cold sitting in the dark like that," she said. "Come on into the sun."

"A'right," Jackie answered. "I only got two pages to finish the chapter."

He did not lift his head from the book he was reading. She looked over his shoulder — *David Copperfield*. It looked a long book; it was wonderful how he read such long books; such a slip of a kid. She didn't know what to think about Jackie. He was doing well in County School — fourth in the form last terminals and the Headmaster said on his report "Very promising." But it was five years before he could go to college, and then another few before he'd be qualified for a job. And all that time he'd have to be kept. Her soul seemed to wilt inside her and tear in two in the darkness like an outworn garment when she thought of all those years ahead. It made her dizzy. And his legs were so thin; his knees little bony lumps like the stalks of the seed cabbage; and his shoulders hunched over his books in the evenings were frightening to look at; skinny little collarbone and protruding blades. And when he put his books away at bed time, and looked up short-sightedly and sleepily, his pretty brown eyes with a bluish pallor glowing through the skin underneath them melted all her heart. You just couldn't tell what would come to him — whether he'd win loose from here and live, really live, somewhere else away from it all, or whether it was asking too much of his little body. You just couldn't tell. Penry said he ought to come out of school and work in the allotment for a bit; it would do him more good.

And then Mervyn, podgy little savage, crept softly behind Jackie and shoved him off the block with a blood-curdling whoop.

"Come on," he said, imperiously. "Let's go and spend."

"Tell him to stop it, Mam," Jackie said quietly. "He's always messing."

"Never mind," she said softly, smoothing his hair and straightening his black and amber school tie. "Go on with him to Granny Geake's and buy some loshins."

"Oh alright," Jackie said, with querulous resignation. "Come on, messer." He stuffed his book under his jersey, caught Mervyn by the hand and led him down the path to the back door.

*****

The garden was so barren and lonely when they had gone. Myfanwy stood in the shed, in the semi-darkness, suddenly trembling. She didn't know what to do with herself for the rest of the afternoon. She stood there for a long time, and the feeling got worse, making all her limbs weak and shaky; her knees had no strength and her heart pounded like an hysterical limed bird. She sat down on the block, and her thoughts went down from her like roots. And then, with a terrible effort, she thrust the black wave back and walked slowly down the path and out into the back lane.

It was better in the back lane. The high dry stone walls of the allotments which enclosed the lane on the other side gave her a solid reassurance; she tossed her head back and told herself she was being silly. She wondered whether the children were giving Granny Geake any trouble. They could never decide what to buy. They climbed onto the footstool in the old woman's parlour in order to see over the counter, and then asked her innumerable questions. She remembered buying at Granny Geake's herself. The smelly little parlour with its oilcloth counter ranged with great paradisical glass bottles, smooth and round and filled with coloured sweets; and the thrilling moment when Granny took the thick glass lid off and plunged her hands into the bottle, sifting the sweets like diamonds; and then at the last moment changing your mind and deciding instead to buy a bag of sherbet or a barley stick or a Turkish Delight; whereupon Granny replaced the lid with a vexatious click of her tongue, and shuffled across the parlour in her carpet slippers to get some coppers out of her little tin box. She had a big white wen on her neck that fascinated the children, and behind her silver-rimmed spectacles her eyes hid in her pouched and wrinkled flesh. She had been like that when Myfanwy went there to spend; nothing was changed in Granny Geake's, neither the delight of the sweets nor the fascination of the wen; when she thought of the children Myfanwy thought of her own childhood; nothing had changed. She hoped Jackie would not forget to offer Granny a loshin; there was no danger of her taking one; her withered old gums would have bruised themselves on a boiled sweet; but she liked to be offered one, and she gave you better measure for it.

She was glad she had the children, although she knew it would be better for them if they hadn't been born. She hadn't intended having any; before their marriage she had told Penry that she wouldn't have any until he got a job somewhere — Slough or Dagenham or anywhere — but Jackie was already forming inside her when she said it, and their marriage had to be hurried up. And now the children were repeating her own first days. It was like being caught in a winding belt in the colliery, going round and round, never getting loose....

★★★★★

She left the back lane and climbed the wet path up the mountain, following its twisting through the gorse bushes. In the big bush by the gate they had found a hedge sparrow's nest last summer — or the summer before — and Jackie had taken one of the eggs, pricking it on a thorn and blowing it out. He had taken it to the school museum. She parted the stinging green branches to see whether the nest was still there. There was a sodden little pile of matted grass and leaves caught on the thorns, no more. She looked at it for a minute without moving or thinking, then sighed and went on up the path.

★★★★★

From the mountain side she could see the whole village. The black and swollen stream running down from the ravine at the head of the valley split the village in two. The lower part consisted of three straggling parallel rows of dirty grey houses, built by the Colliery Company in the '80's when the bottom pit was sunk. Myfanwy could only see the back gardens — a long row of bare patches, with nothing growing. In one of them — five doors up from her own house — a man was chopping sticks. He was wearing a pair of blue serge trousers, and a waistcoat buttoned over a collarless Welsh flannel shirt. A woman was bending over a pile of baking utensils two doors away. She washed the dishes under the tap, soaking her stockings and old blue skirt. When she had finished she stood up and watched the man chopping sticks. She had flabby shapeless breasts and her hair blew in long rat tails over her spectacles. Myfanwy could hear the dull echo of the axe on the chopping block. She thought, "I wonder what else they could be doing, those two." But looking down on them from above, she saw that they had no choice but to be there, part of the composition of broken-down sheds and barren backs, fulfilling a predestined role.

There must be some way of getting away. An easier way than the one facing Jackie — years of study and borrowing and doing without, poor kid. If they could tear themselves loose, rip the old cloth, get away from the rut of pig sties and idle collieries and dreary monotonous days. What sort of a life was this? House work, gossiping over the garden wall, child-bearing, patching and darning, making ends meet, putting a little aside to get the children's shoes tapped before the winter, looking bleakly ahead, narrowly, timidly. Ever since the pit closed down it had gone on changelessly, a gradual decline which the people faced with the self-defensive cheerfulness of consumptives. Penry wouldn't stir himself out of it. He didn't fret and nag like Granny; he hadn't got her wicked turn of mind; no, there was just no fire in him. He'd spend hours carving a wooden boat out of a strip of bark for Mervyn; nothing was too much trouble; he'd help his mates to mend their sheds. But he wouldn't get out. She'd nagged him into a temper time and again, but he wouldn't budge. He had his allotment, his pigs and his chickens; he had his old mother, his wife and children. And he'd always lived there, from the day of his birth. It's hard to leave the place if you've never left it before.

I must stop fretting against it all the time, she told herself. It's no good. I must say, deep inside me, "I accept; I have accepted." I must give myself some peace, let my soul grow solid, so that the children will have something real and durable to cling to. I have never been a mother to them; when they sucked my milk they sucked at my soul, at my restless fears. I must settle down in my soul.

She looked over the block of red-bricked council houses on the other bank of the stream at the derelict rusty overhead haulage of the top pit. It had been idle for six years; the wheel had been dismantled; there was nothing left but the drifting coal dust, which still blew down the valley on gusty days when the wind whipped it off the crest of the tips. Only the dust and the people....

She scoured the back lane with her eyes, trying to spot the children. Then she saw them, crossing the river by the little bridge, and picking their way through the tangled web of rusted lines and disused sidings, going further away from her. She watched them pass the front gate of the Vicarage, the tiny red smudge of Mervyn's jersey crawling slowly along by the privet hedge. The Vicar's three monkey trees towered stiffly over him. The red blob moved on until it reached the church, the ugly church with its five side chapels built in a row against the north wall of the nave, like a huge angular sow lying on its side with its dugs flopping on the ground. The children looked like flies, settled on the carcass, probing the flesh, moving a little round the wound. They must be waiting for choir practice.

Well, she must accept the idle pits and the faded window curtains, the inanimate church and the slow denudation. She continued her climb along the hill side, making for Penry's allotment.

She could see him in the distance, shovelling pigs' dung into the soap box which he had fitted onto the axle and wheels of Jackie's tricycle. Then suddenly he hurried through the gate into the allotment. She wondered what had made him move so quickly. Perhaps the sow had started to farrow. She shivered. The thought revolted her. The fat fertile sow, lying grunting in the mud, dung caked on its fat flanks, fat heaving flanks with distended, oil-filled pores. It was more disgusting than the malicious old woman who sat muttering to herself by the kitchen fire. And the way Penry tended it, talked about it, saved the week's peelings for it; when he was sitting by the fire in the nights he was wondering to himself how many she would bear next time, and whether it was worth trying another boar with her.

As she got nearer the pig sty her disgust mounted so that she tasted in her mouth the fried bread and dripping they had had for dinner. The allotment was surrounded by a huge stone wall, two feet thick. When she was small she used to marvel at the thickness of the walls, believing that they must enclose something precious beyond words. The men who went inside seemed to her to be demigods, passing in and out of Eden. There was still something unreal about the thick walls, and about the white hens strutting outside, pecking viciously at the cabbage stumps that littered the ground, and about the intolerant cockerels with their rusty-red neck feathers and pink scalloped combs. Something comic and desultory and feckless.

The sty had been built at odd moments, with odd shillings and wood scavenged from the pit top. It looked like a little tarred ark, hastily constructed after the deluge had begun, with a drain pipe poking out of the roof instead of a chimney. The roof was a sheet of corrugated iron, the walls were covered with a tarred felting; the wood at the base had rotted and a thick yellow ordure oozed out, foul-smelling. She could hear Penry's boots squelching inside, and the sow breathing in grunts. Swallowing her bile she pushed open the green-rotting gate and picked her way through the mud of the sow's forecourt to the low aperture of the shed.

Penry was kneeling in the mud with the lantern at his side. The sow lay prostrate under his hands.

"Is it coming alright?" she asked.

He did not look up. There was a disgusting stink in the little shed, infecting the darkness, making it difficult to breathe. She lifted her skirt to her nose and let the air filter through to her nostrils.

"They're staying in," he said, "they won't drop."

The sow lay very still, breathing heavily, waiting. Then it jerked its trotters, writhing convulsively and squealing, squealing. It pressed its snout into the mud in the agony of its labour. Myfanwy bit her teeth together and clenched her fists. She wasn't going to faint, nor puke. The squealing stopped; the fat flanks shuddered involuntarily. Penry was making inarticulate sounds, of encouragement and endearment and fear.

It went on for a long time, long after it got dark outside the shed. Penry never once got up from his knees and Myfanwy stayed watching. At last the labour overwhelmed the sow, and her squealing suddenly ended with a choking shudder. She died with her litter inside her. It was the first time she had seen Penry cry.

"You can't do anything to it now," Myfanwy said. "Put a sack over it and come down to the house. It's perishing cold up here."

He did not move, so she covered the corpse herself, and putting her hands under his armpits, lugged him to his feet. His body was limp. She couldn't move him.

"Come on up, Penry, for God's sake," she said sharply. "Don't be such a woman."

He put his hand on the sow's rump and pushed himself to his feet.

"It's the ruin of us, this is," he said dully. "We'll never be able to afford another."

"Let's get out of here quick," she said, covering her mouth with her hand and squeezing through the low aperture, bent almost double.

After they had had tea she touched Jackie on the shoulder. He looked up from his book with a hasty irritated toss of his head.

"Come to the pitchers with us?" she said.

"Pitchers?" Granny snapped. "You ought to stay in decent-like, with the sow dead like it is."

"Are you coming, Jackie?" Myfanwy said, ignoring the alert wizened face.

"Alright."

Jackie put his book carefully away in the table drawer and took down his coat from the passage hooks. Meanwhile, Myfanwy rolled up the sleeves of Mervyn's jersey and scrubbed the dirty water mark off his fat wrists. They had to hurry. Mervyn ran by her side, too preoccupied with the task of keeping pace with her to speak. Jackie took long strides, his hands thrust in his coat pockets, his eyes on the ground.

"You're like an old man to-night, Jack," she said. "What are you thinking about?"

She hoped he would laugh, but he just walked on as before.

"Is it a sad book, that *David Copperfield*?" she asked.

Still he did not answer. His silence vexed her, making her silent too.

Just as they reached the end of the back lane he caught her by the sleeve, hesitatingly.

"Mam," he said.

"What's the matter?" she asked.

He dropped his eyes, tucking his chin into his little woollen scarf.

"Granny had her head in the gas oven again this afternoon," he said. "She said she'd put me inside if I told you anything."

"Next time you see her," Myfanwy said in a dead voice, "leave her to it. It's time she knew her own mind at seventy-five."

"You won't say I told you, Mam, will you?" He was pulling at her sleeve, passionately.

"No, I won't say anything," she said.

He brushed his head against her side with a warm frightened gesture.

"Come on," Mervyn said, "we'll be missing the serial if we don't watch."

The threepenny seats were right in front, under the screen. The big picture was just ending. The faces of the characters seemed to stretch for miles, like faces in the convex mirror of a spoon. It was grotesque and beastly, and sitting in the dark she felt the nausea of the pigsty coming over her again. Miles of cheap fleshy faces. The whole audience suddenly roared with laughter, Mervyn jumped out of his seat with merriment.

"Did you see that man then, Mam?" he said, tugging her sleeve. "'E fell into the pond."

"Shh," she said, "sit down, there's a good boy. There's people behind you wanting to see."

And sitting taut and stiff in the darkness, Mervyn and Jackie on either side of her following the movements on the screen with devout attention, she had to shut her eyes and bite her lips to keep back the words that surged through the gorge of her throat.

"I won't accept," the words beat, "I won't, I won't..."

And then the film ended, the bare electric lamps were switched on, and the audience stood up with sweaty, smiling faces while the pianotrope lurched into the first bars of the national anthem.

"Come on, little husband," she said to Jackie. "Bed's the place for you. It's nearly time for school."

Acting-Captain

The detachment was a very small one, a single platoon sent from the battalion to guard the dock gates and perimeter, but they had a bugle. Acting Captain Cochrane, the detachment commander, had indented persistently for one, and after two months' nagging on his part, D.A.D.O.S. had grudgingly coughed up a brand new one. It was hanging over old Crocker's bed in the fuggy blacked-out Nissen hut in which the administrative staff were sleeping. There was Crocker, an old soldier who had served in Flanders, Gallipoli, India, and the Far East; he was the cook, Acting Lance-Corporal, C.3, and used to it. Next to him Taffy Thomas was snoring; the air had grown slowly thicker and more corrupt with fumes from the stove, last night's fish and chips, cigarettes and beer, and all the coming and going since black-out time on the previous evening; so you couldn't breathe it into your lungs without a snore as it squeezed and scraped past your uvula. The fire was still flickering under a weight of grey ash and cinders in the stove.

For no apparent reason Crocker woke up, groaned, yawned, pushed his dirty blankets off and sat up, vigorously scratching his thin hair. He was wearing his thick winter vest and long pants with brown socks pulled up over the legs so that no part of his flesh was showing except where the heel of his sock was worn through. He listened a moment, to discover whether it was raining; then, finding it wasn't, he unhooked his bugle from the nail above his head, turned the light on to make sure that the office clock, which he always took to bed with him, indicated 6.30 a.m., put out the light again, shuffled to the door, spat, breathed in, closed his lips inside the mouthpiece of the bugle, and blew reveillé. He found he was blowing E instead of G, but after faltering an instant, laboured through with it in the same key. It was too dark for anyone to notice; not a streak of grey anywhere.

"Gawd curse the dominoes," he grumbled, shuffling back to his bed. He shook Taffy Thomas hard, relishing the warm sleeping body's resistance.

"Get up, yer Welsh loafer," he shouted in his ear. "You'll 'ave the boss on yer tail if you don't get down there wiv 'is shaving water double quick. Get up. You ain't got yer missus besidejer now."

Taffy didn't get up as philosophically as Crocker. He was still young enough to resent and rebel against things the old cook had long ago ceased thinking about. Most things were a matter of course to Crocker; air raids, sinkings, deaths were as normal as cutting rashers of bacon in the dark and peeling potatoes in his ramshakle corrugated-iron cooking shed.

However, Taffy got up. He put his hand on his head to feel how hot his hangover was, and then in a fit of irritated energy pulled on his trousers and pullover and searched about for his razor. "Well, we're a day's march nearer home," he said, dipping his shaving brush in the jam-tin of cold water he kept under his bed and lathering his face in the dark.

"You pups are always thinking about leave," Crocker said, fed-up. "D'you know I didn't see my old lady for three and a 'alf years in the last bust-up, nor any English girl. Plenty of dusky ones, of course, and Chinese ones that'd scarcely left school — "

"Yeh, I know," Taffy interrupted. "You're a real soljer. I know."

"Well, I didn't want to write 'ome every time I found a flea under my arm," Crocker scoffed. "I've sat in the mud scratching my arse from one Christmas to the next wivout arsking to see the O.C. abhat it."

"It wasn't your fault we didn't lose the war, then," Taffy said, wiping his shaved face in his dirty towel. "And if you're moaning about me asking for leave and asking for a transfer, you'd better shut your trap, old soljer, 'cause I'm not going to sit in this dump doing nothing while my missus freezes in the Anderson and coughs 'er guts up every time Jerry drops a load on Swansea."

"What are you going to do, then?" Crocker taunted. "Stop the war?"

"No," Taffy answered hotly. "Win the bleeding thing."

"Garn," Crocker laughed jeeringly. "Get off and polish the cap'n's Sam Browne. Win the war, be damned. What was you doing at Dunkirk, if it wasn't rude to ask? We never scuttled out of it, we didn't."

"Aw, shut up and get a pail of char ready for the lads," Taffy said. "I reckon you'd still be in your little dugout if somebody hadn't told you the war was over."

He slammed the door after him, pulled his cycle from under a ripped tarpaulin, and tucking his bag of cleaning kit under his arm, peddled through the muddy pooled ruts, past the sentry shivering in his greatcoat and flapping groundsheet like a spider swollen by the rain, down the lane past the knife-rest and Dannert wire obstacle that ran from the sidings to the quay where the Irish packet boat lay moored, and out onto the bleak tarred road that was just beginning to reflect a mildew-grey light along its wet surface. The detachment commander was billeted in an empty house on the hill above the harbour. Taffy's first job was to boil him some water for shaving and tea, make a cup of tea with a spoon infuser, shake him respectfully, salute, collect his Sam Browne and yesterday's boots or shoes, and retire to the scullery to clean them up. Then he swept the downstairs rooms, looked round to see whether there were any chocolate biscuits hidden in the trench-coat pocket, threw his sweepings outside for the starlings to swoop and grumble over, and then back upstairs to fold the blankets and sheets, empty the wash basin and jerry, and let the clean air of the ocean revitalise the room. The whole operation was conducted in silence, broken only by odd grunts and monosyllables from the officer and a sort of absent-minded whistling by the private. Taffy knew his man well enough to leave him alone while he pulled himself together; a glance at his reflection in the shaving mirror was enough to inform him as to the patient's condition. He had a young face, but his narrow eyes and almost pointed teeth, combined with the thin bony forehead and cheeks, gave him an astringent intolerant sharpness that only wore off after he had warmed up to the day's task. He was a regular officer who had been commissioned a few months before the war began, and because of his martinet appearance and the facility with which he could fly into an abrupt temper he had spent most of the war drilling recruits on the square at the regimental depot. He had got the square in his blood by the end; muddy boots or tarnished buttons, an indifferent salute, the lazy execution of a drill or an order provoked him immediately to a violent reprimand; all his actions were impatient and smart, his appearance immaculate and important, his opinions unqualified and as definite as they were ill-informed. His nature was bound to insist sooner or later on action; he had got into a bad state at the depot and asked to be posted to a battalion. He considered it a rebuff when he was posted to this small harbour on the featureless north-west coast, and it hadn't improved his frame of mind to consider that a further application for posting would be impolitic while an indefinite stay in his present post could only blur the image of a forceful disciplined soldier which he had so assiduously striven to impress on the depot command. He endured his inactive isolation with some acerbity and sought compensation in other quarters. He was careful of his career, knowing how easy it is to fall down the Army ladder; he paid court to the daughter of the Battalion's colonel with the same regard for tact and a proper keeness as he employed in his conduct towards his senior officers. But he was not of a firm enough mould to subsist on long-term expectations of advancement. He had to have his fling. And, what with one thing and another, he usually got out of bed on the wrong side and had to work a little bad blood out of his system before he could sit on his table and argue politics or swop dirty jokes with Sergeant Crumb, his principal stooge, or Private Norris, his clerk general who had a classics degree, an LL.B., a mind of his own and a stoop that barred him from promotion.

"Quiet night last night, sir," Taffy said amiably when the hair-combing stage had been reached and a measure of civility might be expected.

"Was it, hell!" the O.C. replied, wincing his face. "Mix me a dose of Andrew's Health Salts, Thomas. They're in my valise."

"Very good, sir."

"What sort of a morning is it?"

"Nothin' partic'lar, sir. What do you want for to-night, sir?"

"My S.D. suit and my Sam Browne; best shoes and walking out cap. I don't want any silvo stains on it , either."

"Very good, sir."

The vexed look left the harsh young face as he tilted the bubbling glass down his throat; beads hooked to the uncombed hairs of his moustache; it was pink at the roots and gold-brown at the tips. "Gosh!" he said, "it makes you want to live a clean life always, tasting this stuff. God bless Mr. Andrews."

Having returned and breakfasted with the rest of the lads on old Crocker's lumpy porridge and shrivelled bacon and greased tea, Taffy strolled off to collect his wheelbarrow and begin his second task, cleaning the lines. He had sharpened a beech-stick to pick up the chip papers and litter; Curly Norris had suggested the idea, saying it gave the camp a better tone, made it more like a royal park. Curly also wanted to indent for a couple of fallow deer, or if D.A.D.O.S. refused to supply them, purloin them from the grounds of Magdalen College, Oxford. He said Taffy should lead the raiding party, singing the War song of Dinas Fawr.

"You will probably be put on a charge," he said. "But what is a charge *sub specie aeternitatis*?"

He was always laughing behind his twinkling spectacles, and even if you didn't know what he was talking about, which was most of the time, his gaiety infected you and you laughed as well or wrestled with him.

When Taffy arrived outside the office Curly Norris was just completing his housework. The office was swirling with smoke from the newly-lit fire and dust from the floor. Curly's first task was to sweep all the dust from the floor onto the tables and shelves and files. This ritual was always performed alone, before Sergeant Crumb arrived for the day.

Taffy halted his barrow and respectfully tapped the office door.

"Any old match-sticks to-day?" he shouted. "Any old match-sticks?"

"Take your dirty boots off my porch," Curly shouted. "A woman's work is never done, don't you men know that yet?"

Taffy jumped in and screwed his arm round Curly's neck. They were wrestling on the table when Sergeant Crumb appeared. At his bull's bellow they stopped.

"What the hell d'you think this is? A tavern?"

"Sorry, sarge."

"You'll apologise to the O.C. if I catch you at it again, either of you." He smoothed the underside of his waxed moustache with a nicotine-stained forefinger. "What sort of a mood is he in this morning, Thomas?" Sergeant Crumb always arranged the morning programme on the basis of Taffy's report.

"Got a liver on this morning, sarge," Taffy replied. "Shouldn't be surprised if it turns to diarrhoea."

"I saw him in the Royal at closing time," Sergeant Crumb said. "He was buying drinks all round, so I expected he'd be off his food. Get cracking, Norris. Get the correspondence sorted out, let's see what there is. Then get down to the stores and warn Rosendale to appear before the O.C. I saw him in town last night when he should have been on duty. Make a charge-sheet out before you go. Section 40 — conduct prejudicial to good order. Get weaving."

Curly thought it a pity there wasn't a mantelpiece for the sergeant's elbows and a waistcoat for his thumbs.

"Very good, sarge."

"And you get down to cleaning the lines, Thomas. What are you hanging about here for?"

"Want to see the O.C." Thomas said.

"Too busy," the sergeant replied, stiffening his weak chin. "Get out."

"I can see the O.C. if I want to," Thomas replied.

"A-ah!" laughed the sergeant, his shallow blue eyes turning foxy. "Getting a bit Bolshie, are you? What with you and Rosendale in the detachment we'd better hoist the Red Flag, I'm thinking." He straightened up, blew out his chest, hardened his characterless eyes. "Get out!" he shouted.

Curly wasn't laughing now. He looked serious, bothered and unhappy. The way these foolish and unnecessary rows blew up, these continual petty litigations springing from bad temper and jealousy and animosity; why did they allow their nerves to become public? Why couldn't they hold their water?

Taffy stayed where he was, stubborn and flushing. He had a bony ridge at the base of his neck, a strong chin and a knobbly receding forhead. Huge-shouldered and rather short and bandy in the leg, he gave the appearance of animal strength and latent ferocity.

"That was an order," the sergeant said.

"O.K." Taffy replied. "But I'm asking to see the O.C. You can't refuse."

The sergeant began to hesitate, grew a little sick at the mouth, fiddled with the paper-cutter.

"What d'you want with him?"

"I want to get into a Commando," Taffy said.

"You'll get into a glasshouse, maybe," the sergeant laughed unpleasantly, not at all sure of himself now.

"Yes, for knocking you between your pig's eyes," Taffy said.

An immediate tension, like the shock of an electric charge, and silence.

"You heard what he said, Norris," the sergeant snapped. "I'll want you as witness."

"Hearsay doesn't count as evidence," Curly said quietly.

"What did you say?" Sergeant Crumb swung livid on him. "You bloody little sea-lawyer, are you trying to cover him?"

"No. I'm not covering anybody. I simply happen to know that legal procedure excludes my repeating something alleged to have been said by a person not formally warned."

Sergeant Crumb wrote some words on a sheet of paper.

"We'll see," he said, uncertainly. "Now get out."

Taffy shrugged his shoulders and slouched out. He hadn't meant to say that. Not out loud. All the same, it was O.K. by him. He pushed his barrow down the muddy path to the stores shed.

Rosendale was shaving in his shirt-sleeves. His mirror was a splinter of glass an inch long stuck into a packing case. There was a heap of straw in one corner of the shed; the men were changing the straw of their palliasses; he, as storeman, was in charge; he gave more to some than to others — not to his friends, for he had none, but to the important people, the lance-jacks and the lads with a tongue in their heads who determined public opinion in the camp. Rosendale was very sensitive to public opinion, partly because it affected his own advancement, partly because he was politically conscious and wanted to form a cell to fortify his somewhat introvert ideas. He was inept as a soldier, too untidy and slow to get a stripe; consequently he posed as a democrat refusing to be bought over to the ruling classes by a stripe, as one of the unprivileged millions who would be deprived of power and exploited by the boss class for just as long as they were content to endure it. He wasn't making much headway in his campaign. His ideas were too dogmatic to convince men who saw life as a disconnected series of circumstances and poverty as a natural ill and active political opposition as both unpatriotic and unpleasant, something that might get you C.B., or your application for a week-end pass rejected. He was popularly known as Haw-Haw.

"Morning, Rosie," Taffy said, having recovered his equanimity. "Had a tidy sleep, love?"

"Be damned I didn't," Rosendale grumbled. "I slept in that bleeding straw in the corner there and a goddamn mouse crawled under my shirt and bit me under my arm. I squeezed him through my shirt and the little sod squirted all over it."

"Well, you'd better brass yourself up, Rosie," Taffy commented, "'cause the snoop has pegged you for being out of camp last night when you were on duty. I'm on the peg, too. So don't start moaning." At such moments Rosendale lacked the dignity and calm bearing of the representative of the unprivileged millions. He became an anxious frightened little man seeking an excuse, a lie, an alibi. "Curly'll come down with the charge in a minute," Taffy said reassuringly. "He'll tell us what to say, Curly will."

Curly brought the mail with him when he came. There was a letter for each of them. Rosendale was too het up to read his letter; he threw it without interest onto the table and bit his nails until the other two had read theirs. Taffy was a slow reader. Rosendale fiddled and shuffled, tears almost touching the surface of his eyes. "My missus is bad again," Taffy said, staring at the solid cheap paper on which a few slanting lines had been pencilled in a childish scrawl. Big crossed kisses had been drawn under the signature. "She can't touch her food again and her mouth is full of that yellow phlegm I told you about, Curly. And the rain is coming in since the last air raid."

"Why doesn't she go into hospital?" Curly said. "She's on the panel, isn't she?"

"I don't know proper," Taffy said, rubbing his face wearily. "I used to pay insurance when I was in the tinplate works, an' she's been paying twopence a week to the doctor. But *he* don't know what's up with her. I fetched him down last time I was on leave; anybody could see that she was bad. All yellow and skinny, pitiful thin she was. Not eating a bite, neither, not even milk or stout, but only a drop of pink pop when she was thirsty. I made her bed for her in the kitchen to save her climbing the stairs. I stayed in every night with her. Had to go drinking in the mornings with my brother and my mates. And she was spitting this yellow stuff all the time, see? Very near filled a pisspot with it every day."

"Well, you've got to get her to hospital," Curly said. "What the hell is that doctor doing? It sounds criminal to me."

"I told her to see another one," Taffy went on. "But my mother-in-law it is, she swears by him, see? He's delivered all her kids for her, and he helped my missus through with the twins. So she won't change him. She won't go against her mother, see, Curly?"

"What the hell does a mother-in-law matter?" Curly said sharply. "Look here, Taff. You've *got* to get home and *carry* her to hospital *yourself* if you don't want her to die. D'you understand? Especially with all these air raids. It's cruel to leave her alone."

"But what about the kids? She can't take them to hospital with her."

"Get them evacuated. Or send them to your mother-in-law's."

"What? That bastard?"

"I'd like to knock your head off, Taffy," Curly said with cold and exasperated anger.

"I wouldn't care much if you did," Taffy replied, suddenly plunged in despondency. Like his temper, which had flared against the sergeant, his blues came on without warning.

"Come on," Curly insisted crossly. "Pull yourself together. It doesn't matter about you. It's your wife and kiddies I'm thinking about. Get up to the office and show this letter to the O.C. You've *got* to get home."

"Catch him giving me a forty-eight hours leave after Crumb has told him what I said," Taffy said, hang-dog.

"I'll see Crumb at once and ask him to hold the charge back," said Curly, turning to go.

"What about my charge?" Rosendale asked. He had been hanging around the fringe of Taffy's trouble, like an uncomfortable curate with a dyspepsia of his own. "Can't you talk it over with me, Curl?"

"Your charge isn't important," Curly said, hurrying out.

"Bloody intellectuals! They're all the same, the pack of them," Rosendale muttered.

Sergeant Crumb was already closeted with the O.C. when Curly got back to the office. The Nissen hut was divided into two rooms by a central plywood partition with a door. Curly stood by the door listening.

They were talking about Sergeant Crumb's wife. It was a matter of long standing, and Curly knew enough about it from the sergeant's occasional confidences to see that he had been ruined by it so gradually and completely that he himself didn't know the extent or nature of the damage. He had joined the Army eight years back to get away from a powerful woman who had him tucked into her bed whenever she wanted him and who was pushing him to divorce his wife. He was afraid of ruining his business, a small garage, by the publicity of a divorce; moreover, he wasn't in love with either of the women though he slept with each in turn. So he joined up to let time and distance settle the mess. Oddly enough it was still unsolved. His wife had gone back to a factory job and taken a small flat. After several years he had called on her on leave, having been discarded by the other woman who preferred a civilian lover. He was very proud of that night. He had wooed his wife back to him; Gable had nothing to show him, he told Curly, recounting it in some detail. So things reverted to the old ways for a while, until he received information from a sister of his who lived near his wife that his wife had another man, somebody in the works, a young fellow in a reserved occupation. It wasn't definitely established; Sergeant Crumb wasn't one to beard lions; he hadn't asked his wife point-blank, nor did he intend offering her a divorce. He preferred to use the welfare machinery of the Army. Through the O.C. he had got in touch with the regimental paymaster and requested him to investigate his wife's conduct through the local police with a view to stopping her allowance, to which he contributed fourteen shillings a week, if her guilt could be established. Meanwhile he continued to prove his manhood and independence by making love promiscuously wherever he was stationed, and displaying a definite penchant for married women. His heart wasn't affected by the affair any more, his affections weren't involved. That was the whole trouble, it seemed to Curly. It was simply a matter of pride, of getting his own back. He took it out of his staff in the same way, blustering at them, telling the O.C. of their disloyalties and delinquencies, keeping well in with his chiefs, at once toady and bully. At the same time he was efficient and hard-working, smart at drill and a master of office routine and military red-tape. His files were neat and complete, correspondence properly indexed, A.C.I.'s and Battalion Orders always to hand. Messing indents, pay rolls, men's documents were all open for inspection. The only man who knew that Sergeant Crumb depended entirely upon Private Norris, his clerk general, was Curly Norris himself. And because of his peculiar comic outlook on life he had no desire to split. It amused him to contemplate the sergeant's self-importance and it paid him to be useful in a number of small ways. He could get a weekend pass for the asking. He could use the office at nights to type out his private work — some learned bilge he was preparing for a classical quarterly — and as the war was a stalemate and the Command board had rejected his application for a commission after one look at his stoop, he had grown to consider these small amenities as perhaps more important than the restless discontent that produces poets or heroes or corpses.

Having discussed his marital affairs and got the O.C. to write another letter to the paymaster, Sergeant Crumb, as was his wont, made deposition against the malcontents, on this occasion Rosendale and Thomas. He suggested that each should be charged under section 40 of the Army Act. Curly, hearing the O.C. melt under the sergeant's reasoned persuasion, shrugged his shoulders and lit a cigarette. He knew it was a poor look-out for Mrs.Thomas's cancer of the throat. Certainly it was no use making any application at the moment. The O.C. had given him two week-ends leave in the last six weeks, after air raids, to see that his wife was alright. It was Taffy's own fault, the fool, for not getting her into hospital when he was home last. And now they had no money. Curly had already lent him his last train fare, and had no more cash to spare.

Rosendale came in with a pail of specially sweet tea at that moment, hoping to mollify the powers. But Sergeant Crumb's voice was unsweetened as he told him to get properly dressed and be ready to answer a charge in five minutes time.

The upshot of it was that both men got seven days' C.B. and Curly a severe unofficial reprimand for attempting to shield Thomas. The O.C. always enjoyed a little adjudication. It gave him strength.

"Sod the Army!" Rosendale moaned, bitter and outraged. "King's Regulations be damned. Better if they'd spent their time in strengthening the League-a-Nations or finding a living job for the unemployed or making things better somewhere, not pottering around with King's Regulations."

"What wouldn't I do to Mr. bleeding Crumb if I met him in Civvy

Street after the war," Taffy murmured fondly.

"A lot of use that is to your wife," Curly snapped.

"Go on. Rub it in," Taffy flared up, goaded to feel anguish at last. Disconsolate, he wheeled his barrow off to the incinerator, and Curly returned to the office to write letters to his friends.

Acting Captain Cochrane was sitting on the clerk's table, tapping his swagger cane against the brown boots Taffy had brought to a nice shine and chatting to Sergeant Crumb over a cup of luke-warm tea.

"Well, Norris," he said with a sardonic grin. "You see what comes of playing the barrister to a pair of fools."

"They're not particularly fools, sir," Curly replied with proper deference. "They're both men. Thomas has worked in pits and steel-works, he's taken the rap in Belgium, he's trying to maintain a wife and two kiddies — that's more than most of us have done."

"He's still a fool," the O.C. said. "He's like the rest of the working people. They've been too blind and stupid to help themselves when they had the chance. They could have had Socialism any time in the last twenty years. They've got the vote. Why don't they use it to get a Labour government? Because they can't be bothered to lift a finger for their own interests. I'm a Socialist at heart, but it's not a bit of good trying to help the people. They don't want to be helped."

"It isn't entirely their fault, sir," Curly replied. "The middle class hasn't helped them very much — the teachers and clergy and newspaper proprietors and business executives. They've all thrown dust in their eyes, confused or denied the real issues and disguised selfish interests and reactionary politics to appear progressive and in the public interest, as they say. They keep the world in a state of perpetual crisis in order to crush internal oppostition by the need for national unity, and they buy off their critics by giving them minority posts in the Cabinet. Appeasement at home and abroad; give the beggar a penny and expect him to touch his cap."

"Hot air," the O.C. answered, offering Curly a cigarette. He always came in for a chat after giving anybody a dressing down; Curly surmised that it was a maxim of his that a man who is alternatively severe and humane wins the respect as well as the affection of his subordinates. As a matter of fact the men distrusted his geniality and called him two-faced. They never knew how to take him; before asking a favour of him they always consulted Taffy or Curly about his mood. They were nervous of him in a surly way; not from fear, but because they disliked being treated curtly without being able to retort on natural terms. "Would you like England to become Communist?" he continued.

"I should be quite acclimatised to the change after serving in the Army," Curly replied. "We live a communal life here; all our clothes and equipment are public property; nobody makes any profits; we serve the state and follow the party line."

"You think the Army is based on Lenin's ideas, do you?" the O.C. said. "That would shake the colonel if he knew it."

"He needn't worry," Curly said, laughing. "The Army hasn't got a revoluntionary purpose. It has no ideas worth speaking of except a conservative loyalty to the throne and a professional obligation to obtain a military victory. King Charles I.'s ideas with Oliver Cromwell's efficiency. That's England all over. They never settle their differences, they always keep both sides going. The Royalists were beaten in the field, yet they dominate the Army. The Germans were licked, yet they've got Europe where they want it. There's plenty of class distinction in the Army, black boots versus brown shoes, but no class conflict. I could go on quite a long time like this, sir. It's more interesting than football." He laughed to hide his seriousness. He hadn't been speaking in fun, but he preferred to be taken lightly. He knew himself to be a perpetual student, introspective, individualist, an antinomian with a deep respect for the privacy of others. His gentle and slightly neurotic liberalism took the edge off his revolutionary convictions. He lacked the strength to defy what is powerful in men, and he had no heart for extreme action. So he always preferred to be left in peace, to think and observe; his conflicts were within him. He had his own anguish.

"I tell you what's wrong with you, Norris," the O.C. said largely. Curly felt something wince in him. To be told again what was wrong with him. People were always presuming to do that, nearly always people who knew too little about him and about themselves. It wasn't so bad if they spoke from kindness and a desire to help; that hurt, but it was understood by him. But when a man, like this young fascist type with his muddled democratic ideas and his desire to exercise his power over men proffered him advice, he writhed like a split toad.

"You haven't got enough *push*, Norris. That's what's wrong with you. Too soft-hearted, not enough keeness. You don't go for things as if you wanted them."

Curly laughed.

"My ambitions aren't as tangible as yours, sir," he replied.

"Well, get some ambitions, then, for God's sake. Your life won't go on for ever. Get cracking."

"Very good, sir. I'll submit my scheme for defeating Germany to Sir John Dill immediately."

The O.C. shrugged his shoulders, confessing to himself that here was another man who wasn't worth helping because he refused to be helped. He was browned off with fools.

"If you want to help anybody, you might help Thomas to get his wife into hospital, sir."

The O.C. snorted and narrowed his eyes.

"I know the difference between seven days C.B. and a weekend leave," he said curtly. "Thomas won't pull that old gag over me again." Curly hadn't enough vigour to insist. He clenched his fists on the table, knowing how important it was that Taffy should get leave, knowing it suddenly with anguish. But, as so often, the conflict smashed itself up inside him like two contrary tides, and he said nothing because the intensity of his feelings made him impotent.

The door opened and Sergeant Crumb came in, followed astonishingly by a very dashing young lady. The sergeant was all smiles and deference, inclining his body courteously to her and pointing with a wave of his hand to the O.C. Curly stood to attention. The O.C. stood flushed.

"Lady to see you, sir," Crumb said urbanely.

"Hector," the lady said, her rouge parting in a slow private smile. She held out her gloved hand, letting her fur coat fall open.

"But — but come in," the O.C. stumbled. He pushed open the door of his room and she swept through in a swirl of fur and silk and interesting perfumes. He closed the door after her, humbly.

"Gives you the impression of expensive cutlery," Curly said softly, "though I doubt whether she is stainless."

"It's the colonel's daughter," Crumb whispered, his head inclined and movements subdued as though he were in the presence of the saints.

Curly hoped she wanted some love, so that he'd have a little peace to write his letters. But he had scarcely started when the door opened and she came out again.

"Don't trouble to see me to the gate," she said. "I'm sure you're busy. This private will escort me."

"Not at all," said the helpless captain, following her out with her gloves.

"Stand easy, stand easy," Crumb said as the door closed behind them. "She must have been jilted or something," he sneered.

The O.C. came back in a hell of a tear.

"Where's that bloody fool Thomas? Tell him to go to my billet and polish my shoes and Sam Browne till he can see his face in them. And tell Rosendale I want him to take a message for me. At once."

"Very good, sir." Sergeant Crumb leaped to it, realising the situation was urgent. The room was suddenly in a turmoil, as though the young lady had been a German parachutist.

The O.C. took a sheet of paper and scribbled a quick note, put it in an envelope and threw it into the OUT tray.

"Tell Rosendale to deliver that when he comes, Norris."

He put on his service cap, took out his stick and gloves and went out. He was excited and flustered. Probably going to cool off by catching the sentry sitting down or the cookhouse staff eating the men's cheese rations, or the fatigue party throwing stones into the cess pool they were cleaning.

Rosendale came and collected the letter.

"Forgot to lick the envelope," he said. "What is it? Is there a war on?"

"Run away," Curly said, weary of everything.

Rosendale cycled out of camp and down the road till he was out of observation. Then he opened the letter and read it through.

"Dear Eva," it said. "Sorry I can't meet you to-night as we arranged. I'm on duty again and won't be able to see you this week. I seem to have so little free time these days that I doubt whether it's worth our while carrying on any more. What do you think? Affectionately yours, Hector Cochrane, Capt."

"Hector Cochrane, Capt." Rosendale repeated, curling his lip. He cycled down coast to the town, knowing where to go; he had been to the little street behind the gasworks on other occasions. Miss Barthgate was the name, and very nice, too. Smart little milliner, deserved better luck than to fall in love with *him*. Rosendale's mind was working by devious ways. He'd seen the flash dame in the fur coat with rich smells about her. Maybe he'd get a bit of his own back for that seven days' C.B.

He knocked at the door, propping his cycle against the wall. She worked in the parlour; he could see the sewing machine through the window. But the place sounded quiet to-day, as though she hadn't started working yet.

There was some delay before she opened the door. She was in a loose-fitting frock let out at the waist. Her face was nervous, her dark eyes looked dilated. Her beauty seemed agitated, on pins. "Yes?" she said, almost breathing the word, at the same time holding her hand out for the note he held between his fingers. Grinning a little, Rosendale handed it to her, watched her read it, waited a long time while she tried to raise her head....

At last she looked up. She wasn't bothering to hide anything. He could see it as clear as daylight.

"There's no answer," she said.

"No," he replied. "No answer." He shuffled, half turning to go. Then he looked up at her shrewdly.

"He isn't on duty," he said. "I thought I'd tell you. I shouldn't mind about him if I were you."

"No," she said, looking at him vaguely with her unutterable distress.

He had intended to say more, but her look confused him. He turned, mounted his cycle and pedalled off. She didn't move all the time.

There was a new sensation buzzing through cookhouse, stores, office and guardroom when he returned. The sentry told it him as he cycled through the gate; and because of it he decided to withhold his own bits of gossip till the chaps would be readier to appreciate it. He didn't want any competition.

The news was that Taffy Thomas couldn't be found anywhere. His denim overalls were on the floor by his bed, his best battledress and respirator were missing. He hadn't answered Crocker's quavering version of Defaulters bugle, he hadn't come forward to shine the O.C.'s Sam Browne. He'd done a bunk.

Curly was waiting for Rosendale with another message, this time for the Swansea police, asking them to visit Taffy's house at night and instruct him forcibly to return by the next train. The O.C. had said something about a court-martial; it would be the colonel's charge at least. That meant probably 28 days' detention and no pay for himself or his wife. It was a bad business, all things considered; but Curly was glad Taffy had gone. Perhaps he'd save his wife's life: 28 days was cheap at that price.

Acting Captain Cochrane had a considerable liver by the end of the afternoon. The men had been dozey and idle all day. He'd gone round bollucking them right and left. The latrines hadn't been cleaned, the washbasins were still littered with rusty blades and fag-ends when he inspected them after lunch. The cesspool stank and the fatigue party complained that there wasn't any hot water for them to clean up afterwards. All the plugs for the washbasins were missing, the kit was untidily laid out on the beds, the rifles hadn't been pulled through since he inspected them last. He was in no mood to be accosted. When he saw Eva waiting for him at the bottom of the lane he had already had too much.

She was wearing a plain mackintosh, a loose-fitting burberry, and a little green hat with turned-up brim like a schoolgirl. Her hands were in her pockets, her eyes on the ground. He knew she'd seen him, but she wasn't able to look at him approaching. He walked smartly towards her, very military in his swish greatcoat and service cap flat over his eyes. His face looked narrow and sharp under the severe cap, his fair moustache and rather pointed teeth giving him a stoatlike appearance. When he was within a couple of yards she looked up and her eyes were wide and lambent, looking at him for some sign.

"Well, Eva," he said. He coughed and looked at his wrist-watch. "You got my letter, didn't you?"

She stayed looking at him with her pale searching face and her dark transparent eyes. Damn it all, she had a nice face. Was she going to cling? Why did she take things so seriously?"

"Well? Say something, Eva."

His voice was softer, the least bit softer.

"I got your letter," she said. "That's why I came to see you."

"Well, you know I'm on duty, then?" he tried it out, not so sure that he wanted to finish it for good just yet.

"That's what you said," she replied.

He flushed, but she had turned away from him.

"Well?" he queried, his voice hardening. He wasn't going to be pried into. If his word wasn't enough for her, O.K. chief!

She looked up again. He noticed she hadn't powdered herself very carefully; her nose had a thick patch on it.

"Hector," she said, putting her hands on the immaculate breast of his greatcoat. "Don't you understand, darling?"

He was swept with impatience. His success with women was about to equal his ignorance of them. He wasn't going to have any sob stuff, thank you.

"How the blazes d'you expect me to understand?" he said roughly.

"Well," she said. "There is something to understand."

He quailed under her sudden precision of mood; she knew what she was going to do now; she wasn't leaning on him, beseeching him with her eyes. She was very quiet and firm.

She looked at him and he got scared.

"There's nothing serious, Eva, is there?" his fear prompted him.

"It is serious," she said.

"Darling," he gasped.

He was horrified of the consequences, infuriated with her for getting into this mess, and, for the first time in his life, even if only for a minute, in love.

He spoke slowly, stopping to think.

"Can't you see a doctor, Eva? There are some doctors, you know — "

"I don't want to," she said, still with this ridiculous composure.

"But — but you ought to," he said.

"I can do as I choose," she replied.

He said nothing, sensing a hopeless deadlock.

"Eva," he said at last.

"Well?"

"We could get married at the Registry Office next weekend if you like," he said, slowly, never taking his worried eyes off her. She was silent, as if listening to his words again and again in her mind.

He felt a growing exhilaration, a new and wonderful simplicity in him, like sunlight slowly breaking.

"Shall we?" he asked, holding his hand out.

She looked up again. This was always the most active thing she did, disclosing her eyes. Her hands all the time in her burberry pockets. She was reluctant to answer; there was a sweetness in the possibility, a reflection of his own momentary sincerity. It was what she had come for, to hear him say that; because he had said these words she was happy. She had no sense of tragedy or shame. She felt indifferent to the future.

"No, we can't get married," she said slowly at the last.

Something in him was suddenly overpoweringly relieved. He had no sense of a durable daily happiness, of a long companionship in love; but only romantic impulses, like sunlight, and harsher emotions.

"But why not?" he asked, trembling.

"Because — oh well," she mumbled, seeking blindly to bind up her thoughts into the certainty that was still inchoate in her, "because you — don't — " she turned away, and in profile he saw her lips finish the sentence — "love me."

Her courage shamed him into a greater confusion. He flushed and lost his head and was just about to gallop into the breach with protestations of devotion when a four-seater army car swung round the bend and pulled up with a screech and a shudder.

"Christ," he gasped, this time in a real fluster. "Look out."

He sprang to the car and saluted.

The colonel half-opened the door.

"Just coming to see you, Cochrane. Expected to find you in your office, not flirting on the roads."

"Yes, sir."

"Hop in. Quickly. I want to get back."

"Yes, sir."

The car surged forward.

Eva watched it go. By herself. She pushed her hair back, rubbing her cheeks, rubbing the cold sweat off her forehead. Heavily she turned and walked slowly along the road.

The colonel looked into the first Nissen hut.

"These bricks round the fireplace," he said. "I sent an order to all detachments that they be whitewashed. Why haven't you done it?"

"No whitewash, sir."

"Get some. Christ. What are you here for?"

He picked up a pair of boots from one of the men's beds.

"These boots. Burnt. Look at the soles. Burnt through. Drying them by the fire. Is this man on a charge?"

"Er, no, sir."

"Why the hell not? Nation can't afford to waste boots every time they get wet. Christ. Send him to me to-morrow under escort."

"Yes, sir. I don't believe they *are* burnt, sir. The man has been waiting for a boot exchange for five weeks. He's worn them out — "

"I tell you they're burnt. Christ man, you're not a cobbler, are you?"

"No sir."

"Then talk about something you know."

By the time the old man drove off Captain Cochrane was utterly emasculate. He saluted with so pathetic and servile a gesture that the old colonel didn't even return the salute. And so his day ended. The duties of the evening confronted him. Dinner in mess, then dance attendance on the old man's daughter. Poleworth was the name. Less respectfully, when the subalterns were hidden away in a pub, the name was sometimes garbled to Polecat. She certainly had a pungent odour. Still, hardy men said she was a good sport. She liked to play, they hinted, twisting the yellow ends of their moustaches. Captain Cochrane emptied his whiskey flask before deciding on his tactical plan. Marvellous thing, whiskey.

Curly took a walk after drinking his mug of tea and eating a piece of bread and marge and a Lyons' fruit pie. He didn't wash or brass up. He wasn't going to town. He wanted some peace of mind, along the sand dunes running from the harbour to the boarding house promenade where the ferro-concrete seaside resort began. Faintly, as though his tedious preoccupations had taken a musical form, the distant sound of hurdy-gurdy jazz songs blaring in the fun-fair touched his quietness, accompanying him unobtrusively as he climbed the loose sand.

Thinking of the industry of pleasure he watched the sea, fuming like a thin grey smoke far far out beyond the mudflats, and it seemed as though the purpose of the town had been lost, the balance between sea and land ruined, the fundamental element forgotten. Pleasure had broken away from simplicity, the penny-in-the-slot machine had conquered the sea, people had turned their backs and were screaming with laughter. Watching the sea fuming and grey he found himself suddenly investing the solitary person walking slowly and with downcast head across the wet wormcast mud with all the attributes which humanity, he decided this evening, had rejected. He wanted to speak to this lonely person; it was a woman; heavy she was; heavy with the rejected attributes of humanity; pregnant she must be, and pale with a serious beauty, bearing so much in her.

Following his fantasy, he walked down from the dunes and across the slimy front towards the girl. He walked quickly, keeping his attention on her, refusing to allow the usual inhibitions to stop him accosting her.

Eva felt no particular strangeness at his approach. A little soldier with spectacles and curly hair like a wire brush. It was quite natural. She said good evening. She was glad he had come.

"I was standing on the dunes," he said. "And there was nobody but you anywhere at all. And so you became important to me, so that I came to ask you something."

"Don't ask me anything," she said.

"No, I don't want to," he said thoughtfully.

"Will you take me back to the land?" she said, looking at him, holding her hand out to him uncertainly.

Her face was as he had imagined it, young and hollow, large hollow-eyed, luminous and vague with distress.

He took her cold hand and led her back to the firm land, the grass and rocks and walls and telegraph poles and houses. In silence.

"Have you ever tried to die?" she asked.

"Yes," he said.

"What shall I do now, then?" she asked again.

"Walk," he said. "Pick a flower. Hurt your shin against a rock. Keep doing things like that for a bit. Do you like coffee?"

"Yes," she said, thinking back to the taste of such things. "Yes. I like coffee."

"Shall we go and have some, and some chocolate biscuits, in the Marina?" he asked.

"Yes," she said, very seriously. "That would be nice."

She looked at the people having coffee and peach melbas and spaghetti on toast at the little green tables, soldiers and girls, commercial men, ponderous wives on holiday with children past their bedtime. The waitresses rustling and slender and deft, rotund and homely and competent; the warm shaded lights falling on the flowery wallpaper. The strangeness and the fear gradually left her eyes like sugar melting in a lemon glass. She tasted the hot coffee slowly, and its warmth led her to smile.

"Why do you look so serious?" she asked Curly.

He looked at her all the time. She could see the gathering of his thoughts in the dark blue eyes magnified and concentrated by the curved lenses of his spectacles.

"Funny, you having blue eyes," she said.

Looking at each other over the wispy coffee steam, each wanted to be confessed in the other, each desired to share a new yet ancient community of interest. Neither of them could think now of how different they were, the one from the other, how insulated by separate compulsions and circumstances.

"I live near here. Shall we go and sit by the fire?" she asked.

"I'd like to," he answered....

"It's only an electric fire," she said, as he opened the glass door for her.

There were two photographs on the mantelpiece of her little bedsitter. Curly noticed they were both men in uniform. Brothers? Or lovers? Also a sewing machine and dresses half finished. A reading lamp and *Picture Post* and *Lilliput* and a *Sunday Pictorial*.

"I haven't got a shilling for the meter," she said.

He produced one.

"You're very good," she said to him, putting the shilling in the slot, bending down as she spoke. "You stopped me committing suicide and now you've given me food and money and — and what else?"

"What else?" he repeated, his sensitive mind crushed by the sledge-hammer blow of her casual confession.

"I don't know," she said, standing up and smoothing her navy skirt down, picking bits of fluff off her knees. "I don't know what I'm talking about."

Her sick soul was in her eyes.

He stayed with her till late in the night, putting another shilling in the meter, going and queuing outside the chip-shop for some fish cakes for their supper while she set the little table and boiled the kettle and cut some bread and butter. The reading lamp on the table, and she telling him about dress making, and the poverty she was in now there was no material purchasable, and the requirements of her clients, and their sexy confidences. She was recovering herself and he watched her judgment returning gradually as her comments on people and things reached further and futher out from the touchstone of herself, radiating like ripples from a stone dropped into a pond. She had no politics or plans, no criteria; except herself, her intuitions and feelings and aversions. He wanted to restore her self to her, so that she could continue living from day to day, thought to thought, with continuity.

They were talking about the army; to-night it seemed a remote unreal topic, a social problem which could be discussed or dropped as they chose. In the same unreal mood she said:

"My husband liked the Army. He's the one on the right there. He had a good time in France, till suddenly it all happened."

Curly crossed to the mantelpiece and looked at the smiling R.A.C. sergeant in his black beret; a powerful smiling man, confident and untroubled.

"He never bothered about things," she said. "He liked tanks and so he liked the war. I don't think he bothered about dying, or being away from me. He just married me one leave, that's all. He wouldn't have a baby. It never occurred to him. And now he's dead. A whole year now he's been dead. I've forgotten nearly everything about him."

Curly looked from the second photograph in consternation.

"You know Captain Cochrane?" he asked.

"He's been coming here a lot," she said. "He's had enough of me now, though."

How weary she sounded, telling him all these elemental facts in a flat indifferent voice.

"I should have thought you'd had enough of him," he said. "He's a poor piece of work. You shouldn't have let him take you in. He's nothing at all, just cardboard and paste."

She smiled, lighting one of his cigarettes.

"Would you have saved me, if you'd known me six weeks ago?" she asked. "I met him in the Plaza at a dance, just six weeks ago. Would you have stopped him touching me?"

"It's your own affair," he said. "If I'd known you I would have."

"Could you have?" she teased him. "Could you make love as gifted as he did?"

"I don't suppose so," he said. "I am not a cinema fan. Nor am I very enthusiastic about that sort of thing. You know what he used to say? He used to say he had a lot of dirty water on his chest and he knew a woman who would swill it out for him."

"You're preaching to me, anyway," she said. "You're hitting hard, aren't you?"

"I could hit much harder," he replied.

"I can't help it now," she said, dejected. "He offered to marry me; there's that to be said for him; only he didn't mean it."

Curly went hot and sticky, as though there were filthy cobwebs all over him. And at once the old despair touched him with its dry unavailing fingers, as when he had tried to get a short leave for Taffy Thomas to see his wife.

It was difficult for him to go now. Yet she didn't want him to stay. She was normal again, and consequently beginning to understand the task that was on her, the mess she had made, the immense fatigue. She turned on the wireless, late dance music, mawkisk and sticky. They both stood up.

"Shall I come and see you again?" he asked.

"Yes," she said. "Yes. Unless I go away from here."

"Where to?"

"I don't know," she said. "Where do you go to have a baby? Are workhouses open for that? Or I'll go to my sister-in-law. She's evacuated to her father's farm in Borrowdale. I won't go yet. Not for a few months. Perhaps I won't go at all."

She was only talking round and round.

On his way downstairs he bumped into somebody, stood against the wall to let him pass, recognised Captain Cochrane, smelt his hot whiskey-sweet breath, and hurried out into the black streets and the unhurried stars.

Anglo-German hostilities, held in abeyance during the day-light, resumed at a later hour than was customary this particular night. The operational orders of the Luftwaffe gave a certain unity to the experiences of Taffy Thomas, Curly Norris, Captain Cochrane and the women with whom they were connected — a unity which would not have existed otherwise. Taffy reached Swansea on a lorry conveying sheep skins from slaughterhouse to warehouse just as the first Jerries droned eastwards along the Gower coast, droned lazily towards the dark sprawling town and released beautiful leisurely flares into the blackness below. Taffy was hungry and thirsty and broke, not even a fag-end in his field dressing pocket. So he didn't mind a few extra inconveniences such as air raids. Life was like that at present. He wasn't expecting anything much. He hurried past his habitual pubs, past the milk-bar where he had eaten steak and kidney pies on his last leave and been unable to get off the high stool on which he sat, drunk at one in the afternoon and his kid brother just as bad at his side, bloody alright, boy; and as the first bombs screamed and went off with a sickening shuddering zoomph down the docks way, he turned into his own street and kicked the door with his big ammunition boots. It was about the same time as Curly went into Eva's flat, and Captain Cochrane bought the polecat her first gin and lime. Taffy's missus was in bed on the sofa in the kitchen; she couldn't get up to let him in, she'd gone two weak. He had to climb the drainpipe to the top bedroom and squeeze through the narrow sash. She knew who it was as soon as he kicked the door with his big boots, so she wasn't frightened when he came downstairs; only ashamed, ashamed that she was such a poor wife, so useless a vessel for his nights, skinny thighs and wasted breasts and dead urges.

"Hallo, mun," he said with his rough vigour, picking up the newspaper and glancing at the headlines. "Still bad? Where's the kids? Up in your mothers?"

"She fetched them up after tea," she said, "'gainst there's a raid."

"By yourself, then?" he said. "Good job I come. Got anything to drink?"

"No," she said, ashamed at being such a poor wife. "I'd 'ave asked mam to go down the pub for a flagon if I'd thought you was coming."

"What about yourself?" he asked. "Still drinking that old pink lemonade? Can't you drink a drop of milk or tea or oxo or something yet? Still spitting that old yellow phlegm up, too, by the looks of that pisspot. I don't know, bach." He sat on the edge of the sofa and put his hand idly on her moist tangled hair. "I don't know what to do. Curly said for to take you to the hospital. I think I'd better, too. Shall I carry you to-night?"

"No," she said, frightened. "You can't now. It's blackout and there's bombs again, and I doubt there won't be a bed there. And you got to pay, too" She pushed her bony hand slowly across the soiled sheet and touched his battledress. "I don't want to go there," she said.

She was too weak to wipe the tears out of her eyes.

"Oh Jesu!" he said, getting up in a temper. "Don't cry, then. I was only suggestin'. Do as you like. Wait till to-morrow if you like. Only I was thinking the redcaps will be coming round to look for me to-morrow."

"Never mind about to-morrow," she said.

"The cat's been pissing in the room somewhere," he said, sniffing about him. He sat down again and wiped her eyes with the sheet.

"You got to mind about to-morrow," he said.

"Remember you was jealous of me in a dance at the Mackworth when we was courting?" she said. "You took me out and slapped me in the face, remember?"

"What about it?" he asked slowly, nonplussed.

"Slap me now, again," she said.

He laughed.

"I'm not jealous of you no more," he said. "You get better, and then p'r'aps I'll get jealous again, see?"

She smiled and let her neck relax on the cushion.

"You'll never be jealous of me again, " she said, looking at him with her far away eyes.

Her soul was in her eyes, and it wasn't sick like her body.

The bombs had been falling heavier and heavier, and neither of them seemed to notice. Till the light went out, and then he cursed filthily. The fire was nearly out, it was cold sitting with her all the time. He tucked her icy hands under the blanket.

"I'm going out for some coal," he said.

"There's none there," she said. "The coalman's killed."

"Christ, there's plenty more men not killed," he said. "I'll get some from next door, then."

"Don't go," she whispered.

The house shivered and plaster fell in a stream of dust, as if from an hour-glass.

"Can't sit in the cold all night," he said. "And the dark. I won't be a minute."

He slipped the latch and went out into the burning night, straight out into a screaming bomb that tore the sky with its white blade and flung him onto his face in the little backyard and brought the house crashing down with its mighty rushing wind.

The Luftwaffe's secondary objective concerned Captain Cochrane's harbour. The raid began at midnight, by which time Swansea had nothing to do except stop the big fires spreading and wait for the morning to come. Taffy had called at his mother-in-law's, and seen the children; and at the police station, to tell them his wife was buried and ask them to inform his unit; and he was just walking around, trying to keep himself from freezing and crying and lying down in a doorway, when Captain Cochrane, who had also suffered some emotional disturbance, was getting out of Eva's bed and hastily pulling on his shirt and trousers in the dark. When he was half dressed he pulled the blind back to see what was happening. The searchlights were stretching their white dividers over the harbour; and yes, by God, they had a plane in their beam, a little tinsel plane, and the red tracer bullets were floating up at it from the Bofors by the sidings. Christ, it was a marvellous sight. He was thrilled stiff, trembling to sink his teeth into it, to draw blood. Where the hell were his shoes?

"I'll have to run," he said brusquely, grabbing his cap and greatcoat.

Eva, motionless and dark in bed, said nothing at all. Of course he had to go; a soldier like him.

"Good-bye," he said, stumbling on the stairs.

Eva lay quietly, heavy and as though waterlogged, thinking of the Germans and the English, the soldiers of both sides, her husband and the excitement, the professional coolness with which, firing his two-pounder from the revolving turret of his pct tank, he died. And Hector Cochrane — she always thought of his surname as well as his Christian name — that boy with the glasses was right; he wasn't much of a man. When he had come in to-night, drunk and abased, begging her forgiveness — as if *that* was anything to give or withhold — her infatuation had dissolved like a sudden thaw, leaving everything slushy. And as she stroked his spiky bryll-creamed hair and let him sob into her lap she had felt how small and worthless the two of them were, clumsy bungling people of no moment, passive and degraded by their own actions. She had let him take her to bed. Anything was as good as nothing. He had written her a cheque.

Captain Cochrane had a haggard jauntiness arriving at the office the next morning. The ethical code of his profession forbade a man to allow a hangover to take the edge off his morning smartness. He behaved in the exemplary manner of a commissioned officer, inspecting the sleeping huts and the cookhouse and the sump, chewing up slovenly old Crocker for overflowing the swill bins, chasing the fatigue party who were rat-hunting round the sump, getting a shake on everywhere. Then to the company office for his morning correspondence. Ration indents, pay requisition, arrangements for boot and clothing exchange, a glance at the medical report to see who was scrounging to-day. Sergeant Crumb had everything in order, non-committal and deferential, soothing.

"Damn good show last night, sergeant," he said when he had finished his business. "Got a cigarette?"

"Certainly, sir." (Bloody cadger). "The Bofors crew are going on the beer to-night, sir, to celebrate knocking that Jerry down."

"Yes. Damn good show it was. All burnt to death, weren't they?"

"Yes sir. The plane was too low for them to parachute."

"Well, that's burnt their fingers for them. Something towards winning the war."

"Yes sir."

A phone message. Trunks. Captain Cochrane speaking. Good morning, sir.

This is Swansea police. A private Thomas from your company, sir. Yes? Called in at 0025 hours last night, sir. Said his wife had been buried under a bomb, sir. Christ, has she? That's bad luck. Have you confirmed it yet? Not yet, sir. Check up on it, please. He's a bit of a scrounger. If it's O.K., put him in touch with the barracks. They'll give him all the dope he needs. Money. Railway warrant. O.K.? Yes sir. If he's bluffing hand him over to the redcaps. He's absent without leave. Very good, sir. Good-bye. Good-bye sir.

"Thomas's wife. Killed. They must have had a raid as well."

"That's bad luck, sir. I'll look up the A.C.I. about coffins. I think the civil authorities supply them, don't they, sir? R.A.S.C. only issue them to soldiers. She was ailing anyway, sir, I know."

"Check up on it, sergeant. Also ring through to battalion and inform them. We'll send him a leave pass if necessary. Keep the charge sheet, though. He'll have to go before the colonel for absence without leave just the same."

"Very good, sir."

"Anything else, sir?"

"No. I don't think so. Oh yes, there's that return to the adjutant about the anti-gas deficiencies. I'll inspect all respirator contents at 1100 hours."

"Very good, sir."

"Christ, that reminds me. I've left mine in town. Where's Norris?"

"Up at your billet, sir, I sent him to clean your kit, sir, being that Thomas your batman isn't available."

"Send a runner up, then. Tell him to go to this address" — he scribbled it down, Sergeant Crumb hiding the faintest wisp of a smile as he did so — "and ask for my respirator. Miss Eva Barthgate is the name."

He smiled too. They were both men.

"Very good, sir."

Sergeant Crumb saluted smartly and withdrew.

Captain Cochrane yawned and put his feet up for a few minutes, and thought, well, that was that.

Maybe he'd ask the old man to put him in for a transfer to the Indian Army. There were better prospects out there, on the whole.

The Children

I

"Can I go out *now*, then?" the child asked, sulky and heavy with impatience.

His mother wiped the big meat dish carefully dry before replying. "I think you're a tidy little boy at last," she said. "Have you got a clean hanky?" She put the meat dish into the crockery cupboard on the kitchen wall and picked up the hand brush to dust the grate. "Well, wipe your nose, then."

He stubbed his nose furiously, his eyes leaping with tears.

"I'm late,"he said bitterly.

She laughed softly at him, then knelt down to clean the twinkling grate and the worn rag mat she had made seven winters ago; the winter of the little boy's birth, of her husband's death.

"Alright," she said. "This grate eats a lot of coal. I don't know how we can buy another load this month. You'll have to bring me brushwood from the forest. Don't be away long."

Released formally, he still hung there, sulkily waiting, unsatisfied. He wanted her voice to be *real* again, not absent-minded, empty, as though she wasn't in her voice any more, and he was nothing but an old breakwater the high careless tide swept over listlessly. He was more important than the grate or the coal or the house that always demanded attention from her, always, always.

"I won't go far," he said thoughtfully; he made no promise about *time*, he would stay out all day, he only promised not to go far. It was her own fault if she was so careless of him that she didn't notice that his answer was an evasion, not a promise. He felt like tearing her pinafore to bits, but to *bits*.

"Alright," she said, still absorbed in sweeping. "Go and play with the girls if you'd rather not help me peel the apples and pluck the fowl."

He went. Like a thunderbolt.

On the way to the meeting place at the bottom of the dusty white lane he forgot his anger and his misery. There were white flints on the path, strange shapes, odd colours — not colours, either, but gleams, thrills, changes of texture, harmonies like the sky in the distance, in the evening from his bedroom window, tingling like silk on the flesh-tips of his fingers. He put the prettiest ones in his pocket, as a present for her. He forgot about the pebbles when he saw her. He didn't even notice they were slipping through his frayed trousers pocket as he ran to meet her. And that is as it should be, for Hansel and Gretel were neither sweethearts nor brother and sister, but simply children; and as children they did not know whether their parents were wicked and unkind, or good and gentle, nor whether their father was less to blame than their stepmother; nor did they drop the white pebbles behind them cunningly and with conscious resource. When they were together they forgot about when they were unhappy, or hungry-to-bed, did Hansel and Gretel.

She was sitting on the gate, dangling her tiny feet in their dainty home-made slippers.

"Where *have* you been?" she said with mock anger, deceiving even herself. "I've been waiting for ages," she lied.

Scratch a lie and you find the truth. Maybe she *had* only just arrived before him. Nonetheless she had been waiting all day for this moment, this being together to plot and laugh and pretend, all the long morning, all the slow noon while dinner was preparing. She had waited for the potatoes to boil, and had fretted with anger at her mother's measured ease, her mother's refusal to test the potatoes every five minutes with a fork to see whether they were soft enough, her mother's refusal to be hurried or show any concern for the ticking of time. No wonder she was angry with him. She was in love with herself; she demanded his homage.

"Sorry," he said, flushing miserably; he hated apologising, it hurt him so, he felt ugly and clumsy.

Something was tickling her nostril; she scratched with her little finger, delicately, inside her nostril.

"Where shall we go and live to-day?" she asked, forgiving him capriciously, like Queen Elizabeth.

"In the castle of the rocks in the meadow?" he suggested, eager with happiness now.

"No. I think we'll make a new house to-day," she said, picking her nose again, this time angrily with her thumb and forefinger.

"Let's go into the middle of the forest, shall we?"

Her daring and resolution made him sway.

"I promised not to go far," he said, doing his conscience the honour of mentioning its existence.

"You're afraid," she taunted.

"Silly idiot," he snapped. "I'm not afraid. You're the one who's always afraid."

"I'm not," she yelled back. "Let's prove it. Come on."

She slipped off the gate, exposing her pink cotton knickers.

"We'll go right to the middle of the forest, into the dark part, where the owls and the jaguars and the slinks are," she said, looking terribly reluctant now.

But he wouldn't release her. He knew she'd be frightened when they got to the thicket where the sun was shut out by the dense branches, where there was no sun or sound, but only strange furry sounds, disturbing the cruel sleeping eagles of the silence. She would clutch his hand and keep close to him, and *he* would be the strong one then. *He* would lead her back. He saw his greatness in her, and gladly went into the forest, into the dangerous unknown.

"There are soldiers in the forest," she said. "I heard them shooting this morning."

II

In the mind of man tale and truth and time are symbols of himself, of his ever-changing everlasting constancy. Many years pass between the telling of the tale and its recollection, between the act and its moral. Who can measure the time the two children spent in the forest? Who knows how long they were in the darkness, learning the taint and touch of terror?

The children got lost in the forest. They lost each other. Eternity of terror.

It was getting dark. The trees massed and deepened, roughed out in the dusk. The searchlights plotted the sky with bluish shifting diagonals, the enemy aircraft filled the low rain clouds with anger and doom, the anti-aircraft guns roared with thwarted uncertain malevolence. The clouds shredded and the soldiers lying on their bellies behind the hurried parapet noted the glitter of the stars.

Like a dream, like a bad dream, Hansel said in his mind. The mountains fade like dying cultures, the trees fall away like the doomed fleets of Tyre; the violent red flash behind the hill's black spine is merchandise going to heaven, robes of white velvet.

We are lost. Ichabod, wail the prophets as they cower in the crannies, in the caves among the mountains. We dream that we are lost. We dream of war.

The searchlights switched off and his mind fell into darkness.

Gripping his rifle, he became aware of its impersonality, its mechanism, its impartial judgments, its refusal to discriminate between one man and another. How strange that death should be so impersonal; *his* death.

It was difficult to see; their patrols could come right up to the barbed wire without being seen. If they didn't crack a twig, or stumble, they would be as pervasive as dreams, dreams of death.

He couldn't think; not *think*; but only feel, like a blind-worm. He kept feeling the same things, again and again.

Her face, her loved face came to him again and again; it had no features, her features were sponged out, drawn over; and she was trying passionately to reach him, to be visible to him. He felt the passion of her, the trembling calm of her, the terror beneath her pride. It disturbed him terribly, not seeing her face distinctly. His mind was an embryo, struggling for release, for wholeness and form. There was weeping, darkness of mind, locked and empty chambers in deserted corridors and pain moving in the blue vague light, roughing the blankets in the dim disinfected wards. Babies crying indecently like trapped rabbits, and men whimpering, and some beds silent, silent. And the sisters noiseless and starched, smoothing the blankets that pain had pinched and disturbed. Like a bad dream, the trance of terrible anguish.

It is all like a dream, he kept on saying. We had such a wild and beautiful courtship; life revealed itself as incredibly beautiful, passionate, wonderful, terrible; like a dream. We have married, signed the register in the vestry, paid the fee. We have made house; and she is with child by me, beautiful with child.

Like a bad dream this war came, refusing to be averted, and we parted at the railway station. She got smaller and smaller, waving all the time her useless and pathetic handkerchief; and then the endless journey.

But it is not as simple as that. That is only fact; history, not life.

Life. LIFE, he said, exorcising the dream. He chose to suffer, to live. He suffered her absence; the ignorance of her health, her child, her mind, her dress consumed him. Longing for her, longing... But not like the first ignorant longing when his sex sang unsatisfied in him, and love was a brutal imperative in his blood. And she withheld herself, leaving him sucked-out and vapid, without conversation for daily deeds or spirit for daily routine, imagining nothing, enjoying nothing, animal in food and breath. Saying "I do not love her. I do not love her. I only want her, to draw her into the darkness, into the destruction in me."

Ah! It was better, now he remembered that all that terror had been lived away, lived out. She had come to him in the darkness, in the boarding-house bedroom at the week-end village and helped him, begging him to help her. In the darkness of tossed sheets and heated bodies, blind with nakedness and desperate with failure he had lain in her soft voice, believing against himself that her words were true because *she* spoke them. Her voice was the only thing he still knew in his immense unbearable agony. She quieted his sobbing and held him close in sleep.

The second night, the third night, and after a month of other things, the fourth, fifth, sixth nights they were alone together she guided and loved him out of his hell, and by her faith she made apparent the miracle of beauty. And on the sixth night she slept in his arms at last and he became the possessor of truth. He had been so lonely, so lost and beaten; and then success had been so violent, so hungry; and now he lay in the darkness, forgetting the two naked bodies, voyaging into infinite distances timelessly, beyond the intuitions and limits of sense and thought, wondering, wondering.

And then, with a tremendous leap of joy he knew the truth. The truth that all the attempts that are made to convince us that the flesh, the network of sense and nerve and appetite, is the dominant motif, had failed. The spirit took on itself the knowledge and power of flesh, its power to move and act and be. Every fatigue the army imposed on him, from cleaning latrines to burying his mates, was a test, a proof of the spirit. How he loved his mother when he thought of her, those few years he grew up with her before she died, sitting by the fire in the clean-swept kitchen, darning the worn-out darns in his socks, patching the frayed patches of his trousers, neatly concealing the poverty of the garment with deft patient fingers; her tired bony hands had a soft life, a pride, a self-reliance that was also in her yellowing wasted face and grey dying hair, a grace. But she had worked, understanding the necessity for work. It was the manifest of her spirit, her achievement: the cottage, the child of her marriage, the poverty that purged her of grossness.

And there he lay in the boarding-house bed, thinking of his mother darning by the fire, until his beloved stirred sleepily and woke softly to the gentle feel of his kisses.

And love achieved its harmony with life at that moment. He could think of it now, as he lay against the parapet of the trench, simply and clearly, remembering the cottage in the woods, the northern pines that came down to the roof and brushed the mossy tiles whose green was a continuation of the forest's floor. And a magpie slanting across the clearing and his mother waving good-bye with the dishcloth in her hand as he went along the path to the meeting place, wondering whether she would be merry or teasing, secretive, wanting love, or excited with something, wanting to tell him about it....

He could see her face alright now, and hear her voice, the inflexions of her joy, the quiet of her when she was thinking of something she would soon say. Thinking of the child in her, the child in her eyes, in her womb. The earth was wet, it soaked through his elbow, making his fingers cold as they gripped the small of the rifle butt. The cold was inside his greatcoat, and he was dimly aware of hunger and the whispering of soldiers in the fire bay beside him in the starry night.

It was a dream, this wet earth, this loaded rifle, this danger. A dream easily thrown off, a flimsy veil. His spirit was awake and glad, glad of his birth, of his pain, his childhood, his joy, his calm manhood. For him there was no war, no darkness; and no suffering but the pure suffering of children.

When the grenade lobbed over the parapet and got him, the darkness was pure light, pure power. Her face, her presence.

III

It was nearly dark when they came out of the wood. They could just distinguish the white lane. The owls were crying in the darkness of the high trees. They were still trembling, and too relieved to talk. They hurried, hand in hand. They were thinking of the witch in the forest, how she had locked them in a cage of thorns and lit a great fire and fattened them as geese are fattened; and how Gretel had tricked the old hag, pushing her into the fire and releasing Hansel. But of course they would never *tell* anyone of this; not for years would they mention it even to themselves. Fear goes through the blood many times before it reaches the mind.

"Do you think we'll get a smacking for being late?" she asked.

"I 'xpect so," he said. "I said I wouldn't go far."

"I promised to slice the apples, too," she said.

They hesitated at the turning where they would part.

"I don't expect mummy'll give me any supper," she said.

"Never mind," he replied. "I won't eat any either."

But when he stood blinking in the fire-lit lamp-lit kitchen and saw the flames twinkle on the knob of the poker and the noses of the fire-dogs, and the whited starched table cloth laid with meat pie, and apple tart sprinkled with sugar, and brown bread and butter piled on the board, he forgot. He loved his mother then, as he climbed the big wooden chair she had drawn up to the table.

"And don't think you can always spend your days playing in the fields with girls and come home to find the table groaning with meat pie, my boy," she said. "Life isn't all fairy tales. Life isn't."

He liked the sound of her voice; its love and warmth and comfort. He didn't hear what she was saying; only the sound of it he understood. It was right, whatever she said. She *knew*.

"Children!" she said smilingly, pouring the boiling water on his cocoa and stirring at the same time. "I don't know how God ever dared let children come into this world. I don't indeed."

She didn't mind, then. *She wasn't angry with him for being away from her.* The bread was thick with salty white butter.

Ballerina

The stray dog that had picked up with the soldier as he strolled along the fields made fierce barking darts at the little spaniel from the whitewashed cottage, yelping and salivating and pawing it in a frenzy. The soldier stood smiling.

She came tripping through the short garden track in her usual negligée, bell-bottomed navy trousers and cable-stitched white jumper fitting warmly about her breasts, hair long and smooth down her neck, turning up in an even wave above her shoulders.

"Tony, Tony," she cried, "come away, you immoral little beast."

She picked the spaniel up before it fell to the male blandishments of the stray dog.

"Worse than death," she said, kissing his hot black snout. And then seeing the soldier, "Hallo, soldier," she said. "Won't you come in? Have a beer?"

"O.K." he grinned, like a big bear.

He followed her into the exquisitely simple whitewashed cottage.

She was alone in the house, except for him.

She put a great juicy log on the wide hearth; it spluttered at once; flames spurted out.

"You belong to the searchlight detachment in Windy Copse?" she said.

He grinned like a big schoolboy, taking the tankard of beer from her.

"That's right," he said. "How did you know?"

"I've seen you passing," she said. "You're the signals man, aren't you?"

"That's right," he said, grinning. "You know a lot."

"You shouldn't take my maid to the pictures if you want to remain a mystery," she said, laughing and refilling the beer mugs.

She was very fine in the concealed smooth lamplight, a soft white glow against her delicate firm profile, the whitewashed wall behind her, her hair falling straight and silken to the curl in the nape of her neck.

"All of us are crazy about you," he said. "Up at the searchlight we call it a day if one of us has seen you. We always tell each other if we've seen you, what you were doing and when and where."

She smiled, archly as a queen. She was a great lady, no doubt of that, a painter or an actress or something unique.

"They'll never believe I've been in your parlour," he said. "Not actually in your house."

"Better take my hanky then," she said, handing the little lace kerchief tucked into her sleeve.

"Thanks," he said, breathlessly. When he was embarrassed his neck began twitching, his chin rubbed against the rough collar of his battle dress. He was heavy and simple in appearance.

"How about some supper?" she said. "I gathered some fresh mushrooms this morning, the dew is still fresh on them."

He smiled like a great fawn, bashful, wanting to go.

"You're not on duty just yet, are you?" she said.

"No," he said simply.

He looked at the painting over the plain oak mantel and warmed his hands at the open hearth and looked at the open bookshelves and the delicate array of noble books. The soft lamplight covered him like the presence of a sheepdog. The little spaniel slept with his nose in the white fleece of the rug.

They ate mushrooms on toast and beer and black coffee.

"I'm not like the rest of them up there," he said, his chin twitching. "They like beer and dances and women and jokes, but I like being by myself. I like sad things," he said, "the stars and music you can't hear."

"Yes?" she said, intrigued, her dark luminous eyes upon him. "Will you sing to me?"

"Yes," the soldier said. "If you want me to."

He stood up in his worn battle dress and his green gaiters, listening to the music he could not hear. His mouth paused on the brink of a song. He began singing. Being a Welshman he sang with the great sadness that is in faith and understanding, the hiraeth of a people that has seen the goodness in itself going away, away. "Dafydd Y Carreg Wen" he sang for her in the lamplit whitewashed room with the books and the spluttering wood fire and the spaniel waking up and moving restlessly outside them, and she in her soft black silk and the darkness where the lamp didn't reach, but cast a soft shadow.

When he had finished he lit a cigarette by the fire, stooping over the flames quietly and naturally, and she watching him from the edge of the darkness.

"Are you happy to-night, soldier?" she asked.

"My wife was killed last month," he said, "in the blitz."

"Oh," she said, and all the glass crumpled and splintered inside her.

"I wasn't living with her," he said. "We were separated, you know. She was wrong in herself, you know."

"Oh," she almost sobbed, leaning her white hands out in pity from the shadow, and he smiled like a great boy.

"You're young," he said, looking at her. "Nineteen, maybe?"

"Yes," she said.

"I'm old," he said. "Thirty-eight I am. That's a lot, if what happens means much to you."

"I'm a ballet dancer," she said.

"You won't dance if I sing?" he asked her.

"If you sing with that sadness on you," she said. "I will."

She danced as he sang the song of the dying poet, dying among the white boulders. Her dance was dark flame moving in the darkness of the dying flowers and the white walls and the stillness.

"There," she said, when she had finished, falling on the couch, lying on her back and closing her eyes.

"My husband is in Libya flying a plane," she said. "He doesn't love me now. He is only flying."

"I know how it is," he said, picking up his respirator and forage cap from the corner. "Well. Nos da, 'nghariad 'i."

"Good-night, soldier," she said. "And God bless you, for when I dance I know my husband is thinking of me and trying to get back to me."

"We are all like that," he said, crushing her lace handkerchief into his pocket. "I don't know indeed whether they'll believe me when I get back to camp."

"The searchlight is beautiful on starry nights," she said.

And let him go.

Cold Spell

Gracie worked in the Naffy on the aerodrome and it had begun with him buying coffee from her during the morning break, or before taking off of a winter morning on practice, or after dark on a raid. She always saw to it that his coffee was piping hot; the very first time she served him a cup she had heated it up for him.

"It's the first hot cup I've had in this joint," he said. "I reckon I ought to treat you to the pictures on the strength of that, Marlene." And that's when it really began, when she refused, disdainful at his banter. He had to wait till they met in a Paul Jones in one of the station dances. Maybe he *was* a flight sergeant and she a two-penny Naffy girl. Just the same she knew one man from another and the different attitudes the same man might contain. He flowed along like a river, altering as the ground altered, naturally, with never a thought about it. If it was beer and women he knew his stuff, or if it was just beer, or if he was browned off, and just wanted to talk to somebody quietly for a little. She made sure she became the sort he wanted to talk quietly to, so they sat in a corner, dust in their nostrils from the dance, talking a bit. Not about anything much — just the manageress of the canteen threatening to sack her for giving one of the boys credit, and why she never bothered with lipstick, and how they had told him to be a clerk in the R.A.F. and he'd made so many typing mistakes that they put him to flying to get him bumped off, and the different kites he'd been in, and the ropey pilot who scared him to death so that he picked a fight with him at a dance and broke his ribs and got transferred to another kite whose pilot was as safe as a minister in the pulpit. Just chatting about each other's jobs, quietly; and at the end of the dance he said it was the first time he'd finished up sober since Christ knows when and he reckoned he ought to treat her to a drink on the strength of that. To which she was quite amenable.

You wouldn't think there were any complications, anything to snag the smooth current. They were both single, both unattached. He'd been on the station for eight months, which is an eternity these days, and he'd taken a few Naffy girls out in his time; and one of the girls told Gracie with thin-lipped spite that he was too fast for her, and another told her with a voluptuous serpentine triumph that he could certainly satisfy a girl. But Gracie wasn't so concerned with what he was before she fell in love with him. What mattered really was what he thought of *her*, whether she was more to him than a little dirty water to get off his chest. She knew pretty soon that she wanted him just like hell, and she knew she would go with him as far as ever she could. Only she knew herself, too, and she became afraid of him finding her out as she had found herself out. Somewhere in the part of a person that melts and flows and overwhelms there was a lump of ice in her that wouldn't melt, you see, just wouldn't; she had to stop, and go back, shamefully, because she never went far enough to realise herself. The only other complication was his job. Naturally they never knew when; nor did they think about it consciously. But it was like a fan in a room, blowing their hair a little even in the quietest hours. It got on his nerves sometimes, the long flights and the flak and some of his mates not getting back, and he might be a lot of things then. He might be indifferent to her, or restless, wanting to get drunk, or peevish and sarcastic about love and settling down and that, or cynical. Only one thing he never was, in those unpredictable moods; he was never fast with her.

It was alright in summer; when she was free the same time as he they were happy enough to go into the pinewoods and lie in the moss or the warm brittle ferns with soft beds of needles under their sides. They didn't want to be indoors. But autumn turned wet on the country and there was nowhere they could go. She never came off till nine-thirty, which was too late for them to go to the pictures five miles away. He couldn't take her into the sergeant's mess, and she only had the top bunk in a little partitioned stall she shared with another girl in the Naffy hut. She wouldn't take him there although the other girl was always telling her to; "only don't use the top bunk, you might break it," her room-mate said, or something suggestive like that. She'd die rather than take him to her poky little stall.

But they got fed up with living in the hedges, and the rain, and shivering when they got up and brushed their clothes. He was getting to look ill, too, and his nerves were upsetting his system, he got real anaemic-looking. The food wasn't passing any goodness into his blood, and his body was getting full of hungers, and his mind began starving, too. If he got a shrapnel wound in that condition it wouldn't heal healthy, perhaps. She was worried for him, and got him to go to the M.O. for some drugs. It made him better, but he still had stomach trouble, and in the end she said she wouldn't go out with him any more if it rained or was cold. She kept her word, too. She went to bed the first wet night they had a date. She went to bed and wept herself to sleep. And he went and got drunk.

So the next evening they were off together they decided to ask for a room at the few cottages strung across the rough land outside the drome. She loathed doing it. But he said: What the hell, darling, why not? And they needed some place badly, so she went with him.

When they walked up the garden to the first house, a little new ferro-concrete house with an Anderson in the vegetable garden, and he rang the bell and somebody got up inside and came along the passage, she shrank back behind his shoulder in the darkness.

"Good evening," he said, in his politest.

"Good evening," the woman replied, planting herself flat in the narrow passage. "What is it?"

"I was wondering whether you could hire us your spare room for the evenings," he said. "Just for now and again."

"Heavens above," she said, taking a hissing deep breath. "What do you think I am? This is a respectable house, do you understand? And that's enough."

She slammed the door. They heard her bolt it.

"Phew!" he whistled, pushing his cap back off his forehead the way he had. "That's another bit of England I'm not fighting for. There's quite a tidy bit of this island in that category by now, Gracie."

She didn't say a word, and he felt her trembling under his arm. He bent to kiss her but she averted her face.

"Silly Gracie," he said softly, loving her for being wrongly ashamed.

"Come on Garbo. Let's try again."

She took a lot of persuading, but she went in the end, under duress, not speaking to him except yes and no.

There was a cottage he knew along a lane, in the pinewoods south of the drome. He took her there. It was like Hansel and Gretel in the wood in the moonlight, walking down the rides where the felled trees lay in bright pools of water and the chopped wood was white as the breast of a chicken, and he was telling her how the south coast looked in the moonlight when you were coming home. They could see the hens sleeping on one leg in the run, and a little foal followed behind them. It was a nice place.

He knocked at the door after listening a moment to voices and good honest laughter. The door opened straight into the kitchen. "Come in, dear, because of the light," the woman said. "Somebody with you?" She peered out through her pebble glasses. "Come in, dear. I can't see you well. I'm like my blind hen."

They stood blinking in the yellow light of the paraffin lamp. The brown little kitchen was vague with smoke from the curling fire. She was a great Falstaff of a woman, a pinafore tied round her bulging body under her heavy bosom. She smiled at them, and it was a homely smile on her red pointy face. Her shoes looked as if they must split under the weight of her dropsical ankles.

"Do you want a room, dears?" she said.

Gracie nodded her head.

"Well, we can manage that, I'm sure. Sleeping out, or just for the evenings?" — Gracie had woollen gloves on.

"Just for the evenings, mother," he said.

Gracie took her gloves off, so she could see there were no rings on her thin hands.

"You can have the parlour. It's got a sofa, and you can get wood from outside if you don't mind the fire smoking. It's an old cottage, see, but I wouldn't change it, not for a mansion. I always say: Do what you can for people, specially for you boys and girls. We haven't got no neighbours, you see. There's only us, and it's a bit quiet just me and Walter — that's my husband — and our Muriel, that's an invalid since she was so high. And you get a rotten time, don't you, away from home? So sit down and have a warm. Give the young lady a bit of the fire, Walter."

She was asthmatic and stopped for breath. Her husband stood up with the slowness of a countryman, rubbing his bald head with his earth-rough hand and grinning amiably.

"Thank you so much," Gracie said, feeling ashamed of herself at such kindness.

"Well, we're very happy, Walter and me," the words flowed on a new breath. "Not sentimental, but we're very happy, ain't we, Walter?"

Walter grinned and scratched his head more.

"Aye," he said.

"Don't scratch, it'll get worse,"she said. "I always say you don't know how happy you are till something bad happens to you. Like one day Walter was taken with a stroke, digging in the garden and his shovel struck a stone and the shock sent him into a stroke. And I wasn't crying, but the tears was rolling down my cheeks. It was a Monday, the Monday before Whit-Sunday, and I didn't eat a bite of food not till the Friday, when the doctor said he'd be alright. Did I, Walter? See, you can never tell in this life from one day to the next, so I say do what you can for people, I do."

So they used to go to the cottage, to Millie's, that was her name, and maybe they'd have a bit of supper with her, or she'd bring a tray of cocoa and biscuits into the parlour where they lay on the sofa by the smoking wood fire. She told them a lot of things, especially Gracie, who sometimes came along there in the afternoons by herself, the Naffy being shut from two to six every day. She was always ready for a laugh, Millie was; she was a bit simple, Gracie thought sometimes, the way she imagined things and laughed helplessly at them. And then other times she'd be very sorry for herself and tell Gracie her secrets. Walter was never in the house, except for meals; he was shepherd on the estate and had a little lambing shed where he kept all the prize-cards he'd won at the agricultural shows with his Suffolk ewes, and he spent most of his time there with his prizes; she didn't know what he did there, long after it was dark. And when he came home he went straight to bed after supper and asleep before she'd washed the things up; never any love, like.

All the time Gracie was waiting for winter to make the flying field too muddy or icy for the planes to take off. She wanted a rest from the nightly vigil that began when she heard the engines splutter and roar and saw the flare path light up suddenly and the great dark vultures run forward and disappear into the night. And the long, long silence that went on and on till she thought the world must have grown exhausted with the endlessness of turning and turning; and at last the distant buzz that was like a child smiling in her, and the increasing drone and the great heavy shapes coming down in the haggard light. And he'd always wave to her window, and she'd turn to sleep then for an hour, before getting up to sweep the fagends and ash and dust out of the Naffy with queer thoughts in her light head. It was hard, going on and on. Only it was hard for him, too.

And all the time life got deeper and wider, deeper and wider than she had ever dreamed it could be; she was perpetually amazed at the inexhaustible wonder and gentleness of it. She got breathless, it was queer, as if she'd run a long way with him — she got short of breath just sitting and talking to him.

One evening when Walter was out in the lambing shed Millie stood looking at them a minute very seriously, and Gracie saw her exchange a glance with her lover, and she felt all a tremble. And she knew they'd been talking to some purpose. She half-guessed; and when Millie put a candle and a box of matches on the table and went out without a word, she knew for certain. And to save him getting embarrassed she stood up and lit the candle herself and took his hand.

He followed her upstairs and pushed open the bedroom door Millie had shown him and he marvelled at Gracie being so cool and quiet and matter-of-fact. She put the candle on the washbasin and after a long pause turned quietly to his arms.

The pain and panic of that hour broke the dream in her. She had wanted to please him, that was the deepest thing she wanted; to please him by perpetuating and confirming the world their association had evoked, to make it flesh. But there was no pleasure in it, no love even; it was the ice in her, that which even then would not melt, a lump of ice blocking the stream. Sordidly sobbing on the ruffled quilt — she had removed her shoes to keep it clean — she wrestled with reality and unreality in a Jacob's dream. And he, so accomplished in this, whispered to her advice which she felt herself hating, hating. And then accepting, but as if she were accepting defeat. It would be alright in time, he murmured, kissing her, kissing her — *she would choke if he didn't let her go* — it was bound to be like that at first. Oh yes, he knew all about it, of course. Yet whom did she hate? Not him, after all, but herself.

So the bread had become a stone, as the Bible said. He had taken what she could neither give nor withhold. And he was disappointed in her, told her not to be hysterical and old-fashioned; said it kindly, but it was still an insult. Stiffened by it she sat up and combed her hair, dabbed her face with water and powder, tidied herself, said, Let's go, and could not meet his eyes that followed her every action. She couldn't face Millie either, waiting in the kitchen for them with the kettle boiling for cocoa, so she slipped out through the front door.

And gradually, by herself, she made terms with life, figuring out just how it was. He had never said a word about the future. Marriage wasn't in his mind. And how could it be when he didn't expect to live? She wasn't blaming him for that. Their whole life was so limited in a way, limited to the aerodrome, its routine and conventions and personnel and operations. When he went on leave in November she couldn't go with him even if he'd wanted to take her. They were just part of the aerodome, that was all, a little corner of the war. And he was more a part of it than she. He belonged to his kite, and was part of its crew. He talked of her engines and controls and guns with the intimate quietness of a lover. When she came back with her fuselage riddled with flak he was sorry for her and proud of her airworthiness, keeping her nose doggedly for home, shaking the flak off her back and never faltering. He'd been through a lot with her, and he knew every fixture and cylinder and mounting in her. She meant more to him than Gracie did. And she wasn't blaming him for that, either. Nor for going off on the razz with the rest of the crew after a big flight and a dogfight back. It was natural for him and she knew her only chance was to keep her proper place in his life. No, she didn't blame him, but she couldn't help hating. Hating the war more than the danger, the continuance of the risk more than its ending; it would go on and on, just like that, and there would be no peace. Only war.

He did his best to comfort the distress she couldn't always conceal from him. When one of the crew got the D.F.M. he took her to the private little dinner they had in town. But she felt it was a special privilege, and his mates treated her with the quixotic respect due to a friend's mistress. She was unhappy in the midst of their courtesy and merriment and wine, a raven at the feast.

Yet she wanted him avidly; she dried up without him, was parched and dry and demagnetised unless he came with her to Millie's and Walter was out in the lambing shed. Millie was immensely maternal to them both; one day she'd have shot a rabbit for supper for them, another day the blind hen she kept in the coalshed would have laid them a couple of eggs. And she'd talk to them as they ate the hot supper by her fire, telling them how she was terrified of the little brown deer that slipped noiselessly through the pinewoods and would attack her one night, she felt sure; or how she'd told Walter's mother to get out of her house when the old blighter accused her of giving Walter the toothache. Gracie knew how Millie wanted to look after her, no matter what happened. She was a melodramatic kind-hearted creature, Millie, and she was starving in herself.

So she figured it out that she wouldn't risk more than she must. And she felt herself shrinking and shrinking into something small and hard and cunning; her eyes grew puckered a little, as if with watching from a corner, watching his actions and mannerisms, his comings and goings, his free and easy laughter, his dangerous journeys. She saw him as his mates saw him, and as the girls in the Naffy saw him, and as Millie saw him. And watching him moving through his life and his duty she waited for something to happen to him, some little incident in his life, some casual necessity of the war.

The ground froze up in mid-December and he had a lot of time on his hands. He used to sit in the Naffy for hours, reading the paper, playing doolies and dominoes, leaning on the counter when the rush hour was over, talking to Gracie behind the manageress's back, looking lethargic and preoccupied and browned-off. She felt the same old resentment at him wanting to be in action, with his mates and his kite, in his fleece-lined jacket and straps. The inaction got on her nerves as well.

At the end of the second week he said "Let's go into town this afternoon, Gracie. I want to do a bit of shopping and maybe your taste is better than mine by now. I don't seem to know the difference between genuine things and sham any more. Too much flying, most likely."

So she put her best Herschel costume on and her Dutch shoes and her black straw hat that turned up all round with her curly fringe in front of it, and she felt like new paint for once. When they got off the bus he said "Let's go along the lake for a bit first. The shops are all too crowded. They get on my nerves."

Walking along by the lake the sun came out and touched the willows on the island to red flames. School-boys sailing boats and dragging butterfly nets for minnows to put in their jam-jars. Soldiers and their girls strolling past. A woman sitting knitting in the cold. An old man with a beard, gathering herbs in brown paper. Gracie let him lead her quietly to the copse of northern pines, where the wind was singing to itself.

"Look, Gracie," he said, stopping and turning to her and kicking a stump of gorse with his toe. "I've been thinking it out this week. Shall I tell you what I think?"

"Yes," she said, her whole life suddenly pausing. If after all it was just this Saturday afternoon beside the lake for which she had been waiting with such fixed frightened endurance?

"Well, I've been thinking about the kite and about the boys," he said.

Something flared up in her, blind anger, like a heath fire half-stamped-out that breaks again into flame with a gust of wind.

"Yes?" she said. "That is not unusual, is it?"

He didn't notice the spleen in her voice.

"You didn't see her come in from the last trip, did you?" he said. "She crash-landed. She had half the port wing shot away over Hamburg and the undercarriage was busted. And when we got out we found Micky in the rear- gunner's blister couldn't get out. So I went in after him. I told you he'd gone to hospital, didn't I?"

"Yes," she said.

There was no spleen in her now. She watched his face; he was looking across the choppy sun-flash of the lake, pulling his sight back from where his thoughts were, pulling it back towards her. She had a queer impression that he was in the plane, a speck in the clouds over the world trying to bring her back to the landing field, the sleeping bunk, the breakfast and bath, Gracie's window — to the solid fixed point on the earth where the odd clues made a human reality and he was able to be something familiar and simple. He wanted to make the airport, and find it not the scientific centrifugal force that sent planes out like shuttles on a loom, but *home*, *his* home.

"Well, he died to-day," he said.

After kicking the stump of gorse for a long time he said "I can't forget the stink of blood, and the clots of black flesh congealed in his clothes and the mess on the floor his face was sprawled in — I can't get it out of my mouth, Gracie, the filthy mess it was, and the stink."

She could see Micky alright as he used to be in the station dances and the Naffy. Always acting and telling stories that made the table listen and then burst out laughing — dirty stories, no doubt, but a good spirit in them — and suddenly getting up and doing an Egyptian dance with his wrists at right angles and his body a triangle and one arm stretched forward, the other to the rear. Always calling the girls "Love" and never bothering with them *really*. Turning out everything in his pockets onto the counter to find a couple of pennies to pay for his char, and a funny pocketful he usually had — marbles that he'd won from the kids in the village, a locket, once even a dead bird. Micky was a good name for him.

"Micky and I used to go on leave together," he said. "And pool our wages when we were going on the razz. I sat his wireless exam for him because he had a hangover, and wrote his paper out with a sloping hand when I'd finished my own. We had some times together."

"Yes," she said.

"Well," he said. "It doesn't make sense, see, Gracie; but I didn't cotton on to what this war is, and what killing is, until I smelt that gore in Micky's cabin and saw him screwed up on the floor. And I've been thinking — Well, Christ Almighty!" he turned and put his big hands on her shoulders — "Why didn't you tell me before, Gracie? Why didn't you make me see? *You* could see, couldn't you?"

"What, darling?"

"Well," he said. "I can't say it exactly. What I mean is, well, how *casual* we are; blokes like me, I mean. We don't realise what we're dragging in the muck, most of the time."

And she knew that this was her big moment; one way or the other something was going to break.

"I'd got used to the idea of dying," he said. (Why must he go on kicking that stump of gorse? Dust was curling up between the fine ice-film, over his toecap). "It's *living* is what puzzles me. I've fooled around all the time. It's a kind of habit I've got into."

She waited, her head bent down like a worn-out doll.

"I was thinking," he said, "what if I could make a start, now; it's a sort of opportunity, when the ground's frozen up and there's no chance of taking off for a week or two. What do you think?"

"You're a funny boy," was all she could say.

"So was Micky," he said. "But he's serious now." (The gorse broke at last. He stopped kicking). "Well, I was thinking of proposing to you, Gracie, see?"

She didn't answer.

"Will you take a chance with me?" he said, his hands hurting her.

"Haven't I taken one with you already?" she said.

His lips stroked her fringe; he took her round little hat off.

"Oh, look!" he said. "Look at those two swans."

A brace of swans, swift and white, cut like arrows slantwise through the lemon clouds of misty sunlight over the pines, wings firm-spread and glittering white in their downrushing and furling, scarcely disturbing the surface of the lake.

"Perfect landing!" he said. "Wasn't it? Couldn't have done better myself."

Dusty Hermitage

She had the key of his cottage ever since his death, and at least once a week she had gone in and dusted it, opened the windows, put fresh flowers in the music room, and run the brown water out of the taps. She did this for three years; and when his brother or mother or friends were coming down they dropped her a line and she got everything ready for them — coal and firewood, milk and bread and groceries; also she asked the butcher boy to call for orders, the butcher boy who was waltzing on his bicycle across the heath when the great Brough Superior roared round the bend flat out, and swerved to avoid him, and threw its rider, and killed the owner of the cottage just like that. She didn't worry about the future of the cottage as long as his family lived; she knew they wouldn't sell it; besides nobody would want to live in that arid twilit stretch of dusty rhododendrons and scrub and tank lanes, except perhaps an officer from the R.A.C. camp. But she didn't want it to fall back into the uninhabited decay in which he had found it. So that when the National Trust took the cottage under their aegis and converted it into a museum, she admitted to herself that it was perhaps the best solution, even though it was incongruous that the dusty little hermitage should be given the official status of a "Place of Historic Interest." And when they asked her, very deferentially and respectfully, whether she would still keep the key and let people in and tend the place, she being the only person living within a mile of it, she said Yes, of course.

And for four years she showed people round the cottage. Sometimes she listened to their remarks, sometimes she shut her ears. Their comments built up such a vulgar grotesque image of him; an inflated public figure, a national hero, a great man, a human paradox, a Jekyll and Hyde, a mixture of a glamorous desert sheikh out of *Desert Song* and a boorish solitary playing pseudonymous games. When the visitors gossiped in that way she didn't listen, unless the effect of their words cast its cheap neon light not on him but on themselves and she saw how their minds were full of headlines and sensations and Hollywood hungers. It amused her to listen to them then. Particularly if it was somebody "great"; a general glittering with polished jackboots and Sam Browne and red epaulettes and drooping moustaches, or a Cabinet Minister with his wife and chauffeur, or some long-haired person with a big velvet bow-tie. How hungrily they looked round for the Visitors' Book, sometimes even asking her if there was one, and how they were irritated or disappointed when she said "No, there's no Visitors' Book I'm afraid" — as though they particularly wanted *him* to know they *had* called. What a pleasant relief it was when his mother came down, or one of his delightful friends, and they talked together for the afternoon; quite different, *quite* different.

Fewer people came down since the war, and now that private cars had all been laid up scarcely anybody came at all. A few soldiers from the camp, an occasional hiker or cyclist, that was all. She was by herself once more, with her flowers and vegetables and hens and kittens, which was as she liked it.

On June 13th, the anniversary of his death, she preferred nobody to call for the key. She performed the same orderly little ritual each year. In the morning before breakfast she cut her best late roses, some sweet peas and carnations and antirrhinums and a few tall yellow hollyhocks, and filled the flower bowls in his dark low-ceilinged library downstairs and the beautiful moss-coloured music room upstairs. She opened all the windows and left it all so. At four in the afternoon she shut the windows. The bike had thrown him just then.

This year somebody called in the middle of the afternoon. As a matter of fact she was lancing a little sac of pus that had been making the tabby kitten limp for the last few days, and when the bell rang she deliberately didn't answer it until she had unhurriedly finished the operation. Then she opened the door and it was as she feared, a middle-aged man and his wife wanting the key. She looked at her watch. It was half-past three. She said she'd come with them directly, wanting to get them out of the way by four. And she went straight down the lane, not even taking her pinafore off.

She opened the door and gave them one of the green brochures for threepence each and they stood in the library looking at the outside of the brochures and at all the photographs at the same time. The big divan with its worn leather coverlet and his sleeping bag so filled the room that the visitors had difficulty in moving. And they were both of a middle-aged corpulence, he in his black suit and celluloid collar chafing his chins and she in her flouncing summer frock with

diaphanous frills camouflaging her bulges. They must have walked up
from the station, they looked hot and dusty; the wife fanned herself
with a *Daily Mirror* and looked longingly at the divan; they were going
to have a rest. She'd be lucky if she got them out by four.

"This is a small place for a great man," the husband said, wiping his
forehead along the line of his hatbrim with a large damp handkerchief.
"You can't swing a cat here." He blew hot air out of his cheeks with a
puff like a bicycle valve. "But then, I gather he wasn't very strong on
the financial side, was he?" He looked without interest at a photograph
of excavations at Carchemish. "Funny, too. I believe his book was a
best seller, wasn't it? *Somebody* must have got the money."

She stood in the shadows by the door, her back against the wall, very
slender and straight and quiet, her grey hair fastened neatly in a small
bun above her long neck, effacing herself. It wasn't quite clear whether
the husband was speaking to his wife or to her, or just to an audience.
She imagined the latter and made no reply.

"I wouldn't like to live here, anyway," the wife said. She looked
round. "There isn't even an indoor lavatory, is there?"

She heard the gate click, and the sound of boots on the gravel, army
boots by the sound of it. Somebody else.

She didn't move from the shadow just inside the door. Then the
light from the open hall door was obscured by the newcomer. It was a
low door and his head must have nearly touched the lintel. He was
wiping his boots on the mat. How unusually considerate.

She turned to face him. He was in battledress, with the red and
yellow flash of the Armoured Corps on his arm, one pip on his
shoulder, motoring goggles round his neck, and his black beret in his
hand. He looked young and wiry,with wide perceptive eyes that were
more contemplative and sensitive than inquisitive.

She knew she had seen his face before. Still, that was not in itself
uncommon among visitors to the cottage.

"Good afternoon," he said. "May I come in?"

"Of course," she replied, automatically picking up a brochure and
handing it to him. Contacts with people sometimes embarrassed her,
so that she went through the formalities of introduction, or as in
this case, the threepenny entrance fee, without being consciously
aware of it. She only regained her serenity when he turned from her
to look at the photographs and the portraits by Kennington and John
that lined the library shelves. She had not moved. The married couple
were sitting empirically on the edge of the divan in front of the
portraits.

"What a marvellous face," the woman said, fanning herself. "Isn't it a *shame* he had to die like that. You'd think he'd have been more careful, wouldn't you? And he'd have been so useful to us in *this* war, too."

"They say he didn't care," her husband replied. "He was cheezed off with things. He was a miserable sort of chap." He turned to the door, looking at the shadow there. "Did you know him?" he asked.

She nodded Yes in the shadow.

"Was he?" he asked with the directness of a man who expects his employees to have it at their fingertips.

"Not with me," she said. "He was different with different people."

The soldier looked round at her a moment, quickly.

"Did he smoke?" the wife said.

"Would you mind if I had a look upstairs?" the soldier asked her.

"Of course not," she said. "I'll come with you."

As they were going up the stairs they heard the man say he was going outside to have a pipe while she finished looking at the "snaps".

Upstairs, as down, there were only two rooms. A small guest room on the right with a sleeping bag marked "Thine" and a water cistern, and the spacious, tranquil "music room" on the left with its cool mossy carpet and soft leather door like an Arab's temporary habitation.

"He made the door himself," she said. "Listen." She let it swing closed. "It doesn't make a sound. He made that Jacobean chest, too, when he was a boy. He was ill."

"It's good carving," he said, considering the formal entwinement of grapes and leaves.

"He didn't like it," she said. "But of course he never liked his own work. He said it was never *innocent*." She shrugged her shoulders.

"He was an artist," the soldier said slowly, looking out through the window onto the dusty thicket of rhododendrons. "But an artist who couldn't commit himself to his choice."

"How do you mean?" she asked, swinging the door to again, soundlessly.

"Well, the artist has the best chance of pursuing the good," he said, "because as an artist he has no vested interests in the warring elements. He is just so much an artist as he is disinterested. But that is only his potential. His actual power depends on the vigour with which he pursues his choice once he has made it. He couldn't make a positive choice. That's why he was unfulfilled."

"You have chosen?" she said, smiling a trifle ironically.

"In so far as one can," he said, laughing a little and standing up.

"My trouble is — " and he laughed again, evading her without being evasive. That was a habit she had met before also. "Oh well, we grow up by the time we die. One learns self respect after learning to respect other things. It's just the order in which things happen that puts you all wrong."

"Do you think she really knew him?" a voice came from the gravel path. "An ordinary woman like that?"

"Hush," the husband said. "Your voice is too loud."

"I suppose he borrowed milk from her, and a loaf of bread sometimes," she continued. "I meant to ask her, was he a *sight* after his accident? Oh well, never mind now. I didn't think much of the place, did you? I mean, not all that long walk."

Their voices faded away, dusty as the road.

"I always kept some milk on one side for him," she said. "And a little wholemeal loaf. She's quite right."

"Heavens," the soldier said, looking at his watch. "It's five to four. I've got a tank trial at four in the camp. I'll have to fly."

"Have you got a bicycle?" she asked.

"Better still," he said. "I've got a motorbike."

Something jumped inside her, like a dark fist. She trembled, stilled herself, and tossed her head.

"I apologise for poking my nose into another man's house like this," he said. "I won't intrude again."

She smiled. "Few people say that," she said. "Most of them are only too glad to." She held the door open for him.

"Yes," he said, looking at her. "But few houses have such a living presence in them."

She returned his look.

"You feel that about this place?" she asked.

"Yes," he said, still looking at her. "You ought to be proud of that, you know."

He smiled and slipped past her. He turned at the bottom of the stairs.

"Good-bye," he said, waving his beret and smiling.

"Good-bye," she waved back.

She followed him down stairs and watched him set the controls of his motor-bike.

Before the engine made speech impossible with its roar, she called out to him.

He turned his head towards her.

"Be careful on that motor-bike," she said. "The road is still oily where he was killed. The tanks cross it there. Be *careful*."

"Yes," he said, laughing back, fresh and suddenly carefree. "Good-bye."

The engine roared at his kick. He revved her up, put her in gear, let the clutch out. He was gone with a whirl of dust.

She looked at her watch. It was four o'clock.

She knew she wouldn't see him again. But she was inexplicably happy despite her unreasoning agitation as the sound of the motor-bike died away. And quietly she turned back to the empty cottage to close the windows. Another such as he had come and gone.

She was remembering his last letters. "I find myself wishing all the time that my own curtain would fall... There is something broken...my will, I think... As for fame after death, it's a thing to spit at; the only minds worth winning are the warm ones about us. If we miss those we are failures." And how some evenings he watered her flowers.

The Prisoners

The wooden blinds black-out the light hanging over the card game. The military police loosen the necks of their battledress and flick their cards onto the stained baize, and salivate as they wait for supper. In the next room, behind the locked door, the prisoners lie on their straw palliasses, easily and uneasily, looking for sleep in the darkness....

In the morning, when the sun shone, the prisoners marched back and fore in threes along the patch of dusty earth fenced with barbed wire. Back and fore, back and fore, about turn, about turn under the police corporal's whipped commands, exercising themselves as the Medical Officer instructed. Their blankets, neatly folded on groundsheets, lay in the sun, square piles of grey and blue beneath the trees. The trees towered in new leaf, two chestnuts waking to summer, green palaces of sighing down-hanging leaves momently exhausted with burgeoning. Maybe the prisoners noticed this morning that there was less sunlight patching the dusty compound; the green leaves have been sucking the sun, reaching forth their fine fingers and folding the sunlight away.

Being Sunday, the prisoners sang hymns after their exercise. The padre only asked them to sing hymns on Sundays, visiting them after the big church parade and putting a hymn on their silent tongues, giving them a nice change.

And after the hymns and the benediction the prisoners cleaned the buckets that had been filled with water overnight and left to rust through their sleep. And after dinner the browned-off corporal marched them down the dusty road through the camp area to scrub the company offices and quartermasters' stores, the latrine seats and ablution rooms, and the back stairs of the officers' mess. When they had done, he marched them to the tin shanty where the cold showers were, and made each man bath himself while he leaned against the zinc sheeting and spat thoughtfully and scratched his chest and his neck.

Then back for tea, which was brought up in deep tin boxes, bread, cake, a tin of jam, a pail of tea. The corporal kept the tea waiting till its cheering warmth had taken a chill — it was a favourite gag of his.

And then, after tea, for a whole beautiful hour, the prisoners were free to do exactly what they liked, bar smoking. They could write a letter — though not more than one — to whom they chose; or they could read the yellow Westerns the padre had brought them from Woolworths. Or they could lie on their palliasses and talk. They could do just as they pleased, in fact.

Then lights out at dusk, black-outs up, no talking allowed. The thin partition and the ill-fitting door through which the light streaked allowed every sound to pass. So there was silence, then whispers in the silence, and the uneasy movement of lethargic bodies. In the police room the sound of talk, obscene talk, polishing and tidying, the corporal of the day going out for a booze, the corporal of the night taking over. He was a decent chap, the night bloke, he let the prisoners talk themselves to sleep, and if they had threepence he'd sell them a Woodbine.

"Thank God that bastard's gone," said a rough voice in the darkness of the prisoners' room, sighing with relief as the day corporal slammed the door behind him and hurried down the road. "I'll get that bastard stone cold once I get back to civvy street."

It is a psychological characteristic of soldiers with a grudge, this revenge vow they link up with a return to egality.

"That won't be to-morrow, Nicky, so don't promise yerself nothink; yer might ferget abaht 'im by then," a cracked Cockney voice from the corner replied.

"Not me I won't," the rough voice shot back. "I don't forget no faces, boy" — this with a smear of pride — "when I started work in the lamproom in Durham pits at fourteen I knew every man's face and where 'is lamp was within a fortnight. No need to look at their number plates; knew three 'undred faces I did."

"Aw, shurrup," the cockney retorted. "If you're such a bleeding miracle 'ow come you're in 'ere doin' a bit of time?"

"Got to pay for yer pleasures, Tommy, that's fair enough. How was I to know it was the O.C.'s car I was spooning in? 'E should 'a locked the door of it, the dozey cow."

They were quite at ease in detention, these two. Nobody did more than twenty-eight days in the camp jail. Longer punishments were served in the glass-house at Aldershot. These two had just settled down to a month's clink. They weren't missing much. The old cockney was nearing his discharge, actually waiting his final medical board. He had fought the last war out to the bitter end; this time he wasn't bothering. His job was to polish the officers' brown boots and belts and stoke the boilers. He was proud of his record, no convictions for anything except his solitary failing, drunkenness. He was a bit ashamed of that; not of being hauled before the C.O. regularly, but of finding himself less and less able to hold his beer. His head was as weak as his bladder and he was seriously perturbed at this softening of his most valued faculties. He was garrulous with a touch of senility, and boastful and crammed with violent exploits. He had killed men in France, in Flanders, in Asia Minor; after the war he had killed men in Egypt and Russia; it never seemed to have occurred to him that he himself ought to have been killed by any reasonable law of averages; consequently, he related his bloody stories and pranks impersonally, ironically, like a laughing malicious daemon.

The Durham boy was a young conscript, one for the fleshpots, with a long lean face and a squat body, strong and agile, a monkey of a lad. He took things as they came. He was at home anywhere, simple and genuine, carrying no regrets in his mind to veil or give pause to his zest. His company commander had found him spooning in the back of his car outside the town hall a week back, and had taken a humourless view of the matter. "Serve 'im right if 'e can't take a joke," Nicky had muttered to the girl he was with, quietly putting the O.C. also on his revenge sheet for civvy street.

There were two other men lying in the darkness. One had been there for a fortnight, waiting trial. He was in for a packet, he was. Kong was his nickname, a heavy retarded man with a thick corrugated forehead receding to curly hair, a flat nose, a fat little mouth with lips like cherries, and a hairy ape-like body, bandy with heavy labour.

He never grinned, never did anything spontaneous; before speaking he always shifted his body, raised his shoulders, lifted his head up on his short bullneck — and then he said something slowly, brooding on his words. He never drank or went to town on Saturdays or read — maybe he couldn't read; he had no curiosity about the war, and no physical fear, for he had stood and watched an odd plane dive-bomb the working party he was with the August after Dunkirk and it seemed to have amazed him in a slow wondering way. Six men had been killed and he was so impressed that he never said a word. He was as ingenuous and gullible as any cockney could have wished; if anyone advised him to do a thing he did it. He followed people like a child, every day, in every detail — to meals, to draw kit, to parades, to bed.

Generally his mates looked after him and quickly shut up any smart alick who tried to make a guy of him. But this time he was in one hell of a mess. He'd hit a policeman with a blunt poker, and they were waiting to see whether the policeman would recover. When he was out of hearing, Tommy would immediately start thinking aloud about the policeman, wondering whether he'd fractured his skull, asking the corporal of the guard every day whether any news had come from the hospital, watching and listening at the keyhole every time anyone came into the guard room in case they had news. With a taste for violence and drama he half-hoped the policeman would die. All *his* murders had been legal and authoritative. He had never slept with a real murderer before. In a way it would be interesting. And when Kong was in a docile innocent mood, after tea when they had a spare hour sometimes, he would try artfully to make him talk about how it happened. So far in vain.

"Sleeping, Kong?" Tommy asked, reaching over and prodding the heavy silent body.

"Naow," Kong grunted. As a matter of fact he scarcely slept at all.

"Didn't 'ave enough food," Tommy said sympathetically. "They don't never give us a man's rations in 'ere; think because we're indoors we don't get 'ungry, I s'pose. Blimey, they ought to know our bellies get bigger and bigger in jail. There ain't much else to think of."

Nobody joined in. They were all fed up with his moaning about food. As it was he always tried to serve out the dinner so that he could give himself more than the others.

"Sociable lot," he grunted. "Reel chatty. Like to meet you lads in the old boozer in Kentish Town after the war. 'Ave some fun together, w'at do you think?" Silence, then, imperturbably — "When I was in 'ospital in Newport wiv a blighty in the last do, that's w'en I 'ad the food. I was a 'ero then, of course. Ladies bringing me chocluts an' jelly an' custard every arternoon. Coo! An' I stayed there eight months, boy, long arter my leg'd got better. There was a sister in my ward, see, an' I sedooced 'er as you might say, an' she didn't 'alf like it. So she moved me into a private ward and always gave me a temperature so's the M.O. couldn't send me out, an' many a merry night she warmed my bed for me. But the food. Lummee!"

Still nobody spoke. He sighed sorrowfully and turned over. "Luvly, tell yer mam," he concluded, yawning and spitting against the wall.

Somebody came into the guardroom and warned the N.C.O. that there was an air raid message purple on. Later, five or ten minutes, and the first distant tremor touched their ears. Then slowly, beautifully, the air began throbbing, growing wider and deeper, a vibrant dynamic throb that touched their veins and bodies where they lay in their scruffy blankets, touched them like a drop of brandy, sensitising and liberating their imprisoned bodies so that they were part of the throbbing air, the pulsing night, the feeling slender searchlights, the vast dangerous purpose and counter-purpose of the war.

"Santa Claus," sneered Tommy, "takin' a present for my missus in Kentish Town, bless 'er 'eart. Jerry ain't concerned over us. We're only soljers."

A distant muffled thud; the door rattled.

"Pompey," said Tommy. "Green-grocer's on the corner. Wumph. Wumph." The other three lay listening, very still and relaxed.

"'Taint nothing," he said deprecatingly. "We ain't 'ad nothing yet. Not to the last time. It's Russia wot's getting it this time. All the Bolshies. I reckon a man wot stays a Bolshie after 'e's eighteen ought to be *forced* to work. I was there last time, and I know wot I seen. I was there in the Rasputin do, boy. I seen the soldiers coming back from the front an' the women coming out of the brothels. Alright, too. Alright."

"Aw, shut your long trap," Nicky shouted, suddenly angry. "Shut your trap and let's 'ave some peace. I want to sleep."

"Aw awlright, Geordie, 'ave yer bleeding sleep."

Humming Esquimaux Nell, Tommy slowly and easily glided into sleep.

For half an hour flak and bombs and naval guns thundered and rattled thirty miles south of them, on the coast. Then the night closed its eyes again.

The darkness of the prison room grew fuggy with the snoring breath of the sleepers. Next door was quiet, except for the murmured words of the card game. The light lay like a bright yellow rapier across the dark room and the scrubbed floor. Apathy swirled slowly about and about, like stale tobacco smoke; nothing seemed to be happening in the silent down-pressing four-walled darkness; nothing; no conscious thought, no human qualm of hope or faith or fear; apathy like a stale drain wandering stagnantly through all attrition, through all the land. Through darkness and windows of darkness, through the slums and the promenades of the night, merging and dissolving all effort and identity and resolve. The prisoners turned uneasily.

A heavy hairy hand tugged the sleeping blankets. Kong couldn't sleep. Perhaps he was having a living nightmare and needed desperately some human help. He tugged the blankets of the boy next to him, the fourth of the prisoners. He was a newcomer, not interesting to Tommy because he spoke like a clerk, with a quiet gentleness that was mammy's boy to Tommy; too civil he was. He had only been in two days; he was doing a seven days' stretch for absence without leave; Tommy disliked him further because he wouldn't tell them why he'd done a bunk; politely he evaded all leading questions. And he only needed to shave every three days, soft downy skin he had like a girl's, and brown eyes so liquid and sensitive you couldn't look at them in case you hurt him; little cissie.

"Sleeping, mate?" Kong whispered hoarsely.

"No," the boy answered quietly.

"Nor me," Kong assured him, his voice swimming with relief, "I i'n't sleeping, neither."

"I can't feel tired, somehow," the boy said.

"Let's talk, is it?" Kong asked with the wishful timid voice of a child.

"Yes," the boy replied. "If you can think of anything to say. I can't think."

"You don't like it in 'ere, mate, do you?" Kong said.

"No," said the boy.

Kong listened like an animal; he could hear the boy weeping; he could hear the tears running down his cheeks, the slight swallowing noises he was making trying to control his tear ducts.

Kong waited patiently until he felt the boy compose himself. Then he spoke slowly, half to himself.

"They're always asking you what you're in jail for, same as me. I don't tell them what 'appened, see? I'm not arstin' you, neither."

The boy was silent.

"I'll tell you what it was with me, though," Kong said, speaking easily, miraculously confessing. "I won't tell the judge nor nobody. Only I'll tell you to-night. My missus, see? She's only eighteen. Well, my mother, she wrote to me. She said my missus was 'aving a man in every night, in the dark, see?"

He waited a little.

"Yes," the boy said softly.

"Well, my mate, see, 'e read the letter to me. Then 'e thought it out, and arsked the sarge, an' sarge said tell the O.C. about it. The O.C. will stop 'er allowance, sarge said, and I'll get full pay, not ten bob like I'm getting now. See?"

"Yes," the boy breathed.

"But I went 'ome myself, walked it I did. Only I didn't want to get there at night. I wanted to get there at dinner time, and 'ave dinner

164 *Collected Stories*

with 'er. There'd be nobody there then I thought. But there was a policeman on the corner; knew my name and number, 'e did. Said 'e 'ad orders to arrest me and send me back. Without me seein' 'er, see?

"An' 'e tried to stop me.

"But 'e didn't stop me.

"She said it was all lies, so I don't care now.

"If 'e dies I don't care."

"He won't die," the boy said.

"You don't think 'e'll die?"

"No, he won't die," the boy said, praying.

"I don't care," Kong said.

He lay quietly for a time.

"I went away to see my girl, too," the boy said.

"Did you see her?" Kong asked eagerly.

"Yes."

"Good kid," Kong relaxed, happy.

"My sister've got a baby," Kong said. "W'en it was one year old its 'air turned from yellow to brown it did. It was all bones at first, she wouldn't let me touch it, little thing. But it got fat an' strong and laughing and kicking."

"My sister's got two children," the boy said. "Denis and Maureen. They wear green rompers and yellow bonnets, like daffodils."

Kong turned over.

"Are you going to sleep?" he asked.

"Yes, now," the boy said.

"It must be late," Kong said. "I don't care."

The night composed itself again.

Kong lay very still, too still to be sleeping.

The boy knew this, and didn't get up as he wanted to, and walk round. He lay still, thinking of his girl and his home and his father's anger because he had deserted, the scene on the lawn in front of the library windows, and kissing her good-bye, oh his heart breaking in him, and the Army again, the Army, the Army. Which was the way to the front to fight, to fight and be killed? This way? He was afraid of going this way, a deserter sent abroad in punishment; he loathed being killed this way....

The white of his cheeks turns pallid as the fine ashes of dawn fall grey on his skin; all his vain barricades waver as the grey tide strokes his delicate head and its passionate error.

Dawn is rough against the outer wall.

The cards fall softly in weak pools of light.

But the four prisoners tremble and turn uneasily, and smile in their sleep in the darkness, unknowingly, beautiful as children.

Dawn is distant, distant as the origin of the smile on their sleeping lips.

The bugler also sleeps.

They Came

The evening was slowly curdling the sky as the soldier trudged the last mile along the lane leading from the station to the Hampshire village where he was billeted. The hedgerows drew together in the dusk and the distance, bending their waving heads to each other as the fawn bird and the black bird sang among the green hollies. The village lay merged in the soft seaward slope of the South Downs; the soldier shifted his rifle from left to right shoulder and rubbed his matted eyelashes with his knuckles. He was a young chap but, hampered by his heavy greatcoat and equipment, he dragged his legs like an old clerk going home late. He cleared his throat of all that the train journey, cigarettes and chocolate and tea and waiting, had secreted in his mouth. He spat the thick saliva out. It hung on a twig.

Someone was following him. When he heard the footsteps first he had hurried, annoyed by the interfering sound. But his kit was too clumsy to hurry in and he was too tired. So he dawdled, giving his pursuer a chance to pass him. But the footsteps stayed behind, keeping a mocking interval. He couldn't stop himself listening to them, but he refused to look back. He became slowly angry with himself for letting them occupy his mind and possess his attention. After a while they seemed to come trotting out of the past in him, out of the Welsh mining village, the colliers gambling in the quarry, the county school where he learned of sex and of knowledge, and college where he had swotted and slacked in poverty, and boozed, and quarreled in love. They were the footsteps of the heavy-jawed deacon of Zion, with his white grocer's apron and his hairy nostrils sniffing out corruption.

But that was silly, he knew. Too tired to control his mind, that's what it was. These footsteps were natural and English, the postman's perhaps.... But still they followed him, and the dark gods wrestling in him in the mining valley pricked their goaty ears at the sound of the pimping feet.

He turned the corner into the village and went down the narrow street past the post office and the smithy, turned the corner under the A.A. sign and crossed the cobbled yard of the hotel where the officers' and business men's cars were parked. A shaggy old dog came frisking out of its straw-filied barrel in the corner, jumping and barking. He spoke to it and at once it grovelled on its belly. He always played with the dog in the mornings, between parades. The unit did its squad drill in the hotel yard, kitchen maids watching flirtatiously through the windows, giggling, and the lavatory smelling either of disinfectant or urine.

He pushed open the little door in the big sliding doors of the garage which had been converted into a barrack room for the duration. Thin electric bulbs high in the cold roof dangled a weak light from the end of the twisted, wavering flex. Grey blankets folded over biscuits or straw palliasses down both sides of the room. Equipment hanging from nails on the whitewashed wall — in one corner a crucifix, over the thin, chaste, taciturn Irish boy's bed. He was the only one in the room, sitting on his bed in the cold dark corner writing in his diary. He looked up and smiled politely, self-effacingly, said "Hallo. Had a good leave?" and bent his narrow head again to read what he'd written.

"Yes, thanks," said the soldier, "except for raids. The first night I was home he raided us for three hours, the sod," he said, unbuckling his bayonet belt and slipping his whole kit off his shoulders.

Last time he returned from leave, four months back, he had sat down on his bed and written to his wife. They had married on the first day of that leave and slept together for six nights. This time he didn't ferret in his kitbag for notepaper and pencil. He went straight out.

The hotel management had set a room aside for the soldiers to booze in. It was a good class hotel, richly and vulgarly furnished with plush and mirrors and dwarf palms in green boxes. The auctioneers and lawyers and city men, the fishermen and golfers and bank managers, most of whom had week-end cottages or villas of retirement in commanding positions at the local beauty spots, spent the evening in the saloon bar and lounge, soaking and joking. So the soldiers were given a bare little bar parlour at the back, with a fire and a dartboard and two sawdust spitoons. The soldiers were glad of it. It was their own. They invited some of their pals from the village to play darts with them — the cobbler, the old dad who lived by himself in the church cottage and never shaved or washed, the poacher who brought them a plucked pheasant under his old coat sometimes — all the ones the soldiers liked popped in for an evening. A few girls, too, before the dance in the church hall, on Tuesdays.

Fred Garstang, from Portsmouth, and Ben Bryant, from Coventry, the two eldest soldiers in the unit — regulars who had never earned a stripe — were playing darts, two empty pint glasses on the mantelpiece by the chalk and duster.

"'Owdee, Taffy?" they said in unison. "'Ave a good leave, lad?"

"Yes thanks," he said automatically, "except for raids. The sod raided us for three hours the first night I was home."

"Damn. Just the wrong side of it," said Fred, examining the quivering dart. "I deserve to lose this bloody game, Ben. I 'xpect you're same as me, Taff; glad to get back to a bit of peace and quiet and a good sleep. My seven days in Pompey's the worst I've ever spent in India, China, the Rhineland, Gallygurchy or anywhere. But we're nice and cosy here, thank God. They can keep their leave. *I* don't want seven nights in an Anderson. I'd rather stay here, I would."

Old Fred never stopped talking once he started. The soldier tapped the counter with a shilling and leaned over to see whether the barmaid was on the other side of the partition. He saw her silky legs and the flutter of her skirt. He hit the counter harder, then, while he waited, wondered at his impatience. His body wasn't thirsty; it was too damned tired to bother, too worn-out. It was something else in him that wanted to get drunk, dead, dead drunk.

The barmaid came along, smiling. She was natural with the soldiers. She smiled when she saw who it was and held her pretty clenched fist to him across the counter. He should have taken it and forced it gently open, of course. Instead, he just put his flat palm underneath it. She looked at him with a hurt-faun reproach in her sailing eyes, and opening her hand let a toffee fall into his.

"One from the wood, Madge," he said.

"I'll have to charge you for *that*," she said.

"That's all right," he replied. "You always pay in this life."

"Why don't you take the girl, Taffy?" said old Fred as he came and sat by them, their darts over. "If I was your age — "

He had been in the army since he was fifteen. Now he was past soldiering, wandering in the head sometimes, doing odd jobs; in peacetime he kept the lawns trimmed at the depot, now he was tin-man in the cooking-shed, cleaning with Vim the pots and pans Ben Bryant used for cooking. "Vermicelli tastes all right," he said. "Better than anything you can pick up in the streets. Yellow or black or white, German or Irish. I've never had a Russian though, never. It's not bad when you're young, like a new crane when the jib runs out nice and smooth; it's better than sitting in the trenches like an old monkey, scratching yourself and not knowing whose leg it is or whose arm it is, looking in his pockets to see if there's anything worth taking, and not knowing who'll win the race, the bullet with your number on it or the leaky rod you're nursing. But I like it here. It's nice and peaceful up here, in the cookhouse all day. We ought to try some vermicelli, Ben, one day."

"Don't you get impatient now, Freddy," Ben said with the calmness of a father of many children. "We'll stuff your pillow full of it next Christmas and put a sprig of it on your chest. Don't you worry, boy."

But old Fred went on talking like an old prophet in a volcanic world, about and about. "There's no knowing when you've got to fight for your king and country," he said. "No matter who you are, Russian or Frenchy or Jerry — and the Yankee, too. He'll be in it, boy. I've seen him die. It's only natural, to my way of thinking. I wore a pair of gloves the Queen knitted herself, she did, last time. The Unknown Soldier I was, last time."

None of us are ourselves now, the Welsh boy sat thinking: neither what we were, nor what we will be. He drained his pint glass and crossed to the counter, to Madge smiling there.

"You never looked round all the way up from the station," she said, pulling her shoulder-straps up under her grey jumper and exposing the white rich flesh above her breasts.

"So it was you followed me, eh?" he said, sardonic.

"Why didn't you turn round?" she asked. "Did you know it was me? You knew someone was behind you, I could tell."

"I didn't turn round because I didn't want to look *back*," he said.

"And you mean to say you don't know how the Hebrew puts out the eyes of a goldfinch?" Freddy's aggrieved voice swirled up.

"Afraid of being homesick for your wife, eh?" she jeered.

He covered his eyes with his hand, tired out, and looked up at the vague sensual woman playing upon his instincts there like a gipsy on a zither.

"Not homesick," he said drily. "Death-sick."

"What d'you mean?" she said.

"Well, she was killed in a raid," he shouted.

He went up to the orderly room then, having forgotten to hand in his leave pass to the orderly corporal. The room was in the corner of an old warehouse. The building also housed the kitchen and the quartermaster's stores. About the high bare rooms with their rotten dry floors and musty walls rats galloped in the darkness; in the morning their dirt lay fresh on the mildewed sacks and the unit's cat stretched her white paws and got a weak and lazy thrill from sniffing it.

The orderly corporal was dozing over a Western novelette from Woolworth's, hunched up in a pool of lamp-and-fire-light.

"Hallo, Taffy," he said. "Had a good leave?"

"Yes thanks," he replied. "Except for raids. Am I on duty to-morrow?"

"You're on duty to-night, I'm afraid," the orderly corporal replied with the unctuous mock-regret of one who enjoys detailing tired or refractory men for unexpected jobs. "Dave Finley had a cold on his chest this morning and didn't get out of bed. So they fetched him out on a stretcher and the M.O. gave him pneumonia pills before Dave could stop him; so he's got pneumonia now. You'll go on guard duty at midnight and at six hours."

"O.K."

He turned to go.

"Better get some sleep," said the orderly corporal, yawning noisily. "Hell! I'm browned off with this war."

The soldier yawned too, and laughed, and returned to the barrack room to lie down for a couple of hours. He rolled his blankets down on the floor and stretched out.

Old Ben and Fred were back, also, Ben fixing bachelor buttons into his best trousers and singing Nelly Dean comfortably to himself, Fred muttering by the stove. "There's some mean and hungry lads in this room," he said; "very hungry and mean. It's an awful nature, that. They'll borrow off you all right, but they won't lend you the turd off their soles. And always swanking in the mirror, and talking all the time, saying Yes, they can do the job easy. The fools! Whip 'em! Whip 'em!"

Ben was toasting bread on the point of his bayonet and boiling water in his billy. A tin of pilchards left over from tea was for them all.

"Come on, Taffy. Have a bellyful while you can," he said.

"No thanks," said the soldier, restless on his blankets. "I don't feel like food to-night, Ben, thanks."

"Ain't you never bin hungry?" Fred shouted angrily. "You don't know what food is, you youngsters don't."

"I've been without food," the soldier said, thinking of the '26 strike; and going without peas and chips in the chip shop by the town clock in college when a new book must be bought. But not now, when everything is free but freedom, and the doctor and dentist and cobbler send you no bills.

What survives I don't know, the soldier thought, rubbing his hot eyelids and shifting his legs on the spread-out blankets. What is it that survives?

He got up and buckled his battle order together, adjusting his straps, slipping the pull-through through his Enfield, polishing boots and buttons, tightening his helmet strap under his chin.

"There was a religious woman used to come to our house," Ben was saying, "and one day she said to me, sociable like, 'You're a Guinness drinker, aren't you, Mr. Bryant?' and I says 'I am, mum,' and she says 'Well, can you tell me what's wrong with the ostrich on them advertisements'?'"

The soldier went out to relieve the guard.

They were only twenty soldiers altogether, sent up here to guard a transmitting station hidden in the slopes of the Downs. A cushy job, safe as houses. There was a little stone shed, once used for sheep that were sick after lambing, in a chalky hollow on the forehead of the hill, which the guard used for sleeping in when they were off duty. Two hours on, four hours off, rain and sun and snow and stars. As the soldier toiled up the lane and across the high meadow to the shed, the milky moon came out from grey clouds and touched with lucid fingers the chopped branches piled in precise lengths at the foot of the wood. The pine trees moved softly as the moon touched their grey-green leaves, giving them a veil that looked like rainy snow, grey-white.

The lane running up through the wood shortened alarmingly in perspective. A star fell. So surprising, so swift and delicate, the sudden short curved fall and extinction of the tiny lit world. But over it the Plough still stayed, like something imperishable in man. He leant against the gate, dizzy and light-headed, waves of soft heat running into his head. He swallowed something warm and thick; spitting it out, he saw it was blood. He stayed there a little, resting, and then went on.

He went along the sandy lane, noticing as he always did the antique sculptures of sea and ice and rain, the smooth twisted flints, yellow and blue and mottled, lying in the white sand down which the water of winter scooped its way.

At the top of the lane was the lambing shed — guard room. He slipped quickly through the door to prevent any light escaping. There was gun-fire and the sound of bombs along the coast.

The sergeant of the guard was lying on a palliasse in front of the stove. He got up slowly, groaning lazily. "So you're back again, Taffy, are you?" he said, a grudge in his too hearty welcome. "Relieving Dave Finley, eh? He's swinging the lead, Dave is. I've a good mind to report him to the O.C. It's tough on you, going on night guard after a day's journey. Have a good leave, Taff?"

"Not bad," the soldier replied, "except for the raids. Raided us the first night I was home."

"It's a sod, everybody's getting it," the sergeant replied, yawning. "They dropped two dozen incendiaries in our fields in Lincs. last week."

He was drinking a billy can of cocoa which he had boiled on the fire, but he didn't offer any. He had weak blue eyes, a receding chin, fresh features of characterless good-looks, wavy hair carefully combed and brilliantined. He was always on edge against Taffy, distrusting him, perhaps envying him. He lived in terror of losing a stripe and in constant hunger to gain another promotion. He sucked and scraped the officers for this, zealously carrying out their orders with the finnicky short temper of a weak house-proud woman. He polished the barrack room floor and blackleaded the stove himself because the boys refused to do more than give the place a regulation lick. And he leaped at the chance of putting a man on the peg, he was always waiting to catch somebody cutting a church parade or nipping out of camp to meet a girl when he should be on duty. Yet he was mortally afraid of a quarrel, of unpopularity, and he was always jovial, glassily jovial, even to the Welsh boy whom he knew he couldn't deceive.

"Who am I to relieve on guard?" the soldier asked.

"Nobby Sherraton. He's patrolling the ridge."

"O.K." He slipped his rifle sling over his shoulder and put his helmet on. "You marching me out? Or shall I just go and see Nobby in?"

For once laziness overcame discretion.

"There's nobody about. Just go yourself," the sergeant said, smiling, posing now as the informal honest soldier. "I'll be seeing yer."

"Some day."

He left the hut and crossed the dry dead-white grass to the ridge where Nobby was on guard.

Nobby was his mate.

He had only been in the unit about a month. Before that he had been stationed just outside London and had done a lot of demolition and rescue work. He was from Mile End, and had roughed it. His hands and face showed that, his rough blackened hands, cigarette-stained, his red blotchy face with the bulbous nose, and the good blue eyes under tiny lids, and short scraggy lashes and brows. His hair was mousy and thin. He had been on the dole most of the time. He had been an unsuccessful boxer; he cleared out of that game when his brother, also a boxer, became punchdrunk and blind. He had plenty of tales of the

Mosley faction. He was sometimes paid five bob to break up their meetings. He always took his five bob but he let the others do the breaking up. Who wants a black eye and a cut face for five bob? 'Tain't worth it. He rarely said anything about women. He didn't think much of lots of them; though like all Cockney youths he loved the 'old lady,' his mother. He wasn't married. No, sir.

He was a conscript. Naturally. He didn't believe in volunteering. And he didn't like the Army, its drills and orders and its insistence on a smart appearance. Smartness he disliked. Appearances he distrusted. Orders he resented. He was 'wise' to things. No sucker.

Taffy felt a warm little feeling under his skin, relief more than anything else, to see Nobby again. He hadn't to pretend with Nobby. Fundamentally they shared the same humanity, the unspoken humanity of comradeship, of living together, sharing what they had, not afraid to borrow or talk or shut up. Or to leave each other and stroll off to satisfy the need for loneliness.

Nobby was surprised so much that he flung out his delight in a shout and a laugh and a wave of his arms. "Taffy, lad!" he said. "Back already, eh? Boy!" Then he became normal.

"Can't keep away from this bloody sannytorium for long, can we?" he grumbled.

Taffy stood looking at him, then at the ground, then he turned away and looked nowhere.

"What's wrong, kid?" Nobby said, his voice urgent and frightened, guessing. "Anything bad? Caught a packet, did you?" He said the last two phrases slowly, his voice afraid to ask.

"*I* didn't," Taffy said, his voice thin and unsteady. "*I* didn't. *I'm* all right. *I'm* healthy."

Nobby put his hand on his shoulder and turned him round. He looked at the white sucked-in face and the eyes looking nowhere.

"Did *she* get it?" and he too turned his head a little and swallowed. "She did," he said, neither asking a question nor making a statement. Something absolute, the two words he said.

Taffy sat down, stretched out. The grass was dead; white, wispy long grass; Nobby sat down,too.

"They came over about eight o'clock the first night," Taffy said. "The town hadn't had a real one before. I've told you we've only got apartments, the top rooms in an old couple's house. The old ones got hysterics, see, Nobby. And then they wouldn't do what I told them, get down the road to a shelter. They wouldn't go out into the street and they wouldn't stay where they were. "My chickens," the old man was blubbering all the time. He's got an allotment up on the voel, see? Gwyneth made them some tea. She was fine, she calmed them down. That was at the beginning, before the heavy stuff began. I went out the back to tackle the incendiaries. The boy next door was out there, too. He had a shovel and I fetched a saucepan. But it was freezing, and we couldn't dig the earth up quick enough. There were too many incendiaries. One fell on the roof and stuck in the troughing. The kid shinned up the pipe. It exploded in his face and he fell down. Twenty odd feet. I picked him up and both his eyes were out, see?"

He had gone back to the sing-song rhythm and the broad accent of his home, the back lanes and the back gardens. He was shuddering a little, and sick-white, sallow.

Nobby waited.

"I took him into his own house," he said, controlling his voice now, almost reflective. "I left him to his sister, poor kid. Then I went in to see if Gwyneth was all right. She was going to take the old couple down the road to the shelter. She had a mack on over her dressing gown. We'd intended going to bed early, see? So I said she was to stay in the shelter. But she wanted to come back. We could lie under the bed together.

"I wanted her back, too, somehow. Then some more incendiaries fell, so I said 'Do as you like' and went at them with a saucepan. I thought sure one would blow my eyes out. Well, she took them down. Carried their cat for them. Soon as she'd gone the heavy stuff came. Oh Christ!"

Nobby let him go on; better let him go on.

"It knocked me flat, dazed me for a bit. Then I got up and another one flattened me. It was trying to stop me, see, Nobby. I crawled out of the garden, but it was dark as hell and buildings all down, dust and piles of masonry. Then he dropped some more incendiaries and the fires started. I knew she must be somewhere, see? I knew she must be somewhere. I began pulling the masonry away with my hands, climbed on to the pile of it in the fire. I couldn't see with the smoke and I knew it wasn't any use, only I had to do it, see?

"Then suddenly the masonry fell downwards. The road was clear on the other side. I thought it was all right after all, then. I thought she'd have reached the shelter.... But she hadn't.

"I found her about twenty yards down the road.

"She wasn't dead. Her clothes were gone. And her hands. She put them over her face, I reckon.

"She couldn't speak, but I knew she knew it was me.

"I carried her back in my arms. Over the fallen house. The fire wasn't bad by then. Took her home, see, Nobby. Only the home was on fire. I wanted her to die all the time. I carried her over a mile through the streets. Fires and hoses and water. And she wouldn't die. When I got her to the clearing station I began to think she'd live.

"But they were only playing a game with me, see?"

He stood up and made himself calm.

"Well there it is." He rubbed his face with the palm of his hand, wiping the cold sweat off.

"I knew she was going to die. When they told me she was — I didn't feel anything, Nobby."

"But she died while they were messing her body about with their hands, see?

"And she never said anything. Never said anything to me.

"Not that it makes any difference, I suppose. We never did speak about those things much. Only, you know how it is, you want a word somehow. You want it to keep."

"Sure. I know," Nobby said.

"What's it all for, Nobby?" he said in a while. He looked so tired and beat. "I used to know what it was all about, but I can't understand it now."

"Aw, forget all about that," Nobby said. "You're here, aincher, now?"

He put his hands on his mate's shoulders and let him lean against him for a bit.

"I reckon you belong to each other for keeps, now," Nobby said.

"You believe that, Nobby?" he asked, slow and puzzled, but with a gathering force as his uncertainty came together.

"Yes. For you and 'er, I do. It wouldn't be true for me, or the sergeant in there, but for you two it is."

Taffy was still against his shoulder. Then slowly he straightened himself, moved back onto himself, and lifting his face he looked at the milky-white fields and the sentinel pines and the stars.

"I knew it was so, really," he said. "Only I was afraid I was fooling myself."

He smiled, and moved his feet, pressing on them with his whole weight as if testing them after an illness.

"I'm all right now, Nobby. Thank you, boy."

"I'll go, then," Nobby said. He slipped his rifle over his shoulder and as he moved off he hesitated, turned back, and touched his mate's arm lightly.

"Two's company, three's none," he said, and stumped off slowly to the lambing shed through the dead straw-grass.

And the soldier was left alone on the flat upland ridge.

Below him the valleys widened into rich arable lakes on which the moonlight and the mist lay like the skeins which spiders spin round their eggs. Beyond the pools another chain of downland lay across the valleys, and beyond those hills the coast. Over him, over the valleys, over the pinewoods, blue fingers came out of the earth and moved slanting across their quarters as the bombers droned in the stars over his head and swung round to attack the coastal city from inland. The sky over the coast was inflamed and violent, a soft blood-red.

The soldier was thinking of the day he received his calling up papers, just a year ago. Sitting on the dry-stone wall of his father's back garden with Gwyneth by him; his ragged little brother kneeling by the chicken-run, stuffing cabbage stumps through the netting for the hens to peck, and laughing and pulling the stumps out as the old hen made an angry jab; his father riddling the ashes and the ramshackle garden falling to bits, broken trellis and tottering fence; his mother washing her husband's flannel vest and drovers in the tub, white and vexed. He had taken Gwyneth's hand, and her hand had said, "In coming and in going you are mine; now, and for a little while longer; and then for ever."

But it was not her footsteps that followed him down the lane from the station.

Now over his head the darkness was in full leaf, drifted with the purity of pines, the calm and infinite darkness of an English night, with the stars moving in slow declension down the sky. And the warm scent of resin about him and of birds and of all small creatures moving in the loose mould in the ferns like fingers in velvet.

And the soldier stood under the pines, watching the night move down the valleys and lift itself seawards, hearing the sheep cough and farm-dogs restlessly barking in the farms. And farther still the violence growing in the sky till the coast was a turbulent thunder of fire and sickening explosions, and there was no darkness there at all, no sleep.

"My life belongs to the world," he said. "I will do what I can."

He moved along the spur and looked down at the snow-grey evergreen woods and the glinting roofs scattered over the rich land.

And down in the valleys the church bells began pealing, pealing, and he laughed like a lover, seeing his beloved.

IN THE GREEN TREE

Night Journey

An hour before the midnight train left Paddington all the seats were full, the blinds all drawn, the corridor full of kitbags and suitcases and the burning ends of cigarettes. Several Welsh soldiers were singing Cwm Rhondda and Aberystwyth and the more maudlin hymns of the Evan Roberts Revival. Every compartment was hooded and blue with smoke. Just before the train started a young captain with the badge of an infantry regiment on his black beret opened the door of one compartment, a third-class one, and was about to make his way through into the corridor when a private soldier sitting in the corner said, "Here you are, sir, squeeze in here." He said, "Thanks a lot," and sat down. He was perspiring and dead white, he had no luggage, not even a respirator. He looked done in.

The crowded compartment looked at him with the same reserved inquisitiveness as the inmates of a small boarding-house covertly examine a new resident at his first meal. There were two WAAF's. The bespectacled one simply wondered why he wasn't travelling first and thought he looked distressed. The one with lipstick, who had been interrupted in her tale of her boy friend Bob, a pilot who didn't give a damn and was a wizard with a kite, patted her set waves self-consciously and looked at him with wide filmstar eyes. The tanks corps sergeant-major, a young sandy-haired man with facile features and the cocksure glance of the too successful, raised his fair eyebrows knowingly, discerning some irregularity. "Good evening, sir," he said politely. "Good evening, sergeant-major," the officer replied. Finally the R.A.F.corporal and his companion, a blonde civilian girl cuddled close under his shoulder, disturbed themselves sufficiently to crane forward a moment before reposing again. The officer wiped his face with a dirty handkerchief, and then noticed that an aircraftman was standing up in the compartment.

"I'm very sorry," the officer said. "You were here before me. I've taken your seat." He stood up, deferentially.

That's all right, sir," the corporal said, craning forward again, the hooded light full on his Brylcreemed curls. "He's a prisoner. I'm escorting him to detention barracks, sir. He don't sit down."

"Oh, surely, that's not fair," the officer insisted, still offering his seat.

"He's standing up on my orders, sir," the corporal retorted.

The officer shrugged his shoulders.

The train slid a little, imperceptibly beginning its long journey, then jerked forward with a puff.

"My God," said the WAAF with lipstick. "It's actually moving. Well, as I was saying, when I asked Bob to take me up, he said, 'If you were fat and ugly I wouldn't mind risking it. But you — no, I won't risk you,' he said. Sweet of him, I thought."

"Maybe he just wanted something for nothing," the sergeant-major said with a naughty gallantry.

"You men," countered the WAAF, very haughtily. "Your thoughts never rise any higher than your manners. Well, Bob isn't that sort, thank you." She wanted to assert her value; she wasn't going to let him knock her price down; she sulked and considered what was best. The other WAAF was reading a Penguin.

"Got a penknife, sir?" the private asked. "I've lost my corkscrew." He had a bottle of liqueur whisky between his knees; he was evidently a man of importance in the compartment. They all looked at him, for the first time really; he'd only been a private soldier before. Now he had a bottle of liqueur whisky. The sergeant-major was the first to produce a knife.

"Here you are," he said with alacrity.

"Thanks, major," the private replied. He was a tall groomed man, with smooth hair, a big chin blue with shaving, a clever surface smartness in his nodding glance. He scraped away at the cork, smiling to himself. The WAAF hadn't considered him before. She looked interestedly at him now. After all, she hadn't actually *cut* him before.

"Would you ladies like a chocolate while I'm opening this?" he asked, passing a box of chocolates round. The WAAF fell on it with little girlish cries of delight.

"Now, gentlemen, a toast to us all," he continued, lifting the bottle to the light. "You, sir, first."

They all demurred; he reassured them. Sure, he had two more such bottles in his respirator, and 500 Players. They were welcome.

"Go on, sir. Sorry there's no wine-glasses. Nice drink, isn't it? Got connections, see, sergeant-major. Go on, drink it up. My connections wouldn't give me poor stuff, don't you worry. Come on, lady, drink to that pilot boy of yours. Come on, corporal, sweeten your breath. What? Not allowed to drink on escort? What a sense of duty. Blimey. Well, what about the prisoner. Come on, prisoner. Sweet as your mother's milk it is. Take a good swig now. I won't be calling round in the morning, you know. Oh come on, corp, let the poor sod have a drink. Being alive isn't much fun for him. Yeh, why not?"

"If the prisoner's going to have one I don't see why I should go without," the corporal said, anxious as a man who has bought a shirt too big for him and hurries back to the shop, blustering and dubious, to revoke the deal.

"Sure, that's the spirit, that's swell," the soldier pattered. "Now that's how I like it. We're all social now."

"Or do you mean socialist?" the officer asked.

"Oh no, sir, begging your pardon, we're not socialist. Here's the capital, sir, here" — he patted the golden bottle — "and wherever you find capital you find the black market, and wherever you find the black market you find yours truly, sir. I'm not proud of being a capitalist, sir. It's just an inescapable fact, that's all, sir. Calls for another drink, I think, sir."

Here's a case, the sergeant-major's grin seemed to say, I'd like to get him on a fatigue, by God I'd shake him. He took a second draught with a friendly and local condescension.

"What shall I drink to?" the WAAF said coquettishly.

"You don't need to drink to anything," the soldier said. "You just want to drink, that's all, lady. However, drink to the rebuilding of Stalingrad, if you want to."

"Why in particular Stalingrad?" the officer asked. "Why not London?"

"Sure, London if you like. I don't mind. Every city's a job of work to me, sir. I'm an internationalist. Paid by America, Dupont of America, via the Chase National Bank — heard of it, sir? — no income tax on my salary, two thousand a year I get, sir. Before the war I put half the machinery into the Red October factory in Stalingrad, and I'll go and put it back there after this little shake is over. I built factories in Magnitogorsk, too. Hitler won't see them, sir."

"Say, you're talking big," said the sergeant-major.

"Not particularly big, major. I'm small fry. Only I get around, you know."

"And you're only a private, eh?"

"That's right, sir. I'm not ambitious. I'm all right. I've got connections in the Army. Got a living-out pass, got a suite of rooms in the Swan in Dorchester and a taxi to take me to camp every morning. I'm sitting the same course for the fourth time. Usually they send you back to your unit if you fail it once, but they're letting me stay on because I'm keen to get through, you know, real keen. Very comfortable down there. Course I volunteered for the Army, you know. Only I'm not ambitious, not like you, sir, or you, major."

"Are you married, soldier?" the WAAF asked clumsily.

"Married, lady? What, me? I've only got the best wife in the world, that's all. Look, here she is." He fished a wallet out of his trousers and hunted among the white five-pound notes for a couple of photographs. "There she is, lady. That was taken in Shepheard's Hotel, Cairo. Here we are, both of us again, in the garden of the Grand in Bucharest."

"You look much nicer in tails than you do in battledress," she said.

"My battle dress wasn't made in Saville Row, lady," he laughed. "How do you like my wife?" (She was a beautiful voluptuous woman in a glittering evening gown.) "She's a fine wife. Sends me 600 Players a week, and I love her like I'd just married her, though I got a son of seventeen. He's in the States, he is, apprenticed to Henry Ford. Good kid he is, too."

The stuffy compartment, overheated with the breath and talk and whisky, swaying a little with the advance of sleepiness and the unreality of the big names he flung out like attracting stars leaving their proper orbit, rocking with the gathering motion of the train, played a cartoonist's trick on them all. How absurd and how amiable they seemed, these little people with long and short noses, with vanities and illusions and daydreams, with their fatigues and desires and routines, their religion and bewilderment and pettiness! There was a gradual relaxation in them all, a common impulse to stretch their limbs and loose their guard. The WAAF leaned up against the sergeant-major; he took her hand; her regulation underwear crinkled the tight blue skirt against her thighs. He took her at his own valuation, pilot or no pilot. O.K., big boy. O.K., baby. The bespectacled girl let her Penguin lapse. She looked at the officer, dreamily, disinterestedly, as though there was something there that distressed her and wouldn't let her alone. Only the prisoner stood like a great dull bull, holding on to the strap, dark and swaying. His great sullen head and shoulders were in shadow, over-powering. He was a miserable devil. The whisky didn't seem to improve him at all.

"I'm an internationalist," the private soldier said. "I don't agree with wars between one country and another. I don't believe it. I got nothing against Russia. I worked there. Nothing against Germany. They're a smart lot, I take my hat off to them. America's the best of the bunch for a living. England's the salt of the earth. I didn't make this war, and I'm not fighting it. Ever had your fortune told, lady? I'll tell it for you with this pack of cards. O.K.?"

"I believe you're a fifth columnist," the WAAF said lazily, snug in the sergeant-major's arms. She shuffled uneasily, paused, sat up, looked at him with a frown, puzzling over him. Certainty dawned in her silly eyes. She pointed a hand at him, hard and splenetic. "That's what you are, you're a fifth columnist. I know you are." Her hard grasping voice had the high pitch of hysteria. "You can't fool me," she jeered. "You dirty fifth columnist. And they'll get you."

"Aw, shut up," he said. "I never had no education but I don't make a fool of myself in public like you, lady. Ever been in the Ritz?"

"What do I want with the Ritz?" she shouted, screaming with laughter. In the unreality of the moment the dark prisoner moved towards the corridor. The door was open into the corridor.

She was laughing uncontrollably.

"The fifth column dine in the Ritz," she shouted, waving her arms and body from the waist upwards like a snake.

"Look here, lady, I never been insulted like this before. Look here, I got Commander Anthony Kimmins's autograph here, see? He gave it to me when we were playing billiards after lunch in the Ritz."

"He's a liar," she shouted, terrible tears in her eyes. "They're all liars. Bob took me to the Ritz for a week-end, and I'm going to have a baby now, I'm going to have a baby," she was weeping now, "and he got himself posted to another squadron, he did."

"Your prisoner's gone, corporal," the sergeant-major said with the coolness of a man in the thick of mechanized battle.

"Christ," the corporal gasped, suddenly white, his enjoyment of the scene sucked out of him. He jerked himself to his feet, pulling out his revolver. "I'll get the swine."

The officer pulled him back by the neck of his jacket.

"Put it back, you fool," he said quietly, and slipped past the corporal into the corridor.

The Welsh soldiers were singing their national anthem in harmony, softly and most tenderly, alto and tenor and bass moving back and forth like searchlights over the range of sound. The prisoner was leaning by an open window, looking at the misty moonlit fields.

"Hallo, prisoner," the officer said. "They've just missed you."

"I was born just over them fields, sir," the prisoner said heavily, slowly, peaceably. "See that level crossing there? Used to go over that to school every day."

"Never mind," said the officer. "We'd better go back now. Both of us." Both men sighed, and turned away from the misty white fields, and returned.

The Raid

My platoon and I were on training that morning. We've been on training every morning for the last three years, for that matter. On this occasion it was Current Affairs, which always boils down to how long the war is going to last, and when the orderly told me the C.O. wanted me in his office I broke the lads off for a cup of tea from the charwallah and nipped over to the orderly room, tidying myself as I went. I didn't expect anything unusual until I took a cautionary peep through the straw window of his matting shed and saw a strange officer in there. So I did a real dapper salute and braced myself. Self-defence is always the first instinct, self-suspicion the second. But I hadn't been drunk since I came to India and I hadn't written anything except love in my letters. As for politics, as far as they're concerned I don't exist, I'm never in. The other chap was a major and had a red armband.

"Come in, Selden," the colonel said. "This is the D.A.P.M. Head of military police. Got a job for you. Got your map case?"

"No sir. It's in company office."

"Hurry off and fetch it."

When I came back they were hard at it, bending over the inch map. The C.O. looked up. His face got very red when he bent.

"Here's your objective, Selden. This village here, Chaudanullah. Eighteen miles away. Route: track south of Morje, river-bed up to Pimpardi, turn south a mile before Pimpardi and strike across the watershed on a fixed bearing. Work it out with a protractor on the map and set your compass before you march off. Strike the secondary road below this group of huts here, 247568, cross the road and work up the canal to the village. Throw a cordon round the village with two sections of your platoon. Take the third yourself and search the houses methodically. Government has a paid agent in the village who will meet you at this canal bridge here — got it? — at 06.00 hours. The agent reported that your man arrived there last night after dark and is lying up in one of the hovels."

"What man, sir?" I asked.

"Christ, didn't I tell you? Why the devil didn't you stop me? This fellow, what's-his-name — it's all on that paper there — he's wanted. Remember the bomb in the cinema last Tuesday, killed three British other ranks? He's wanted for that. Read the description before you go. Any questions so far? Right. Well, you'll avoid all houses, make a detour round villages, keep off the road all the way. Understand? News travels faster than infantry in India. He'll be away before you're within ten miles if you show yourself. Let's see. Twenty miles by night. Give you ten hours. Leave here at 19.30 hours. Arrive an hour before first light. Go in at dawn, keep your eyes skinned. M.T. will R.V. outside the village at dawn. Drive the prisoner straight to jail. D.A.P.M. will be there.

"Very good, sir. Dress, sir?" I said.

"Dress? P.T. shoes, cloth caps, overalls, basic pouches, rifles, 50 rounds of .303 per man, and grenades. 69 grenades if he won't come out, 36 grenades if he makes a fight of it. Anything else?"

"No sir."

"Good. Remember to avoid the villages. Stalk him good and proper. Keep up-wind of him. I'm picking you and your platoon because I think you're the best I've got. I want results, Selden."

"I'll give you a good show, sir."

"Bloody good shot with a point 22, Selden is," the C.O. said to the D.A.P.M. by way of light conversation. "Shot six mallard with me last Sunday."

"Of course we want the man alive, sir, if it's at all possible," the D.A.P.M. said, fiddling with his nervous pink moustache. "He's not proved guilty yet, you see, sir, and with public opinion in India what it is."

"Quite," said the colonel. "Quite. Make a note of that, Selden. Tell your men to shoot low."

"Very good, sir."

"Got the route marked on your talc?"

"Yes, sir." I'd marked the route in chinograph pencil and the Chaudanullah place in red as we do for enemy objectives. It was all thick.

"Rub it all off, then. Security. Read his description. Have you read it? What is it?"

"Dark eyes, sir. Scar on left knee. Prominent cheekbones. Left corner of mouth droops. Front incisor discoloured. Last seen wearing European suit, may be dressed in native dhoti, Mahratta style."

"And his ring?" said the C.O. He's as keen as mustard the old man is.

"Oh yes, sir. Plain gold wedding ring."

"Correct. Don't forget these details. Invaluable sometimes. Off with you."

I saluted and marched out.

"Damn good fellow, Selden," I heard the C.O. say. "Your man is in the bag."

I felt pretty pleased with that. Comes of shooting those six mallard.

The platoon was reassembling after their tea and I felt pretty important, going back with all that dope. After all, it was the first bit of action we'd seen in two and a half years. It would be good for morale. I knew they'd moan like hell, having to do a twenty-mile route march by night, but I could sell them that all right. So I fell them in in threes and called them to attention for disciplinary reasons and told them they'd been picked for a special job and this was it...

They were very impressed by the time I'd finished.

"Any questions?" I said.

"Yes, sir," said Chalky White. He was an L.P.T.B. conductor and you won't find him forgetting a halfpenny. "Do we take haversack rations and will we be in time for breakfast?" He thinks the same way as Napoleon.

"Yes," I said. "Anything else?"

"What's this fellow done, sir?" Bottomley asked, then. Bottomley always was a bit Bolshie, and he's had his knife into me for two and a half years because I was a bank clerk in Civvy Street and played golf on Sundays.

"Killed three troops, I think," I said. "Is that good enough?"

I felt I'd scored pretty heavy over his Red stuff this time.

"Right," I said. "Break off till 19.00 hours. Keep your mouths shut. White will draw rations at the cookhouse. No cigarettes or matches will be taken."

I did that for disciplinary purposes. They didn't say a word. Pretty good.

We crossed the start line dead on 19.30 hours and everybody looked at us with some interest. I felt mighty "hush-hush." My security was first class. Hadn't told a soul, except Ken More and Ted Paynter.

"Bring 'em back alive," a soldier jeered outside the cookhouse.

Somebody's let the cat out of the bag. Damn them all. Can't trust a soul in the ranks with the skin of a sausage.

Anyway, we got going bang away. I knew the first stretch past Morje and Pimpardi and we did about three miles an hour there. The night was breathless and stuffy; we put hankies round our foreheads to keep the sweat out of our eyes. And the perpetual buzzing of the crickets got on my nerves like a motor horn when the points jam and all the pedestrians laugh. I suppose I was a bit worked up. Every time a mosquito or midge touched me I let out a blow fit to knacker a bull. But I settled down after a while and began to enjoy the sense of freedom and deep still peace that informs the night out in the tropics. You've read all about tropical stars; well, it's quite true. They're marvellous; and we use some of them for direction-finding at night too. The Plough, for instance, and one called Cassiopeia that you bisect for the Pole Star.

Then there was the tricky bit over the mountain by compass. I just hoped for the best on that leg. Luckily the moon came up and put the lads in a good mood. I allowed them to talk in whispers for one hour and they had to keep silent for the next hour for disciplinary reasons. We halted for half an hour on the crest of the watershed and ate our bully beef sandwiches with relish, though bully tastes like a hot poultice out here. It was a damn fine view from that crest. A broad valley a thousand feet below with clusters of fires in the villages and round a hill temple on the other side. Either a festival or a funeral, obviously. I could hear the drums beating there, too; it was very clear and echoing, made my flesh creep. You feel so out of it in India somehow. You just slink around in the wilds and you feel very white and different. I don't know... You know, I'd have said that valley *hated* us that night, on those rocky crests. Queer.

I didn't know which group of huts was which, but I could see the canal glittering in the moonlight so I was near enough right, praise be. The jackals were howling too, and some creature came right up to us, it gave me a scare. I knew that bully had a pretty bad stench. Anyway we got on the move again, Chalky White saying next stop Hammersmiff Bridge, and we slithered down as quietly as we could, hanging on to each other's rifles on the steep bits. We made our way between the villages and the drums beat themselves into a frenzy that had something personal about it. Then we went up the canal for about four miles, keeping about a hundred yards off the path and pretty rough going it was. Then we came to what I felt must be our objective, a cluster of crumbled huts on the foothills, pretty poor show even for these parts, and the boys were blistered and beat so I scattered them under the bushes and told them to lie low. It was only 5.30 a.m. and the agent fellow wasn't due until six. I had a nap myself, matter of fact, though it's a shootable offence. I woke up with a start and it was five past six, and I peered round my tree and there wasn't a sound. No drums, no jackals, no pie dogs. It was singing in my ears, the silence, and I wished to God we'd got this job over. It could go wrong so easily. He might fight, or his pals might help him, or he might have got wind of us, or I might have come to the wrong place. I was like an old woman. I loaded my Colt and felt better. Then I went down the canal to look for the chowkey fellow. I took a pretty poor view of a traitor, but I took a poorer view of him not turning up. He wasn't there and I walked up the path and just when I was getting really scared he appeared out of nowhere and I damn near shot him on the spot.

"Officer sahib huzzoor," he said."Mai Sarkar ko dost hai," or something. And he said the name of the man I was after, which was the password.

"Achiba," I said, meaning good show. "Tairo a minute while I bolo my phaltan and then we'll jao jillo." He got the idea.

I nipped back and roused the lads quietly from under the trees and we moved up like ghosts on that village. I never want to see that village again. It was so still and fragile in the reluctant grey light. Even the pie dogs were asleep, and the bullocks lying on their sides. Once I travelled overnight from Dieppe to Paris and the countryside looked just as ghostly that morning. But this time it was dangerous. I had a feeling somebody was going to die and there'd be a hell of a shemozzle. And at that same time the houses looked so poor and harmless, almost timid somehow. And the chowkey bloke was like a ghost. It was seeing him so scared that put me steady again. He was afraid of being seen with us as far as I could make out, and said he'd show us where this fellow was lying up and then he'd disappear please. I said never mind about the peace, let's get the war over first, and I told Bottomley to watch the bloke in case he had anything up his sleeve.

We got to the ring of trees outside the village without a sound, and the two section leaders led their men round each side of the village in a pincer movement. All the boys were white and dirty and their eyes were like stones.I remember suddenly feeling very proud of them just then.

I gave them ten minutes to get into position and close the road at the rear of the village. And then a damned pie dog set up a yelp over on the right flank and another replied with a long shivering howl. I knew things would start going wrong if I didn't act quickly. We didn't want the village to find out until we'd gone if possible. For political reasons. And for reasons of health, I thought. So I gave the Follow-me sign and closed in on the huddled houses. There were a couple of outlying houses with a little shrine, and then the village proper with a crooked street running down it. The chowkey seemed to know where to go. I pointed to the single buildings and he said, "Nay, sahib," and pointed to the street. So I posted a man to picket the shrine and led the rest through the bush behind our scruffy guide. He moved like a beaten dog, crouching and limping, bare-foot. There was a dead ox in the bush and a pair of kites sleeping and gorged beside it. It stank like a bad death. Turned me. We hurried on. The bushes were in flower, sort of wisteria, the blossoms closed and drooping. We crept along under a tumbledown wall and paused, kneeling, at the street corner. I posted two men there, one on each side with fixed bayonets, to fire down the street if he bolted. The other two sections would be covering it from the other end. Then I nudged the chowkey man and signalled to my grenade man and rifleman to cover me in. I slipped round the corner and went gingerly down the street. Suddenly I feel quite cool and excited at the same time. The chowkey went about fifteen yards down the street and then slunk against the wall on his knees, pointing inwards to the house he was kneeling against. It was made of branches woven with straw and reed, a beggared place. He looked up at me and my revolver and he was sweating with fear. He had the pox all over his face, too. I took a breath to steady myself, took the first pressure on my trigger, kicked the door lattice aside and jumped in. Stand in the light in the doorway and you're a dead man. I crouched in the dark corner. It was very dark in there still. There was a pile of straw on the floor and straw heaped in the corner. And some huge thing moved ponderously. I nearly yelped. Then I saw what it was. It was a cow. Honestly. A sleepy fawn cow with a soft mild face like somebody's dream woman.

"She never frew no bomb," Chalky said. He was my rifleman. Cool as ice. His voice must have broken the fellow's nerve. There was a huge rustle in the straw in the corner behind the cow and a man stood up, a man in a white dhoti, young, thin, sort of smiling. Discoloured teeth. Chalky lunged his bayonet. The chap still had plenty of nerve left. He just swayed a little.

"Please," he said. "Have you got a smoke upon you?"

"Watch him, White," I said. I searched him.

"Please," he said. "I have nothing." He was breathing quickly and smiling.

"Come on," I said. "Quietly."

"You know you are taking me to my death?" he said. "No doubt?"

"I'm taking you to Poona," I said. "You killed three of our men."

The smile sort of congealed on his face. Like a trick. His head nodded like an old doll. "Did I?" he said. "Three men died? Did I?"

"Come on," I said. "It's daylight."

"It's dreadful," he said. He looked sick. I felt sorry for him, nodding his head and sick, sallow. Looked like a student, I should say.

"Keep your hands up," Chalky said, prodding him in the back.

We went quietly down the street, no incident at all, and I signalled the two enveloping sections together and we got down the road out of sight. I was in a cold sweat and I wanted to laugh.

The trucks weren't there. God, I cursed them, waiting there. They might bitch the whole show. The villagers were going to the well quite close.

"What did you do it for, mate?" I heard Bottomley ask.

After a long silence the chap said very quietly, "For my country."

Chalky said, "Everybody says that. Beats me." Then we heard the trucks, and Chalky said, "We ought to be there in time for breakfast, boys."

The Earth is a Syllable

"What I say is, if you're in trouble, take it easy," the ambulance driver said. "Always have done. Once I got a girl in trouble and I wasn't going to get grey hairs over that. And now I've bust the gasket and she won't budge and maybe the Jap is nearer than our own boys, but there you are, you're no better off if your nose bleeds, are you now?"

He'd often thought he'd die; it was a familiar idea; why shouldn't he, if there's a war on and you're young and you try to be in it, somewhere? It had taken him a long time to succeed. He'd got into the army easy enough, but the war seemed to elude him all the time. If he was in England it would be in France in hot summer weather and he'd be eating Wall's ice cream outside the barracks. If he was in India it would be in Egypt and he'd think of the Eighth Army glowing in the desert, attracting him like a moth to its fiery circle. He used to fancy himself flying there like a queen ant on her nuptial flight and shedding his wings when he alighted, and going to ground there. And now that he *had* caught up with it, here in Burma, well, it hadn't been much of a show. But he'd never liked the idea of Burma. He'd always known he'd die if he caught up with it in Burma.

"Can't you stop tossing and kicking those blankets?" the ambulance driver said. "Wear yourself out quicker like that. Take it easy, I say. I've been in some bad spots off and on. Narvik for a kick-off, and Crete for a birthday, and a bloody narrow escape from going into Libya with Ritchie; thought I was lucky once, being sent out here instead. But I reckon it's all the same where I go. There's sure to be a war there." He spoke very mournfully, a sort of thoughtful incantation. "I've had more crump than crumpet this war. That's why I take it easy, mate. You got to last a long time, you know. A long time."

The driver had given up trying to repair the damage to the cylinder head of his 15-cwt. Bedford; the tropical heat and the dust of the bumpy track that cavorted through the misleading jungle had dried up his water and blown the gasket . It was useless. They were on their way to the rendezvous where the wounded from the advanced dressing-stations were handed over to the main dressing-station ambulances. To-morrow they'd have to find out where the new rendezvous was; it changed daily, same as everything else changed daily; the situation was very confused, the Japs were said to have worked right round their left flank somewhere up the Sittang, and to have landed above Rangoon. To-morrow they'd have to find out where the new rendezvous was, if it still mattered.

He was lying on a stretcher in the back of the truck and it was a bit awkward because the truck tilted steeply, one side in the ditch so as to let the traffic pass up the track to the front, what front there was. The rear flaps were strapped up to give him some air and he could see the darkness of the jungle encircling them. It was dark and soft like a mass of congealed blood. If you put your hand in it, it would give like a sponge. If the Japs were there they'd be sleeping. They had to sleep. Or a snake or a tiger would get them, they weren't all that clever. Any case you could hear them if they were there, calling each other like owls, because they were lonely, maybe. And the jungle was utterly silent, dark and shimmering with darkness like ebony, and malevolent. And he was quite at peace. He'd been more nervous in India than he was here. It was lonely in India, no friendship there, nor any active hostility to brace you. Just loneliness and strangeness. It wasn't dangerous there: just nerves, that's all. You couldn't walk into a native village and have a good time there like you wanted to. QUIT INDIA they painted on the walls. Quit India, the silly fools. How can we? India is part of the world. It's the world we can't quit. No, it was just nerves in India. Riding back to camp after the pictures in a trotting tonga with bells tinkling on the skinny mare's neck, it was so dark it was like riding to your death. Just nerves. Here he was quite peaceful.

There was a sudden murmur in the jungle, a sigh, a growing perturbance. Dust. The wind puffed up with a hot dry sigh and the dust came riding in on them in a thick irritating column, into their eyes and mouths, making them swear, sweat and blink and extinguishing the petrol cooker on which the driver was brewing some char. His own lamp spat a high flame and cracked the glass and then subsided. He didn't move. He liked the dust storms by day, the whirling cylinder of tall red dust moving across the plain, the moving red towers that touched the blue sky. He didn't like it at night so much; now when he put his hand over his face his skin was dry and dusty like a statue in a dilapidated museum, like an embalming. The blanket was filthy, it set the skin of his fingers on edge, and he saw with sudden distaste that it was covered with hairs and dandruff under his cheek. It made him think of his wife, she'd written to say he'd left some hairs on his pillows the time he was on embarkation leave and she felt terribly cruel to shake them off, she said. But she was so beautiful and fresh always and the house always so clean and simple, with the sun or the snow always lighting it. She wouldn't like this dust.

"Well, we'll have to go without a cup of you an' me," the driver said, grinning and sweating as he leaned over the tailboard to stow the cooker away. " 'Tisn't the first thing I've done without by a long chalk. Christ, I've been without work before now. That's a real nasty thing; being without work. I don't suppose you've been without work, chum, being an officer?"

His mouth was bitter and dry and it hurt him when he smiled. It was the lump the shrapnel had taken out of his throat was hurting now when he smiled. Life had been pretty heartless off and on, but you usually got a laugh out of it. When he'd written three novels one after the other and failed to sell any of them, and gone round to an agency for a job and the old clerk asked him if he could type and he said, "Two fingers only," and the clerk said, "No good," and he went to sea then as a trimmer. He'd never thought of dying in those days, though, it didn't seem a physical fact at all. Just something you wrote and theorized about. Not like this.

"Speaking for myself," said the driver, "I've found it a bloody sight easier with a war on. You don't have to bother now. It's all buttoned up. Food and clothes and dentists, trucks to drive, loads to carry, allowances for the missus. It's all laid on for you now. You don't have to bother."

Yes, he thought, it's been pretty easy. You sink your scruples in conscription, and then there's always something interesting if you take the trouble of finding it. Infantry schemes, sleeping under hedges, swimming a river in full kit, being hungry, talking to a stranger. And since his regiment had been mechanized the tanks had him by the hair — the iron maidens — he'd never tire of pulling on the tiller bar and stamping on the clutch and pulling like hell on the gear lever and the thrill as she surged softly forward, grunting peacefully and bellying over a slope so sweet and easy. And the big 75 mm. gun and the voices of your friends in your headsets coming over the air. And the queer consolation of the other things he'd tried and written off for failures and now recalled — the little meetings he'd tried to run, debates round a hurricane lamp on the FUTURE, talks he'd carefully put together on

RECONSTRUCTION, gramophone records he'd borrowed and played for the lads, the choir he'd tried to make something good of; naturally it was no good for a few odd men to sit round and discuss how to prevent another war, naturally they couldn't "succeed." Still, it was all right to remember it.

No. The terrible struggles had been quieter and less obvious than voyages and armoured regiments. They were just something inside you — simply whether to say Yes or No to a thing — to chastity or pity or love or drink with another man's wife. Maybe if you could avoid saying Yes or No to Life, and yet be free, you'd be stronger, better? Would you? How did the dust columns form? What did the Upanishads say? The Earth is a syllable.

"I'm turning in, mate," the driver said. "There ain't nothing I can do till a truck comes along. Get you back, then, if a truck comes along. It's so bleeding quiet in these parts, that's what I don't like. Makes you think we missed the road back somewhere, or missed the war or summat. I never did like the quiet. Give me a pub that can sell its liquor, not keep it. Give me a call if your pains come back, chum, though there ain't nothing I can do. Jesus, I'm tired. Goodnight, cocky."

He stumped up the road a few yards to where he'd slung his mosquito net among the bushes. He sighed aloud as he pulled each boot off.

Now he was left alone and whatever he had he was alone with it. It was all right, as long as he was alone. Whatever he had he could manage it now. His lamp still burned calmly and it might last an hour yet. He didn't want the dark to come any nearer. He could see exactly where it started, just this side of his feet. And then it went on and on. The dawn is the head of a horse. He lay quietly among the crickets and the darkness and the moths came suddenly tilting head on against his lamp and righted themselves on his face, and flew on again. It was very still, except for the pain. There was a translucent golden influence at the core of his being. He could see his wife. She'd wanted a child before he left England, but it hadn't turned out that way. And now in a way he was glad. There was only her left, besides himself. She would understand. He'd tried bloody hard; he'd roughed it and now he was cut up a lot and he could smell the poison where his left shoulder and arm had been. But there was still her little house. That was all. He didn't want to go to Burma; he knew it would be a bad place for him. But all striving is a blind guess, and he wasn't in Burma now, he was in the night, in the common ground of humanity, and he wasn't alone now.

He wanted to get up and enter the darkness and enter the silent village under the hill and enter it with his wife alone. Not in a tank, for that was a schoolboy's thrill, nor in Burma, because it was a bad place for him. So he pushed himself up on his spare arm and sweated all over; Judas! it hurt. But he hated the dirt and hair on his blanket, and being hot in bed and he wanted to have this little walk.

So he went across the plain in the night and the darkness was hot and tepid and after a while he didn't know where the hell he was; but he knew he was all right; and he loved her so much that he knew he could throw the darkness over the hill.

The driver found him five yards away from the truck.

Ward 'O' 3 (b)

I

Ward 'O' 3 (b) was, and doubtless still is, a small room at the end of the Officers' Convalescent Ward which occupies one wing of the rectangle of one-storied sheds that enclose the "lily-pond garden" of No. X British General Hospital, Southern Army, India. The other three wings contain the administrative offices, the Officers' Surgical Ward and the Officers' Medical Ward. An outer ring of buildings consists of the various ancillary institutions, the kitchens, the laboratory of tropical diseases, the mortuary, the operating theatres and the X-ray theatre. They are all connected by roofed passage-ways; the inner rectangle of wards has a roofed verandah opening on the garden whose flagstones have a claustral and enduring aura. The garden is kept in perpetual flower by six black, almost naked Mahratti gardeners who drench it with water during the dry season and prune and weed it incessantly during the rains. It has tall flowering jacquarandas, beds of hollyhock and carnation and stock, rose trellises and sticks swarming with sweet peas; and in the arid months of burning heat the geraniums bud with fire in red earthenware pots. It is, by 1943 standards, a good place to be in.

At the time of which I am writing, autumn 1942, Ward 'O' 3 (b), which has four beds, was occupied by Captain A.G. Brownlow-Grace, Lieut.-Quartermaster Withers, Lieut. Giles Moncrieff and Lieut. Anthony Weston. The last-named was an R.A.C man who had arrived in India from home four months previously and had been seriously injured by an anti-tank mine during training. The other three were infantry-men. Brownlow-Grace had lost an arm in Burma six months earlier, Moncrieff had multiple leg injuries there and infantile paralysis as well. "Dad" Withers was the only man over twenty-five. He was fourty-four, a regular soldier with twenty-five years in the ranks and three in commission; during this period he had the distinction of never having been in action. He had spent all but two years abroad; he had been home five times and had five children. He was suffering from chronic malaria, sciatica and rheumatism. They were all awaiting a medical board, at which it is decided whether a man should be regraded to a lower medical category, whether he is fit for active or other service, whether he be sent home, or on leave, or discharged the service with a pension. They were the special charge of Sister Normanby, a regular Q.A.I.M.N.S. nurse with a professional impersonality that controlled completely the undoubted flair and "it" which distinguished her during an evening off at the Turf Club dances. She was the operating theatre sister; the surgeons considered her a perfect assistant. On duty or off everybody was pleased about her and aware of her; even the old matron whose puritan and sexless maturity abhorred prettiness and romantics had actually asked Sister Normanby to go on leave with her, Sister deftly refusing.

II

The floor is red parquet, burnished as a windless lake, the coverlets of the four beds are plum red, the blankets cherry red. Moncrieff hates red, Brownlow-Grace has no emotions about colours, any more than about music or aesthetics; but he hates Moncrieff. This is not unnatural. Moncrieff is a University student, Oxford or some bloody place, as far as Brownlow-Grace knows. He whistles classical music, wears his hair long, which is impermissible in a civilian officer and tolerated only in a cavalry officer with at least five years' service in India behind him. Brownlow-Grace has done eight. Moncrieff says a thing is too wearing, dreadfully tedious, simply marvellous, wizard. He indulges in moods and casts himself on his bed in ecstasies of despair. He sleeps in a gauzy veil, parades the ward in the morning in chaplies and veil, swinging his wasted hips and boil-scarred shoulders from wash-place to bed; and he is vain. He has thirty photographs of himself, mounted enlargements, in S.D. and service cap, which he is sending off gradually to a network of young ladies in Greater London, Cape Town where he stayed on the way out, and the chain of hospitals he passed through on his return from Burma. His sickness has deformed him; that also Brownlow-Grace finds himself unable to stomach.

Moncrieff made several attempts to affililate himself to Brownlow-Grace; came and looked over his shoulder at his album of photographs the second day they were together, asked him questions about hunting, fishing and shooting on the third day, talked to him about Burma on the third day and asked him if he'd been afraid to die. What a shocker, Brownlow-Grace thought. Now when he saw the man looking at his mounted self-portraits for the umpteenth time he closed his eyes and tried to sleep himself out of it. But his sleep was liverish and full of curses. He wanted to look at his watch but refused to open his eyes because the day was so long and it must be still short of nine. In his enormous tedium he prays Sister Normanby to come at eleven with a glass of iced nimbo pani for him. He doesn't know how he stands with her; he used to find women easy before Burma, he knew his slim and elegant figure could wear his numerous and expensive uniforms perfectly and he never had to exert himself in a dance or reception from the Savoy in the Strand through Shepheard's in Cario to the Taj in Bombay or the Turf Club in Poona. But now he wasn't so sure; he wasn't sure whether his face had sagged and aged, his hair thinned, his decapitated arm in bad taste. He had sent an airgraph to his parents and his fiancée in Shropshire telling them he'd had his arm off. Peggy sounded as if she were thrilled by it in her reply. Maybe she was being kind. He didn't care so much nowadays what she happened to be feeling. Sister Normanby, however, could excite him obviously. He wanted to ask her to go to a dinner dance with him at the Club as soon as he felt strong enough. But he was feeling lonely; nobody came to see him; how could they anyway? He was the only officer to come out alive. He felt ashamed of that sometimes. He hadn't thought about getting away until the butchery was over and the Japs were mopping up with the bayonet. He'd tried like the devil then, though; didn't realize he had so much cunning and desperation in him. And that little shocker asking him if he'd been afraid to die. He hadn't given death two thoughts.

There was Mostyn Turner. He use to think about Death a lot. Poor old Mostyn. Maybe it was just fancy, but looking at some of Mostyn's photographs in the album, when the pair of them were on shikari tiger-hunting in Belgaum or that fortnight they had together in Kashmir, you could see by his face that he would die. He always attracted the serious type of girl; and like as not he'd take it too far. On the troopship to Rangoon he'd wanted Mostyn to play poker after the bar closed; looked for him everywhere, couldn't find him below decks, nor in the men's mess deck where he sometimes spent an hour or two yarning; their cabin was empty. He found him on the boat deck eventually, hunched up by a lifeboat under the stars. Something stopped him calling him, or even approaching him; he'd turned away and waited by the rails at the companionway head till Mostyn had finished. Yes, finished crying. Incredible, really. He knew what was coming to him, God knows how; and it wasn't a dry hunch, it was something very moving, meant a lot to him somehow. And by God he'd gone looking for it, Mostyn had. He had his own ideas about fighting. Didn't believe in right and left boundaries, fronts, flanks, rears. He had the guerrilla platoon under his command and they went off into the blue the night before the pukka battle with a roving commission to make a diversion in the Jap rear. That was all. He'd gone off at dusk casually as if they were on training. No funny business about Death then. He knew it had come, so he wasn't worrying. Life must have been more interesting to Mostyn than it was to himself, being made that way, having those thoughts and things. What he'd seen of Death that day, it was just a bloody beastly filthy horrible business, so forget it.

His hands were long and thin and elegant as his body and his elongated narrow head with the Roman nose and the eyes whose colour nobody could have stated because nobody could stare back at him. His hands crumpled the sheet he was clutching. He was in a way a very fastidious man. He would have had exquisite taste if he hadn't lacked the faculty of taste.

"Messing up your new sheets again," Sister Normanby said happily, coming into the room like a drop of Scotch. "You ought to be playing the piano with those hands of yours, you know."

He didn't remind her that he only had one left. He was pleased to think she didn't notice it.

"Hallo, Sister," he said, bucking up at once. "You're looking very young and fresh considering it was your night out last night."

"I took it very quietly," she said. "Didn't dance much. Sat in the back of a car all the time."

"For shame, my dear Celia," Moncrieff butted in. "Men are deceivers ever was said before the invention of the internal combustion engine and they're worse in every way since that happened."

"What is my little monkey jabbering about now," she replied, offended at his freedom with her Christian name.

"Have you heard of Gipsy Rose Lee?" Moncrieff replied inconsequentially. "She has a song which says 'I can't strip to Brahms! Can you?'"

"Course she can," said Dad Withers, unobtrusive at the door, a wry old buck, "so long as she's got a mosquito net, isn't it, Sister?"

"Why do you boys always make me feel I haven't got a skirt on when I come in here?" she said.

"Because you can't marry all of us," said Dad.

"Deep, isn't he?" she said.

She had a bunch of newly cut antirrhinums and dahlias, the petals beaded with water, which she put into a bowl, arranging them quietly as she twitted the men. Moncrieff looked at her quizzically as though she had roused conjecture in the psychoanalytical department of his brain.

"Get on with your letter-writing, Moncrieff," she said without having looked up. He flushed.

"There's such a thing as knowing too much," Dad said to her paternally. "I knew a girl in Singapore once, moved there from Shanghai wiv the regiment, she did. She liked us all, the same as nurses say they do. And when she found she liked one more than all the others put together, it came as a terrible shock to her and she had to start again. Took some doing, it did."

"Dad, you're crazy," she said, laughing hard. "A man with all your complaints ought to be too busy counting them to tell all these stories." And then, as she was about to go, she turned and dropped the momentous news she'd been holding out to them.

"You're all four having your medical board next Thursday," she said. "So you'd better make yourselves ill again if you want to go back home."

"I don't want to go back 'home,'" Brownlow-Grace said, laying sardonic stress on the last word.

"I don't know," Dad said. "They tell me it's a good country to get into, this 'ere England. Why, I was only reading in the *Bombay Times* this morning there's a man Beaverage or something, made a report, they even give you money to bury yourself with there now. Suits me."

"You won't die, Dad," Brownlow-Grace said kindly. "You'll simply fade away."

"Well," said Sister Normanby. "There are your fresh flowers. I must go and help to remove a clot from a man's brain now. Good-bye."

"Good-bye," they all said, following her calves and swift heels as she went.

"I didn't know a dog had sweat glands in his paws before," Brownlow-Grace said, looking at his copy of *The Field*.

The others didn't answer. They were thinking of their medical board. It was more interesting really than Sister Normanby.

III

Weston preferred to spend the earlier hours in a deck chair in the garden, by the upraised circular stone pool, among the ferns; here he would watch the lizards run like quicksilver and as quickly freeze into an immobility so lifeless as to be macabre, and the striped rats playing among the jacquaranda branches; and he would look in vain for the mocking bird whose monotony gave a timeless quality to the place and the mood. He was slow in recovering his strength; his three operations and the sulphanilamide tablets he was taking had exhausted the blood in his veins; most of it was somebody else's blood, anyway, an insipid blood that for two days had dripped from a bottle suspended over his bed, while they waited for him to die. His jaw and shoulder- bone had been shattered, a great clod of flesh torn out of his neck and thigh, baring his windpipe and epiglottis and exposing his lung and femoral artery; and although he had recovered very rapidly, his living self seemed overshadowed by the death trauma through which he had passed. There had been an annihilation, a complete obscuring; into which light had gradually dawned. And this light grew unbearably white, the glare of the sun on a vast expanse of snow, and in its unbounded voids he had moved without identity, a pillar of salt in a white desert as pocked and cratered as the dead face of the moon. And then some mutation had taken place and he became aware of pain. A pain that was not pure like the primal purity, but polluted, infected, with racking thirsts and suffocations and writhings, and black eruptions disturbed the whiteness, and coloured dots sifted the intense sun glare, areas of intolerable activities appeared in those passive and limitless oceans. And gradually these manifestations became the simple suppurations of his destroyed inarticulate flesh, and the bandaging and swobbing and probing of his wounds and the grunts of his throat. From it he desired wildly to return to the timeless void where the act of being was no more than a fall of snow or the throw of a rainbow; and these regions became a nostalgia to his pain and soothed his hurt and parched spirit. The two succeeding operations had been conscious experiences, and he had been frightened of them. The preliminaries got on his nerves, the starving, the aperients, the trolley, the prick of morphia, and its false peace. The spotless theatre with its walls of glass and massive lamps of burnished chrome, the anaesthetist who stuttered like a worn gramaphone record, Sister Normanby clattering the knives in trays of lysol, the soft irresistible waves of wool that surged up darkly through the interstices of life like water through a boat; and the choking final surrender to the void his heart feared.

And now, two and a half months later, with his wounds mere puckers dribbling the last dregs of pus, his jaw no longer wired up and splinted, his arm no longer inflamed with the jab of the needle, he sat in the garden with his hands idle in a pool of sunlight, fretting and fretting at himself. He was costive, his stockings had holes in the heel that got wider every day and he hadn't the initiative to ask Sister for a needle and wool; his pen had no ink, his razor blade was blunt, he had shaved badly, he hadn't replied to the airmail letter that lay crumpled in his hand. He had carried that letter about with him for four days, everywhere he went, ever since he'd received it.

"You look thrillingly pale and Byronic this morning, Weston," Moncrieff said, sitting in the deck chair opposite him with his writing-pad and a sheaf of received letters tied in silk tape. "D'you mind me sharing your gloom?"

Weston snorted.

"You can do what you bloody well like," he said, with suppressed irritation.

"Oh dear, have I gone and hurt you again? I'm always hurting people I like," Moncrieff said. "But I can't help it. Honestly I can't. You believe me, Weston, don't you?"

Disturbed by the sudden nakedness of his voice Weston looked up at the waspish intense face, the dark eyebrows and malignant eyes.

"Of course I believe you, monkey," he said. "If you say so."

"It's important that you should believe me," Moncrieff said moodily. "I must find somebody who believes me wherever I happen to be. I'm afraid otherwise. It's too lonely. Of course I hurt some people purposely. That dolt Brownlow-Grace for example. I enjoy making him wince. He's been brought up to think life should be considerate to him. His mother, his bank manager, his batman, his bearer — always somebody to mollycoddle him and see to his wants. Christ, the fellow's incapable of wanting anything really. You know he even resents Sister Normanby having to look after other people beside himself. He only considered the war as an opportunity for promotion; I bet he was delighted when Hitler attacked Poland. And there are other people in this world going about with their brains hanging out, their minds half lynched — a fat lot he understands." He paused, and seeming to catch himself in the middle of his tirade, he laughed softly, "I was going to write a letter-card to my wife," he said. "Still, I haven't got any news. No new love. Next Thursday we'll have some news for them, won't we? I get terribly worked up about this medical board, I can't sleep. You don't think they'll keep me out in India, Weston, do you? It's so lonely out here. I couldn't stay here any longer. I just couldn't."

"You're in a state, monkey," Weston said, perturbed and yet laughing, as one cheers a child badly injured. "Sit quiet a bit, you're speaking loudly. Brownlow'll hear you if you don't take care."

"Did he?" Moncrieff said suddenly apprehensive. "He didn't hear me, did he? I don't want to sound as crude as that, even to him."

"Oh, I don't know. He's not a bad stick," Weston said. "He's very sincere and he takes things in good part, even losing his arm and his career."

"Oh, I know you can preach a sermon on him easily. I don't think in terms of sermons, that's all," Moncrieff said. "But I've been through Burma the same as he has. Why does he sneer at me?" He was silent. Then he said again, "It's lonely out here." He sighed. "I wish I hadn't come out of Burma. I needn't have, I could have let myself go. One night when my leg was gangrenous, the orderly gave me a shot of morphia and I felt myself nodding and smiling. And there was no more jungle, no Japs, no screams, no difficulties at home, no nothing. The orderly would have given me a second shot if I'd asked him. I don't know why I didn't. It would have finished me off nicely. Say, Weston, have you ever been afraid of Death?"

"I don't think it's as simple as that," Weston said. "When I was as good as dead, the first three days here, and for a fortnight afterwards too, I was almost enamoured of death. I'd lost my fear of it. But then I'd lost my will, and my emotions were all dead. I hadn't got any relationships left. It isn't really fair then, is it?"

"I think it is better to fear death," Moncrieff said slowly. "Otherwise you grow spiritually proud. With most people it's not so much the fear of death as love of life that keeps them sensible. I don't love life, personally. Only I'm a bit of a coward and I don't want to die again. I loathe Burma, I can't tell you how terribly. I hope they send me home. If you go home, you ought to tell them you got wounded in Burma, you know."

"Good God, no," Weston said, outraged. "Why should I lie?"

"That's all they deserve," Moncrieff said. "I wonder what they're doing there now? Talking about reconstruction, I suppose. Even the cinemas will have reconstruction films. Well, maybe I'll get a job in some racket or other. Cramming Sandhurst cadets or something. What will you do when you get home?"

"Moncrieff, my good friend," Weston said. "We're soldiers, you know. And it isn't etiquette to talk about going home like that. I'm going in where you left off. I want to have a look at Burma. *And I don't want to see England.*"

"Don't you?" Moncrieff said, ignoring the slow emphasis of Weston's last words and twirling the tassel of his writing-pad slowly. "Neither do I, very much," he said with an indifference that ended the conversation.

IV

The sick have their own slightly different world, their jokes are as necessary and peculiar to them as their medicines; they can't afford to be morbid like the healthy, nor to be indifferent to their environment like the Arab. The outside world has been washed out; between them and the encircling mysteries there is only the spotlight of their obsessions holding the small backcloth of ward and garden before them. Anyone appearing before this backcloth has the heightened emphasis and significance of a character upon the stage. The Sikh fortune tellers who offered them promotion and a fortune and England as sibilantly as panders, the mongoose-fight-snake wallahs with their wailing sweet pipes and devitalized cobras, the little native cobblers and peddlers who had customary right to enter the precincts entered as travellers from an unknown land. So did the visitors from the Anglo-India community and brother officers on leave. And each visitor was greedily absorbed and examined by every patient, with the intenser acumen of disease.

Brownlow-Grace had a visitor. This increased his prestige like having a lot of mail. It appeared she had only just discovered he was here, for during the last four days before his medical board she came every day after lunch and stayed sitting on his bed until dusk and conferred upon them an intimacy that evoked in the others a green nostalgia.

She was by any standards a beautiful woman. One afternoon a young unsophisticated English Miss in a fresh little frock and long hair; the next day French and exotic with the pallor of an undertaker's lily and hair like statuary; the third day exquisitely Japanese, carmined and beringed with huge green amber stones, her hair in a high bun that only a great lover would dare unloose. When she left each evening Sister Normanby came in with a great bustle of fresh air and practicality to tidy his bed and put up his mosquito net. And he seemed equally capable of entertaining and being entertained by both ladies.

On the morning of the medical board Brownlow-Grace came and sat by Anthony among the ferns beside the lily pool; and this being a gesture of unusual amiability in one whom training had made rigid, Weston was unreasonably pleased.

"Well, Weston," he said. "Sweating on the top line over this medical board?"

"What d'you mean?" Weston asked.

"Well, do you think everything's a wangle to get you home or keep you here like that little squirt Moncrieff?"

"I don't think along those lines, personally," Weston said. He looked at the long languid officer sprawled in the deck chair. "The only thing I'm frightened of is that they'll keep me *here*, or give me some horrible office job where I'll never see a Valentine lift her belly over a bund and go grunting like a wild boar at — well, whoever happens to be there. I got used to the idea of the Germans. I suppose the Japs will do."

"You're like me; no enemy," Browlow-Grace said. "I didn't think twice about it — till it happened. You're lucky, though. You're the only one of us four who'll ever see action. I could kill some more. What do I want to go home for? They hacked my arm off, those bastards; I blew the fellow's guts out that did it, had the muzzle of my Colt rammed into his belly, I could feel his breath, he was like a frog, the swine. You, I suppose you want to go home, haven't been away long, have you?"

"Six months."

"Six months without a woman, eh?" Brownlow-Grace laughed, yet kindly.

"Yes."

"I'm the sort who'll take somebody else's," Brownlow-Grace said. "I don't harm them."

Weston didn't reply.

"You've got a hell of a lot on your mind, haven't you, Weston? Any fool can see something's eating you up." Still no reply. "Look here, I may be a fool, but come out with me to-night, let's have a party together. Eh?" Surprisingly, Weston wasn't embarrassed at this extreme gesture of kindness. It was so ingenuously made. Instead he felt an enormous relief, and for the first time the capacity to speak. Not, he told himself, to ask for advice. Brownlow-Grace wasn't a clergyman with a healing gift; but it was possible to tell him the thing simply, to shift the weight of it a bit. "I'm all tied up," he said. "A party wouldn't be any use, nor a woman."

"Wouldn't it?" Brownlow-Grace said drily, standing up. Weston had a feeling he was about to go. It would have excruciated him. Instead he half turned, as if to disembarrass him, and said, "The flowers want watering."

"You know, if you're soldiering, there are some things you've got to put out of bounds to your thoughts," Weston said. "Some things you don't let yourself doubt."

"Your wife, you mean?" Brownlow-Grace said, holding a breath of his cigarette in his lungs and studying the ants on the wall.

"Not only her," Weston said. "Look. I didn't start with the same things as you. You had a pram and a private school and you saw the sea, maybe. My father was a collier and he worked in a wet pit. He got rheumatism and nystagmus and then the dole and then parish relief. I'm not telling you a sob story. It's just I was used to different sounds. I used to watch the wheel of the pit spin round year after year, after school and Saturdays and Sundays; and then from 1926 on I watched it not turning round at all, and I can't ever get that wheel out of my mind. It still spins and idles, and there's money and nystagmus coming into the house or no work and worse than nystagmus. I just missed the wheel sucking me down the shaft. I got a scholarship to the county school. I don't know when I started rebelling. Against that wheel in my head. I didn't get along very well. Worked in a grocer's and printer's, and no job was good enought for me; I had a bug. Plenty of friends too, plenty of chaps thinking the same as me. Used to read books in those days, get passionate about politics, Russia was like a woman to me. Then I did get a job I wanted, in a bookshop in Holborn. A French woman came in one day. I usually talked to customers, mostly politics; but not to her. She came in several times, once with a trade union man I knew. She was short, she had freckles, a straight nose, chestnut hair, she looked about eighteen; she bought books about Beethoven, Schopenhauer, the Renaissance, biology — I read every book she bought, after she'd gone back to France. I asked this chap about her. He said she was a big name, you know the way revolutionary movements toss up a woman sometimes. She was a Communist, a big speaker in the industrial towns in North France, she'd been to Russia too. And, well, I just wanted her, more and more and more as the months passed. Not her politics, but her fire. If I could hear her addressing a crowd, never mind about wanting her in those dreams you get.

"And then the war came and most of my friends said it was a phoney war, but I was afraid from the beginning that something would happen to France and I wanted to hear her speaking first. I joined up in November and I made myself such a bloody pest that they posted me to France to reinforcements. I got my war all right. And I met her, too. The trade unionist I told you about gave me a letter to introduce myself. She lived in Lille. She knew me as soon as the door opened. And I was just frightened. But after two nights there was no need to be frightened. You get to think for years that life is just a fight, with a flirt thrown in sometimes, a flirt with death or sex or whatever happens to be passing, but mostly a fight all the way along. And then you soften up, you're no use, you haven't got any wheel whirring in your head any more. Only flowers on the table and a piano she plays sometimes, when she wants to, when she wants to love."

"I've never been to France," Brownlow-Grace said. "Hated it at school, French I mean. Communists, of course — I thought they were all Bolshies, you know, won't obey an order. What happened after Dunkirk?"

"It was such burning sunny weather," Weston said. "It was funny, having fine weather. I couldn't get her out of my mind. The sun seemed to expand inside the lining of my brain and the whole fortnight after we made that last stand with Martel at Cambrai I didn't know whether I was looking for her or Dunkirk. When I was most exhausted it was worse, she came to me once by the side of the road, there were several dead Belgian women lying there, and she said 'Look, Anthony, I have been raped. They raped me, the Bosche.' And the world was crashing and whirring, or it was doped, wouldn't lift a finger to stop it, and the Germans crossing the Seine. A year before I'd have said to the world, 'Serve you right.' But not now, with Cecile somewhere inside the armies. She'd tried."

"And that was the end?" Brownlow-Grace said.

"Yes," said Weston. "Just about. Only it wasn't a beautiful end, the way it turned out. I had eight months in England, and I never found out a thing. The Free French didn't know. One of them knew her well, knew her as a lover, he told me; boasted about it; I didn't tell him; I wanted to find her, I didn't care about anything else. And then something started in me. I used to mooch about London. A French girl touched me on the street one night. I went with her. I went with a lot of women. Then we embarked for overseas. I had a girl at Durban, and in Bombay: sometimes they were French, if possible they were French. God, it was foul."

He got up and sat on the edge of the pool; under the green strata of mosses the scaled goldfish moved slowly in their palaces of burning gold. He wiped his face which was sweating.

"Five days ago I got this letter from America," he said. "From her."
Brownlow-Grace said, "That was a bit of luck." Weston laughed.
"Yes," he said. "Yes. It was nice of her to write. She put it very
nicely, too. Would you like to read it?"

"No," said Brownlow-Grace. "I don't want to read it."

"She said it often entered her mind to write to me, because I had
been so sweet to her in Lille, that time. She hoped I was well. To enter
America there had been certain formalities, she said; she'd married an
American, a country which has all types, she said. There is a Life, she
said, but not mine, and a war also, but not mine. Now it is the Japanese.
That's all she said."

"She remembered you," Brownlow-Grace said.

"Some things stick in a woman's mind," Weston said. "She darned
my socks for me in bed. Why didn't she say she remembered darning
my socks?"

Brownlow-Grace pressed his hand, fingers extended, upon the
surface of the water, not breaking its resistance, quite.

"I don't use the word," he said. "But I guess it's because she loved
you."

Weston looked up, searching and somehow naïve.

"I don't mind about the Japanese," he said, "if that were so."

V

Dad Withers had his medical board first; he wasn't in the board
room long; in fact he was back on the verandah outside "O" 3 (b) when
Weston returned from sending a cable at the camp post office.

"Did it go all right, Dad?" Weston asked.

"Sure, sure," Dad said, purring as if at his own cleverness. "Three
colonels and two majors there, and the full colonel he said to me 'Well,
Withers, what's your trouble? Lieutenant-Quartermaster, weren't
you?' And I said 'Correct, sir, and now I'm putting my own body in for
exchange, sir. It don't keep the rain out no more, sir.' So he said,
'You're not much use to us, Withers, by the look of you.' And I said,
'Not a bit of use, sir, sorry to report.' And the end of it was they gave me
a free berth on the next ship home wiv full military honours and a
disability pension and all. Good going, isn't it now?"

"Very good, Dad. I'm very pleased."

"Thank you," Dad said, his face wrinkled and benign as a tortoise.
"Now go and get your own ticket and don't keep the gentlemen
waiting...."

Dad lay half asleep in the deck chair, thinking that it was all buttoned up now, all laid on, all made good. It had been a long time, a lifetime, more than twenty hot seasons, more than twenty rains. Not many could say that. Not many had stuck it like him. Five years in Jhansi with his body red as lobster from head to toe with prickly heat, squirting a water pistol down his back for enjoyment and scratching his shoulders with a long fork from the bazaar. Two big wars there'd been, and most of the boys had been glad to go into them, excited to be posted to France, or embark for Egypt. But he'd stuck it out. Still here, still good for a game of nap, and them all dead, the boys that wanted to get away. And now it was finished with him, too.

He didn't know. Maybe he wasn't going home the way he'd figured it out after all. Maybe there was something else, something he hadn't counted in. This tiredness, this emptiness, this grey blank wall of mist, this not caring. What would it be like in the small Council house with five youngsters and his missus? She'd changed a lot, the last photo she sent she was like his mother, spectacles and fat legs, full of plainness. Maybe the kids would play with him, though, the young ones?

He pulled himself slowly out of his seat, took out his wallet, counted his money; ninety chips he had. Enough to see India just once again. Poor old India. He dressed hurriedly, combed his thin hair, wiped his spectacles, dusted his shoes and left before the others came back. He picked up a tonga at the stand outside the main gates of the hospital cantonment, just past the M.D. lines, and named a certain hotel down town. And off he cantered, the skinny old horse clattering and letting off great puffs of bad air under the tonga wallah's whip, and Dad shouting "Jillo, jillo," impatient to be drunk.

Brownlow-Grace came in and went straight to the little bed table where he kept his papers in an untidy heap. He went there in a leisurely way, avoiding the inquiring silences of Weston and Moncrieff and Sister Normanby, who were all apparently doing something. He fished out an airgraph form and his fountain-pen and sat quietly on the edge of his bed.

"Oh damn and blast it," he said angrily. "My pen's dry."

Weston gave him an inkbottle.

He sat down again.

"What's the date?" he said after a minute.

"12th," Moncrieff said.

"What month?" he asked.

"December."

"Thanks."

He wrote slowly, laboriously, long pauses between sentences. When he finished he put his pen away and looked for a stamp.

"What stamp d'you put on an airgraph?" he said.

"Three annas," Moncrieff said patiently.

Sister Normanby decided to abolish the embarrassing reticence with which this odd man was concealing his board result. She had no room for broody hens.

"Well," she said, gently enough. "What happened at the board?"

He looked up at her and neither smiled nor showed any sign of recognition. Then he stood up, took his cane and peaked service cap, and brushed a speck of down off his long and well-fitting trousers.

"They discharged me," he said. "Will you post this airgraph for me, please?"

"Yes," she said, and for some odd reason she found herself unable to deal with the situation and took it from him and went on with her work.

"I'm going out," he said.

Weston followed him into the garden and caught him up by the lily pool.

"Is that invitation still open?" he asked.

"What invitation?" Brownlow-Grace said.

"To go on the spree with you to-night?" Weston said.

Brownlow-Grace looked at him thoughtfully.

"I've changed my mind, Anthony,"he said — Weston was pleasurably aware of this first use of his Christian name — "I don't think I'd be any use to you to-night. Matter of fact, I phoned Rita just now, you know the woman who comes to see me, and she's calling for me in five minutes."

"I see," Weston said. "O.K. by me."

"You don't mind, do you?" he said. "I don't think you need Rita's company, do you? Besides, she usually prefers one man at a time. She's the widow of a friend of mine, Mostyn Turner; he was killed in Burma, too."

Weston came back into the ward to meet Sister Normanby's white face. "Where's he gone?" she said.

Weston looked at her, surprised at the emotion and stress this normally imperturbable woman was showing.

He didn't answer her.

"He's gone to that woman," she said, white and virulent. "Hasn't he?"

"Yes, he has," he said quietly.

"She always has them when they're convalescent," she said, flashing with venom. She picked up her medicine book and the jar with her thermometer in it. "I have them when they're sick."

She left the ward, biting her white lips.

"I didn't know she felt that way about him," Weston said.

"Neither did she," said Moncrieff. "She never knows until it's too late. That's the beauty about her. She's virginal."

"You're very cruel, Moncrieff."

Moncrieff turned on him like an animal.

"Cruel?" he said. "Cruel? Well, I don't lick Lazarus's sores, Weston. I take the world the way it is. Nobody cares about you out here. Nobody. What have I done to anybody? Why should they keep me here? What's the use of keeping a man with infantile paralysis and six inches of bone missing from his leg? Why didn't the board let me go home?"

"You'll go home, monkey, you'll go home," Weston said gently. "You know the Army. You can help them out here. You're bound to go home, when the war ends."

"Do you think so?" Moncrieff said. "Do you?" He thought of this for a minute at least. Then he said, "No, I shall never go home. I know it."

"Don't be silly, monkey. You're a bit run down, that's all." Weston soothed him. "Let's go and sit by the pool for a while."

"I like the pool," Moncrieff said. They strolled out together and sat on the circular ledge. The curving bright branches held their leaves peacefully above the water. Under the mosses they could see the old toad of the pond sleeping, his back rusty with jewels. Weston put his hand in the water; minnows rose in small flocks and nibbled at his fingers. Circles of water lapped softly outwards, outwards, till they touched the edge of the pool, and cast a gentle wetness on the stone, and lapped again inwards, inwards. And as they lapped inwards he felt the ripples surging against the most withdrawn and inmost ledges of his being, like a series of temptations in the wilderness. And he felt glad to-night, feeling some small salient gained when for many reasons the men whom he was with were losing ground along the whole front to the darkness that there is.

"No," said Moncrieff at last. "Talking is no good. But perhaps you will write to me sometimes, will you, just to let me know."

"Yes, I'll write to you, monkey," Weston said, looking up.

And then he looked away again, not willing to consider those empty inarticulate eyes.

"The mosquitoes are starting to bite," he said. "We'd better go now."

The Orange Grove

The grey truck slowed down at the crossroads and the Army officer leaned out to read the signpost. *Indians Only*, the sign pointing to the native town read. *Dak Bungalow* straight on. "Thank God,"said Staff-Captain Beale. "Go ahead, driver." They were lucky hitting a dak bungalow at dusk. They'd bivouacked the last two nights, and in the monsoon a bivouac is bad business. To-night they'd be able to strip and sleep dry under a roof, and heat up some bully on the Tommy cooker. Bloody good.

These bungalows are scattered all over India on the endless roads and travellers may sleep there, cook their food, and pass on. The rooms are bare and whitewashed, the verandah has room for a camp bed, they are quiet and remote, tended for the Government only by some old khansama or chowkey, usually a slippered and silent old Moslem. The driver pulled in and began unpacking the kit, the dry rations, the cooker, the camp bed, his blanket roll, the tin of kerosene. Beale went off to find the caretaker, whom he discovered squatting amongst the flies by the well. He was a wizened yellow-skinned old man in a soiled dhoti. Across his left breast was a plaster, loose and dripping with pus, a permanent discharge it seemed. He wheezed as he replied to the brusque request and raised himself with pain, searching slowly for his keys.

Beale came to give the driver a hand while the old man fumbled with the crockery indoors.

"The old crow is only sparking on one cylinder," he said. "Looks like T.B.," he added with the faint overtone of disgust which the young and healthy feel for all incurable diseases. He looked out at the falling evening, the fulgurous inflammation among the grey anchorages of cloud, the hot creeping prescience of the monsoon.

"I don't like it to-night," he said. "It's eeric; I can't breathe or think. This journey's getting on my nerves. What day is it? I've lost count."

"Thursday, sir," the driver said, "August 25."

214   *Collected Stories*

"How do you know all that?" Beale asked, curious.

"I have been thinking it out, for to write a letter to-night," the driver said. "Shall I get the cooker going, sir? Your bed is all ready now."

"O.K." Beale said, sitting on his camp bed and opening his grip. He took out a leather writing-pad in which he kept the notes he was making for Divisional H.Q., and all the letters he'd received from home. He began looking among the letters for one he wanted. The little dusty driver tinkered with the cooker. Sometimes Beale looked up and watched him, sometimes he looked away at the night.

This place seemed quiet enough. The old man had warned him there was unrest and rioting in the town. The lines had been cut, the oil tanks unsuccessfully attacked, the court house burnt down, the police had made lathi charges, the district magistrate was afraid to leave his bungalow. The old man had relished the violence of others. Of course you couldn't expect the 11th to go by without some riots, some deaths. Even in this remote part of Central India where the native princes ruled from their crumbling Mogol forts through their garrisons of smiling crop-headed little Ghurkas. But it seemed quiet enough here, a mile out of the town. The only chance was that someone might have seen them at the cross roads; it was so sultry, so swollen and angry, the sky, the hour. He felt for his revolver.

He threw the driver a dry box of matches from his grip. Everything they carried was fungoid with damp, the driver had been striking match after match on his wet box with a curious depressive impassivity. Funny little chap, seemed to have no initiative, as if some part of his will were paralysed. Maybe it was that wife of his he'd talked about the night before last when they had the wood fire going in the hollow. Funny, Beale had been dazed with sleep, half listening, comprehending only the surface of the slow, clumsy words. Hate. Hate. Beale couldn't understand hate. War hadn't taught it to him, war was to him only fitness, discomfort, feats of endurance, proud muscles, a career, irresponsible dissipation, months of austerity broken by "blinds" in Cairo, or Durban, Calcutta or Bangalore or Bombay. But this little rough-head with his soiled hands and bitten nails, his odd blue eyes looking away, his mean bearing, squatting on the floor with kerosene and grease over his denims — he had plenty of hate.

"....tried to emigrate first of all, didn't want to stay anywhere. I was fourteen, finished with reformatory schools for keeps... New Zealand I wanted to go. There was a school in Bristol for emigrants... I ran away from home but they didn't bother with me in Bristol, nacherly... Police sent me back. So then I became a boy in the Army, in the drums, and then I signed on. I'm a time-serving man, sir; better put another couple of branches on the fire; so I went to Palestine, against the Arabs; seen them collective farms the Jews got there, sir? Oranges...then I come home, so I goes on leave... We got a pub in our family and since my father died my mother been keeping it...for the colliers it is...never touch beer myself, my father boozed himself to death be'ind the counter. Well, my mother 'ad a barmaid, a flash dame she was, she was good for trade, fit for an answer any time, and showing a bit of her breasts every time she drew a pint. Red hair she had, well not exactly red, I don't know the word, not so *coarse* as red. My mother said for me to keep off her. My mother is a big Bible woman, though nacherly she couldn't go to chapel down our way being she kept a pub... Well, Monica, this barmaid, she slept in the attic, it's a big 'ouse, the Bute's Arms. And I was nineteen. You can't always answer for yourself, can you? It was my pub by rights, *mine*. She was *my* barmaid. That's how my father'd have said if he wasn't dead. My mother wouldn't have no barmaids when he was alive. Monica knew what she was doing all right. She wanted the pub and the big double bed; she couldn't wait... It didn't seem much to pay for sleeping with a woman like that... Well, then I went back to barracks, and it wasn't till I told my mate and he called me a sucker that I knew I couldn't... Nothing went right after that. She took good care to get pregnant, Monica did, and my mother threw her out. But it was my baby, and I married her without telling my mother. It was *my* affair, wasn't it? *Mine*."

How long he had been telling all this Beale couldn't remember. There was nothing to pin that evening upon; the fire and the logs drying beside the fire, the circle of crickets, the sudden blundering of moths into the warm zone of the fire and thoughtful faces, the myopic sleepy stare of fatigue, and those bitter distasteful words within intervals of thought and waiting. Not until now did Beale realize that there had been no hard-luck story told, no gambit for sympathy or compassionate leave or a poor person's divorce. But a man talking into a wood fire in the remote asylums of distance, and slowly explaining the twisted and evil curvature of his being.

"She told me she'd get her own back on me for my mother turning her out... And she did... I know a man in my own regiment that slept with her on leave. But the kid is mine. My mother got the kid for me. She shan't spoil the kid. Nobody'll spoil the kid, neither Monica nor me... I can't make it out, how is it a woman is so wonderful, I mean in a bedroom? I should 'a' murdered her, it would be better than this, this hating her all the time. Wouldn't it?..."

"The Tommy cooker's O.K. now, sir," the driver said. "The wind was blowing the flame back all the time. O.K. now with this screen. What's it to be? There's only bully left."

"Eh? What?" Beale said. "Oh, supper? Bully? I can't eat any more bully. Can't we get some eggs or something? Ten days with bully twice a day is plenty. Can you eat bully?"

"Can't say I fancy it," the driver said. "I'll go down the road and see if I can get some eggs."

"I shouldn't bother," Beale said. "The storm will get you if you go far. Besides, it is dangerous down the town road. They've been rioting since Gandhi and Nehru were arrested last week. Better brew up and forget about the food."

Beale was by nature and by his job as a staff officer one who is always doing things and forgetting about them. It was convenient as well as necessary to him. His *Pending* basket was always empty. He never had a load on his mind.

"I'll take a walk just the same," the driver said. "Maybe I'll find a chicken laying on the road. I won't be long."

He was a good scrounger, it was a matter of pride with him to get anything that was wanted, mosquito poles, or water or anything. And every night, whether they were in the forest or the desert plains that encompass Indore, he had announced his intention of walking down the road.

Some impulse caused Beale to delay him a moment.

"Remember," Beale said, "the other night, you said you saw the collective farms in Palestine?"

"Aye," said the driver, standing in the huge deformity of the hunch-backed shadow that the lamp projected from his slovenly head.

"They were good places, those farms?" Beale asked.

"Aye, they were," the driver said, steadying his childish gaze. "They didn't have money, they didn't buy and sell. They shared what they had and the doctor and the school teacher the same as the labourer or the children, all the same, all living together. Orange groves they lived in, and I would like to go back there."

He stepped down from the porch and the enormous shadows vanished from the roof and from the wall. Beale sat on, the biscuit tin of water warming slowly on the cooker, the flying ants casting their wings upon the glass of the lamp and the sheets of his bed. An orange grove in Palestine.... He was experiencing one of those enlargements of the imagination that come once or perhaps twice to a man, and recreate him subtly and profoundly. And he was thinking simply this — that some things are possible and other things are impossible to us. Beyond the mass of vivid and sensuous impressions which he had allowed the war to impose upon him were the quiet categories of the possible and the quieter frozen infinities of the impossible. And he must get back to those certainties... The night falls, and the dance bands turn on the heat. The indolent arrive in their taxis, the popsies and the good-timers, the lonely good-looking boys and the indifferent erotic women. Swing music sways across the bay from the urbane permissive ballrooms of the Taj and Green's. *In the Mood, It's foolish but it's fun,* some doughboys cracking whips in the coffee-room, among apprehensive glances, the taxi drivers buy a betel leaf and spit red saliva over the running-board, and panders touch the sleeves of the soldiers, the crowd huddles beneath the Gateway, turning up collars and umbrellas everywhere against the thin sane arrows of the rain. And who is she whose song is the world spinning, whose lambent streams cast their curved ways about you and about, whose languors are the infinite desires of the unknowing? Is she the girl behind the grille, in the side street where they play gramophone records and you pay ten chips for a whisky and you suddenly feel a godalmighty yen for whoever it is in your arms? But beyond that? Why had he failed with this woman, why had it been impossible with that woman? He collected the swirl of thought and knew that he could not generalize as the driver had done in the glow of the wood fire. Woman. The gardener at the boarding school he went to used to say things about women. Turvey his name was. Turvey, the headmaster called him, but the boys had to say *Mr.* Turvey. Mr. Turvey didn't hold with mixed bathing, not at any price, because woman wasn't clean like man, he said. And when the boys demurred, thinking of soft pledges and film stars and the moon, Mr. Turvey would wrinkle his saturnine face and say, "Course you young gentlemen knows better than me. I only been married fifteen years. I don't know nothing of course." And maybe this conversation would be while he was emptying the ordure from the latrines into the oil drum on iron wheels which he trundled each morning down to his sewer pits in the school gardens.

But in an intenser lucidity Beale knew he must not generalize. There would be perhaps one woman out of many, one life out of many, two things possible — if life itself were possible, and if he had not debased himself among the impossibilities by then. The orange grove in Palestine....

And then he realized that the water in the biscuit tin was boiling and he knelt to put the tea and tinned milk into the two enamel mugs. As he knelt a drop of rain the size of a coin pitted his back. And another. And a third. He shuddered. Ten days they'd been on the road, making this reconnaissance for a projected Army exercise, and each day had been nothing but speed and distance hollow in the head, the mileometer ticking up the daily two hundred, the dust of a hundred villages justifying their weariness with its ashes, and to-morrow also only speed and distance and the steadiness of the six cylinders. And he'd been dreaming of a Bombay whore whose red kiss he still had not washed from his arm, allowing her to enter where she would and push into oblivion the few things that were possible to him in the war and the peace. And now the rain made him shudder and he felt all the loneliness of India about him and he knew he had never been more alone. So he was content to watch the storm gather, operating against him from a heavy fulcrum in the east, lashing the bungalow and the trees, infuriating the night. The cooker spluttered and went out. He made no move to use the boiling water upon the tea. The moths flew in from the rain, and the grasshoppers and the bees. The frogs grunted and croaked in the swirling mud and grass, the night was animate and violent. He waited without moving until the violence of the storm was spent. Then he looked at his watch. It was, as he thought. The driver had been gone an hour and twenty minutes. He knew he must go and look for him.

He loaded his revolver carefully and buckled on his holster over his bush shirt. He called for the old caretaker, but there was no reply. The bungalow was empty. He turned down the wick of the lamp and putting on his cap, stepped softly into the night. It was easy to get lost. It would be difficult to find anything to-night, unless it was plumb in the main road.

His feet felt under the streaming water for the stones of the road. The banyan tree he remembered, it was just beyond the pull-in. Its mass was over him now, he could feel it over his head. It was going to be difficult. The nearest cantonment was four hundred miles away; in any case the roads were too flooded now for him to retrace his way to Mhow. If he went on to Baroda, Ahmedabad — but the Mahi river would be in spate also. The lines down everywhere, too. They would have to go on, that he felt sure about. Before daybreak, too. It wasn't safe here. If only he could find the driver. He was irritated with the driver, irritated in a huge cloudy way, for bungling yet one more thing, for leaving him alone with so much on his hands, for insisting on looking for eggs. He'd known something would happen.

He felt the driver with his foot and knelt down over him in the swirling road and felt for his heart under his sodden shirt and cursed him in irritation and concern. Dead as a duckboard, knifed. The rain came on again and he tried to lift up the corpse the way he'd been taught, turning it first on to its back and standing firmly astride it. But the driver was obstinate and heavy and for a long time he refused to be lifted up.

He carried the deadweight back up the road, sweating and bitched by the awkward corpse, stumbling and trying in vain to straighten himself. What a bloody mess, he kept saying; I told him not to go and get eggs; did he have to have eggs for supper? It became a struggle between himself and the corpse, who was trying to slide down off his back and stay lying on the road. He had half a mind to let it have its way.

He got back eventually and backed himself against the verandah like a lorry, letting the body slide off his back; the head fell crack against the side wall and he said "Sorry," and put a sack between the cheek and the ground. The kid was soaking wet and wet red mud in his hair; he wiped his face up with cotton- waste and put a blanket over him while he packed the kit up and stowed it in the truck. He noticed the tea and sugar in the mugs and tried the temper of the water. It was too cold. He regretted it. He had the truck packed by the end of half an hour, his own bedding roll stretched on top of the baggage ready for the passenger. He hoped he'd be agreeable this time. He resisted a bit but he had stiffened a little and was more manageable. He backed him into the truck and then climbed in, pulling him on to the blankets by his armpits. Not until he'd put up the tailboard and got him all ready did he feel any ease. He sighed. They were away. He got into the driving seat to switch on the ignition. Then he realized there was no key. He felt a momentary panic. But surely the driver had it. He slipped out and, in the darkness and the drive of the rain, searched in the man's pockets. Paybook, matches, identity discs (must remember that, didn't even know his name), at last the keys.

He started the engine and let her warm up, slipped her into second, and drove slowly out. The old caretaker never appeared, and Beale wondered whether he should say anything of his suspicions regarding the old man when he made his report. Unfortunately there was no evidence. Still, they were away from there; he sighed with relief as the compulsion under which he had been acting relaxed. He had this extra sense, of which he was proud, of being able to feel the imminence of danger as others feel a change in the weather; it didn't help him in Libya, perhaps it hindered him there; but in a pub in Durban it had got him out in the nick of time; he'd edged for the door before a shot was fired. He knew to-night all right. The moment he saw that dull red lever of storm raised over his head, and the old caretaker had shrugged his shoulders after his warning had been laughed off. You had to bluff them; only sometimes bluff wasn't enough and then you had to get away, face or no face. Now he tried to remember the route on the map; driving blind, the best thing was to go slow and pull in somewhere a few miles on. Maybe the sun would rise sometime and he could dry out the map and work out the best route; no more native towns for him; he wanted to get to a cantonment if possible. Otherwise he'd look for the police lines at Dohad or Jabhua or wherever the next place was. But every time he thought of pulling in, a disinclination to stop the engine made him keep his drenched ammunition boot on the accelerator pedal. When he came to a road junction he followed his fancy; there is such a thing as letting the car do the guiding.

He drove for six hours before the night stirred at all. Then his red-veined eyes felt the slight lessening in the effectiveness of the headlights that presaged the day. When he could see the red berm of the road and the flooded paddy-fields lapping the bank, he at last pulled up under a tree and composed himself over the wheel, placing his cheek against the rim, avoiding the horn at the centre. He fell at once into a stiff rigid sleep.

A tribe of straggling gipsies passed him soon after dawn. They made no sound, leading their mules and camels along the soft berm on the other side of the road, mixing their own ways with no other's. The sun lay back of the blue rain-clouds, making the earth steam. The toads hopped out of the mud and rested under the stationary truck. Land-crabs came out of the earth and sat on the edge of their holes. Otherwise no one passed. The earth seemed content to let him have his sleep out. He woke about noon, touched by the sun as it passed.

He felt guilty. Guilty of neglect of duty, having slept at his post? Then he got a grip on himself and rationalized the dreadful guilt away. What could he have done about it? The driver had been murdered. What did they expect him to do? Stay there and give them a second treat? Stay there and investigate? Or get on and report it. Why hadn't he reported it earlier? How could he? The lines were down, the roads flooded behind him, he was trying his best; he couldn't help sleeping for a couple of hours. Yet the guilt complex persisted. It was a bad dream and he had some evil in him, a soft lump of evil in his brain. But why? If he'd told the man to go for eggs it would be different. He was bound to be all right as long as he had his facts right. Was there an accident report form to be filled in immediately, in duplicate, Army Form B — something-or- other? He took out his notebook, but the paper was too wet to take his hard pencil. 23.00 hrs. on 23 August 1942 deceased stated his desire to get some eggs. I warned him that disturbances of a political character had occurred in the area.... He shook himself, bleary and sore-throated, in his musty overalls, and thought a shave and some food would put him right. He went round to the back of the truck. The body had slipped with the jolting of the road. He climbed in and looked at the ashen face. The eyes were closed, the face had sunk into an expressionless inanition, it made him feel indifferent to the whole thing. Poor sod. Where was his hate now? Was he grieving that the woman, Mona was it, would get a pension out of him now? Did he still hate her? He seemed to have let the whole matter drop. Death was something without hate in it. But he didn't want to do anything himself except shave and eat and get the whole thing buttoned up. He tore himself away from the closed soiled face and ferreted about for his shaving kit. He found it at last, and after shaving in the muddy rain-water he ate a few hard biscuits and stuffed a few more into his pocket. Then he lashed the canvas down over the tailboard and got back to the wheel. The truck was slow to start. The bonnet had been leaking and the plugs were wet in the cylinder heads. She wouldn't spark for a minute or two. Anxiety swept over him. He cursed the truck viciously. Then she sparked on a couple of cylinders, stuttered for a minute as the others dried out, and settled down steadily. He ran her away carefully and again relaxed. He was dead scared of being stranded with the body. There wasn't even a shovel on the truck.

After driving for an hour he realized he didn't know where he was. He was in the centre of a vast plain of paddy-fields, lined by raised bunds and hedged with cactus along the road. White herons and tall fantastic cranes stood by the pools in the hollows. He pulled up to try and work out his position. But his map was nowhere to be found. He must have left it at the dak bungalow in his haste. He looked at his watch; it had stopped. Something caved inside him, a sensation of panic, of an enemy against whose machinations he had failed to take the most elementary precautions. He was lost.

He moved on again at once. There was distance. The mileometer still measured something? By sunset he would do so many miles. How much of the day was left? Without the sun how could he tell? He was pannicky at not knowing these things; he scarcely knew more than the man in the back of the truck. So he drove on and on, passing nobody but a tribe of gipsies with their mules and camels, and dark peasants driving their bullocks knee-deep in the alluvial mud before their simple wooden ploughs. He drove as fast as the track would allow; in some places it was flooded and narrow, descending to narrow causeways swept by brown streams which he only just managed to cross. He drove till the land was green with evening, and in the crepuscular uncertainty he halted and decided to kip down for the night. He would need petrol; it was kept in tins in the back of the truck; it meant pulling the body out, or making him sit away in a corner. He didn't want to disturb the kid. He'd been jolted all day; and now this indignity. He did all he had to do with a humility that was alien to him. Respect he knew; but this was more than respect; obedience and necessity he knew, but this was more than either of these. It was somehow an admission of the integrity of the man, a new interest in what he was and what he had left behind. He got some soap and a towel, after filling his tanks, and when he had washed himself he propped the driver up against the tailboard and sponged him clean and put P.T. shoes on his feet instead of the boots that had so swollen his feet. When he had laid him out on the blankets and covered him with a sheet, he rested from his exertions, and as he recovered his breath he glanced covertly at him, satisfied that he had done something for him. What would the woman have done, Monica? Would she have flirted with him? Most women did, and he didn't discourage them. But this woman, my God, he'd bloody well beat her up. It was her doing, this miserable end, this mess-up. He hadn't gone down the road to get eggs; he'd gone to get away from her. It must have been a habit of his, at nights, to compose himself. She'd bitched it all. He could just see her. And she still didn't know a thing about him, not the first thing. Yes, he hated her all right, the voluptuous bitch.

He slept at the wheel again, falling asleep with a biscuit still half chewed in his mouth. He had erotic dreams, this woman Monica drawing him a pint, and her mouth and her breasts and the shallow taunting eyes; and the lights in her attic bedroom with the door ajar, and the wooden stairs creaking. And the dawn then laid its grey fingers upon him and he woke with the same feeling of guilt and shame, a grovelling debased mood, that had seized him the first morning. He got up, stretching himself, heady with vertigo and phlegm, and washed himself in the paddy flood. He went round to the back of the truck to get some biscuits. He got them quietly, the boy was still sleeping, and he said to himself that he would get him through to-day, honest he would. He had to.

The sun came out and the sky showed a young summer blue. The trees wakened and shook soft showers of rain off their leaves. Hills showed blue as lavender and when he came to the cross-roads he steered north-west by the sun, reckoning to make the coast road somewhere near Baroda. There would be a cantonment not far from there, and a Service dump for coffins, and someone to whom he could make a report. It would be an immense relief. His spirits rose. Driving was tricky; the worn treads of the tyres tended to skid, the road wound up and down the ghats, through tall loose scrub, but he did not miss seeing the shy jungle wanderers moving through the bush with their bows, tall lithe men like fauns with black hair over their eyes that were like grapes. They would stand a moment under a tree, and glide away back into the bush. There were villages now, and women of light olive skin beating their saris on the stones, rhythmically, and their breasts uncovered.

And then, just when he felt he was out of the lost zones, in the late afternoon, he came down a long sandy track through cactus to a deep and wide river at which the road ended. A gipsy tribe was fording it and he watched them to gauge the depth of the river. The little mules, demure as mice, kicked up against the current, nostrils too near the water to neigh; the camels followed the halter, stately as bishops, picking their calm way. The babies sat on their parents' heads, the women unwound their saris and put them in a bundle on their crowns, the water touched their breasts. And Beale pushed his truck into bottom gear and nosed her cautiously into the stream. Midway across the brown tide swept up to his sparking plugs and the engine stopped. He knew at once that he was done for. The river came up in waves over the sideboards and his whole concern was that the boy inside would be getting wet. A gipsy waded past impersonally, leading two bright-eyed grey mules. Beale hailed him. He nodded and went on. Beale called out "Help!" The gipsies gathered on the far bank and discussed it. He waved and eventually three of them came wading out to him. He knew he must abandon the truck till a recovery section could be sent out to salvage it, but he must take his companion with him, naturally. When the gipsies reached him he pointed to the back of the truck, unlaced the tarpaulin and showed them the corpse. They nodded their heads gravely. Their faces were serious and hard. He contrived to show them what he wanted and when he climbed in they helped him intelligently to hoist the body out. They contrived to get it on to their heads, ducking down under the tailboard till their faces were submerged in the scum of the flood.

They carried him ashore that way, Beale following with his revolver and webbing. They held a conclave on the sand while the women wrung out their saris and the children crowded round the body. Beale stood in the centre of these lean outlandish men, not understanding a word. They talked excitedly, abruptly, looking at him and at the corpse. He fished his wallet out of his pocket and showed them a five-rupee note. He pointed to the track and to the mules. They nodded and came to some domestic agreement. One of them led a little mule down to the stream and they strapped a board across its bony moulting back, covering the board with sacking. Four of them lifted the body up and lashed it along the spar. Then they smiled at Beale, obviously asking for his approval of their skill. He nodded back and said "That's fine." The gipsies laid their panniers on the mules, the women wound their saris about their swarthy bodies, called their children, formed behind their men. The muleteer grinned and nodded his head to Beale. The caravanserai went forward across the sands. Beale turned back once to look at the truck, but he was too bloody tired and fed up to mind. It would stay there; it was settled in; if the floods rose it would disappear; if they fell so much the better. He couldn't help making a balls of it all. He had the body, that was one proof; they could find the truck if they came to look for it, that was the second proof. If they wanted an accident report they could wait. If they thought he was puddled they could sack him when they liked. What was it all about, anyway?

Stumbling up the track in the half-light among the ragged garish gipsies he gradually lost the stiff self-consciousness with which he had first approached them. He was thinking of a page near the beginning of a history book he had studied in the Sixth at school in 1939. About the barbarian migrations in pre- history; the Celts and Iberians, Goths and Vandals and Huns. Once Life had been nothing worth recording beyond the movements of people like these, camels and asses piled with the poor property of their days, panniers, rags, rope, gramm and dahl, lambs and kids too new to walk, barefooted, long-haired people rank with sweat, animals shivering with ticks, old women striving to keep up with the rest of the family. He kept away from the labouring old women, preferring the tall girls who walked under the primitive smooth heads of the camels. He kept his eye on the corpse, but he seemed comfortable enough. Except he was beginning to corrupt. There was a faint whiff of badness about him.... What did the gipsies do? They would burn him, perhaps, if the journey took too long. How many days to Baroda? The muleteer nodded his head and grinned.

Well, as long as he had the man's identity discs and paybook, he would be covered. He must have those... He slipped the identity discs over the wet blue head and matted hair and put them in his overall pocket. He would be all right now, even if they burned him... It would be a bigger fire than the one they had sat by and fed with twigs and talked about women together that night, how many nights ago?

He wished, though, that he knew where they were going. They only smiled and nodded when he asked. Maybe they weren't going anywhere much, except perhaps to some pasture, to some well.

The Reunion

In the afternoon the sun uncurls his sting as a scorpion its tail. Like the scorpion the sun is animate and animal and vicious, making for his habitat stones and dust. Out of the stones and dust here, now, emerge slowly roads, pavements, bazaar, hotels, railway station, car park, canteens, cinemas. Before crumbling under the uncurling tail of the sun they poise, pause for a century, containing people. Contain people who emerge, pirouette, incredible palaver and goings-on, poise, pause, revert. The hotel is in the middle of the town, at the crossroads, walled in, a taxi rank at its doors. Central, convenient, slovenly. British officers and white women lunching, damp fish, cold gravy on red beef, soiled white of the waiters, their bare feet stirring the dust. The rice was boiled to death to-day, the curry is watery, fetch the manager at once. The sweeper drives the fag-ends before him slowly with twig brush, bending dustily. The chowkeydar contemplates the shade with green eyes, the room boys lie on the inner pavement, smoking brown leaf, spitting red betel juice, eyes indolent with submerging consciousness. The violence of the sun makes inertia ominous. There must be violence, curled in the cracked stones perhaps. to sleep to dream, aye there's the rub. Like a jackdaw a child swoops on the shaking of table cloths and seizes a crust to allay the hardness in its shrunken belly. The beggar women, old timers, infamous, Lazarene, pester the emerging guests, bakshish, bakshish, rajah sahib, their bellies drawn tight as though with worry. A tonga driver becomes vociferous, demands more than the soldier will give, snatches, is pushed away. At noon an altercation, at night a fight, a knife. Wealth retires to its rooms, the high rank, the red tabs, the civil servant in lounge suit, the bourgeois with an emergency commission, sleep tickles them, washes out the sandpaper quality of their bustle, the hardness of their dubious currency. For two hours money withdraws itself from circulation.

Obviously brothers, the eyes at the tables said, considering the saturnine boyish faces of the two chatting amid close and tranquil silences, exchanging snaps and airletter-cards, smiling slowly, unaware of the eyes. Both boys, the one a captain with a limp, a loose mouth, devastating darling, so sulky, simply divine, I wonder who: the other raw, hair strong and ungroomed, little almond eyes, broad cheekbones, such very thick eyebrows, hunched shoulders, funny little private soldier, of course they say in England private soldiers can go anywhere, simply anywhere, Savoy, Berkeley — obviously brothers, that explains how it is. Sweet, rather. In the canteen, when one has to, sometimes some of them are really rather, you can't help but...but how nice for their mother to think, brothers together to-day.

"I didn't think I'd see any of the family again."

"What? Never again?"

"Maybe."

"You mustn't say that, kid."

"Only to you."

"Did you want to?"

"What? See you or Eunice or Mums again? I should say."

"I got so I didn't want to."

"But that's very bad for you."

"Oh yes, I know."

"What shall we do this afternoon?"

"Don't mind."

"Neither do I. Let's not do it, then."

"What?"

"Whatever we were going to do. Did you have a rough voyage? Was Durban O.K.?"

"The ship was terrible. For us. The officers were all right. Cabins, and a smashing dining saloon, menus in French; I saw them because we used to have Urdu classes in the saloon. What French! Petits pois Navarre, potage Henri Quatre. The barber's shop had a notice, 'Out Of Bounds To Third Class Passengers. Third Class Passengers May Make Purchases Through The Porthole.' The sea was lovely, though, and the stars. I slept on deck as soon as the sea turned blue."

"Yes, I know."

"The troop train was the next thing. It was waiting for us at Ballard Pier. Six days of it. No fans, wooden racks. I had a whole rack. There was a man wouldn't take off his boots for four days. We were on to him all the time. When he did take them off we made him put them on again till we got to a platform. You don't notice another smell on a platform."

"You had it raw."

"We had it tinned. Bully and biscuits for six days. If it had been an electric train we'd have had no tea, either. I enjoyed tea made from the engine boiler."

He's a little boy and he's a man; you can't tell his age any more than a tortoise's. The world has hit him. He's taking it, he's got a good stance, must have been there all the time. How we used to fight, hate each other, refuse to share things, he resenting having to wear out my suits while I had the new ones, he rejecting the opportunities, failing the exams, indifferent to jobs, capricious and wary of any gambits to tame him; me making the most of my luck, my few talents, finding out the short cuts, taking the jobs, playing tennis with the daughter, working when necessary, never looking too hard at anything, sham or lovely. Funny. He with a wife, a nice girl in the snaps he showed me, he with a child, how did it happen to him?

"Did your wife try to put Brylcreem on your hair?"

"No. Nor make a fighter pilot out of me."

"Does she like you as a private soldier?"

"She doesn't mind me. She might be uppish with you at first. You give that impression."

"Do I? Ha, ha, how bloody funny! Well, I earn five hundred and fifty a month."

"That's five hundred more than me. I can't get into my trousers with my shoes on."

"I've got some spare trousers."

"What? Wear your bloody cast-offs again? No, sir."

He's different. Sometimes he's the same, just for a flash, but he's changed. Deep deep down he's got some shrapnel in him. He's shy of it. I don't try to find it, but when I look I touch some iron in him with my eyes and I stop looking then. It isn't the thing for one's family to see. Mother would be worried. She'd think it was women, she'd be frightened, she'd be relieved to think it was Burma, the Japs, the limp. It's both. It's an animal, it's terror, it's having killed. I want to take his face in my hands. I suppose that's what women want to do. I wonder what his wound looks like. I won't like it when we're undressing. I used to hate Daddy's wound, the sucked-in holes cratering his thigh. Now he's got it. But Daddy never had any iron in him. That's what was so horrible about Daddy's wounds, because he was so gentle himself.

"Sometimes it's hard to tell which of us is which. It doesn't seem to matter which of us is which. I've never felt that before except with a woman."

Night comes with its moods indigo, enfolding the streets in its blues.

The man with the mongoose and the snakes in wicker baskets, and the man with the monkey, the drum, the patter of villages, both of them vacate their dry perches on the corner, giving way to the tongas, the footsteps, the lorry loads of troops coming in for the night, the brightly lit cafés and clubs, windowless, verandahed, cool. The tableaux of hunger lie grotesque on the sidewalks, the old women under the trees. The colonel shouts for the water- bearer, shouts in vain, rings the bell that won't ring, takes his trousers off and puts them on again. The brothers clean their teeth under the tap. The women behind drawn curtains powder and paint, considering a wardrobe of gowns. Only the hard-boiled have any tranquillity, know what they are about. The others don't know at all, haven't the faintest idea, are spiritually deserted, emotionally unstable, when they rub their eyes hard there are lights here, there, where, dancing lights beyond closed eyelids. There is such a thing as Nothing. To handle it requires considerable *savoir faire*.

"It's healing all right now. The M.O. in the hospital knows his stuff up there, he used to spend half his time flying to critical operations in Civvy Street. Pity to waste him out here."

"He's healing you. That isn't a waste."

"Oh, I don't know. Everything seems a waste out here."

"You talk great foolishness."

"I'm thirsty. Shall we have a peg?"

"Water's all right when you're thirsty. Your wound is a nicer one than Daddy's."

"His was a German one. This is Japanese. They're both pretty nasty. The mark of the beast. If I had a wife, would she like it?"

"It would purify her."

"You talk like a parson. Put some trousers on and let's eat."

The tawdry chandeliers suspend their cheap icicles over the frigid assembly. The eyes reconnoitre with the swift thrust and withdrawal of highly trained troops. Never leave your flank unprotected. Feel along the line for the weak point. Use the ground to give you the maximum cover and advantage, always go for the high ground, all's fair in love and war. In a society dominated by the military caste it is proper to make life conform to correct tactical principles. Lots of these boys are new from home. Emergency commissions; very few regulars; surprising how quickly they settle down. Get to know the ropes, join the club as temporary members, get invited to parties, hullo stranger, what have you got to offer? Nothing? But I couldn't. It isn't worth it. I ask you. Is it? Yes, for you maybe. Well, just for you, then. Look, there are those two again. The brothers. Of course the troops don't settle down quite so easily. There are so many of them and so little for them to do. Things weren't intended for them, unfortunately. It's a shame how they get rooked by these hawkers; I'm sure they send some awful trash to their wives; and they can't afford it, I'm sure. I wonder how much they get. How much does a soldier get, George? God, I don't know. Ten rupees a week, something like that. Look at that kid's khaki drill. Like drainpipes. That's what you call issue trousers, isn't it, George? We really must have a couple of them up to Christmas dinner this year. Find two nice ones for me, George, I'd simply love it.

"You don't tell me much about your baby."

"You don't tell me much about Burma, either."

"You'll find out about Burma in good time."

"So will you about a baby."

"Not much! My leg will be all right in two months. I'll be back before the dry weather comes. I can pull strings. I'll get back to the regiment, before they go in again."

"Do you want to?"

"What have one's personal wants got to do with it?"

"Pretty well everything. You're daring yourself to go back."

"Shut up. Don't catechise me."

"Well, you are. Remember how we were terrified of diving from the Black Rock in Carris Bay and when you'd dived how you used to swagger."

"It's different now. Look at that woman just coming in. The one in velvet. She's clinical. She's arithmetic. She adds up lots of little sums, calculates other people's interest and lives on it. If there's a difference she takes it away."

On the troopship the air stank with the bottoms of many lungs, stenches hung over men's feet, the oaths stank of lechery, you couldn't move; when she rolled there was a sick smell. This country has some smells too. In the troop train it was too hard to mind very much, time got lost, there were platforms and beggars and cripples. I wonder whether he'll tell me what happened in Burma. I don't think he will. I'll be off at first light to-morrow, to catch that early train. I hope I wake. Sleeping on a spring mattress between sheets for the first time since I slept with Eunice on embarkation leave, perhaps I'll over sleep. Be on the duff when I get back. Mustn't be on the duff, don't like justice one bit. Mark time, halt, left turn. While on active service returning late from short leave. I wish he'd tell me about Burma.

"Look at those two over there. I know the man. He's a man who hates sleeping by himself. Bad soldiering that. I bet they'll come in late for breakfast and he'll bully the waiter with the big sahib act till he gets some bacon and eggs. I wonder where he met her. She looks rather nice, doesn't she? He's got a loud voice, can you hear him? She doesn't like loud voices. I like that red in her hair."

"Oh I forgot. Mother said if I met you I was to give you this."

The boy put a pure white seashell on the table, on the soiled cloth under the bruised flowers, a seashell. His elder brother looked at it, looked at it, looked harder at it than he looked at most things, put out his hand and softly stroked it. "You must have been very careful with it, not to break it," he said.

"Mother said if I met you I was to give it to you."

The elder boy stroked it with his long middle finger, softly caressed it, let his finger stay on it.

"Hallo, Eric. Fancy meeting you here," a woman's voice broke into his dream, and he jerked himself up and he had a grin on his face.

"Hallo, Pamela," he said. "Just fancy. This is my brother. Pamela, Vincent." The younger boy hardly noticed her at all, because the little seashell was crushed under his brother's finger, it crumbled on the soiled cloth, and he was frightened by it.

He went to sleep as soon as he slid his naked body between the delicious sheets.

Now he is asleep and my thoughts do not harm him, he's oblivious to them now. He isn't offended when I admit that it wasn't real, we didn't really meet, I didn't respond, didn't say with my heart, "This is my kid brother." I hope he enjoyed it, I think he did. He wasn't self-conscious of his rough misfitting trousers and shirt any more than of his ungroomed hair. Some gentleness in his nature sees injustices and inequalities as if they were human maladjustments, the tragedy of a bad marriage, not to be condemned. It's comforting when he talks in his sleep, in this vast darkness. It's a warm night, yet there's always this coldness in me, this lurking. Just past the village above Pegu it was quiet, the bamboo copse utterly still, the bodies of the Japanese and white men motionless, dead, done with. Violence back in its earth, under the surface, lying doggo, waiting for a step, a jerk, the renewal of itself in movement, a cryptic shot, a puff of smoke, a fool. We will make good the clearing. Orders. Number one section right flanking, number two section fire section. I will go with number one section. I crushed the seashell under my finger. It crumbled. I hardly pressed it at all. I didn't think I'd see him again. When I wake he'll be going. What chance does he stand? What does it mean to *him*?

The clock has chimed twelve, the clock has chimed one, the clock has chimed two. For two hours the stag party has been going on in the room on the right. They've been singing for two hours now. I can't settle down, I can't sleep, life is being wasted in me, going round and round on its empty repetitive journeys, avoiding the encounter, identifying itself with nothing, avoiding love, refusing socialism, rejecting a better world because my self is worse, worse, worse, but doesn't matter, my self doesn't matter, it wasn't because I wanted to, it was bound to be hell, I couldn't, I had to, if only they'd stop singing. It's an hour since they shouted at the manager when he asked them to make less noise, and threw him out with the clatter of tables and the angry sound of feet and fists, calling his skin black, aware of their whiteness, making me worse, worse, worse. It's a jolly good show and I say, I take a dim view of that bloody little chichi trying to turn us out. Kick him in the teeth next time. Aye, aye, aye, I love you ve-e-e-ry much. There'll always be an England. Blue-birds over the cliffs of Dover. Say that everything is still O.K. dear. I'll be loving you always. Red, white and blue, what does it mean to you? Who could ask for more in sleepy valley?

He could have shot me, but he didn't. All the time I was crossing the clearing he could have got me with his pistol. But he didn't. He waited until I was right by him, till he could make his magnificent thrust. Then he leapt out of the brake and his sword was raised above his head.

So near me I couldn't miss. I've never hit anything with my pistol, except him. It was absurd. Just the reflex action of my trigger finger, before I thought about it, before I screamed. I wish I hadn't screamed.

I'll get up and stop them singing. If I push the narrow door open from the verandah, just one leaf of the door, and switch the light off, the switch is by the door the same as in this room, and kick the table over and get out of the door, I can belt the first one in the teeth as he comes out, I should be able to get away, if I put my tennis shoes on. He'd still be sleeping when I came back. He wouldn't know. It won't disturb him at all...

The fools! They looked at me with their inane grinning faces, in the fug among the fag-ends and the glasses in the ugly room. And I kicked and I hit. My knuckles are burning and wet. It's cold in pyjamas. I'm shivering. Nobody saw me dive into these palms. They're scared of me. They're arguing. They're nothing. I used to think: If they catch me, I'm done for. If they catch me... They... They... But he waited for me with his sword and it was too late. It was simple. And the thing is that you must be the first. Get him first. Otherwise keep away.

What are they doing? Creeping along the verandah...maybe they're going to bash open the door of the lovers... *They've gone into our room.* One with a torch, one with a lathi.

They're beating up my brother. Oh God, oh God, they got him first. He wasn't awake, was he, he wasn't aware of what goes on in the world. Listen, I'm screaming again... I'll kill... I'll kill. Kill now. Kill.

The whole hotel wakes because it is its business, but the world does not wake because another hotel brawl is none of its business and there are plenty of officials and an established procedure for settling that sort of thing, to-morrow and to-morrow and to-morrow.

II

from THE BOVIAN

The Death of Monga

"Cheep-a-chuk, cheep-a-chuk," came a sweet little chirrup from amongst the blooming beauty of the honeysuckle. "Cheep-a-chuk, cheep-a-chuk," there it was again, further down the hedge now. "Cheep-a-chuk, cheep-a-chuk," came another trolling burst, and out of the interwoven branches of the weeping willow, hanging melancholily over the lazy little stream, a fluttering bundle of bright blue and red feathers scrambled to the highest twig. There it crouched up against the green leaves, nestling against the moss-grown branches, while ever and anon, with head proudly uplifted and little ruffled breast expanded, it filled the air with its glorious, crooning song, preening its feathers the while. "Cheep-a-chuk," it went, "cheep-a-chuk," and the gipsy and his son, lying half concealed amongst the sedges which grew in stately profusion along the bank of the rivulet, smiled a crafty smile, and into those narrow eyes crept a vicious gleam of anticipation.

All unaware of the nearness of his danger, the little stranger sent his joy, full-throated, down the scented breeze, and old Groat the heron, immovable as a statue as he perched one-legged over the crystal pool, beneath whose mossy stones and beauteous water-lilies the trout had fled in terror at the sight of that ominious figure on the brink, winked his eyes and almost imperceptibly ruffled the feathers at the nape of his neck as if he, too, were intoxicated with those fairy notes.

The loud booming of the bittern down by his nest in the solitude of the marshes silenced the little songster for a moment, for he was unaccustomed to the raucous song of the big bird as he hailed his mate, now perched at his side with a trout in her beak. Overhead, hanging immovable in the sunny blueness of the heavens, his two wings outstretched as if to gain more support, a kestrel hawk was watching with his cruel eye the drama that was being enacted below.

Suddenly his keen eye espied a little brown creature hopping about on the top of the bluff, about a mile from the stream, now hidden amongst the long grass, now jumping free and lying for a moment in the warm sunshine, content to listen to the age-old song of the breeze as it whispered through the dead leaves. Silently, without effort, the kestrel swung over and, making a wide circuit, swooped down on the unsuspecting animal, swift and sure as grim death itself. A frightened, terrified squeak from a broken little heart and all was over. The kestrel made off to his nest up on the cliffs, where his mate was solemnly sitting on the six reddish-brown eggs, lying haphazard amidst the bundle of twigs which served them for a nest. Landing on the rough ledge with strong leisured beats, he quietly and methodically ripped off the little buck rabbit's head, and the two fierce birds of prey fell to gorging on the little creature's still warm entrails. Five minutes later he was once more suspended in his old place, scanning the landscape with greedy eye, but the rabbits had learnt their lesson for the present.

All the time the gipsy, his brown, dirty face pressed close against the loamy earth, his callous bitter eyes glinting dangerously in the rays of the sun, was quietly moving on, inch by inch, foot by foot, never making a sound, never snapping a single twig, like some venomous snake, towards the hedge, where a certain willow was sprayed with a scented mass of honeysuckle. Enthroned at its very top, a little bird was perched, basking in the cheering warmth of the late afternoon, his dainty head cocked to one side as he gazed with wondering eyes at old Groat as his long razor-bill suddenly pierced the waters, returning immediately with a trout transfixed, still vainly wriggling.

Monga — for that was its name — was a little stranger bird who had fled across the sea from the sun-baked plains of Spain during the winter, with a band of fellow-companions. They had seen the swallows departing in hundreds, and had followed them to find where they were going. But the swiftly-flying birds soon left them behind, and Monga and his little friends had found themselves in the middle of a deep blue sea which sparkled and rolled in the rays of the sun. They could see no change on any side, nothing but endless stretches of this queer, beautiful land which moved and danced. They recognised the sun, but the rolling white horses tickled their fancy, and a score of them flew down to rest on its bosom. They never rose again, for there were hordes of greedy fish waiting under the treacherous surface, and, frightened and very, very tired, Monga and his fellows flew on wary and distracted, where they knew not, only on and ever on. Gradually the weaker dropped behind and fluttered half-resisting into the ocean, while others perished when they flew full-tilt into the blinding glare of the Lizard, falling back on to the cruel, wave-tormented rocks, blinded, battered, dazed. When at length they came in sight of a long line of sunny cliffs, their white sides crowned with grassy meads, only a few sorry little creatures remained of the gorgeous, feathered throng that had set out from Spain on that illfated voyage.

But the sight of this new land, its green grass forming an inviting luscious carpet for them, its little wooden dingles with anemones and delicate snowdrops ringing the little streams, which always came bubbling up in the centre, its twisting hedgerows glorious with their spring attire of budding ashes and rustling little flowers, violets, daisies, primroses, and many other fragile blooms, was ample recompense for all the toil they had undergone. Like Christian after climbing Hill Difficulty, Monga and his little friends, weary and tired, with their gaudy plumage sorely bedraggled and upset, for a few days enjoyed a well-earned rest. While, heedless of all else, they whiled away the time in innocent song, two cruel weasels, hunting around for food, came upon them, and with catlike bounds snapped two frail necks and tore open two faintly-quivering breasts. Another, fascinated by the stare of a venomous adder, curled motionless round the fork of an alder, allowed itself to be caught without any effort. The kestrel had carried off half-a-dozen to its ledge above the sand dunes, until finally Monga only was left. Not for him to mourn over his lost comrades; not for him to think with sad heart of the little companions who had gone from him. He still roamed at large over the hedgerows and glittering, gleaming cornfields. Sometimes he would stare out across the sea to where a graceful yacht, its white sail bellying in the wind, was bowling over the gentle swell like a stately swan in its native reaches. But now, with Autumn drawing to a close, his days of freedom were well-nigh over. Even as he hopped along the top of the hedgerow, still trilling his glad song, "Cheep-a-chuk," a cruel noose descended over his proud head, and, with a little frightened gasp, Monga, the last of his race, the pride of his land, fell from his lofty seat. With a smile of satisfaction on his harsh features the gipsy sprang up and dashed across the brook to the insignificant little figure, which dangled limply at the end of a long wire noose. Old Groat, alarmed at the unprecedented noise, rose from his pool and flapped his way with slow beating wings across the

long stretches of marsh before him. The kestrel slowly swung over
and sailed easily along the silent miles of coast, while the cliff rabbits,
seeing the ominous shadow above them, scurried for safety to their
burrows. And, as the gipsy hurried off through the hedges to his van,
where a rudely constructed bird cage was waiting on the door, out of
the gloaming came the hollow boom of the bittern, as, down by his
lonely nest, deep in the marshes, he warned off the weasel that had
scurried over his path. The last rays of the setting sun were glinting
on the golden sea and lighting up the sails of the little smack which
cruised about in the offing, when the gipsy in his tent spat forth a
venomous oath, for Monga, the proud, the beautiful, was dead.
There was no need for a cage!
(*1930*)

The Tale of a Dwarf

The world was a glitter of lights and vulgar music. The crowded throng jostled roughly between the stalls, threading the roundabouts and swings with noisy clamour. The gondolas had just started the round and the pagan tongues of the huge organ shook the black night with a paean of noise that harmonised strangely with the gay scene. Men on the verge of ruin threw their last pennies at the coconuts with careless abandon; women who had left their children, uncared for, in the cold darkness of a cheerless home, shouted hysterically and hurried on from booth to booth, tossed from side to side, irresponsible queens in an unreal world. Little children stared up in mute awe at the swinging blaze of lights, the swiftly revolving horses, and the red-faced gipsy, who cried out from a point of vantage, "This way, ladies and gen'l'men; this way to Madame Vobansky, the internationally famed clairevoyante." The ringed booths, lit up with dazzling bulbs, were exposing their attractions to a spendthrift mob, which surged on from tent to tent like a huge moth ringing the glinting candelabra. The big crowd on the right, behind the swings, was laughing at the drunken efforts of a middle-aged man, hurling wooden balls at the leering row of coconuts, dancing elusively in his fuddled vision. "'Ard luck, sir, 'ard luck. Come on, sir, try agen, try agen," rang out the raucous voice of the grimy attendant, and the poor fellow threw and missed again. Next door to the coconut stalls, the crash of bottles bespoke men wreaking paltry vengeance at "twopence a bottle, no change." Further down, the pennies were rolling on to studded tables, while every now and then a red light shone and money was handed back.

High up on a shaky platform a timid, berobed negro was advertising the presence of the "African Village — a modern-mir'kle-fust-time-shown-fo'-the-li'l-price-of-six-pence," by repeatedly clanging a camouflaged saucepan and dancing a fiery war song. And all the time the lights whirled round and round faster and faster, shooting up clear pencils of light into the blackness, now lighting up the phantom image of a passing crow, now startling the brooding hells which surely must have hemmed in the laughing arena of tragedy below. The roundabouts clanged fierce warning, the gondolas dashed up and down, up and down; the Gothic faces that started out from the hub of ringed flame beat out a steady wild chant; the crowd cheered and jostled, the gypsy caretakers, grimier and sweatier than before, bellowed their encouragements; the lights dashed round and round. Away they went in a mad rush, whizzing through the dark, laughing at the brazen hooters and the screaming throng. Away they ran, chasing each other and passing each other; faster and faster as the night sped on, blending into one mad haze of lightning; green chasing red, red chasing green; blue fleeing from the raging purple; yellow crying terror-struck at the cruel rush of purple. God! what are they doing? Spirits of magic and awe, look at them! Shut your eyes, shut your eyes — they are evil, cruel, heartless. God! Run home to your houses, lock your doors, shut out the lights that call and kill! Can you not see them? Can you not hear the mad cry?

> "Death, Chaos, and Night
> From the sound of our flight
> Shall flee, like mist from a tempest's might."

Can you not feel them, blinding your eyes, haunting your brain, shaking your senses, exulting with heathen blare? Can you not? Round they dash and round; faster, ever faster; swifter than the winds of heaven, swifter than the angels of Death. Are they the angels of Death? Like the rout of Bacchus, like the sinner fleeing from the Judgment... Mad... Fierce... Blinding... Harsh... Insensate....

*****

The Furies have fled; the lights are quenched. The crowd has straggled home. Night, pitch-black, ineffable night, shrouds the clustered caravans, the canvas stalls, and the sentinel booths. Here and there a dim light still flickers, accentuating the darkness and the silence. Out of the shadows a dog barks fiercely, as if straining after sights not meet for man to see. The spirits of night are abroad; they have whispered "Silence"; all is quiet as the grave. The spirits of night and futurity are thronging phosphorescent, intangible over the empty space; are marshalling their unseen ranks outside the door of a tiny wagon; are crowding the roof and crowding the window, crowding the steps and crowding the lattice, while on the chimney a shrieking owl is crying a message of horror, two baleful green eyes standing in a sea of blackness. The silence is unbearable, agonising. It is battering against the door and striking against the window. It is moving restlessly in the opaque unknown. It is the silence of death, of the tomb of Pharaoh. Suddenly a wild prayer breaks the stillness, shuffling the invisible ranks outside, dispersing them in the mists of night, the wraiths of the morning, leaving the little drama inside to be carried to its end.

On the little wooden stool inside sat a human figure, like a small child, hugging the darkness, indistinct and fantastic in the fitful light of the little stove. Hunched up as he sat, in the gloom, distorted by a hundred quips of light and shade; a creature of angles and mystery as he rocked to and fro in silent misery, beating a ceaseless echoing tattoo on the unseen floorboards. Felix the dwarf he was, price 2d. for the fairgoer. "Felix means happy," he thought, eyes brimming with tears of irony. Every night he had stood on a stool of straw in the evil-smelling booth while a vulgar, ignorant crowd looked their two-penn'orth at him and mumbled some hideous joke to each other. Every five minutes some boor had shouted across "'Ullo, Carnera," at which toothless old men and wrinkled old busybodies had nudged each other familiarly and laughed loudly or smiled a condescending smile, as much as to say, "Poor little feller." Every night, for three years, he had wiped back the tears and steeled his frame as Volmar Jackson, his "owner," had cried out, "Fearless Felix, ladies twen'y-three year ol', twen'y-three hinches 'igh, twen'y-three pun's 'eavy — orl for tuppens." He had been twenty-three years old when Volmar first captured him from his home in the Apennines — he was still twenty-three as far as the showmen were concerned. He had refused at first to expose his ugliness to the eyes of every town, for he still remembered his boyhood, passed away from the rest of the race of man among the hills and dales of his country home, where he had been a constant and eager companion of rabbits and thrushes, friend of everything defenceless as himself. Thus he was brought across Europe, still a friend of the wild, still sharing that timid reticence which characterises the harmless creatures that scamper from the approach of man, still burning with shame and Herculean indignation as he sat on his stool and muttered "Mon Dieu" under his breath. Every night, for three years, he had humoured those he would have killed; cried "Pass along, please," in broken English, seared countenance set in expressionless smile, as gluttons fed their glassy eyes on his puny frame. And every night a new pain was added to his mutilated soul as new eyes and new faces stared at him and new voices cracked the age-old joke.

Lately, the life had become unbearable; he was shrinking and dying slowly, quietly, in this flurry of hot air and festering disease. He slept but little in his caravan; sleep to him was no gentle balm, conjuring up, as it did, grim visions of a dying dwarf, acting his humiliation in the centre of a crowded stall. And sometimes, when in the quiet of midnight he lay back and thought, the remembrance of the days of yore, of kind deeds and happy words, of feeding the rabbits with lettuce and tickling the playful cubs of the vixen of the Black Peak, of lying in the sunny brake, half-asleep under the blue warmth of an Italian sky, came back to him and shook his soul with vain longing.

The lights, too, had entered his heart, leading him on with purple riot to thoughts of liberty and fierce deeds of night. They were hardening, alluring him, calling him to the freedom of death, these devils in tinsel. "Mother of God," he cried, "show me the way of light." But in the stillness of the night was no answering cry, no soft assurance; only the black spirits of the future crept nearer and nearer, listening...listening... The loud noise of the evening, the shouting mob, and the fiercely-pealing drum, the organs that thundered and rattled and roared were all creeping in a jumble through his heart, deranging him, maddening him, seducing him.

"Mother of God," he whispered, "is there no path of life? Son of God, is there no goodness in life?" A long silence and then a long drawn cry of joy. "God of Gods, I have heard... I am coming." And the spirits stood up and chuckled like fiends stretching their skinny talons and chanting a siren song. The door was dashed open; the little dwarf came out, straight into the midst of the ghastly throng, oblivious of all but the vision of God that he followed. And the heavens opened up and the moon shone a pale beam of gold through the murky clouds. A cock crew and the spirits of blackness rose and hovered over the little figure as he stepped quickly through the solitude of the morning twilight with eyes and hands uplifted. "Son of God, I am coming.... Ah, yes to Thy bosom, God of Gods.... I am tired and fain would sleep." On he stumbled over the fields, careless of himself, chattering a broken prayer, while the spirits melted and faded into the sunrise.

*****

His body was found, floating in a little reach of the river, nestled against the bank, and kissed by a sheaf of honeysuckle. A thrush was singing on a tree near by; the grass was bright and green. A peaceful look, as of one who has seen and is happy, was spread over his countenance, and the lines of worry were smooth.

That night, the lights raced round again and the crowd jostled, but the spirits of the dark were absent, satiated. One little booth, too, was empty and cold.

(*1931*)

The End of the Hunt

The baying of many hounds, the drumming of many hoofs, the cracking of many whips, and the excited shouts of many human beings were the sounds that filled the big red fox with alarm and dismay, as she basked in the hot rays of the sun amongst the hillside gorse. Crouching breathless on her belly, panting, her heart beating, she strove to hide herself among the brown bracken which littered the clearing. At her feet lay the bloody remains of a farmyard fowl, snatched from the hen-coop in the grey of the dawn, when all slept and the dog was dozing on the end of his chain. A frightened blackbird was crying from its vantage point at the top of a clump of gorse, and up in the azure blue of the sky a pair of larks, almost invisible against the cloudless heavens, sang out their glad welcome to the little band of red-coated figures, even at that moment crashing through the yielding ferns. The hounds, led by the gaunt, scarred Wolf-Fang, their noses in the air, their tails streaming out behind them, gave full-throated warning as they dashed forward madly, springing with easy, effortless bounds over the ferns to where, crouching down in the gorse, paralysed with terror, Redshanks, the crafty, lay grovelling.

Suddenly the grim face, the slavering jaws of Wolf-Fang loomed up over the thicket, his fangs bared, his lolling tongue drawn back, his one eye fixed with a leer of gloating vengeance. The sight of that nightmare vision aroused the hunted creature's numbed senses with a rude jerk. With a startled, gasping yelp she lept to her feet and with a lithe bound cleared the surrounding foliage. An excited shout from the red-coated huntsmen met the appearance of the great red shape, and with the hounds baying in front of them and the silver spurs pricking their heaving flanks the horses bounded forward in their chase, hindered now by no restraining bit.

Redshanks was a well-known figure in this land of farms and wolds; feared at every farmyard, uncaught by all the cunning traps which despairing poultry- owners had invented — and uncaught as yet by the most famous pack in the South Countree. Wolf-Fang, it is true, had once come to grips with her when he found her prowling around in a deserted sheep-fold, but she had got away after tearing out his eye with an angry, snarling snap. Thus it was that the old hound, killer of more foxes than any other dog in the pack, leader of a hundred chases, first in at the end of a hundred bloody deaths, had more to get than just another notch in his huge tally.

Now they were out on the moorland, racing across the uneven surface, the fox, straining to draw away, her eyes fixed in a fury of concentration at the wood upon the hill where lay her den and where, perhaps, three pretty little cubs gambolled about in heedless unconcern — the hounds bunched together, some dozen yards behind Wolf-Fang. The scarred leader, with something of the wolf hidden in his nature, raced on with a look of savage anticipation in his eyes, now gaining a yard, now losing a foot, ever following the fleeting shape that skimmed the heather in unfaltering flight. Over the crest of the hill they rushed. Redshanks, panting and trembling, gradually gave ground to the eager pack, still baying their terrifying war-song as they drew nearer to their prey. Down the valley they raced, fleet as the wind, the brown heather dotted here and there with the panting horses and their excited riders.

In the river at the bottom of the vale Redshanks attempted to outwit her pursuers. She still held a lead of about fifty yards from Wolf-Fang, who had now far outpaced the rest of the pack — for he had an eye to revenge. Sliding, slipping down the bank, the red creature, her eyes expressing the terror of a hunted animal, her mouth foaming and quivering, her sides heaving madly, dived into the water and paddled out to mid-stream. In the middle of the current lay a big rock, breaking the force of the stream and forming a patch of smooth water behind it. To this Redshanks scrambled and, crouching up to the stone, her body concealed under the surface except for her snout, waited while the hounds came baying up, slipped into the water, splashed over to the other side and eagerly sought the new scent. Up and down the bank they raced, whining and whimpering, now wading into the water, now running a short way up the slopes. But nowhere could they find any sign of the enemy. Suddenly there was a yelp from the middle of the stream, a churning of water behind the rock, and Redshanks involuntarily cried out as a rat bit into her leg. All along the bank the hounds were running, while the horsemen had drawn up on the other side. Suddenly she shook off the rat and scrambled to the top of the rock. By this time the hounds had all taken to the water and, seizing her opportunity, she sprang right over their heads and set off at a limping run up the steep hillside and over the top. Baying with chagrin, the pack followed now a hundred yards behind. Wolf-Fang, however, had stayed on the bank only a dozen yards from where the fox had lurked, and when they vanished over the edge the big hound was only a yard behind his enemy. Plucking up courage at the nearness of the fiend behind her, Redshanks dashed forward with renewed vigour, over the hedges and bushes, doubling round the big stone walls, slipping to one side and darting off in a new direction. But, try as she might, the nigh-exhausted fox could not shake off the one-eyed hound gliding along ever at her flanks. Up the steep slope, crashing through the brambles on the hill-top, on they ran with unabated speed, with the rest of the field straggling at the bottom. Right on top of the hill was the big Star Rock, the only place of safety for Redshanks, where her three little cubs were querulously calling for food. Nearer and nearer they got to the rock and it seemed that the fox might reach it in time but, when only a dozen yards off, Redshanks slipped. Wolf-Fang leaped, landing fairly on the poor creature's shoulders. Turning, snarling, the fox managed to shake its heavier opponent off, only to be attacked again immediately. Now the hound had a grip round her throat and was slowly getting nearer and nearer the vital jugular. With a snarl of anger, Redshanks kicked up her back foot and two long claws ripped open the furry stomach of the hound.... When the hunt came over the hill they found the two still locked together motionless, their eyes set in a glassy stare, the hound's teeth fixed in an unbreakable hold on the other's throat. The huntsmen quickly severed the brush, the feet, the mask, and, as the mournful horn sounded the mort to the gentle heavens, an almost imperceptible shiver shook the dead hound's body, while from the hole at the foot of the rock a frightened little wailing broke the momentary quiet.

"Fetch the spades and hurry up about it...," shouted the chief huntsman.

(1931)

from THE DRAGON

"If Such be Nature's Holy Plan...."

The day had just broken, amid a flurry of rain. A cold, cruel wind was scurrying in and out of the dripping sheds and mangers, slashing wildly at the drab, leafless drawn trees, tormenting with its bitter sallies the huddled poultry roosting on a plough drawn up in the shelter of a wet, crumbling wall. The wind came from the sea, which could be heard — if any there were to hear in such a place — crashing upon the beach and dragging the screaming shingle into its white mouth, crashing again — a thunderous roar from down the valley. The hedges were naked and bowed, away from the sea, like rows of patient, bent, old men turning their backs to the beat of wind and water. Little streams swirled uncertainly along the muddy cart-track that went from the yard on a mysterious expedition to the big house on the hill. Low down over the thatched roof of the farm, black clouds, ominous, imponderable, cast a cold twilight hue over the country.

The rain hung back for a moment and a man came out from the farmhouse, climbed the steps outside the door and splashed carelessly through the muddy space separating him from the cowshed. He walked with a slight limp, accentuated by his shambling gait, his loose arms, his bowed head and shoulders. His clothes were torn and mud-bespattered. He seemed to have no pride of person, and his thin, white hair, unshaved, bony face, loose fleshless mouth and protruding teeth were sufficient to make a casual spectator turn away at his sullen stare. Such as he was, he entered the cowshed and lighting a storm lantern that lay on a rough ledge, passed the stalls wherein four brown cattle slept, and halted by the last stall, where a white cow lay quietly on its side, suckling a new-born calf, but a few hours old. He bent down and examined the cow tenderly. He was a cruel master at most times, especially to the pigs, whose lazy life enraged him, but now his rough fingers were sensitive and his rocky grey eyes softer than their wont. A swirl of wind and rain through the broken window pane extinguished his lamp. He swore softly. How could the poor cow live when the world was so forbidding? Cold and bleak and unsmiling world. There was something symbolic in the malice of the wind this morning. Everyone whispering scandal, everyone trying to blow their neighbour's light out. All the farm kitchens gossiping for all they were worth. Poor little calf, coming in to such a world. And the white cow a-dying — more bad debts, more sweat of the brow, more pinching and saving until the harvest. He relit the lamp and as he fixed it to an over hanging beam he felt a swift throb of pain in his stomach that made him quiver and perspire coldly. What else could a man expect, working in winter rains and frosts and sleets. Winter — the sulky beast! Still, he wasn't going to spend ten precious shillings on a doctor. He'd worked hard for his money.

The cow half rose to her feet, but suddenly fell back, its limbs shaking strangely. There was froth on its jaw and terror in its eyes. His bony hand caressed the helpless, imploring face. Fancy something asking for his protection! After the cow had died he wrapped the calf in some old sacking, tucked it under his arm and shambled clumsily from the shed. A whisk of rain in his face — blast them all, cottagers, countryside, winter, God to boot, if He liked. Why couldn't they let his best milker grow strong again? They were always like that — the whole universe was against him. Even the old woman living in the nearest cottage, who was pampered by all the folk around, hated him. What had he done then? Only little things. He remembered quarrelling with her over the profits from garaging the cars of summer trippers. And it was the same with the others — miserable little quarrels. Well, he could get on well enough without them. He must stop his blackhaired daughter Millie, with her dancing eyes, from courting that slick-tongued, nice-mannered schoolmaster fellow. Education! What's the good of that. For all the big words and lovely ideas he'd been putting into Millie's head, he couldn't thatch a stack, or build a hedge or relieve the sow of her farrow. He glowered at the rain-soaked sheds and the mist-blurred landscape. The pain caught hold of him again and twisted him. That was like Winter, no relenting, no gentleness. He'd be glad to wash his hands of the world.

★★★★★

The swirling rains of winter have given suck to long fields of green, green grass, to darker green of gorse and to its gay yellow. The snow has melted from the meadows and left the grass magic with blue and yellow iris flowers. The woods are donning a gay green kirtle, the brushwood is springing and the yew trees cast their buds. Here and there among the trees the daffadowndilly, queen of the spring, holds her dewy cup of yellow in a slender green hand. Everything is pulsating with life. The stream prattles energetically, hurrying to meet the leaping, rolling, foamflecked, merry sea. Fat trout play in the muddy water and in every tree, in every hedge, in amongst the grasses, in reeds beside the river, the birds are building their nests, undisturbed, preparatory to performing the age-old miracle of laying eggs and hatching their featherlings.

Sitting on the hill top, overlooking the sand-fringed sea, and the twisting green valley flanked with woods and dotted with cottages, the young schoolmaster watched the spring beauty of Millie. "Look at the colours to-day," he said. "Light green meadow, dark ferns and the blue patches in the sea. And there's a harmony and life about it, too. I believe the valley could sing if we weren't here."

Millie did not answer.

"One of the farm kiddies told me yesterday she saw seven green fairies, with long pointed hats, in the wood yesterday," he laughed. "I wish I could catch a glimpse of them," he added, as if to himself.

Without taking her eyes off the meadow, Millie said, "I've seen them too, long ago, though — dancing around a big gold mushroom down in those bullrushes."

"You're a little mystic, aren't you? Wait till you hear fairies on the wireless, proud lady. Just turn on a switch and lo! Strange voices and fairy strains from out of the Land of Nod," he countered.

"Yes, and they sell wireless sets in prosaic old shops, don't they? And if you're poor you can't buy one! No, you can let the world run away from my little valley. And those people who come here in their cars, with their gramophones and their silly khaki trousers, who ask us questions as if we're curiosities, and give father a shilling — -"

"Look at those cows down there," he interrupted, inconsequently, "don't they look real brown pixies lazing in the grass?"

"Yes," she said, slowly. "But they don't send pixies to the slaughter house."

"Look here, my good woman," he said, "you're getting a horrible cynic. And on a day like this! You must leave your father — because he's to blame — and marry me and off we'll go to see the Queen."

She was silent for a while and then said: "You must wait here till father dies, if you want me. Perhaps by then you'll have seen a field mouse twittering in the corn, or a badger over in the valley, or a big white owl floating after little crawling things."

"That's no answer," he said. "You can tease me as much as you like, but I'll get a promise from you." She shook her head: "Father hates you. He's ill and he's poor and he can't bear seeing youngsters enjoying the life that has slipped past him before he was aware of it. That's why he's as bitter in spring as he is in winter, and I suppose it's why he makes me work among the pigs when he catches me looking for you on the hill side."

"I suppose there's bitter rust in his soul," he said, as if to himself. "Old and at the fag end of life, while others are on the threshold of long days of beauty and happiness. A prisoner in his own body, and impotent to change his prison. But you mustn't let him wither your happiness — 'old time is still aflying.' "

"He thinks there's nothing but malice in life," she said, "and if I were to betray him, he wouldn't have a shred of faith left. So I can't leave him yet. But I know Nature will right things."

"Even though she's 'red in tooth and claw'?" he asked. "Even though," she said.

The young man clasped her hand and appeared about to entreat her further when she suddenly turned and he felt her hand stiffen. He followed her gaze into the valley. A long-limbed man, dressed in the remains of black trousers and waistcoat and a collarless coarse-flannel shirt, was shouting in an impatient, guttural voice at the reluctant cows and striking them with a hazel switch. They lumbered to their feet and started in a line for the gate. He followed them, shambling through the rushes, one hand clasped to his side, as if he was in pain.

"There he goes, your poor father," said the man on the hilltop to the girl who looked into the valley, "driving my little brown pixies away — making miserable realities of all my lovely dreams."

★★★★★

The threshing machine was in the farm yard. The big engine, with its racing wheels and running belts and its brightly painted funnel, was beating out a steady, incessant throbbing. The men of all the valley, from the big farm near the main road to the last farm on the hill side above this very yard, were busy, despite the hot weather.

Some were pitching the corn from the ricks to the ground. Others were lifting it in big sheaves on pitchforks with shining handles, smooth with constant use, to the men on the board of the thresher. Yet others were shovelling away the earless stems thrown out of the machine or substituting empty sacks for the sacksful of coarse flour, which they carried off to an old out house. The young schoolmaster watching at the gate saw a farmer occasionally look suspiciously at the insatiable noisy monster that for the past week had been thundering in every farm yard. Otherwise there was little notice taken of the intrusion of this mechanical apparition into the shrine of old simple customs. Millie was busy handing bread and cheese to the perspiring workers and the dark mechanic who alone presumed to touch the engine. The ducks waddled aimlessly about the yard. The pond was dry and they were upset by the noisy stranger. Millie's father was busy, hurrying from shed to shed, chiding the laggards and supervising operations with careful officiousness. He was flushed and hot; beads of sweat stood on his lined forehead. Hot burning days of dying August! Here was a nice profit! A perfect harvest, a shed full of flour, trees loaded with apples. A happy feeling of pride suffused his attenuated frame. He had been hard at work since three o'clock, but he did not feel tired. As the day advanced he grew gayer, stronger, strangely confident of himself. He had forgotten life held such a vital urge for him.

He shouted to one of the older farmers, a zealous chapel man, so that he might be heard above the engine. "A good crop I'm getting." "To be sure," the other man shouted back, eyeing the bulging sacks appraisingly. And then, as if in confirmation, "Yes, indeed." "You're right there," Millie's father replied. The conversation languished. It was noisy, and uncomfortably warm. Besides, they were too busy to indulge in such a luxury as speech. They finished threshing by four o'clock and were gone by five, labourers and puffing machine. The yard emptied of its busy crowd and as the dusk fell slowly, the ducks waddled down to the dry white stones of the stream. Blackbirds were busy in the deepening dusk, pecking at the great, ripe apples in the orchard. Millie was decking her black hair with a rose plucked from the orchard wall. As she came out she met her father driving out the cows she had milked an hour ago. Instead of giving her some menial task to perform, as she feared, he paused a moment, smiled at her, and went on. He didn't feel like being sharp to-day. There was good money in those full white sacks, and nothing softens the heart of a hard man more than money gained by the sweat of the brow. There was a cool clearness in the air, a visionary gleam over the headland, a red sunset over the sea. He saw the beauty of his surroundings for the first time. His toil had come to a happy end and the weather had been kind. The neighbours had helped him to garner his treasures and his usual sullen hatred for outsiders was softened. He patted a small white cow and plucked a handful of grass for it. "You are not sorry your mother died," he spoke into its ear, "she was willing to die so that you could live happily." He shook its sturdy short horns approvingly. Like a flash, the old pain gripped his body and shook him mercilessly. He slipped to the ground and waited for it to pass. He rose again in a few moments. Somehow he felt that his end was approaching. The old bitter anger rose in his breast, blinded his sight, blotted out the quiet cattle and the sloe trees in the hedge. It *was* kind of the world to rob him of the pleasure he had worked for! And he couldn't defend himself against such a thief.

His anger died down, leaving a soft feeling of regret. Physical agony gave way to a strange languor. He walked slowly over the field, until he came in sight of the bay. The sun was slowly setting into the sea. He watched it disappear. Sinking to rest — into the sea or into the grave — what did it matter? Rest! That was what he yearned for. His mind turned to the barn with its gained wealth. The old anger surged into his mind again. To die just when life was growing pleasant! To be unable to spend his hard-earned gains! They were all he had in the world. Except Millie, of course. The bitterness left his soul at the thought of Millie, fresh, beautiful, decked with a big white rose. Millie — his daughter, for whose sake a woman he loved had died long years ago! He had disliked Millie because she had taken away the one pure joy that life had held for him. He thought of the white cow that had died so quietly on that cold winter dawning, and of the little white calf that even now munched the dewy grass so contentedly. Sacrifice! That must be true happiness. His wife had gone under the ground so that a new life might be started. And he had been trying to kill his child's pleasure. He had forbidden her to meet the young schoolmaster. He couldn't see her so happy while he had been so lonely, and in such pain. He had some dim ideas of a future life and future rewards. Well, he would let Millie have her way. He would go back and tell her she could leave him and wed her young lover. He would be dying soon, anyhow.

He turned back towards the farm. A stripling moon and a few stars paled in the sun-tinged sky. The pain raced though him and he cried aloud. He walked on slowly. Why couldn't he be left in peace? Why should 'they' plague him like this? His stubborn wrath flowed again. He had no control over his own affairs. It was no good him trying to be merciful, when his only reward was pain. Very well, he'd show them that he could stand up for himself. In a silent anger he dragged his way to the outhouse, with the roof half-fallen in, where lay his precious sacks. He felt surer of himself amongst his own wealth. He climbed the ladder to the attic. He grew peaceful again as he rested on the sacks and looked up at the stars. He was uncertain whether to defy the world and assert his own tyrannical powers, or slip away with his pain into the sunset and let Millie live his life over again — for him. He had made a mess of Life, he realised. If only 'they' would take this racking pain away. He couldn't enjoy his rest if they tormented him. By 'they' he meant the sun, the sky, the earth, the spirit that is in all living things. He was, in fundamentals, a real pagan. What else could he be who had learnt to bow before the fury of the storm and reap his crops while the sun shone? Well, he'd let 'them' decide for him. One way or the other, he didn't mind. A falling star caught his eye. It dropped right across the sky. Moved by some strange impulse he stood up and climbed to the open roof. He looked intently at the sky, as if seeking for some strange token. A fury of pain gripped him, twisted him, threw him off balance, hurled him to the stony ground. And he lay still.

Millie was hurrying down the hill. She was a bit late. Father would be impatient. She was going to tell him she had pledged her troth to her lover. It wasn't her fault. Nature had decided for her. She had told her suitor that she would marry him if a star fell over the sky in one minute. He had been afraid to agree until she told him that Nature always ordained the best things. And a big, glowing star had fallen. Nature had decided her life for her, too. So her thoughts raced, tumbling over each other, as she jumped over the stream and entered the farm yard. And overhead the moon waxed silver and the stars smiled.

(1934)

The Whirligig of Fate

The pump handle creaked as Isaac Bowen filled his old bucket. It creaked with a slow, lazy groan, and the water splashed out in sleepy gushes as if forced from the cool well against its will. It filled the sunwarmed bucket at last and was picked up by the horny hand of old Isaac. It knocked against his muddy breeches as he crossed the little path which intersected the churchyard, and it slopped heavily to the dry parched earth. "Hoosh!" sighed Isaac, as he laid the bucket on the ground and stretched his bent back. "Hoosh!" he sighed, stretching his long crooked arms. His joints creaked almost as patiently as the pump handle. "Hoosh," he sighed again, "I'd like a drop o' that water better than me old aunt," and he dipped his cupped hands into the still water and cautiously drew them up to his face. But the water ran through his fingers and down his sleeve, and by the time his hands were level with his wrinkled lips and his five extant teeth, there was only a wee drop left. "Daro bendi," he said to his wet fingers, and promptly climbed down to his knees — for Isaac's limbs could no longer perform a sprightly curtsey — and proceeded to lap up the water with much relish and a like amount of sucking. When his brow felt cooler, Isaac climbed back up to his full length, bent down again with a sigh of exquisite effort, and tottered along with the bucket. He was not a very steady walker, was Isaac, and by the time he had reached the long-maned brown mare that stood meekly between the shafts of a dung-stained gambo, the bucket had splashed itself well-nigh empty.

"Well, me old aunt," said Isaac to the mare, "'ow do me old aunt like the sun? Ah! It's warm alright. You're right enough — for sure you are." Now the brown nag had not so much stirred her tail to flick away the buzzing flies and if a passer-by — rare phenomenon in such parts! — had heard Isaac's conversation, he might have been at a loss to understand the cause for Isaac's last remark. But in truth, 'Lizzie Jane,' as the 'old aunt' had been christened fifteen years before, was on the most intimate terms with Isaac Bowen. She had two quiet brown eyes which sometimes appeared in a chance gap in the straggling mane which drooped over her face. And Isaac could understand everything she said with her eyes. He saw the patient, mild reproach in them as he lifted the bucket to her fly-tormented muzzle. He was unaware that his halting progress had reduced the contents of the bucket so perceptibly. But at that look his wrinkles dropped from a smile to a hang-dog frown and he patted her neck. "I'm a-sorry I drinked your own bucket," he said. "Oh! I'm awful sorry, old aunt. But I'd like to know as 'ow yer found it out, you clever un," he added, ruminatively. "Ye're gotten fat, Lizzie Jane, for certain," said Isaac, playfully prodding the old mare's flanks. "It's not enough to do we're 'avin', the two of us. An' I'm missin' the money we been 'avin', too, Lizzie Jane. Yes, to be sure." He smacked a greenfly whose twinkling crawl across the old mare's belly came thus to a tragic stop. Lizzie Jane started. "Whoa, mare," said Isaac, with authority, and proceeded slowly to translate his vague thoughts into vague words. Isaac had always thought how ineffective were words to express deep broodings of the mind. "Ah! Liz an' me are not driving nobody to Nith-y-llan market! No! not for weeks an' weeks we 'aven't."

A motor horn piped suddenly from somewhere up the Valley. The churchyard was at the foot of a wooded hill, up which a very narrow lane found a tortuous way. In a twinkling Isaac became galvanised into energy. The bucket was flung willy-nilly into the hedge and, perched on the shafts of the gambo, Isaac was hurrying the mare up the twisting path. The path was dusty and its rough white stones were loose. The big wooden wheels, with their steel rims, rolled noisily up the rutted track, groaning as they went at the superimposed weight of the cart and of Isaac, whose trembling hands shook the worn leather of the reins. "Goo on," he urged, "up the 'ill with yer, Lizzie!" He flicked the broad, expressionless backside of the old mare with a peeled branch that lay in the gambo. He was halfway up the hill before the burning sun caught the wind-screen of Parson's new eight-seater and flashed a dazzling lightning. Down the winding path the car scrambled, little stones beating against the mudguards or springing into the honeysuckle hedges as it skidded slowly down-hill. Then Parson came to a sudden stop. For there, laboriously rounding a sharp bend, came the brown mare, stoically dragging the gambo with Isaac enthroned over its two wheels. At the sight of the car, Lizzie Jane stopped and proceeded to deal with the flies which she had hitherto ignored.

Scrambling down from the shaft, Isaac shambled up to the car, deference in every wrinkle of his face and in the bowed shoulders.

"Well, Parson, I dug Mrs. Jenkins, Ty Bach's grave nice an' deep —
deep enough even for her," he said, officiously.

"That's good!" said Parson, "and I'm pleased to see you looking so
well."

"Thank you, Parson, I'm sure," said Isaac, "thank you fawr."

"But I wish you'd lose this distressing habit of yours of bumping
into me on this hill. You know, it's the third time this has happened
within a week," added Parson.

Isaac was uncertain whether a frown or a laugh would meet the
situation best. Left to themselves, his wrinkles curled up to their usual
position and a broad grin sneaked over his face. "Is it, Parson?" he
said. "Well, to be sure! But I'll get Liz. bach to shunt back down."

Retracing his steps to the waiting mare, Isaac addressed her loudly.
"Back, mare, back!" he hurled at her. But the grin was still on his face
and though Lizzie Jane's hooves scrambled and clattered in the shard,
he held the bridle so firmly that the gambo did not go back an inch.

"Too slippy it do be, by far, Parson," he said, with a grave and
portentous nod. "I'm a-feared you'll 'ave to drive back up to the top
road."

It was a long and difficult operation, and Parson was very angry and
hot and fussier than usual by the time he reached the top. And he felt no
better when he was forced to wait a whole fifteen minutes for Isaac and
his companion to rumble up the hill and clatter lazily past him.

Isaac talked much more to himself than to any of the villagers. All
the winding way to his little cottage up in the gorse land, he chuckled
and chuckled, and occasionally leant over to tell Lizzie of his joke.

"Afore cars was, Liz., you an' me made a tidy bit takin' the old ladies
into the market every week. But now that Parson drives 'is flock in
every Wed'sd'y out of the goodness of 'is 'eart — well, we can't do
nothin' to stop 'im." He spat hard on to the shafts and assumed a
concentrated stare.

"But a'm thinkin', Liz., a'm thinkin' furious. And be blowed if I
'aven't got it!" He shook the reins elatedly and spat right over the
mare's head.

"I just remembered as Parson's preachin' afore the Bishop or the
Pope, or somebody, in Llanglas to-morrow. An' I got an idea that's
better'n bumpin' into 'im on the narrow lane or forgettin' the rope to
lower the coffins or sellin' 'im flea-bit rabbits."

He had reached the cottage up in the gorse by this time and
obediently the old mare turned off the road to the ramshackle shed
wherein the gambo rested nightly alongside Isaac's sprightly market

trap. And over the sea the sun dimmed into the mists of evening. We do not suggest for a moment that Isaac's nocturnal expedition concealed any base design. Far be such a crime from a quiet, sleepy sexton's mind. But, none-the-less, it is indisputable that on the glorious epoch-making morn, when Parson walked down the lawn in his very best black suit and starched collar and dark grey spats, with his sermon all ripe and safe for its delivery before the bishop, he found his means of conveyance, the noble automobile, sadly down at the heel. Its tyres were flat — all four of them, and the steering handle had taken flight during the dark hours of the twenty-four. And with archiepiscopal wrath, Parson bounced back to the Parsonage and called down the one great curse upon widow Evans, who was washing up the breakfast things, and upon Tom Thomas, who was shelling the best Parsonage beans. Great was Parson's heart-burning and great was his wrath and loud threats did he utter concerning the pillorying and the cropping off the ears of the tramp who passed that way yesternight. But his wrath had left him when he climbed the long wooded lane with its tumbledown hedges, to beg his sexton's trap for the twelve miles along aimless country roads to Llanglas town. Unfortunately, Isaac was out and the cottage was warm and silent. Even the grandfather clock had suspended its machinations during the master's absence. But dutifully it chimed a spasmodic twelve strokes in Parson's honour; although its lazy hands clung fondly to seventeen minutes past four.

Eventually Parson found Isaac skinning a rabbit under a bower of blackberry bushes. And great was his sympathetic consternation at the bad news. And never did Shylock so magnanimously lend a ducat to hated Antonio as Isaac Bowen lent his trap to Parson. He'd be delighted to drive Parson in. But, of course, he'd have to catch Lizzie Jane first — no, she wasn't in the field — she'd strayed over the cliffs somewhere and he might have a bit of a job to find her. And, of course, he'd have to fetch the harness from Twm Maesgwyn's — but that was only about half-a-mile away. And then he must have a tidy bit of dinner!

"But don't you worry, Parson," he said confidentially. "Isaac Bowen will get you there easy."

But Parson was awfully fidgetty. He was perspiring and annoyed and nervous. His rubicund smooth face grew redder and more restless. He consulted his watch again and again. He nervously twitched at his sermon and couldn't remember sentences which he knew the night before. "A pure heart staining the white radiance of eternity" (underlined in red ink) — the Bishop ought to like that. But Parson had never realised how vast was eternity until he was obligated to wait on this hot noon for Isaac and the brown mare to appear.

But at long last Parson, still miserably perspiring, found himself sitting behind the gaily caparisoned Lizzie Jane. And boldly, like some charioteer of Rome, Isaac held the reins. The mare was a somnolent old lady, however, and soon decided that haste was unseemly under such a noonday glare. And so she plodded on her dusty way, craning her neck for some grassy morsel, tossing her head at the buzzing gnats, standing still at the advent of the postman on his bicycle, stumbling laboriously down stony inclines, shaking the sorry, black-suited parson as the trap rumbled through deep ruts.

Isaac was more talkative than usual. He felt sure Parson enjoyed a nice sunny ride like this. The weather was lovely. Better'n this time last year. Saw a badger, first thing, 'smorning. Piebald, it was. Wise things, badgers. Oh yes! And talkin' about wise 'uns, that man Parson Adams, who preached in Church last Sunday, spoke about — he must 'a bin clever.

"D'you mean Socrates, Mr. Bowen?"asked Parson, trying to cast off his nervousness!

"You got 'im," nodded Issac. "Well, excuse my curiousness, but 'ow did 'e die?"

"He drank hemlock and killed himself."

"Well, no sexton as knew 'is job would bury 'im in Holy ground," said Isaac sternly.

"But there wasn't a Church in those days, Isaac."

"Wasn't a Church, Parson? That's daft." Isaac relapsed into himself to consider a Churchless world. When he emerged again, he had wriggled out of the abstruse.

"Well, Lizzie Jane, by there's a wise 'un. But I 'ope she won't commit no suicide," he chuckled.

It was just at this point that Lizzie Jane lost the road. They had let the mare lead them hitherto, for as Isaac said, "She knowed the road better'n her own face." Horses not being addicted to studying their features in vain mirrors, this was really poor testimony to Lizzie Jane's sagacity. Isaac indeed might have noticed her turning down a little grassy road between sloe trees just outside Nantgwyn hamlet. But he was too deep in a lazy content even to notice the twitching of his right hand which caused Lizzie to turn from the main road. Parson was really furious by now. Quarter past three! And still five miles away. And the Bishop would be fixing his pastoral staff together and putting his mitre on his venerable bald head, and smiling munificently at the choirboys. And then the local Vicar would be fussing about the churchyard, looking up the road and down the road and thinking what he'd tell the late comer and spanking the urchin who'd ventured between the graves in search of a lost tennis ball — and here was Isaac, smiling like Job in the days of his greatness, with the lazy horse half-turned to retrace her way. Half-turned she was — and jammed fast. And so, philosophically, Lizzie Jane proceeded to add a sheaf of foxglove leaves to her already well-filled stomach, while Isaac undid the harness to turn horse and cart separately. Parson had to jump out. It really was most exasperating! And he was hopelessly late. His great opportunity lost and worse than lost! He was ruined. And he'd done nothing to deserve this treatment. He forgot himself so far as to mutter maledictions to the contented Lizzie Jane. "You're as doltish as Socrates was wise, you lazy bounder. I wish you'd take some hemlock for yourself, though," he whispered.

"Come and take a pip at this 'ere snake, Parson," shouted Isaac, dangling a quiet-coloured grass-snake on the end of a sprig of alder. Swallowing his ire, Parson turned and failed to notice the mare crop a beautiful plant whose thick stem wore a necklace of bright red berries. It was, unfortunately for the brown horse's future, a shoot of deadly nightshade, which was the nearest equivalent Lizzie Jane could find for the more classical hemlock.

Isaac was very happy on the return journey. He'd have been willing to take Parson all the way. But apparently it was too late. With his usual tact, Isaac ingenuously added: "But it 'ave learnt you a lesson about cars, I 'xpect, eh Parson? I don't trust no bloodless things. They isn't natural some 'ow." In fact Isaac got happier as Parson got glummer. But poor old Lizzie Jane stepped slower and slower, her long mane hanging over her drooping head, her hooves no longer ringing proudly on the dust-veiled flints. The harness grew loose over her shoulders and heavy underneath. She trailed along at a funeral pace. Until at last she coughed and tumbled over. Isaac, who had just pledged himself to a half-pint of nice bitter ale, was pitched into the hedge along with Parson. But while Parson grew angrier Isaac grew more sorrowful until he actually cried — two hard salty tears that rolled zig-zag down his wrinkled face. And he asked himself what he had done to deserve such cruel treatment at the hand of fate. But, as Twm Maesgwyn said, when they lowered the poor silent Lizzie Jane into a cool deep grave alongside the last Parson but one, "That's 'ow the world goes round, Isaac bach." And but for the sound of Parson's car calling for Mrs. Jenkins the Shop to go to market, Twm might have heard Isaac sobbing.
(*1934*)

Attitude

"Now don't go into a trance until you've posted my letter," Peter whispered, ruffling her black hair with his thin white fingers. "It's most important that Anne should know I'm getting better."

Frieda laughed and kissed his sallow cheek.

"I am the arrow to thy bow O King," she replied, and lifting herself from the bed she took up her handbag and the letter and tiptoed towards the door.

"I'll be back in ten minutes," she smiled.

"No, don't come back," he said, "please. Stay out all the afternoon." He let his hands play in the pool of sunlight on the quilt. "I shall certainly fall asleep — it's awfully tiring to feel well again and know there's sun and birds singing outside the window. Please stay out."

She half-opened the door and looked across at the garden. The Virginia creeper red and ripe against the wall, calling her away from the still, green sickroom; the hedge flowering into a second blooming of honeysuckle; the timid wren singing, suddenly bold; the robin redbreast's alderman's belly; the thrush half hidden amidst the crisp redcurrant leaves — all beckoning to her.

She turned back to Peter. The vitality had gone from his hands, and they lay limp in yellow light, like dead leaves. He smiled his twisted old smile.

"See, I'm exhausted," he said thinly. "You run away and enjoy yourself for me too. And you can kiss me awake when you return."

"Eh bien, mon brave Pierre," she replied, and suddenly stooped over him and closed his eyes with gentle fingers. "Rêve des fées, mon petit."

"Je ne suis qu'un réve," he murmured, not opening his eyes.

She drew the magenta curtains across to dim the sun and went silently from the room, not daring to look at the bed. His tousled brown hair would be lying on the white bolster and his face would be still and clear, transparently sallow, lifted up like a frail flower chalice. She shut the door softly and went down into the garden.

Its lavish beauty set her nerves on edge. It seemed cruel, the warm abundance of it, so unsympathetic with the remote spell of Peter's bedroom. She felt suddenly terrified, standing dazzled in the fertile garden, for it seemed she had been exiled in a distant, disembodied realm and was now, suddenly and irrevocably, returned to the exuberant blood richness of Living. Shutting the door had broken the delicate web that had bound her to the filigree frailty of Peter's kingdom. She stayed uncertain outside the door, but while she hesitated the afternoon took hold of her, the colours of Autumn seized on her senses.

High in the transparent blue sky a lark was singing, and her mind fell to the delight of it. Blue October sky, blue like a hedgesparrow's egg, blue dissolving into the lark's singing — fragile, imperishable, impermanent blue. A pair of starlings grubbed among the dry fall of leaves, the sun dancing on their speckled green and purple throats. A crow flapped over the lush meadow, its head and wings a dancing gold, and after it a white gull, drawing an arc of silver against the dappled wood. She drew in her breath, lifted her arms to the sky, and smiled and felt the love going warm from her body to caress the day. She went slowly, ecstatically, down the path, out into the lane, and down the gentle hill to the village. Past the flowerman's plot, catching up as she walked the warmth of asters, chrysanthemums, coxcombs, begonias and rich Siberian wallflowers. Past the tall yellow ash, her feet rustling through the rut of fallen leaves. Past the churchyard elms, in whose silence lay embalmed the Spring cawing of rooks. Over the humped bridge, her ears aware of the swirl of the green race of water, and the suddenly remembered line re-telling itself in her mind

"Rose moles all in stipple upon trout that swim."

She almost passed the red pillar box nailed against the oak bole. But its garish red caught her and she stopped short. She took the letter from her handbag, holding it in her fingers at the box's mouth. "Miss Anne Kingsley, 17 Fitzroy Square, Bloomsbury" — and against the thin spearhead of recollection the crystal spell shattered. "I'm not going to live on the Heath or in Mill Hill, or anywhere green," Anne said. "I'm going to live in a town, right in the sty. I'll buy cut flowers on Saturdays in memory of you, Frieda, but I don't envy you one bit — you and your Peter and your Welsh cottage. I am a deliberate Cockney." Anne, in her neat, dark green costume, sitting on the rug and flicking ash over the gas fire — how vivid it still was, that year-old moment. She had looked straight up at Frieda with her grey eyes. "And thank you for the invitation, darling, but I really can't come to your wedding. Work — I must work — Research." And she had laughed. It must have been terribly hard to laugh just then. Their lives suddenly concentrated into the moment, taut almost to breaking; a tremor of laughter might easily have — She kept it up, said something fatuous about ringing her up, reached the door, and got out, mazed. Why the devil couldn't Peter marry them both? It was such a waste, for Anne.

She dropped the letter into the box and went slowly along the lane, seawards.

It was a muddle — it always had been, at bottom. You could never tell, in London, whether you were being real or not. It was so turbid, so changeful. Tubes and lectures, the Tate, the National Gallery, ballet and Proms, and people, people, people. Conversations growing taut and hysterical, or flopping like clumsy dead fish into your lap. You couldn't be sure. Rembrandt, Leonardo, Beethoven, Van Gogh, Brahms — all so important, all to be weighed and included in the necessary plan, all reacting on each other like chemical agents till the mind was in a vapour. And work, the diurnal, unmanageable — bending over medieval charters and accounts, transcribing, copying, collating. And all the time trying to make it remote and scientific, this long-dead Thirteenth Century, that must resurrect itself, swell and lour, assume nebulous shapes, of fish and animal . . . . And then suddenly to see it for the clod of dry dung that it was, and try to kick it off the sole of your shoe, and kick and kick in a vain nightmare. And buses and tea parties, and theatres and books, turning in a wild whirlpool . . . . And then, unexpectedly, softly, the calm poised certainty of Peter.

They had met on a dank April afternoon in the Reading Room of the Public Record Office. The green-shaded reading lamps were lit, and she had looked up from her transcripts to consider the bald head of the American professor basking like a shrimp in the yellow pool of light. He was pouring over the Norwich Valuation Rolls, his nose, she thought almost touching the parchment. Perhaps he had a sensitive nose, she thought, something like an anteater's, or sort of snail's horn — but a highly cultured one that could read medieval Latin. They were all dead, the circle of bowed heads petrified into a musty silence. And suddenly she had revolted, and swept her bundle of manuscripts along the table with a rebellious thrust. They shot into the face of a young man at her side. He had looked up, half annoyed, half puzzled, his lean face showing the struggle of his thoughts to leave one concentration for another. She had blushed with embarrassment. He leaned over with a smile.

"Deserter?" he asked.

She nodded.

He chuckled.

"I'm fed up, too" he said. "Let's go and spit in the Thames."

That was Peter, and it was comforting to lean over the Embankment and watch the tugs dip their funnels under Waterloo Bridge, and wander up to Westminster and wonder whether Wordsworth would have objected to Shell Mex House. Peter lived in Jersey, had done Medieval History at Oxford, and then inserted himself into a Junior Lecturership at University College.

"I," he said, "am a specialist on Byzantine History," and he spat beautifully into the river. "What are you?"

"Me?" she said, flurried. "I don't exactly know. I live in Wales, took History at Manchester, and am now writing a thesis on Papal Legates in the Thirteenth Century."

"Most illuminating," he laughed.

"Well, I can't clarify the situation further, I'm afraid," she replied, — "except for my name — I know that for certain — Frieda Thomas."

"Mine is Peter," he answered, "Peter Topaypaul, grand nephew of the Pieman. Do you like fairly warm toast?"

"I like lots of things," she replied, "though I don't know how much."

"Sois tranquille, there's nothing metaphysical about eating toast," he reassured her, "so let's go before the tea rush."

It had been marvellous to climb on Peter's little island, and stretch wet limbs, and forget about the whirlpool out of which he had pulled her. Spring came laughing on their heels and they met it gladly, walking past the National Gallery without an obeisance and strolling through St. James's Park. They would sit on the green benches and watch the children gaze with awe at the perilously thin legs of the flamingoes. Then leisurely on to Hyde Park, a silver thrill in their fingertips at the touch of budding leaves, until at last they were sitting by the Serpentine, collecting passing scraps of conversation like a pair of pickpockets. So many refined delights did they taste that Spring — standing in theatre queues, running up endless steps to secure a vantage point in the fairyland of the Ballet Russe, slipping softly into

the charmed row of eager faces that ringed the Old Vic gallery like a
bower of flowers too lovely to be plucked, visiting the Tower on
Saturday afternoons when Billingsgate was washed clean of all but its
essential smell, listening to Bach and Mozart and the Beethoven
Quartets on Peter's gramophone. And all these things, and something
warm and intangible informing these things drew them closer and
closer together, until they touched in a piercingly sweet burgeoning of
joy, lips and fingers and bodies joining in intensest Life.

She had reached the first bridge, a wooden, rotted thing perched
precariously over the river, with transverse bars across each end to
prevent the cows crossing into forbidden grassing. She leaned over the
wooden rail, tearing the pulpy wood with her polished nails and staring
moodily into the river. The sun was warm on her cheek. It was quite
clear and distinct now, their courtship, recollected without emotion. It
had been, and she remembered it, but she could not bring it to life. Its
deadness disturbed her. She had grown to believe that only what the
heart feels is real, that intellectual perceptions are remote things. But
what use is reality, if it is so transient? Feeling dies and revives and
dies, and may perhaps have no second resurrection. She recognised the
quicksands on which she had built. "Thou art Peter and upon this rock
I will build my Church." She had written that more than once in
examination answers. Funny.

Nothing in her life had permanence. Her poems just came when they
had a mind to it, and she had no more control over their coming than a
tree over a pair of nesting birds. Less than a tree — a tree is always
ready to receive its visitants. But she was often, oh! so often, shut
against poetry. There was the restless preparing, the search for
lucidity, the long vigil before the purification. And then the exquisite,
pure mood of knowing, when the vision was pellucid and Truth naked
to see. But so swiftly on its heels would come the muddling of the
water, the silting, the gradual obscuring, the loss of balance, the
grotesque fall from the eagle poise into the dull, earthworm mood. Into
despair. There was no peace about it, no certainty. And when the
vision was gone, it left no assurance.

In the first happiness with Peter she had seemed to be living the
ecstatic creative mood every day, no break in the clear Shelleian
weather for weeks on end. Even when the poems delayed their coming
she had still waited confidently and unperturbed. And the change came
so gradually that she did not notice it. His remarks had amused her at
first. He expressed his scorn of people with such a fine knife edge that
she could only admire his pungency. One evening they had talked

about the population of medieval England. Peter was calculating it from the number of land holdings — messuages — and qualified his figures by casually remarking that one could only tell approximately how many people *grew* on each messuage. But a week later they had walked through the East End and the sight of ragged children playing at the blousy knees of their slatternly mothers had whipped his hatred. "Damn them,"he said, "if they will go on breeding." And he always took rather a venomous delight in reading out to her the strictures of medieval canonists on women.

It was only after an experience which had turned her sick with shame she had learned how ominous was this coldness in him which she had once found so reassuring. She gripped the bridge with her fingers and shuddered at the memory of that foul night. He should have told her that he needed nothing from her that night. He shouldn't have gone through with it out of courtesy. He must have known it would sicken him. They had both been hurt and disgusted — tender and penitent, too, but willynilly it had happened, unforgettably. Even then his cynicism had come out, whimsically. "The correct phrase, Frieda, is incompatibility of temperament," he said. She felt sorry for him. He reached his conclusions — tentative, negative ones for the most part — so painfully and carefully, analytically, rationally, discounting intuitions, discarding beliefs and conviction. He contented himself with seeking, not wisdom, but information. He considered Communism too optimistic and rounded, education too ambitious, progress too questionable, Shelly, Spengler, Christ — all presumptuous, mystical egoists. "Nothing is absolute, except the ablative," he rebuked her one night, playfully, as if she were a child. He never really sympathised with her will to create poetry; he was just pleased because she found such joy in it.

She stamped her foot. The rotten plank cracked and powdered wood fell into the stream. She watched it float downstream. It was all so confusing, so evanescent. There was nothing to grasp. Except this valley, which lay always in her mind. She had lived in it since childhood, had grown up in it, and returned to it year after year, gladly, easily, knowing its changeless welcome. Its fold and fallow and plough — they were always clear in her mind, the things she knew best. It was the environment of all her intuitions, the image behind all her poetry, the mould in which her thoughts shaped themselves. It would never fade. It would nurse Peter with her and make him well. He would have died in London, but here he would recover. Oh how glad she had been to move him here, to her valley.

But now even the valley was distinct from her, irrelevant to her. She was powerless even to desire its reassuring familiarity. She had no sympathy with it, and so could not understand it. Nothing to give, therefore nothing to take — such was the Law and the Prophets. And then, at one bound, her mind leaped to understanding. It was just this same cold inability to understand her that had spun its death's web round Peter. She hadn't realised the impassability of the gulf before. They were different orders of being, like Aquinas's God and angels and men, neither able to comprehend the other. All the burning things she had told him during the last six months, before he fell ill — that she loved him, would always love him, wanted a child like him — they must have been just words to him, without meaning. He could no more understand her than she could now understand the proffered comfort of the valley.

Oh yes, he had been polite, as Charlotte was to Werther. He hadn't told her how empty her vows sounded, how it irked him, not sharing with her, not even wanting to share. His silences, his sulky moods, his expeditions with Anne, his drinking bouts, his gradual decomposition — the explanation was clear enough now. He must have been whipping himself, like a Flagellant, desperately concealing from her the hair shirt of his impotence to change. How she had been blind.

She stood still on the bridge, looking at the dimpled water, understanding, now all was done, with a finality that had in it neither fire nor bitterness. Yes, it was just like that first day of the Easter vacation, when they had travelled down from London to the cottage. The train was running by a marsh. She was looking across the dry, autumnal grass, feeling the sere calm of it, and her mind grew full of the peace of the river and the grass all rustled in the wind. Peter sat opposite her, alternately reading the *New Statesman* and gazing through the window. He was pale and jaded and uneasy. And then a plover had sped from the sudden incursion of the train, crossed the river, and dropped safely and lightly into the sedge. She saw it fold its dun wings, set its feet firmly on the oozy grass and dip its thin bent beak into the water, so naturally. She laughed with joy to see the bird fall into its appointed place. She told Peter of it, and his curt reply made her feel wretched — "What the hell has a plover got to do with me?"

She pulled a long splinter of live wood from the bridge rail and regarded the white scar. Everything, Peter, if only you can feel it. Not everything, perhaps, but enough. She dropped the splinter into the water and watched it twirl in the eddies. Enough? Was it enough?

Subconsciously she struggled to deny its adequacy. She must choose between Peter and the plover. And she wanted, oh frantically, to feel with Peter, to recognise, like him, nothing but the frustrations and complications, the incomprehensibilities and negations that hedged him in. Perhaps, if she renounced what she knew lay outside the hedge, he would be able to love her again. If they were both in the same corner of Hell, they could love well together. It would be Pain, living Peter's life — their physical needs not identical, the perpetual fear of committing a rape; the precarious reliance on ornaments and tastes — on Mozart recordings, on Dürer wallprints, on green bowls of cut flowers, on the walnut mirror and the frog-like Chippendale chairs, on Peter's embryo biography of Justinian, on her rare, rhapsodic poems. There was no telling when the thread would snap. Her poems were gone already. She had written nothing since their marriage. Her creativeness had taken another turn. It flowed into Peter — she knew it now. She no longer felt the sensual appreciation of paintings and literature and all things grown beautiful that she had once felt. And without its stimulus she knew that she would never create a beauty of her own. She had sacrificed that — he didn't realise what she had given him, willingly, ungrudgingly. She had given him bread. But in the giving, somehow — who knows how? — it had become a stone.

It was all so changing — there must be some element they had overlooked. Time perhaps — Time to grow together?

Well, there it was. She fingered the white scar on the bridge. Peter and Anne. She wasn't blaming them; it was something outside her ken, alien to her. Anne had been in the whirlpool, too, and annoyed with herself for failing to walk the waters. Anne hated wetting her townee shoes. Well, she was welcome to climb on to Peter's island. Peter's wife was there, too, impotently keeping herself captive there, maybe, but none-the-less no dog in the manger. Anne was welcome to take what she could. Besides, she was more useful there than in the water; she gave Peter peace. Just by talking to him she gave him peace. Funny how people re-act on each other, spontaneously.

She walked listlessly from the bridge and followed the winding of the lane to the beach. The sea was asleep in the blue sun, small waves breaking with tiny sighs on the shingle with an incessant murmur that had no intervals of silence. Land and sea lay together, still and continuous, bound up into one crystalline suspense.

It was strange, this not caring much, she reflected, as she turned away from the sea and slowly retraced her steps along the sandy shore. It had been different last Spring. Then there had been hope and quickness and a desperate responsibility to their mutual life. Then there had been illimitable potentiality in them. And the insecurity had pricked her into a boundless care and responsiveness. And Peter had liked the cottage and wrote a delicious letter to her parents to thank them for their wedding gift. And every morning she had stopped delightedly over the flower beds and called him out to see the flowers bursting, fondled excitedly the pure green shoots, described to him how the budleia would soon grow misty blue and honey-scented and bee-sounding. And as the briars on each side of the gate stretched their lithe green fingers to meeting, and knitted and burst together into leaf and red bud, she had felt a new, precious security, as though the binding together of the briars was a love knot holding Peter to her. And always after that, throughout the long London winter, and each night, when the lamp was lit and the green curtains drawn, she knew that outside the cottage window, in the dark, the briars were bound together over the gate, and the flowers were biding their time in the rich earth. It was breath to her, the certainty of this knowledge.

Before she had met Peter, she had loved these things for their very selves. Peter had pushed them away; they had become mere accessories to her desire to perfect her union with Peter. Yet they loved her more than Peter did — much more. How they sang to her this afternoon, when she came reluctantly to them, from the dim green sickroom. He had been desperately ill, the poor boy, ill nearly to dying. And he had changed such a lot during the long, wearying weeks of pain. He had grown ethereal, no longer itched by the flesh, and for longer and longer periods at peace in his mind. Seeing him suffer had purged her, too; nursing him, her child . . . . The sun was going down to the sea — what a shameful squandering of the afternoon. She had wasted all its loveliness and done nothing but watch the old empty thoughts tread their eternal circle in her head. Well, she wouldn't muddle herself any more. For it was all quite simple. She would tell him, now, as soon as she got back, that the plover was enough, that the flowers and trees and birds and animals were enough and more than enough. They had been terribly wrong to neglect these things and to concentrate instead on their own selves. They mustn't feed on each other any more. They must turn again to these essential, beautiful things. For they are realities, the makers of love, the quickeners. Only from them can we draw suck. Peter would see it. He had grown so clear and simple — he would see it at once. And then they would be together again. He would get better slowly and she would nurse him gently, unhurriedly. And Autumn would stay with them, and go slowly about her alchemy in the beech woods and gaze at the blue sky's reflection in the clear pools, day after day, oblivious of winter. Peter could sit in the rocking chair and count the falling leaves and hum small tunes. And then, if he was good, she might let him walk as far as the bridge. He would see there that it was 194½ miles to London, and he'd have to wait a long time before he could walk that far.

Oh how happy she was, and light-hearted. She ran up the lane, over the bridge, pirouetted outside the churchyard, and on past the gardener's plot, skipping, running, flinging her open palms to the sky. It was alright now. There was nothing impossible in loving the valley most. It was in fact the solution. Peter would see it. She would curl up on his bed and tell him about it.

She danced through the garden gate, and stopped to kiss the green briars. The sun slanted goldenly across the meadow, catching the windows in a dazzle. Lucky the curtains were drawn — it would have troubled his eyes if he had wakened. Yes, to-day she would cut it, to-day she would cut it — the last one flower, the single, drooping red flower left on the bowed plant — Love lies bleeding. She stooped over it and broke it off carefully with her nails. She would put it in her bosom, and let Peter get it out, with his lovely, spirit-thin hands.

She opened the door softly and went in like a mouse. She crossed the thick carpet soundlessly and bent over the dark head. She kissed his lips, but he didn't move.

She kissed his lips, but his lips were as cold as death.

(*1938*)

Squibs for the Guy

M r. Gummer was waiting for the boys outside the Infants' School gates at three thirty sharp and the three of them climbed straight up the mountain side along the bank of the noisy little torrent. He let them carry a sack each but he kept the shears tucked under his arm — "case you gets 'urted," as he said. When they reached the 'cwtch' of ferns at the stream's source they worked so hard that they were descending the mountain an hour later, Mr. Gummer with a huge sackful of ferns on his back, Elwyn tugging a smaller one at his heels, and David trailing a branch of gorse with great circumspection — having been admonished by his father to "watch the prickies."

"Well, I'm feeling like a bite o' tea," Mr. Gummer said, as they turned into the back lane. "And a bit o' fire, too. My 'ands is freezing."

"Go on, Dad, we don't want no tea," Elwyn rebuked him. "It's nearly dark now and we'll *never* 'ave time to stuff the guy if we go and 'ave tea first."

"Well, there's plenty of time," Mr. Gummer said, as they went through the back door into the garden. "It's only November the first, mun. We got four days before Saturday."

He dropped his sack against the door of the shed and blew into his cold hands.

"But we'll 'ave to make the guy straightaway, Dad," David nattered, "we got to take 'im round in the cart and collect money for squibs. We only got four nights."

"All right, you little pest," Mr. Gummer said. "There'll be no peace till 'e's set up, I can see. Let's see what we got, then."

Elwyn whooped like a redskin, opened the shed door and dragged his father in after him.

"It's all there, see?" he said, pointing to a pile of old rags in the corner. "Granny's old 'at and my jersey and the trousers you used to wear when you worked underground, 'fore you 'ad the dole. *And* string for tieing 'is legs up."

"O. K. chief," Mr. Gummer replied. "Only let's go down the kitchen first and 'ave a little warm."

"Well, only a minute, then," David conceded.

Granny came hobbling up the garden steps to meet them, holding her skinny finger up to her lips.

"What's up with you?" Mr. Gummer said.

"Ssh!" she quavered, "it's Mr. Beddoes. 'E's in the kitchen." A crystal fresh tear poised in the crows'-feet round her eyes. "'E says 'e *must* 'ave the rent this time or — " She mumbled the rest inarticulately and the tear rolled down the wrinkled channels of her skin.

"It's all right, Mam. Don't go takin' on," Mr. Gummer said. "I've settled with Beddoes before now."

"Come on, Dad, it's very near dark already," David said, dancing with an exquisite impatience.

Mr. Gummer knotted his red scarf under his chin, squared his shoulders and walked into the kitchen.

"Good evening, Mr. Beddoes," he said.

When Elwyn and David saw Mr. Beddoes they stopped chattering. He rose slowly out of the corner chair and in the dim light he seemed to be getting bigger and bigger until his head went through the ceiling and his arms stretched out through the door and the window. And he laughed like a lump of pumice stone, not happily like Dad. David ran back up the garden.

"Very good evening, I'm sure," Mr. Beddoes said. "Sit down a minute, will you, Gummer? I've come up special to see you."

"Brought your little boy along, too, I see," Mr. Gummer said nervously.

"Aye, 'e's with me," Mr. Beddoes said.

Elwyn had not seen the little boy till then. He was sitting in Granny's chair in the darkest corner, his feet miles from the ground. Elwyn went up to him and touched his arm.

"Come and see our guy," he said.

Mr. Beddoes laughed. "Got a guy, 'ave you?" he said. "What's 'is name?"

"Guy Gummer," Elwyn said timidly. The rattle of coins in Mr. Beddoes' trouser pocket emboldened him. "We're going collecting with 'im tomorrow after school," he said cautiously, "to get squibs."

"Are you?" Mr. Beddoes coughed and took his hand out of his pocket. "Well, you can take Daniel to look at 'im, if you like. And then your Dad and me'll be able to talk business in peace."

Elwyn took the little boy's hand and led him up to the shed. David was already stuffing ferns into the trouser legs.

"That's no good, mun," Elwyn said. "You got to tie 'is legs up first and button 'is fly, 'case the ferns fall out."

The three children set to work, squatting on their heels in the dusk.

"When we've collected thrupence we're going to buy two Catherine wheels and a jumper and four sparklets," David said.

"If we collect thrupence, you mean," Elwyn corrected.

"We seen the fireworks we're going to buy," David pursued. "They're in the window of Mrs. James's shop, and she said she'll keep them for us till Friday."

"Gi's that string, Dai," Elwyn interrupted, "and let's tie 'is sleeves."

They began to stuff the jersey with ferns.

"Our Mam's in the cemet'ry," David said. "Is yours?"

The little boy nodded no.

"Can't you speak, mun?" Elwyn said roughly.

The pale little face blushed pink.

"We got a swede for 'is 'ead," David said, "but we're not going to cut 'is mouth and eyes till Friday because Dad says 'e'll be eating all the chicken's food if we do."

"Let's try 'is 'ead on, now," Elwyn said, propping the guy against the whitewashed wall. They set the swede on the neck of the red jersey and stuck Granny's Victorian hat on top.

"'E's fatter than Granny," David said. "Come an look at 'im, Dad. 'E's ready now."

Mr. Gummer came slowly up the path. He put his hand on Elwyn's head and looked appraisingly at their handiwork.

"Aye, 'e's real fine," he said slowly. "Proper gent." He swallowed. "Ow would it be if we burned 'im to-night?" he said.

"But there's four days to go yet," Elwyn said. "And we 'aven't got no squibs, neither."

"It don't matter about squibs much," Mr. Gummer said, "not when you got a guy, anyway. And you never know what may 'appen by Friday. It might be raining, even. Let's burn 'im to-night, is it?"

David pranced about gleefully.

"Aye, burn 'im to-night," he shouted, tasting blood. "Hooray."

"It isn't proper, anyway," Elwyn said.

"Daniel, " Mr. Beddoes called, " come on this instant. You're keeping me."

The little boy nearly jumped out of his skin, turned to go, then stopped and fumbled in the pocket of his corduroy trousers. He held out his hand timidly to David.

"Here's for squibs," he whispered furtively, and ran to join his father.

And in the middle of David's grimy palm was a twinkling threepenny bit.

(1938)

from THE SERPENT

The Monk's Tale

*B*rother Wilfrid died at Jarrow in the year 932, where he had
been chief copyist of breviaries, hour books, and other holy works
monastery scriptorium. The following story is written into the
chronicle which he kept during the last thirty years of his life. Its
fulness and vitality are in striking contrast with his usual cursory
accounts of storms, deaths of kings, and Danish invasions. It is dated
A.D.930.

It is not easy to speak well of the Vikings, who plundered our
orchards and fields and stole the very bells from our belfry. Nor is it
meet that I should honour the memory of a bastard, spawned by the
itch of the Devil in a Godless pair. But I am old, and my days ripen
with peace, and my back is bent like harvest corn, wherefore I
cannot think evil of any man. Nor do I hold it a grievous sin to tell as
well as I can the strange story of Hakon, though his father was a
Norseman and a freebooter, his mother a serving wench at Lisieux,
too pretty to stay virgin. And when I write of him the memory of my
own youth comes to mind, for when my poll was still cold with the
newness of my tonsure, and I was carrying a satchel filled with divers
Holy writings from my native Jarrow to our brother monks in St.
Gall, I met this same Hakon, by the way, at Chalon in Burgundy.
For all that Jarrow has filled its granges with fifty harvests since that
day, I well remember the comeliness of his yellow hair and grey eyes,
and the sweetness of his voice as we shared my rye bread and beans
beneath the trees.

Eating, he told me how, in his childhood, the housewives of
Lisieux threw him crusts and left the doors of their cowsheds
unlocked that he might lie in the straw by night, after his father had
joined the Norse raid on Mercia, and his mother had died — of
shame, he said, and of hunger. He, also, his bastardy barring him
from office, would have fared ill but for his pretty face, his rhyming
tongue, and his cunning on the harp. For when he thirsted he would

go deep into the forest, plucking music from his harp which brought
the wild goats to him and held them charmed while he stole the milk
from their teats. And when he hungered, if it fell that blight of
famine prevented the good wives feeding him with crusts, he would
sup with the birds off berries and leaves and gather lush cresses from
the freshets. The wolves and wild boars molested him not, nor did
the ravens leave their nests when he climbed the ivy-bound
branches. These things he told me, by the roadside, and also how, or
ever his legs had stopped growing, he wandered through comtés and
villages, playing at ale-gatherings and love-days, singing to folks on
holy days and making the old dames fling their heels to the witchery
of his harp. His songs were of heroes and sprites, he said, as he
drained the wine in my pig-skin flask, of birds and maidens and the
seasons of the year.

And when I begged him to play to me, he said, laughing, "Thou
shalt hear the Song of the Frog, good monk, for thy bread and thy
beans and thy wine"; whereat he began his song. And I forgot all
else but the wondrous sweetness of his song, and this was the way it
went —

"Asquat in the mosses where the lake
Is wooing from brown to green the brake,
The Frog through a blur of water spied
The willow catkins bend in pride
To see their pollen-gilded forms
Mirrored in water whence the storms
Of sulky winter all are fled.
His belly rests on the crusted bed
With lily buds above his head.
'Yea I am Beauty, too,' he said,
'See all the colours freak'd on my back
Rust-on-the-rainbow, green-shot black;
See the diamonds on my brow,
My emerald eyes, and notice how
My four webb'd toes hurt not a whit
The tangled water-flow'rs all lit
With the sun's floating, yellow hair
Illuming the gloom of the Lake Sprits's lair.' "

And as he sang his eyes filled with tears, and when he ended he
was long silent. Then he played softly upon his harp, so that the
birds held their chatter to catch his words —

"O have you seen the thorn that grows
An angry red,
On briars when the gentle rose
Is dead?
"Oh have you seen the sly rat go,
Soft, sneaking-paw'd,
Fearing the ever-threatening blow,
Outlaw'd?
"And can you tell me why it should be so?
And must be ever so?
Such beauty intermingled
With such woe?

"My heart is heavy, good monk," he sighed, laying aside his harp, "when I think on the evil and the cruelty in men and women, in bird and animal. I have seen robbers laugh to pillage and rape, and children smile to rid the fly of its wings. I have seen beauty lose the apples on her cheeks and the soft flesh on her arms at the bite of the plague. I have seen the shrike spear a sparrow on the thorns by its nest and watch the blood clotting its feathers. I have seen the sagging bellies and shrivelled udders of kine when the flies cluster on their muzzles in the drought. Why should it be thus, good monk?"

"In sooth, I know not," I replied, "but doubtless the Holy Scriptures will answer your question. Being young, I have read them but little, and know only that you are a goodly poet, that the forest trees are dappled with sun, and that my stomach is well filled with wine of Troyes."

He laughed, commending my spirit, but methought his eyes were still sorrowing when we parted at Chalon, I pressing on with my books, he wending to a feasting in the neighbourhood.

I have not seen him since, which is but natural, for I have not quitted these cloisters for thirty years and upward. But rumours of him have reached my ears from chance pilgrims and merchants passing this way. If they spake true — and why should men lie to a simple monk? — Hakon went a strange way to his death. And this was the manner of it, as I have informed myself.

No prince in France was strong enough to drive off the Vikings, so that everywhere was burning and harrying, poverty and plague and famine. And when even the trees no longer brought forth berries, Hakon, grieving to see the hills littered with corpses of men and cattle, made his way to the north coast, through Champagne and Beauvais and Ponthieu, for he had heard how Alfred of Wessex had worsted Guthrum and the Danes. At Boulogne he went down to the waves, playing on his harp until a mighty stag ran down from the forest and entered the water. Hakon climbed upon its back, holding to its antlers and singing. For two days the stag swam, guided by God, until at length they drew near the English coast, and the stag took heart seeing the forests. But when they reached the shore Hakon saw that the stag's hoofs were wasted in the salt sea so that it could not stand on the dry land. And he stayed weeping by the stricken beast till it died.

Then he made his way north to Benfleet, where the King's army lay. And when he arrived he found the fyrd joyful because they had slaughtered the Danish garrison under King Haestan, slaughtered the Danish women, mothers and maids. This also grieved Hakon sorely, so that he took no pleasure in his harp. But when King Alfred heard at the feast that a French minstrel was without, he would have him play. Thereupon Hakon entered the banqueting hall and played so marvellous sad a song that the revellers, forgetting their triumph and their mead, thought only of those who had been slain, and wept. And when the song was done, King Alfred bade Hakon be fed and paid five mancuses of gold. But Hakon was vanished, like a spirit, and only the sadness of his song lingered in the minds of men.

Wherever he went in the land he saw only evil deeds and hard words, robbing and murder and rape, and the corn was trampled under the warriors' feet. Hakon could not turn his eyes from the horror of it, and he found no peace under the stars. And when he could bear it no longer, he fell to the dry earth and pressed his fingers into the rock, leaving ten marks in the hard rock. "Spirits of cruelty and evil," he said inwardly, "no more scatter thy poison among all things that live; instead, inhabit me alone, that man and beast may have rest and the corn be garnered with laughter." This he spake out of the infinite love for mankind which he felt, and I pray it be remembered in his favour when men recount the deeds that he did. For no sooner had he said his prayer than a mighty tempest came over the forest, driving the leaves in yellow multitudes to the ground, though it was but June, and making the branches writhe in torment. It lasted but a moment, yet mighty oaks were struck down and the rushlights blown out in every cottage. And then the sun broke upon the forest and the birds sang upon the naked branches and men said the tempest entered the heart of Hakon. For when he rose, his body was swollen and mis-shaped, his skin was black and covered with hairs, his arms were as long as spears, his fingers twisting like snakes. Men in those parts, between Severn and Wye, shuddered to hear the gibber of his laughter sounding through the forest, and sought refuge in the churches with their families. And swineherds told how, ere they took to their heels, they saw him tear the wolf limb from limb, and laugh to feel the warm blood spurt in his face.

There came a time when the cruelty within him would not rest content with the slaughter of wolf and brock and deer. On that day he went through the forest laughing to see the flowers wither at his passing, until he came upon the hamlet of Ruardean. It chanced that the villeins were all at work upon the demesne, and none remained in the street save the priest and a cripple boy who were watching the young rooks stand timidly upon their nests, trusting not to their untried wings. These two Hakon slew with the ten snakes that were his fingers, and with his teeth he tore the flesh from their faces,and took himself off to the forest again with the blood drying on his face. And when the villagers returned at dusk, divining who had wrought the horror that they saw, they fled to the church for sanctuary, while one of their number saddled a horse and galloped to find the King.

Alfred was at Wallingford, feasting and hearing the complaints of his subjects, for there was peace in the land and with the Danes; and no man, Saxon or Dane, had evil in his heart — save Hakon. And when the King heard the Ruardean man tell of the monster that ravaged the forest between Severn and Wye and slew the priest and a cripple of Ruardean, he straightway called his fyrd to him, and, donning his armour, set out for the western parts with all speed. Coming to Ruardean, they saw the village empty save for the two corpses and the crows that pecked at them. Then they heard the laughter of Hakon echoing in the forest and so cruel did it sound that all the war-horses whinnied in terror. But the King spurring forward, the rest followed for very shame, and the galloping hooves made the wild doves flutter from their nests. Hakon was eating off a live deer in a meadow deep in the trees, and there the fyrd came upon him, hurling their lances at him like a flinging of seed, and loosing their arrows like a shower of hail. But though the shafts bristled from him like the quills of a hedgehog, and his blood ran down among the ferns, Hakon rose to his feet and ran against the fyrd. And at the sound of his screaming and the sight of his fingers, that were like snakes, the horses turned and fled from the forest. And then 'tis said Hakon made haste in pursuit, trampling down the trees that stood in his path, and bleeding all the while, until he came once more on Ruardean.

The villeins were still huddled in the church, but while they prayed a little girl, too young to walk, had crawled from the church, seeking her crippled brother. And when she came to his corpse, she knew him by his twisted foot, and fell to weeping bitterly. Seeing her wringing her small hands so piteously, Hakon was touched with compassion and knelt down beside her and she nowhit frightened thereat. "This is my brother," she cried, "who alone knew my secret about the brown goblin; and he is dead; and there is no other to share my secret." Saying this, she looked up into Hakon's eyes, and they were clear and grey, for the evil was gone from them, and from that moment he was no more.

Such is the tale I have heard from divers folk, these thirty years, and if it be true or not I cannot tell. This only I know, that peace was up and down the land during the days when 'tis said these evils fell upon the men dwelling between Severn and Wye, and Dane and Saxon plied the scythe together at harvest. This also I know, that war broke out in England on the day when men say Hakon died, and Alfred fought a mighty battle with the Danes in Sussex, near Chichester. Then, too, pestilences struck down churls and thegns alike — Swithulf, Bishop of Rochester and Beorhtwulf, Alderman of Essex, and many another. And though these things befell in my youth, old age has not obscured them, and I joy again to recall my meeting with Hakon near Chalon, and the sweetness of his discourse and the magic of his song.

(*1936*)

Chestnuts

"Get into bed, you swine," Mottram shouted, standing on his bed at the top of the dorm. with the candle held aloft. "Get into bed and shut up or I'll stick you all in the clink."

The occupants of a dozen pairs of striped pyjamas scuttled barefooted across the well-scrubbed floor-boards and disappeared into a grey row of beds, like ghosts into graves. Mottram blew the light out and snuggled under his blankets, as though he were Caesar going into winter quarters.

"I say, Bristow," he called, "saying your prayers?"

"Don't try and be funny," came a voice from the next bed.

"Well, you're soft enough to do that," said Mottram, lying on his back while his legs explored the cold sheets. "A chap that reads Keats and bloody Shelley's soft enough for anything."

"I'm doing them for Higher — got to do them" — Bristow was on the defensive.

"Oh yeah?" Mottram yawned, punching his pillow into softness, "you're always reading the muck. I bet you spend half the hols. reading them."

"Sez you," came the hot reply. "I can drive the old man's car in the hols. and we've got some marvellous bathing pools in the river, and two cinemas — "

"Pictures aren't bad," Mottram conceded, "Mae West's a bit of all right, and some of these leg shows aren't bad — my brother's running a chorus girl in London. She's not bad, I can tell you. Say, Bristow" — he leaned over and lowered his voice, "ever been with a dame?"

"Course I have," Bristow replied, scornfully.

"Not a real hot dame, you haven't," Mottram pressed, "not a real snip. I'll bet."

"How do *you* know what I've done?" — Bristow's voice was full of a knowing reticence.

"Keats and bloody Shelley's about all *you've* done," said Mottram, bitingly. "There's a dame at home I've been out with a few times — you don't know what you're missing. It's much better than that bit you showed me in Lucretius — you know, the one about bodies mingling in a burning lust or something. She's the real thing. You ought to try it."

"How do you know I haven't?" Bristow answered, his voice quivering a little. Mottram's talk always upset him — made him feel sick and disgusted and yet hungry — an inquisitive, frightened, lusting hunger in the pit of his stomach.

"Skiff," hissed a voice from the bottom of the dorm, and a moment later the door opened ponderously. The Head flashed his torch along the double row of beds. Dead silence, while the torchlight wandered like a lost soul seeking its tomb.

"It was an awful cheek on my part, coming up to you after the pictures last night — I hope you didn't mind. I was afraid you'd think I thought you were . . . .I mean . . . .you don't even know my name. It's Wilfred Bristow — you know Bristow the solicitor, don't you? — he's my father." He blurted it out so furiously that she felt quite awkward, standing and smiling and fiddling with her handbag.

"I didn't mind much," she blushed. "I knew who you were and that you're not common."

Wilfred shifted from one foot to the other, smiling and not quite able to look at her small oval face, with the delicate little nose so deliciously *presque retroussé* — Wilfred was doing French for Higher — and the coal black hair and the impudent beret.

"Of course, I know *your* name — you're Anne Ellis — it rhymes with rose trellis. And I simply *had* to speak to you last night, because I'm going back to school to-morrow and I simply *had* to speak to you first. Shall we walk up the river? It's a lovely morning, isn't it? It's always lovely in September if the sun shines, isn't it?" — he stopped suddenly, like an engine seizing, and smiled at her.

She smiled back, lifting her little face and smiling from her bright brown eyes and her white, white teeth.

"Yes, let's walk," she said, in such a pretty voice. "I love walking and there's a whole hour before dinner."

They went through the white gate into the meadow, following the winding stream.

"I love the way the stream drops down in a rush of white, don't you?" Wilfred broke the silence with an effort. "And then it grows so peaceful and still and careless, as though it had never jumped over the moss in its life."

"What ideas you have," she exclaimed, genuinely surprised. "I love pools and things, of course, but I never thought of it like that."

Wilfred flushed with pleasure, but remembered the virtues of modesty. "If I do have ideas, it's because you give me them," he ventured.

But you never knew me before last night!" she objected.

"I've known you all my life," said Wilfred in the solemn tone of one conversing on eternity or the dear departed.

They were passing through a narrow, wooded gorge, filled with the tumbling roar of the waterfall, and they paused to watch the milk-white foam upon the hard green bedrock. Then they came out into a sloping field where light green grass mingled with the heather and ferns of the mountain.

"The hills come down to the water to drink," he informed her.

"Yes, don't they?" she replied. She must be a poet, too, thought Wilfred, for she sounded as if the same image had been in her own mind. Beauty with a poet's soul — Beauty and Truth and a joy for ever. — Anne Ellis — Mrs. Wilfred Bristow — impossible — Anne — the magic name — Anne — Timidly he looked at her, and trod in some cow-dung. She hadn't noticed, thank God.

"Look at that yellow fire running across the rocks," he said, pointing to the chain of gorse, and rubbing his shoe covertly against a tuft of heather.

"When gorse is in bloom, kissing's in fashion," she replied trippingly, and then blushed. "I mean," she added hastily, "that's what mother always says when she sees gorse.'

"Yes, everything's pretty to-day," he said, helping her out. "Look at all the leaves dancing and sparkling and the crab apples shining — ooh! and those brave rowan berries, look at them!"

"Yes, rather," she said, fully recovered, "and that teeny little robin — see — right on the tip top of that tree."

Wilfred quoted:

"One little red leaf, the last of its clan,
That dances as often as dance it can,
Hanging so light and hanging so high
On the topmost twig that looks up at the sky."

"Did you write that?" she asked.

"No, that's Coleridge," he answered, "I didn't write *that*," and taking the cue she enquired:

"But you do write things, I suppose?"

"Yes, I try," he replied. "I want to be a poet."

"That's what you're going in for, is it?" she asked.

"I'd like to," he said "only I don't know whether I'm quite good enough. I wrote one yesterday, about Autumn. Would you like to hear it? — It's quite short."

"I'd love to," she replied.

"All right," he said; and with an introductory cough, began self-consciously:

Corn's in, be praised, and harvest's done,
Heavily lies the flour-filled sack
On miller's back.
Rows of red apples ripe with sun
Cover the floor of the cowshed loft,
And plums grow soft
With suckling drunken wasps. There's none
But hath glad heart — the farmer rides
To town and bides
A fine day boozing; one by one
The leaves, grown russet, gold and brown
Come idly down —

"Sh!" she broke in, "there's a squirrel nutting there — look at his red tail."

"Where?" he asked, fervently wishing all squirrels in hell.

"It's gone now," she answered. "I'm sorry you missed it and I interrupted you. Was there much more of it?"

"Hardly any," he replied, sulkily. "We'd better turn back — it's nearly lunch time."

"I liked the poem ever so much," she said, as they retraced their path reluctantly.

He brightened, grew gay, rising and rising on her smile and the sweet sound of her praise, rising like a puff of down.

"Gosh, it's daft having to go back to school!" he said, almost bitterly. "It's utterly idiotic — will you write to me sometimes, Anne, during the term?"

"D'you want me to?" she asked coyly.

"Rather," he said eagerly. And then, on second thoughts, "Only, d'you think you could get your brother to write the address? The Head wouldn't half kick up if he thought it was a girl's writing. He's terribly narrowminded about things. And can I write to you?"

"I expect so," she said doubtfully, "though I'm not sure about mother — she treats me as though I hadn't grown up."

The path wound round a chestnut bole; the grass was dark green and sunless under the woven roof of branches. Wilfred picked up a green prickly pod from among the fallen leaves.

"Conker," he said, as he inserted his thumb nail and prized it open. Anne bent her head over his hand. Softly the pod opened, softly, softly, as the nail pressed in. The crack widened. He pressed his thumb in. The pod split open, split in half, and there was the smooth, pale brown nut, lying in its soft white bed. He stroked its polished surface, marvelling how gentle it felt under his finger tips. He lifted it out.

"Look where it's been lying all the summer," he whispered, pointing to the concave impress on the white pith of the pod. "It seems a pity to break things open, doesn't it, and steal their fruit?"

He looked at her eyes, with trees and sunlight in them. Yes, and little wings fluttering, and stars coming to birth in the green moss.

"Don't you think it's cruel, Anne?"

"Yes," she replied, "I suppose it is."

"Out with those bloody lights," bellowed Mottram, "and get to bloody sleep."

"Have a heart," piped an over-bold treble, "it's the first night of term."

"I'll push your bloody eye in, Miss Miggs," Mottram replied, "get into bed and shut your mouth."

Miss Miggs, finding no support, acquiesced with commendable discretion.

"Sleeping, Bristow?" Mottram asked, in the dark.

"No," came a voice from the next bed.

"Well, remember I told you last term about that dame I was running? You know — the snip?"

"Yes," — why wouldn't Mottram let him think of Anne, and yesterday, and eternity.

"Well, how much will you pay to hear what I did to her?"

Silence.

"Say, Bristow," Mottram was impatient to begin, "how much will you pay?"

"Oh Christ, I don't know."

"Well, I'll tell you, anyway. She was camping in the same place as me during August and — "

Wilfred stuck his fingers into his ears and turned his face into the pillow. Anne so hopelessly far away, and he wanted to see her so. It was terrible, loving her so much. He took his fingers out of his ears and listened to Mottram. And as he listened the timid, inquisitive lust rose in hot surges, up through his chest and his throat, like a thirst, and into his eyes. And there was Anne, in the hot mist and he in the hot mist too, living together each detail of Mottram's lewd story. It was marvellous — Ugh! it was marvellous.

(*1936*)

The Wedding Breakfast

"Look sharp, gal, with that bre' n' butter," cried Mrs. Merriman in a high-pitched, nagging voice; "it's twenty past nine — they'll be back from chapel soon as winking."

She popped her worn, pinched face, with its long nose and narrow, beady eyes, round the pantry door to make sure that Martha had put seven plates of ham on the table and divided the half bottle of port between the seven glass tumblers.

"Don't fidget, grampa," she said to her seventy-eight year old father; "jest keep quiet an' learn your poem. Martha'll lace your boots up 'fore they come."

Martha entered the kitchen from the scullery, carrying two plates of bread and butter in her rough hands. Her face was a less animated replica of her mother's. Her shoulders stooped. Red rims round her eyes accentuated the sallowness of her skin.

"Surely to goodness you've not bin crying already, gal?" piped Mrs. Merriman. "Is it jealous you are against your younger sister getting married an' off our 'ands before you?"

Martha bent to lace the old man's shoes, saying nothing.

"Oh, well, if some 'ave got rosy cheeks an' plenty of nerve an' others 'aven't — " sighed Mrs. Merriman. And whisking back to the pantry in search of American cheese, she added, "Anyroads, it's a mercy we won't be paying for Menna's frocks no more."

"They're coming in the taxi," cried Grandma's cracked, excited voice from the front doorway, where she had been waiting with a brown paper bag of confetti ever since Menna and her father had left for chapel. And as Albert Groves helped his bride out of the car, Grandma's shrivelled, little hand flung a benediction of white and pink paper over her newly-married grand-daughter. Will Gibbs, Albert's "butty," having fulfilled the dual role of best man and taxi-driver, drove straight off to a funeral engagement, which was just as well, as

Mr. Merriman observed, "what with the back kitchen bein' a bit small
an' one thing an' another."

"'A' pas' nine," said Mr. Merriman loudly; "jest nice time. Soon as
you've gone through the shop to the back kitchen I'll put the blinds up.
Mustn't keep the shop shut, you know — weddings isn't the same as
funerals. You won't mind going through the back yard to the station,
Albert, will you?"

"It's O.K. with me," said Albert, cheerily. He looked
uncomfortably precise in his black suit and starched collar. His
perspiring hands, fumbling with the sweet bottles on the counter,
seemed bewildered by the absence of his mechanic's overalls.
Formerly an unemployed miner, Albert had worked for the last two
years in a factory at Slough, and was predestined to recommence the
manufacture of buttons at 9 a.m. on the morrow. He had booked two
tickets for the Upper Circle at the London Palladium that night. He
couldn't rightly afford such a luxury, but after all, a fellow doesn't
marry every day.

"Well, come right through to the back kitchen, my dear little
pigeons," Mrs. Merriman greeted them, lifting the hem of her
pinafore to her eyes. "Come an' 'ave some breakfast before your
journey. You'll 'ave to sit close — there's seven of us — three married
couples — an' Martha; not too strong for me, please — an' you sit next
to your father, Menna. You won't see 'im for a long time, so make the
most of it."

"Go on, Mam," laughed Menna, her cheeks flushed with
excitement. "Dad an' you'll come up to see us on Bank 'Oliday, when
we're settled down, won't you? Albert says Slough's right by Windsor
— 'Enry the Eighth built *that*. What date, Albert?"

"1302," said Albert emphatically.

"There, Dad, you'd like to see it, wouldn't you?" she pursued.
"You're fond of ancient 'istory. Can I 'ave another lump of sugar,
Martha? — a small one, please."

"Alright, we'll come up," replied Mr. Merriman, his mouth full of
cold ham, "though I expect it's toys for the quintimplets we'll be
bringing then." He laughed boisterously at his joke — giving the bride
away had made him feel unwontedly generous and expansive.

"Well, Albert, it's time for the station," said Menna. "I'll be glad to
be in the train looking at them Carter's Little Liver Pills rushing past, *I*
know."

"Albert," whispered Martha, speaking for the first time, "when I
went up to London thirteen years ago, the fields was all buttercups.

An' though it was cloudy everywhere else, there was one neadow full of sunlight — by a river — between Cardiff an' Swindon, somewhere. See if it's still there, Albert — dear — will you?"

"There's rude it is to whisper, Martha," snapped Mrs. Merriman, "an' don't sniffle neither — you're making me cry too. Anyroads, look sharp, you two, or you'll lose the train. Martha can go to the station with you, being as she 'elped me when the wedding was on. Some one's in the shop, Dad. There's no time to read your poem, grampa, — better give it to Menna to read in the train."

Mrs. Merriman was an efficient bustler, and in five minutes they were saying farewell at the backyard gate.

"Remember your old mam, sometimes, Menna," she sobbed.

"Don't forget about them quintimplets," shouted Mr. Merriman through the scullery window.

Grandma whimpered — she had no confetti left.

Martha, a coat slipped over her pinafore, walked slowly down the lane, ahead of the others, carrying Menna's hat bag. Suddenly she dropped it and ran . . . helter-skelter . . . down the lane, round the corner . . . .

"What's up with 'er, I'd like to know," said Menna; "there's a daft thing to do!"

"It's 'er nerves, that's what it is," said Albert.

"Well, I want 'er 'elp for the washing up, anyroads," said Mrs. Merriman. "There's a pile of dirty dishes."

(*1936*)

from THE MANCHESTER
GUARDIAN

Cardinali Crisis

Ever since the Abyssinian business began in 1935 things had been bad for Antonio Cardinali. They got worse when the Duce started intervening in Spain; the bald patch at the back of his crown widened and his face got to look mouse-eaten. He was afraid of losing business, for all the colliers were violently antagonistic to Mussolini, and when they dropped into his shop on the way home from work they always gibed roughly at Antonio.

"What are you sending Il Duce for Christmas, Tony? Bottle of hair-restorer from Jones the barbers, is it?"

"Seen you practising the goose-step last night, Tony, down the back lane."

"If your hot drinks wasn't so damned good, Tony, we'd impose sanctions on your shop."

So it went on, day after day, and Antonio took it all with a hairy grin, his top lip vanishing under his nose and his forehead wrinkling up into his close-cropped, grizzly hair.

"I'm not a Blackshirt, nor nothing," he rejoined sometimes. "I don't intermeggle. It's a very bad bisniz — I don't know what."

He kept his shop as spick-and-span as ever, the counter well polished, the coffee urn shining like a mirror, the stove banked with coal, the boiling kettle bubbling a perpetual invitation to partake of a hot sarsaparilla. And his trade did not suffer much. After all, he had been in Glanamman for twenty years; he was as much an institution as the Baptist minister or the postman, and his clientele had no faults to find with him. His shop was by the bus stop, opposite the colliery gates, and it was always full. In the mornings he did little, for nobody came in but a few seedy unemployed youths with holes in their pockets. They brought little trade; they just sat by the stove and yarned, thin and bony ankles thrusting out of frayed and patched grey trousers, feet tapping to the music from Antonio's wireless. It was early afternoon that the rush came, from the moment the cage clanged to the top of the pithead with the first batch of the morning shift, until dusk sent the late-lazing gossips home for their baths. Every afternoon he worked hard, mixing the hot drinks — vanilla, lemon, rasberry, rum, — steam condensing on his face, while the miners came in with a clatter of hobnailed boots and a coughing of dust-teased lungs and banged their black fists on his gleaming counter. When they were served they sat by the stove and discussed the daily paper's football forecasts and compared their own pool sheets. Sometimes they submitted a doubtful one to Antonio.

"Fancy the Villa to win at Manchester on Saturday, Tony?"

And when he shrugged his shoulders and grinned and said, "I don't know, I don' do nothin' with it," they all laughed as though he had cracked a joke, for they all knew what his reply would be.

And Antonio liked to see them laugh, even at him, for he depended on their custom. None of the "better sort" would buy from him. The miners who were chapel deacons never entered his shop, not even to buy an ounce of twist, and they belted their children if they caught them coming out of Cardinali's. They might buy a pink cornet from him in the summer, when he trundled his ice-cream cart with its neatly painted Botticelli daisies festooning his name along the village streets. But his shop was taboo. Only wasters and disrespectables went into his shop; people with nothing better to do. Besides, the place was open even on Sundays when every decent tradesman should be in chapel . . .

So Antonio was careful not to offend his customers. "Not in a twenty years I leave my shop," he would boast, "not a Sunday nor early closing day nor nothing. Aways open, eight o'clock to midnight almost, and always what sort of a cordial you like." He was as proud of his record as a child of its attendance certificate.

But, all the same, things were getting very bad. The pit was only working spasmodically, the men were "out" for weeks on end, with little money and sullen faces. They just sat in his shop and spent hardly a penny. Then the Czech crisis came. Antonio could not stand it all.

"Is there nobody in this village at all but Hitler and Franco and Benes and them?" he complained.

"Sure, there's Chamberlain," somebody answered, "and Lord Rushcliffe." Antonio stopped buying a daily paper, and his wireless set went out of order, too. But the silence was worse . . . .

And then one morning — September 23 — his shop was shut. When the habitúes came and found the door shut and the green blinds down they stared increduously for a minute, and then went down to the billiards saloon in the Workmen's Institute. There they heard what had happened. One of the newspaper boys had seen him at the station with a face like a shaken blancmange waiting for the 7.30 with the Italian brothers who kept a chip-shop in the town. They had been summoned to the Italian Consulate in Cardiff. The boy said Tony was crying like a kid.

"Poor old Tony," one of them said, chalking his cue and laughing; "a hell of a lot of use 'e'll be in the front line, polishing 'is bayonet all day."

The day after Munich Antonio presented all his customers with a double Woodbine and a free drink; he grinned all day like a brass band.

"Just from me," he said, "not from Chamberlain nor the Duce nor nobody. Just from me, see."

He switched the wireless on, banked up the stove, bustled about with a tea-towel pulled through his waistcoat buttonhole, humming to himself. And the men sat morosely at the tables, their feet tapping automatically to the music, smoking Antonio's cigarettes and saying nothing.

(*1939*)

The Poetry Lesson

Pedloe stood by the classroom door of VB, holding a duster in his hand and peeping down the corridor.

"Is he coming yet, Ped?" one of the back-row boys called.

"No, he's still in the boss's room." Pedloe answered.

A boy who had been drawing girls' faces on the board slouched lazily to his seat in the corner.

"Looks a bit of a siss to me, anyway," he said. "Still, we'd better be careful. Some new masters start slamming your ear the minute you try anything on."

"Here he is." Pedloe jumped back to the master's desk and stood to attention with exaggerated stiffness.

The new master entered with a swish of his black gown; stern frown.

"Whirlwind Willie." murmured the boy in the corner.

Titters.

"Shh!" Pedloe said, and when the master turned on him he shook the duster out. "Clean the board, sir?" he said deferentially.

"Yes, hurry up."

They weighed the sound of his voice in the ensuing pause. It was rather high pitched and shaky, sounding as if it would crack if he yelled at ar *y*body. He glanced at the drawings on the board and smiled.

"That's the direction your minds work in, is it?" he said.

They roared like bulls, drowning his attempt to shut them up.

He flushed; his temples were sweating and his nose shiny. He put on his spectacles and picked up the form edition of Palgrave's Golden Treasury.

"Now," he said, with emphasis, "suppose we do a little work."

"Yes, sir," they chorused, scrambling in their satchels with a deal of noise and fishing out their Palgraves in a dilatory way.

"I understand you are doing the Elizabethan poets this term," he said.

"Yes, sir; that's right, sir."

"All right, one of you will do. Answer when I ask you. Now, you," he pitched on Pedloe, "what poem did you do last?"

"Page twenty-three sir: 'Take, O take those lips away,' " Pedloe beamed.

"Stop this tittering," he shouted. His voice nearly cracked.

"Matthews generally reads aloud for us, sir," Pedloe added. "He's been trained in elocution. Yes, sir, that's Matthews there, sir." He pointed at a little pale, grey-suited boy with mousy hair who was sitting in the front row. He was the only boy still wearing shorts.

"Will you read the next one, then?" the new master said, standing by Matthews's desk.

The boy stood up, his fingers twisting the strap of his satchel. He did not lift his head.

"Come on, boy; there's nothing to be shy about."

In a tense silence Matthews lifted his frightened, velvety blue eyes, and his quivering mouth formed a tentative word.

"P-p-p-p-l-l-l," tears starting into his eyes.

"I'm sorry," the new master said, passing his hand gently on the boy's shoulder. "Sit down again, will you?"

Nobody made a sound. They realised Pedloe had gone too far.

The new master looked round very slowly. Pedloe studied his Palgrave intently. The whole class fixed their eyes on their desks or their books or their fingers.

"The next poem is by Michael Drayton," he said slowly. "It is the sonnet I like best of all the Elizabethan poetry."

They shuffled their legs and relaxed. Pedloe looked up cautiously.

"Now before we read it, what do you know of the Shakespearean sonnet?" The boy in the corner lazily lifted his hand.

"Sit up, boy, this isn't a harem. Now, what have you got to say?"

"They're all about love, sir."

"Yes, sir," Pedloe interposed. "But love was much broader then than it is now, sir."

"What do you mean by that?" the new master said, smiling.

"That's what the last master told us, sir," Pedloe smirked.

"Well, what other love poets have you read?"

"Please, sir, Sheats and Kelley."

"Haw! haw! haw!" the class scoffed. Pedloe sat down crestfallen. It was an old joke, but with a new master they should have played up to him.

"Your wit doesn't seem to be appreciated to-day," the master said.

Little Matthews looked round at Pedloe and sniggered.

"Now listen carefully while I read the first quatrain," the master said, and holding the Palgrave in the cup of his hand he cleared his throat:

> Since there's no help, come let us kiss and part, —
> Nay I have done, you get no more of me;

His voice had become vibrant and rich, its shakiness converted into something wonderfully sensitive and tremulous. Its high pitch sounded flute-like, making their spines tingle. They watched him with a half-shameful attention. His face was rapt and naked, shiny with sweat:

> And I am glad, yea, glad with all my heart,
> That thus so cleanly I myself can free;
> Shake hands for ever, cancel all our vows,
> And when we meet at any time again,
> Be it not seen in either of our brows
> That we one jot of former love retain.

His voice rang through and through the still classroom, electrifying the sluggish, bookish air and compelling the sprawling adolescents to understand. Silence like a ruined temple at the end of the second quatrain; then a soft melodic sadness as his voice seemed to veil itself before the deathbed of love; and at the end, with a sharp intake of breath that was like a sigh, his voice trembled through the final confession of the heart's thraldom. In the hush of his last words the bell rang down the corridor. He closed the book with a snap, removed his spectacles, and rubbed his eyes with his knuckles.

"You may go," he said sharply, and stood stiffly by his desk while they filed out. When Pedloe passed him he smiled.

"What's he like?" a fourth-former asked eagerly in the hall.

"I dunno," Pedloe answered. "He's a funny chap. You can't tell — yet."

(*1939*)

MISCELLANEOUS

Rain

He shut the kitchen door against the slash of the rain and picked up the crumpled newspaper once more. The midwife had left it open at the Women's Page. Idly he read it. "It is when she is expecting her first baby that the young wife most needs and most appreciates the tender little attentions that show her the depth of her husband's love." He dropped the paper to the floor, went slowly across to the window, and looked out at the dripping trees.

Then the doctor's footsteps sounded on the stairs, the curtain was pushed back and the old man beckoned wearily.

"Come along, young chap," he whispered. "You've got a son to be proud of." In the daytime the monkey tree outside the small window hid the bedroom in a changeless dusk. Only like this, by the light of fire and lamp, did the room recover its identity from the neuter half-light of the fields.

The midwife lifted the white shawl away from the new, small face with one hand and straightened the bedclothes with the other. She looked up for his approval like a professional photographer.

He couldn't see very clearly for the tears in his eyes. Just vaguely her ashen countenance and the smile in her wide, nervous eyes. And by her side the puckered, grotesque little mask of — of the nameless one.

He touched her damp forehead with his finger tips.

The rain had slackened when he left the cottage half an hour later. He breathed deeply the rising smell of mould and freshened leaves. The laden leaning apple boughs showered him with a tinkling laughter of rain. Under the trees the cows lay on their bellies in the soaking grass, steam curling round their flanks. Along the lane the lumps of cow dung had been beaten into a thin, pock-marked paste and the brown earth washed away from the jagged stones. The under leaves of the copper beech had turned green, caught in the tide of green that swept the valley and submerged all flower colours. A cockerel strutted out of the hedge, jerking its crop like a crosspatch, its red comb burning against the grey and dripping green.

He stooped to pick a few gooseberries from the bush that grew at the corner. One hung on its bowed stem, great and transparently ripe, the dark nucleus of seed glowing through the taut skin. A veined globe, suspended in the firmament. And as he watched, a wasp settled on it, vicious and engrossed, and probed into the crystal fruit. Just so feed Love and Imagination, Poverty and Greed.

The rain gathered in full, pellucid drops on the points of the sycamore leaves and, falling into the pond, divided the water into intersecting circles, impersonal geometric shapes that expanded, like the bubbles, into nothing. The water overflowed through a tin grating and ran away through the long shivering grasses, singing to itself like a lonely child, or as a butterfly might sing.

Across the pond the hay lay in wet swathes, waiting the sun. The further half of the field was still under corn, green and immature. Two magpies strutted about on the fringe of the crop. As he loitered one of them rose with a loud cawing. Which way would it go? To the ivied oak in the far hedge? Or over the lane? Oh, which way, which way was it to be? Towards the oak it flapped, over the green corn, and folded its wings and vanished into the leaves. Ah! And its mate after it.

Further up the lane he stopped again to peep through an empty bolthole in the corrugated iron wall of a hay loft. By placing his eye to the hole he could see the whole farmyard, squarely enclosed by the whitewashed stone house and the well-built sheds. In the sodden dung heap brown and white hens pecking, under the porch a tabby licking itself dry. The whole scene in a timeless consummation, the quiet half-tones made one with the simple, habitable perfection of its building.

When he reached the wood the path sank into the grass. Under the thin and twisted oakes grew brambles and whins and tall, red-capped, wind-rocked foxgloves. Out of their motion stillness was fashioned.

Then suddenly, terribly, a scream of pain. A screech-owl? But who could give a bird a cry of such agony?

Silence, trembling and agonised, transcending time.

Again the high mad scream of living pain.

He could not go away for all his sickness and fear.

He plunged through the bracken to the fringe of gorse at the wood's limit.

There he found what he feared to find.

The rabbit's hind leg was in the iron trap, the bone red and smashed. Its ears were laid back against its head, and leaning over he could see only the glazing whites of its eyes. Its nose strained against the earth. Only when the six inch chain broke its leap to escape did it scream. "Don't scream now," he said to it, "oh please don't scream now."

The best way is to take it by its hind legs and flip it on the nape of its neck. But the mangled hind legs, the protruding bone.

He pressed his heel on its head. The skull squelched, its body quivered and bucked. He caught the chain in his fingers, and pulled, oh hard. Its decapitated body came away in his hand, the long bloody spine uncollared. He dropped it and ran back to the path, the brambles ripping his hands and knees. Swaying to and fro, the foxgloves nodded, red sadistic heads.

He ran down the lane, his mind and body a liquid, quivering consciousness, blood-coloured, urgent with recollection.Fear and pity led him out of the labyrinth into which he had wandered out of the ken of his flesh. His shoes slithered on the wet grass. Out of the wood, past the hay loft and the duckpond until his lungs burned with distress. He leaned against a gate and the dusk washed his breathlessness away. For a few minutes he did not see that a heavy brown mare had lifted her grazing head and was staring at him. Then he stared back. Discrete and strange to each other, his ignorance coloured with wonder, the mare's with fear.

The mare began walking up and down before him, lifting her hooves high, watching him all the time. She whisked her tail, whinnied, kicked her huge hooves; her nostrils distended and quivered. He did not move. Suddenly she turned her head and galloped across the field, hooves hysterically drumming. Out of the misty, impenetrable dusk he heard her whinny in terror, — of the unknown, unchanging, un-guessed at thing.

He walked slowly down the lane, through the pit of darkness under the copper beech. His shoes were soaked, his feet and fingers numb. The lamp light from the bedroom window fell palely on the dripping bracken and the bowed and withered alders. As he shut the gate of the cottage garden he heard the child whimpering. And as the door closed after him the rain came on again and lengthened into bayonets of ice.

(Unpublished until: Lewis: A Miscellany of his Writings, 1982)

The Testimonial

The Senate had been in session for over two hours when Professor Adderby pushed his papers into his tarnished leather portfolio — the one his wife had given him before they married forty nine years ago, though it was so much a part of him that he never thought of it in that way — and left the University Library with a sweep of his long doctor's gown. He had nodded asleep once during the meeting; he wasn't going to make a fool of himself by dropping right off; he knew he snored. And when he had caught himself dozing and with a fierce effort had concentrated on what they were saying, it all sounded so dull and distant, so far beyond the weariness of his body, all this discussion of Fellowships and new appointments and next session's syllabus, that he felt overpowered and dispirited by it all. Year after year, always the same, a ponderous complicated treadwheel turned by words — it was beyond him, beyond him. And in any case he didn't count. It didn't matter what he said, an ancient Emeritus professor lost in research. Besides, there was nothing for him to say. So he went. Nobody noticed. They were arguing a nice point.

He still had a room in College, his old room, which he had been allowed to retain after a hard tiff with the incoming professor. He went to it automatically, along the balcony and up the flight of steps which had slowly worn his legs away, year after year. He stopped at the top, sighing for breath, and fumbled about in his pockets for the key. He couldn't find the confounded thing. He fumbled about, on the verge of tears. Ah, of course. It was fastened to his braces. He smiled, trembling with utter relief. It slipped beautifully into the lock, the door opened, a click, and the room flooded with welcoming warm light. And there were his books, in mad piles on the floor and chairs and table, covered by a thin fall of manuscripts, like snow.

And there was a letter for him. Yes, actually a letter. But, of course. He was still a professor. He had educated thousands of students, written five books — the one on demonology had even been reviewed on the front page of the *Times Lit.*, naturally there would be a letter for him. Only one? It was probably that confounded scout — he never delivered the mail promptly — have to tell him about it again, reprimand him, if he saw him. Hadn't seen him for some time, actually. Was he by any chance — ? He remembered his face distinctly, silver-rimmed spectacles, hooked nose. But, of course, how silly. There was a new chap now. He had noticed him vaguely, some time back. What had happened to the old scout? Was he by any chance — ? Oh never mind. Better attend to his correspondence; it was getting late; they'd be shutting the College soon.

He opened the letter with his dear old ivory knife, slowly, fondly, dragging the pleasure out. He opened it carefully and smiled. How silly he had been to get so flustered and frightened in the Senate. Damn them all, the old dry-as-dust crew, so ridiculously self-important. He had done more work than any of them, in his time. This letter, cheap notepaper, cheap ink, sloppy hand, whoever it was. Fellow ought to know better. A girl was it? An old student of his? Signed herself Monica Berriman. Who the devil was she? Some spinster or other. Wanted a testimonial. Thought as much. People never write unless they want something. But, really, on second thoughts, the handwriting was rather sweet — gentle, timid. Even the faded ink had a charm. She must have mixed it with water . . . . And then he saw the date. Almost . . . exactly . . . a . . . year . . . ago . . . . Heavens. Had it been lying there so long? Surely he hadn't been away from his room all that time. He rubbed his eyes, then laughed. "Of course," he said aloud to the empty room, "I'd forgotten about my illness. How silly."

And then he frowned, partly at the fearful sound of his own voice in all the silence, partly because he didn't like to remember that icy mental hospital place . . . What the devil did she want, anyway?

Her hausband had died, leaving her with two children, two girls of ten and thirteen. She was applying for a headship in a village school. She would be deeply grateful if he could find time to send her a testimonial. She had taken her Finals under him in 1914, but had left the College for the V.A.D. before completing her degree.

Oh, *heavens*. He scratched his head in an angry panic. What on earth could he do? If the woman must rush off to the foolish war at the first sound of the kettledrum, what could he do? What was the use of her coming to him, wasting his time? He pushed the letter away and sat in his chair. Was it worth working? Or was it a bit late? The letter got on his nerves. He pushed it under a green file, furtively. There! Now! He took one nervous look at the dusty pile of manuscripts. No, it was hardly worth starting tonight. And then he thought "Poor girl." He got up quickly, crossed to his bureau and pulled out all the files. Papers fluttered all over him, over the floor. Lists of marks, of books of students, research notes, annual reports. He began sweating as he searched impatiently, then frantically, for the 1914 lists. When, by grace, he found them, he trembled all over. Thank heavens. He sat in his chair and sighed, waiting patiently until his eyes got better. Then he read through the names. Yes, her name was there. Monica Berriman. He stared at her name. Berriman. Miss Berriman. Couldn't recall her face. Monica Berriman. He spoke the name aloud, musingly, then querulously. Finally he shouted it out, half expecting her to start, and blush, and say, "Yes, Professor?" But no. Nothing happened. Only silence. He waited a space; then he looked down the list. Bevan, Bickle, Binns, Bowen, Boyce . . . . And he couldn't remember a single one. He tried hard, in an agony of concentration. And failed. Failed to recall a single face, a single voice, of all the students he had taught. He rubbed his knuckles into his eyes. It was hellish, hellish. His eyes danced with bars of deep colour, under the pressure of his quivering fingers. Not a single face, of all the thousands, the lost thousands.

And then a girl laughed from the street below him, from the darkness, saucily, seductively, very young and vibrant. Ah! He felt suddenly still. Quite, quite, at peace. Home again, safe again. He opened his eyes and smiled affectionately at the old room.

Heavy steps mounted the stairs, clop..clop..clop . . . Mercilessly. He broke into a cold sweat, holding his breath, silent as a terrified mouse. A rap at the door. He stopped himself screaming. Another rap, peremptory, impatient. Instinctively he opened a book. If they were coming for him at last he would let them see he still had work to do . . . . He didn't squeal when the key turned and the door opened. Indeed he looked up with super-human calm.

"Sorry to interrupt, sir," said the new scout. "But College is closing now, sir. I seen a light in your room, sir."

His voice came back after a struggle in his throat, quite clearly.

"Thank you," he said, gathering up his papers. "There *was* some work. But it can wait. You . . . you are the new scout?"

"New, sir?" the scout laughed. "I been here ten years, sir, if you call that new, sir. Ever since the old one died, sir . . . . . . "

(*1939*)

UNPUBLISHED STORIES

And At My Departing

I knew quite well that I was spoiling Sophie's holiday, and I felt horrid about it, for I knew how she'd been looking forward to this little fortnight in St. Malo. You see, we'd both had a very trying winter; indeed I think it was more wearing for Sophie than for me. I was ill, it's true, not Sophie; but I don't worry about things as she does. And now, just when the change and the rest began to bring the colour back into her cheeks, I start being 'queer' again. I wish I could stop being 'queer.' It's so tiresome. For instance, the very first day at lunch they served us up a glass bowl of cockles. We had to take them out of the bowl with our fingers and split them open with our knives. And halfway through the course I saw a cockle moving in the bowl. They were *alive*. And it was so silly of me — I screamed and pushed the bowl off the table, smashed it to pieces. And I just *couldn't* forget about it, for days. Things seem to prey on me, somehow, and it upsets Sophie so, too. You see, she nearly always knows what I'm thinking about. I suppose it's only natural, seeing that we've lived together ever since our father died, thirty years ago. We're inseparable. I imagine the St. Malo people say 'Ah, those two little spinsters,' when we go out shopping. At home, in Salisbury, they say 'Good-day, Misses Brook,' and take off their hats. 'Autres langues, autres moeurs,' as it were.

And so, yesterday morning, I made myself tell Sophie about it. Just before lunch, when we were sitting on the beach and Sophie said "Hadn't we better go and lunch before the restaurants get crowded?" and I answered "Yes, dear, in a minute, as soon as I've finished." "Finished what?" she said, rather sharply, I thought, "You've been doing nothing all the morning except watch the kiddies dig sand castles." And then I told her about my dream. I could hardly bear to tell it, especially as I knew it would spoil our lunch.

I was wandering by the edge of the sea at night, and the tide was coming in all silver with moonlight. There was nobody about and I began talking to the waves. Then suddenly a clear child's voice cried "Help, help." So piteously. But I couldn't see a soul. You know how *distinct* a moonlit night is — but no, not a soul. And then I almost trod on him — a tiny little boy, buried up to his neck in the wet sand. The incoming tide licked his frightened little face and flowed back again. You can imagine how terrified I was. "I'll run all the way — fetch a gendarme — dig you out," I said. He smiled — he was awfully pale — and said "Please hurry, Miss Brook. The tide comes in so quickly. Another minute and — " And I ran and ran, slithering over the weed-covered rocks, until I got to the gate of the town. And there I bumped into Sophie and she said "Where on earth have you been?" And I said "Oh, just walking a little." And she said "The tide comes in so quickly, doesn't it?" And I answered "Yes, I suppose it does." And I forgot all about the little boy. When I remembered about him two days later, it was too late.

But Sophie just poo-pooed it all. "Guilty?" she laughed. "Why should you feel guilty about a *dream*?" She says 'dream' so scornfully; it's because she doesn't understand. "We'll ask that nice chemist behind the fish market whether he can get us some Ovaltine rushed over from England," she said. So we called there after lunch, and as it happened he had some in stock. It cost almost twice as much as it did at home, but we bought it in the end. "If it doesn't do you any good, I shall bring it back," Sophie said.

We didn't go out to dine last night because the wind had risen and had brought a misty rain in from the islands. We went to bed soon after nine and I thought I'd read for an hour after drinking my Ovaltine. But Sophie had taken my books away from my bedroom — Mary Rose, Peter Pan and Alice in Wonderland. I always keep them by my bedside. I felt very hurt — she might at least have told me. But I know she thinks it's for my own good, really. So I put the light out and tried to sleep. I don't know whether I did or not. It was all dark, but a turbulent tossing darkness, full of sound and storm. It might have been just the wind and rain against my window, but I don't think so. I think it was real. I know it was. And all the time voices — one voice from lots of places — calling for help. "I'm dying, oh save me. Come at once, oh quickly." And sometimes the voice was drowned in the roll and beat of the darkness. And I couldn't breath until it started again.

And it went on and on, until suddenly I saw that everything was still clear and grey. Like the dawn, the first of all dawns. And then I heard weeping — it seemed to be coming from a bedroom. But I couldn't see. I strained my senses until I thought I could see — Sophie — bending over a bed and weeping. But that wasn't part of the dream, for Sophie was actually bending over me, asking me how I'd slept.

"Like a top, dear," I said. I would have liked to kiss her then. After breakfast we went down to the beach and sat on deckchairs in the bright sun. Children dancing and romping, and beautiful, sun-tanned bathers, and the sea lit with golden torches — I felt oh so *happy*, as if it was all for ever. As if *I* was the sun and all lovely things. And all the time I could hear the sad voices, faint and deep down, as though the sunlight had robbed them of their strength, but not of their reality. "We are waiting," they whispered, "but come soon, soon."

We didn't talk much. I believe Sophie was thinking about next winter and wondering whether it would be as trying for her as last year. At lunch we talked about our garden. Sophie was afraid the weeds would be getting the upper hand during our absence. And after lunch she made me lie down. I must have been very tired for I slept almost at once. Like a top. And when I woke it was dusk in my room. I could hear footsteps outside, and laughter. Sophie would be sewing in her room, crocheting by the fire. And then, as I lay there the voice said "You *will* come, won't you?" There were tears in the voice and I knew that it would die if I didn't go to it. So I soothed it, drew it to me, and said "Yes."

I went into Sophie's room and chatted to her for a little. Then I felt so weak and tired that I kissed her goodnight and went back to bed. Once I thought of calling to her, but it would only have kept her awake for the rest of the night. So I just lay still and waited. And then I heard the siren of the English night boat sounding, down by the Quai de Southampton. I knew then. I slipped out through the window and down through the dark to the docks. The ship was just casting off. The Algerian peddlers on the quayside were screaming their wares — carpets and bangles and nick-nacks — and waving their red fez caps frantically. And silly Englishmen throwing their odd centimes to them and shouting "Voici un pourboire," and smiling in a lordly way.

Then we were in the middle of the waters, rising and falling and leaving a white wound in our wake. And strong, white-winged seagulls gliding downwind, checking and tumbling. And the black, down-pressing night heavy with mist and wild spray. I tried to think of other things — Sophie's lace collars, the roses we had grafted in June, the procession of the Nativity of the Virgin last week, when the tiny, white-frocked children marched singing through St Malo, waving paper flags with 'mystere douloureux' written on them. When they waved their flags it made a dry, bitter sound, like leaves suddenly sere. But the dark icy waves broke over my thoughts, drowning them; I was frightened. Frightened that I wouldn't get back before Sophie came into my bedroom in the morning.

Then in the end the cold grey cliffs and the bleak glassy Solent and the naked land, waiting for warmth. All laid out under the watery-green sky, waiting for warmth, for breath. The passengers waited too, their baggage in piles near the gangway, waited and blew into their cold hands.

There was no sound, except the ship's engines and the gulls' crying. All the waste of water. And no voice. Only weeping; and loneliness, far, far behind, in a bedroom, sea miles away; which I could not reach, nor desire to reach, having cast off the shroud of night, having been discovered by the dawn.

Duration

I

From the nucleus of whitewashed thatched cottages under the church long tentacles felt their way along the dunes, pinned down by new villas and walled-in boarding houses with foreign names and lemonade kiosks covered with tarred felting. The dunes were disreputable with newspaper and crushed serviettes and other litter left by the trippers. Along the beach thousands of tin caps with crimped edges, pulled off lemonade bottles this year, last year, the year before last, lay thick as tide-wrack, rusting. The dusk and the incoming tide were slowly laying a worn dustcloth over the scene; the trippers had gone back to town, but for one solitary car parked under the wall of a small villa. Inside the car a man was dandling a two-year-old baby, tickling it and guffawing like a horse; inside the villa a soldier and a girl were lying on a prim quilted bed. Ornamental texts from the scriptures hung over them in the small room; a virgin carrying a pitcher and lifting her long white shift with one hand entered the framed temple above their feet. The soldier's boots were tied round with handkerchieves so as not to dirty the pink quilt. He was young and ruffled, his battledress unfastened at the neck; she lay ill at ease in his arms.

"Auntie'll be back any minute, Dave," she said nervously.

"She's not been gone half an hour," he said. "Can't you forget about her for five minutes?"

"*You* won't forget it if she finds us in the bedroom," she replied.

"Oh, give her a rest," he groaned. "We can hear the gate open. Look, Gracie, — " he raised himself over her on his elbow — "can't you *see*, darling? There's only this, this now. That's all that's left for us. Can't you see?"

His voice had a rasping intensity in it, an overwhelming urgency; his brown lambent eyes swam through her distracted gaze like great whales in a misty bay, cleaving her. Youth and desire surging desperately over her, his passion and his apprehension of death forcing her hard. She made no answer. Pale and angular, even in her distress she was listening to the sounds outside, listening for her aunt's voice of the creak of the gate. But there was no sound except the loud guffaws of the man dandling the baby in the car.

"That hateful man," she said with a touch of hysteria.

"Oh what does he matter?" he snapped. "What does anybody matter except *us*? There's only to-night left, don't you understand?"

"Where will they send you, Dave?" she asked, taking her folded white hands up to his face. "Perhaps it will be Iceland, or somewhere safe like that?"

"Perhaps it won't," he said angrily. "Perhaps it'll be Tobruk or Russia. In any case, I won't see you again after to-night for the rest of the war. Do you know that?"

His hand moved a little, up from her silken knee, under the hem of her skirt. She took her hand from his cheek and moved it down to stop him. "Why don't they tell you where you're going?" she almost cried, her voice weepy, her eyes watery.

"Thousands of lives were lost in the last war," he mocked.

Then he saw how this was tormenting her and he drew her closer into him. "It's no good, not now," she said, her voice so thin that he bent his head over her to hear.

"Why not?" he asked, his voice hot and loud.

"It's too late," she contrived to say. "We don't know anything; we haven't bought any of those things you need. Oh, can't you see it's no good?"

They both sat up. And she only wanted him to go. She was exhausted with frustrating him, frustrating herself, holding the eye of the needle shut against him, bitterly. If he tried again she must let him have his way. She was exhausted to death.

"O.K." he said with a laugh. "I'll go."

"Dave!" she was terrified, clutching his tunic, leaning white and agonised towards him. "Please, Dave. Please write to me where you are. Will you?"

"Come on," he said, pulling the handkerchieves off his feet and standing up. "Let's get out before your aunt gets back."

The man dandling the baby roared with laughter.

"Let's go, for Christ's sake," the boy said.

II

He found a corner seat near the engine after walking the whole
length of the crowded express. A huge-shouldered sapper with a
bomb-disposal badge on his sleeve and a raw weal across his face
from lip to temple moved up, pulling his pale thin girl gently
closer under his arm.

"There you are, chum," he said in a rough friendly voice.
"Squeeze in." A girl in a cheap mauve hat with a high feather and
a veil watched the newcomer settle himself down. But he wasn't
anything particular to look at, his hair was no particular colour, so
there wasn't anything much there for her. She turned to look at
the crowd on the platform, "Look at that old man on the bench,"
she said aloud to the whole compartment.

An old man in an overcoat and cloth cap was sitting on the
bench, a little girl in black stockings and a fluffy red jersey beside
him. His shoulders were shaking up and down as if he were
laughing, his head was pressed over his quivering hands which
gripped the knob of his walking stick.

"He's crying his eyes out," the girl said, laughing.

Sometimes the old man managed to regain his composure,
obviously by a great and exhausting effort, so exhausting that it
weakened him and he began sobbing again. The little girl stood
beside him became invaded by uneasiness and shuffled her feet and
wriggled on the bench. Nobody seemed to mind the old man. The
rest of the family were standing in front of him, laughing
excitedly, smoking, talking, embracing the two beefy aircraftsmen
they were seeing off. The platform was packed along its whole
length with excited crowded groups of servicemen and their
relatives, hugging, joking, writing addresses in diaries,
exchanging the last injunctions and endearments.

"They shouldn't let old men like that come to the station," the
girl with the mauve hat said indignantly. "They ought to leave
him at home if he can't control himself. Ugh."

The whistle blew and the guard hurried past the window. A
little boy outside the window tugged at his father's waistcoat until
he gave him a big white handkerchief. The train moved with a
slight shudder, a jerk, then a slow puffing roll forward. The old
man broke down, his head slumping forward as the train slid out
of his view. Everybody was waving handkerchieves and hats and
scarves, smiling, reaching on tiptoe, reaching intensely forward

the way the train was going. It was like the Diaspora of the Jews, this
universal leave-taking, this tearing apart of families, this dispersion.
The girl looked through her coarse veil at the quiet soldier in the
corner, as though she were wondering why he had no one to wave to.
And the express settled down to its long impersonal journey.

The two aircraftsmen came into the compartment when they had
finished waving to the diminishing station and grinned apologetically
for all the fuss.

"Got a postcard handy, Ted?" one of them asked his mate. "I
might as well drop them a line now to say I arrived safely."

The train was running by a flat broad stream, dimples of ripeness
and little moles of calm lying in oily streaks along the filmy surface.

Later there were gasometers and rows of red streets and the train
rattling over points in a broad network of tracks.

Then pollarded willows with wands of yellow flame, and girls with
their skirts tucked into their knickers at the brink of green meadows.
Seagulls circling and screaming petulantly over heaps of offal.

The pale girl was getting train-sick. Her face was grey and pulled
tight over her fine white cheekbones, her eyes large and dusky,
underlined with delicate blue veins. Her huge lover caressed her thin
black hair with his great gnarled hand; her head was glossy with
sweat.

"Shall I get her some water?" the quiet soldier asked.

"No, 'salright," the bomb disposal boy replied. "She'll be all right
now, won't you, love?"

The girl smiled and nudged her head against his rough tunic.

"I'm fetching 'er away; she got bombed out two day's ago," he
said, "so she's coming to live by me in Romford. We'll 'ave some
fun, won't we, love?"

The girl lifted her face and smiled with her dark strained eyes.
The soldier cold see the tension of love and of terror tautening her
sallow features. He turned away quickly, seeing again Gracie's
scared flushed face with the ruffled hair over her forehead and the eyes
luminous and wandering with distress. Why had she refused? Oh
Christ, why? Why had they quarreled so bitterly? They shouldn't
have quarreled, they couldn't afford to, the last night before going
East. If it was a quarrel . . . . It was more than that, really. It was a
failure . . . . No. Not that. They hadn't failed, not for ever. It was a
dirty joke. A practical joke of Love. Yet not of Love, but rather of
Life. Or of God. There was something enormous and almost
obscene about it that smacked of God. Two chaste lovers with no

safety appliances, no time to discover and slowly penetrate and understand each other. If she had let him, what else would there have been but a deepening of ignorance, a cruel unfinished violence, an internal injury bleeding and congealing within them? It wasn't pleasant to consider.

"Going on leave?" the big Sapper asked him.

"No, going back to camp," he replied. And then, wanting to speak a little, he added, "We're embarking this week on a draft. So I ran home for the week-end."

"What? Didn't they give you a pass?"

"No. They're scared of news leaking out. There were no passes. Everybody C.B."

"Hells bells. I don't blame you scramming off. Will you get a packet when you get back?"

"Yes, I expect so. I don't care a damn, though. They can do what they like to me. I don't care."

He got up and stood in the corridor gazing through the dirty pane at the twilit fields and smooth green hills fading away. He rubbed his hot wet eyelids with his knuckle, pressing roughly down on the chaotic anguish and vain rebellious defiance that so ached and flustered him.

For now there was a great distance between them, bus journeys and train journeys and time, time had passed between them. And he was returning shamefully to his duty, a deserter; with this hard lump in his guts, this bitter bitter desire urging him to vileness. But also he was hungry and tired, empty and queasy, and the journey stretched ahead of him all night. He was due at the nearest railway station, ten miles from camp, at 6 a.m. There would be a bus to camp at 8.30. Then the music. Standing to attention at the O.C.'s desk with his cap knocked off onto the floor and the C.S.M. giving evidence of absence without leave and he saying he had nothing to say. He was worried and ashamed, fearing he would turn craven. But there was time enough to think about that.

III

The subway was oozing blue-green darkness. In the green subdued light of the lavatory an old man was buttoning himself up. The waiting room was full of sleeping soldiers, sprawled on benches and table and floor, their heads fallen back as though broken-necked, pallid and open-mouthed in the dim light. There was nowhere for him to sleep; the platform benches were too cold. He decided to walk the streets for a couple of hours till his bus turned out.

Grey fans of darkness breaking towards the dawn winnowed the misty air, brushing the coal trucks in the sidings, touching along the glimmering rails and whitewashed buffers.

Planes had been over, they had told him at the barrier, and the all clear had not yet sounded. But there was no sound of planes or gunfire. The pilots would be back home by now. The main street was quiet, the blinds all drawn, the ashbins undisturbed either by cats or dustmen. The town waited a little on the verge of waking, cold and raw and grey, waiting for a slight movement of warm limbs. In the gardens the flowers hung drooping and closed, null and cold in colour. If a bird were to sing, a starling under the troughing?

At the top of the street a policeman came out of the police station, fastening his cloak warm round his neck. The soldier turned down a cobbled lane to avoid him and came into a quiet square where a red-bricked church was islanded in calm. Ivy touched the red walls, and on the grey cornices and the crenellated coping pigeons stood looking out of beady eyes, heads tucked into smoke-blue breasts, cooing, cooing, warm and soothing like a little fireside for his cramped hands. He held his hands out to receive their warmth.

And quietly something began flowing inside him, a warm pain like a haemorrhage, human in him. It percolated like a warm stream, exploring the way through his mind and his veins, his arteries and heart and the whorled drums of his ears. It stung sometimes like iodine, washing away the resistance and badness in him; a gradual liberation, a slow growing exaltation sublimating his hunger and coldness. Neither burdened with desire and contempt nor diseased with corrupt regrets and puffy hates, he saw it all in the calm perspective of manhood, and it seemed to him then that he was going his own way through the gates that had swung noiselessly open upon the world.

Outside the bus station soldiers were leaning against the wall, blowing into their cold hands. Two old men were sorting out the day's newspapers in the little stall, two old men with bent backs sorting out the news. Two soldiers waited for a paper, one of them saying he'd slept with a widow and the other saying he'd slept on a bench. Suddenly the sirens rose in a high shivering wail, sounding the all clear, waking the sleeping town from its private dreams. The pigeons rose in a cloud from the church and circled over the grey roofs.

IV

He came out of the company office at ten. He was smiling; he wanted to laugh, bubbling over with wonderful lightness and relief.

"What did he give you, Dave?" his mate asked, waiting at the corner of the O.C.'s hut to hear the result of the charge.

"Nothing," he said incredulously. "Nothing. He said he'd punish me after the war if I came back to England without a V.C."

"Nice work," his mate said, slapping him on the back. "Good job you've got a good record."

"I can't understand it,"he said, laughing so happily. "I can't understand it. Get me something to eat in the Naffy, Freddy. I want to send a telegram first."

"You want a shave and a bloody good sleep by the look of you," Freddy replied, looking at the pale unshaved face and the hectic boyish eyes. "How much love can you send her for ninepence?"

'It was very warm and welcome'

I t was very warm and welcome to come into the back kitchen from the raw mist of that March afternoon. The day was shrouded in grey swirling vapours puffed out from the maw of the mountain; the children's knees were raw, their cheeks red. They tumbled into the kitchen, laughing and breathless with running, Morlais with his football and Hetty with her teddy. It was a Saturday afternoon; no school; since dinner they had been playing together in the disused quarry half way up the mountain side, high over the grey village.

"Tea ready, mam?" Morlais shouted, thrusting the door open.

Mrs Jenkins was darning her husband's drovers — long pants of grey welsh flannel with white tapes round the legs to tie them tight to the shins.

"Very near," she replied, looking over her needle to see that the children were all right. "Shut that door now, tidy. You're like a pelt of rain the two of you. Been up the rocks?"

"Mam?" Hetty said. She always asked people to listen to her stories.

"Well, what 'ave you got to say now, fuss-pot?"

"Um," she drew in a breath and stuck her tummy out, ready to begin; "Our Teddy wants to know if 'e can go to Porthcawl with the Sunday School."

"Pull your drawers up, gal. Look at that right leg, very near down to your knees," her mother replied.

"Can 'e, mam?" Hetty persisted, snuffling and hitching up her knickers. "It's the 'lastic is busted, mam. It won't stay up. Look."

She lifted her thin black-stockinged leg and her mother caught hold of her heel.

"Your shoes want tapping, too, bach. You'll be ketching cold again if you go out in them when the old man's dribbling." She had told the children that an old tramp lived in the quarry where they played and when the beck that ran down the grey mossed rock was in white spate she said the old man had been drinking in the village and was dribbling down his beard.

"I'll put a fresh bit of 'lastic in for you now, 'fore Dad comes 'ome from work. Get my sewing things out of the settle, Morlais."

Morlais put his football carefully in the corner and lifted up the seat of the varnished elm settle to get her sewing basket out. She kept blankets and sheets in the settle. He rummaged among them impatiently.

"Take your time, boy; always in a temper you are."

"'Tisn't there," he said crossly, his brown eyes bright with vexation.

"Yes it is," she said, getting up and crossing to the settle. "There you are." She took the sewing bag out of a dark corner and pulled a face at him.

"It wasn't there when I looked for it," he said apologetically.

"Now then, Het," she said, returning to her chair by the fire. "Let's see if you're old enough to keep still for five minutes. Let's 'ave your leg."

She took Hetty's leg like a blacksmith shoeing a mare. Hetty tucked the teddy bear under her arm and pulled up her threadbare red coat. Six years old — five years younger than Morlais — she tried her very best to keep still. Her face always showed what she intended doing. It looked very serious now, her blue eyes determined to ignore every distraction, her lips sucked in to show how she was concentrating. She wasn't dark like the rest of her family. Her hair was straight and flaxen, her face delicate and small-featured with a light wax-smooth glow like a Japanese lantern. When she laughed her cheeks and eyes seemed to become transparent and reflect the inner flame of her joy. She had a nervous grace about her, something wide-eyed and apprehensive. Watching her approaching the house one day with the shopping basket on her arm Mrs. Jenkins had said she looked like Little Red Riding Hood stepping through the forest. Whenever she saw any of the family she always ran to them excitedly and if it was one of the grown-ups — Mam, Dad, or Doris her elder sister, — flung her arms round them and pressed her cheeks against their loins. She was friends with Morlais most of all, but she shared secrets with Dilwyn, too. Dilwyn was her twin brother. Morlais hated him.

"It's you 'ad the football, then?" Mrs. Jenkins said, trying a length of elastic round Hetty's spindly thigh. "Dilwyn was looking for it everywhere. 'E was in a proper temper; there was about twelve boys out the back 'e'd got together to play football on the tip."

Morlais pretended to be immersed in his book. She saw him purse his mouth up and glower.

"Been playing yourself with it?" she asked.

He shook his head negatively but wouldn't look up.

"There's mean you are, Morlais, indeed," she said. "You could 'ave left 'im 'ave it."

He looked up, his eyes savage.

"'E'd only puncher it, or bust it," he said. "And it was for me Father Christmas brought it. 'E never lets me touch 'is water pistol."

Mrs. Jenkins threaded the elastic through the eye of the bodkin.

"Oh, all right," she said a little wearily. "I thought you was more of a man than that, that's all."

Morlais went on reading, pouting and obstinate.

"There you are," said Mrs. Jenkins, giving Hetty her leg back, "see if you can be more respectable now."

"Was I good, mam?" Hetty asked relaxing.

"Not bad for you."

"Can teddy go to Porthcawl, then?"

"We'll see, we'll see. There's three months to go yet. You got to fill your missionary card before then, remember. And get rid of that old cough, too, my girl. Six weeks in bed already this year you've been."

Hetty jumped about the kitchen like a grasshopper, holding her teddy in front of her.

"You can come, too, teddy; you can come, too, teddy," she sang. Then, turning to Morlais, she said, "Come and collect for miss'nary cards, Mor, after tea, is it?"

"We're goin' to pitchers," he replied sulkily. "I want to see the serial."

"We can do both if we 'ave tea now straight," she said. "Can we, mam?"

"You go and take your Parrish's Food, my girl," Mrs. Jenkins said. "You can't 'ave food 'fore your father's bathed."

"Oh drusbince balance," Hetty said, — their father's favourite ejaculation, — wringing her hands in exquisite impatience. "Will 'e be long?"

"Go and take your medicine and don't bother."

Mrs. Jenkins picked up the drovers and resumed her darning. Everything was ready in the kitchen. The great iron boiler was bubbling on the fire, ready for her husband's return from the colliery. On the home-made rag mat in front of the glowing hearth his tub was warming — a strong wooden tub made by the copper, Dai Skeewit, as they called him, a Cardiganshire man who had left his native village like thousands of others to go underground; but the darkness of the pit had affected his eyes and fearing to go blind like the pit ponies he resumed his old trade in a white-washed cottage on the side of the hill. Morlais had spent whole Saturdays in the copper's yard, watching Dai.

"Morlais, get my medicine down," Hetty asked.

Morlais enjoyed watching this ceremony. Hetty wasn't tall enough to reach the shelf above the bosh where her Parrish's Food and eggcup were kept, and he felt very tall and capable when he stood on his toes and just managed to get it down. He poured a teaspoonful into the eggcup and carefully diluted it with water. Then he held it out to her.

She looked round swiftly. Her mother was busy darning. She turned back to Morlais and made a quick grimace. He nodded and swallowed the red liquid himself, handing the eggcup to Hetty.

"There you are, mam," she said. "Clean my teeth now to stop them rusting, isn't it?"

"Yes," her mother said. "If you don't your teacher won't let you stay in the Ivory Castle League."

The door burst open and Dilwyn came in with a rush. He flipped his jockey cap across the room, catching Morlais on the nose.

"Ha-ha-ha," he jeered.

"Morlais. Dilwyn. Stop it. No fighting in 'ere, d'you understand?" Morlais relaxed his doubled-up fists, knowing that ominous tone in his mother's voice. It was her kitchen. She had washed it and made it gleam with firelight and intimate with food. She'd put a clean cloth on the table and laid it out with cups and plates bought from the cheap-jack years ago and wooden-handled knives from the country. It was hers. In some mysterious way it was *her*, her self; like her clothes or her hairpins. If you did anything to the kitchen you did something to her too, disarranged her, invaded her. Morlais went back to the settle.

"A wonder you're home in time for tea for once," Mrs. Jenkins said to Dilwyn. "Oh dear, what've you been up to now? Your knee's all dirty and bleeding. Did you fall down?"

"Aye, plenty of times, too," he answered, swaggering like a little bantam. "Been up the tip 'aving bum-slides."

"Have you, then," she said, aspirating her words heavily. "Hand who's going to buy you a new pair of trousers, I'd like to know. Two pounds fourteen a week comes into this 'ouse, my boy, and that's all." She breathed heavily, pulling her dark cotton blouse down over her distended bosom. She had put on a lot of fat in the last year and when she was angry her body seemed to swell. Her face was too full to have the sharp features of wrath, but her eyes burned fearfully.

Dilwyn bowed his head, letting her irritation flow over him. Then he looked up again.

"Mam, you know the boy working for James the grocer" he began carefully.   "The one you were out delivering goods with till midnight last Tuesday?" she replied.

"Aye."

"What about 'im?"

"Can I bring 'im in to show Morlais?" he asked diffidently.

"What, is 'e out in the lane now?"

"Aye."

"D'you want to meet Dilwyn's buttie, Morlais?" she asked.

Morlais, for answer, turned away and put his fingers into his ears, affecting to be engrossed in his book.

She shrugged her shoulders at Dilwyn; he looked disappointed.

"I'll see 'im," Hetty said self-sacrificingly.

"'E don't want to see girls," Dilwyn answered scornfully.

"But I want to see 'im," Hetty said, stamping her foot.

"Keep quiet, Hetty," Mrs. Jenkins said. "Won't you see 'im, Morlais?"

Morlais continued reading although his book was upside down.

Dilwyn suddenly snatched Hetty's teddy bear.

"I'll rip 'is leg off," he shouted, jumping back towards the door. His voice was shakey and high, his pale cheeks flushed.

"Give it back and go and wash your face. You're filthy," Mrs. Jenkins said. "Stop screaming, Hetty. It's all right. Give that doll back, Dilwyn, this instant."

Dilwyn with a savage wrench ripped the teddy bear open; sawdust spilled from its belly. He flung it on the floor and vanished through the door as Morlais and his mother leaped forward and Hetty screamed as though she herself had been torn in half.

There were tears of anger in Mrs. Jenkins's eyes as she lifted Hetty into her arms and smoothed her hair and let her weeping have its way. "I'll give 'im if 'e dares to come back 'ere," she said. "'E's spoiling everything for us, that boy is. Time 'e mended 'is ways. Never you mind, Hetty fach. We'll sew 'er up again for you. She'll be all right to go to Porthcawl, don't you worry."

Hetty's paroxysm of grief abated. Her mother let her down to the floor. Morlais came over and nervously took her hand.

"Never mind, Hetty," he said timidly. He seemed afraid to touch her.   "I'll make you a paper packet of cocoa and sugar for to take to the pitchers with you," Mrs. Jenkins said.

Hetty stopped crying suddenly and stood very stiff and tense. Then her lip quivered and she broke into a sob again.

"Don't Hetty," Morlais said, his own face quivering. His mother watched them both. He was stroking her arm softly, sensitively. He looked up imploringly. "Tell her to stop crying, mam."

"She'll stop in a minute," she replied. "Come on, Hetty, there's enough grown-ups crying their eyes out without a little jenny wren like you joining in. Come on. Don't let dad come in and find the place all sixes and sevens."

The door at the bottom of the garden slammed. Hetty stopped sobbing and hastily wiped her blurred face in her mother's apron.

It wasn't dad. It was only Doris.

"How do, folks," she laughed, flouncing into the kitchen in her smart navy coat and flinging her beret onto the settle. "Hallo, what's gone wrong with the old lady, eh?"

"Dilwyn busted 'er teddy," Mrs. Jenkins said, looking coldly at Doris.

"Diddums, den, bust ums teddy den," Doris said, kneeling in front of Hetty and taking her hands down gently from her face. "Never mind, dear. Come on upstairs with Doris and help her change." She picked Hetty up and took a candle in the other hand.

"Off gallivanting again to-night?" Mrs. Jenkins asked.

"I'm meeting Ben James outside the Plaza at seven," Doris said, "if you do want to know."

There was a sharp hostility between the two.

Mrs. Jenkins shrugged her shoulders.

"You'll 'ave to see Dad first," she said. "I believe 'e's got something to say about you and Ben James."

"What?" Doris said involuntarily, the fresh colour ebbing from her cheeks. Then she caught herself up and laughed defiantly. "I don't care," she said. "It's none of Dad's business."

She pushed the passage door open and carried Hetty through.

"We'll see about that," said Mrs. Jenkins grimly, to herself. Morlais wandered out into the back yard. The darkness soothed his disquiet, dissipated his apprehension. He knelt down by the rabbit hutch. There was no sound. He made kissing noises with his lips; there was a scutter in the straw of the inner compartment. He smiled and pushed his finger through the netting, feeling for and finding the warm damp nostrils that trembled against the pads of his finger tips.

"You're all right, bunny, aren't you?" he whispered. "Not like our Hetty and Doris. Hetty's doll is busted and our Doris isn't a-friends with mam. I'm going now. Solong."

He stayed at the bottom of the garden until he began shivering with cold. Then he went back to the kitchen. Through a chink in the blind he saw his father kneeling in the bath, his mother soaping his back. He didn't want to go in until his father had dressed. He didn't like to see him naked and hairy and black; he was so huge; all that black curly hair under his arms and on his chest and belly, and the soap suds on his neck and ears and eyebrows, and his hand covering his nakedness inadequately. Hetty liked watching it; sometimes she scrubbed his back for him; but Morlais shrank away. This time he stayed by the door, stuffing his hands under his gansey for warmth and listening to their conversation as though that too would dispel the cold.

"Doris is dressing to go out with Ben James," Mrs. Jenkins said.

There was a long pause.

"Pass the towel, there's soap in my eyes," Mr. Jenkins replied in his gruff voice.

"What are you going to do to her?" she asked.

He blew into the towel.

"You won't 'urt the girl, will you?" she said apprehensively. "She don't mean no 'arm, Doris don't. It's that Ben James it is. She's mad about 'im, and 'e knows it. Takes advantage of it, too, the vain dandy that 'e is."

"I'll put a stop to it for good and all," he said at last. "If I got to use my strap on them. I'll not 'ave none of my family being talked about in the pit. Why don't she go with a decent collier boy that earns a living with 'is 'ands, not a grocer that's all 'air grease and rings?"

"We can't always choose the one to marry," she said. "'Tisn't like picking a dress. I don't think Doris do *like* Ben James. She used to laugh at 'im enough, anyroads. She only went with 'im out of spite first of all. Now — I don't know what it is now. It's like as if she can't find 'erself now."

"Pass my shirt off the fender, will you?" he said. "Ta. Well, don't look so worried, missus. Leave it till after we've 'ad food. We'll pull 'er out of the cart if she isn't in it already, don't you worry. She ought to see for 'erself it isn't a wife that Ben James wants, nor a virgin, neither."

Morlais tiptoed back a few feet from the door, then walked forward stamping his feet on the flagstones and pushed the door open noisily.

"'Ow-be, dad," he said.

"Morlais, you're looking perished," his mother said. "Come by the fire, you little twpsin."

But there was no warmth in the kitchen; only an awkward hiatus.

"I'm all right," he said. "I'm going upstairs to get my missionary card.

"Wait a minute," his father said, pulling on his drovers in front of the fire. "Tell me, 'ave you done your lessons today?"

"No," Morlais said, hanging his head.

"Well, no pitchers for you to-night, then. If a man doesn't do 'is work 'e'll 'ave no money to pay for 'is pleasures, will 'e?"

Morlais darkened, turned away, hid his face.

"You got scholarship exam next Monday for county school. You don't expect to pass if you don't do your sums, do you? Eh? Answer me, boy?"

Morlais shoulders twitched under his thin green jersey.

"There you are, making the boy cry again," his mother said. "Leave 'im be now." She put her hand on Morlais's untidy hair and shook his head. "Dad was only joking, bach. Mam will pay for pitchers for you, don't bother."

"I don't *want* to go to pitchers," Morlais said, his voice squeaking between the millstones of his tears. He twisted himself free from her hand whose sympathy was burning him and ran along the passage and upstairs.

He was all right as soon as he was by himself in his and Dilwyn's bedroom. His eyes were burning but he wasn't crying any more. He stood up in the dark and hardened. Then he relaxed and sat by the window. It was too late to see the lamp lighter; the gas lamps were already lit; and nobody passed underneath them, the pavements were all quiet; only a few moths fluttering round and round the white globe, afraid of the dark. The sound of Doris and Hetty talking in the next room brought him back to immediate things. He tapped at their door.

"Who's there?" Doris asked.

"Me," he said.

"Come on in then, me," she laughed.

He pushed the door open and walked in. Doris gave a mock scream of terror and grabbed her blue silk frock to shield herself. She only had a brassiere and tiny french knickers on, and silk stockings. The candle gave a lustre to her bare thighs and the strong white flesh of her arms and shoulders. Hetty, sitting on the bed, laughed as though she were being tickled.

"Why didn't you say you were a man?" Doris said.

Morlais smiled uncertainly. There was a scent of roses in the room, a delicate yet exciting odour. Doris's room was different from the rest of the house. The lipstick, the scent bottle, the vanishing cream and nail varnish in a row on her dressing table, the little mat she had crocheted and on which she placed her tortoiseshell hair brush, the flimsy

underwear all had something to do with it. But they weren't anything.
He had proved that by coming in quietly when there was nobody
upstairs and touching each one of them, taking the stopper out of the
scent bottle and sniffing at it. There was something else, something that
ravished him with its veils and mysteries. Downstairs everything was
solid and itself, the settle, the wash-tub, the table, the food. Mam and
dad were reliable and comprehensible, too; dad with his tempers and
heavy boots and the smell of carbolic, mam with her washing and
cooking and warm gentle body that harboured his troubles. But up
here there were avenues of dusk, swaying and rustling and enticing
him, troubling his chaste little body with strange sensations.

"Well, come in, then," Doris said. "Don't stand there with your
mouth and the door open. What shall we do, Hetty? Read his palm or
paint his lips? Let's put lipstick on him, is it?"

"No," Morlais said, backing against the bed. "Don't touch me."

His fear was so intense that he looked comic. Doris and Hetty went
into peals of laughter. Doris pinned him to the bed, forcing him back
with her beautiful bare body. Hetty uncapped the lipstick pencil.
Morlais stopped struggling. He lay under Doris pale and limp. His
body shivered all over like a dog that has been fondled into a trance.
They were laughing too much to notice.

"There that's enough," Doris said. "It costs three shillings,
remember. It's just the shade for his complexion, too. Come on, then,
Morley porley, up you get. You've got kiss proof lips now, my boy.
Look."

She leaned over and kissed him full on his lips. He shuddered.

Her laughter stopped abruptly when she saw how sick he was.
Revulsion brought a cold sweat out on his face.

"Morlais," she said, all desire to undo whatever she had done.
"Morlais. Don't take on like this. Pass me my handbag, Hetty. Get the
smelling salts out. Quick." Her voice was all in a flutter.

Hetty passed her the salts, and taking Morlais's head in her hand,
she held the bottle under his nose.

He sat up with an immense effort.

"They don't smell very nice," he said, smiling shakily. Then he
sneezed. The two girls seized on the explosion as a pretext for a
renewed fit of laughter, hysterical relief after the sharp and ugly fear
that his shuddering had aroused.

"Oh dear,"Doris said helplessly, spluttering into the pillow. "I
don't know whether I'm laughing or crying. What are we laughing
about, Het.?"

"Come on, you rowdies, your tea's poured this long time," Mrs. Jenkins called out from the bottom of the stairs.

"Look out. There's mam," Doris hissed. "Coming, mam," she sang out.

Morlais and Hetty jumped off the bed and hurriedly smoothed the counterpane. They all acted as though they had been caught in some vicious act. Doris pulled her frock over her head.

"You two go on down," she said, the frock rustling down over her hips. "I'll be along in a sec. Only comb my hair first."

Hetty scuttled down stairs. Morlais paused at the door, his mouth moving as though he wanted to say something, then, giving it up, he too tumbled downstairs to tea.

His father was half-way through his meal and with his head tilted back was draining the lasts dregs of his basin of mutton broth and boiled leeks and potatoes. A morsel of meat had got caught in his teeth and he sucked at it loudly and impatiently. Mrs. Jenkins handed Morlais his plate of fried bread and dripping which was warming on the oven and he sat down quietly beside Hetty on the settle his father had pulled up to the table.

"That cawl was salty," Mr. Jenkins said. "Let's 'ave some tea, mam."

She poured him a cup of tea.

"Hetty'll 'ave to get a new pair of shoes, William," she said. "It isn't worth tapping the ones she's got; the uppers is going."

"How much will that cost?" he asked, pouring the tea into his saucer and blowing on it.

"Nine shilling," she said.

He pulled a wry face.

"No pudding for Christmas at this rate," he said. "We'll 'ave to take Morlais out of school, I can see, and send 'im down the pit."

"No fear you won't," she answered hotly. "I don't want none of my boys getting nystagmus and bad chests and never seeing the sunlight. You stay where you are, Morlais bach, and work hard to get out of this — this valley of darkness."

Mr. Jenkins laughed loudly, spreading out his shoulders and rubbing his flat cheekbones with his knuckles. Morlais looked from one to the other, dumbly aware that they were discussing what to do with him and laughing about it — mam was smiling too.

"You're a tartar you are, mam," his father spluttered, "losing your wool every time I say anything about the kids. You didn't ought to 'ave married a collier, you didn't."

"I didn't marry a collier, neither," she said. "A good-looking young man I married with a tenor voice that was like birds singing in chapel."

"All right, then," he answered. "We don't make a collier out of 'im. We'll send 'im to the Baptist college and make 'im a minister of the Gospel. 'Ow'd you like that, Morlais?"

"I'd like to be a haulier like you, dad, and give oats to the pit ponies."

"There you are, mam," Mr. Jenkins said, slamming his huge fist on the table in triumph. "The boy's all right. A man's job 'e wants, not a lot of tongue-wagging for the women."

"For shame on you, William," she said, "blaspheming the Lord like that. Wouldn't you like to be a missionary, Morlais?" she added softly.

"Oh yes," Hetty broke in excitedly. "I'd collect for you, Morlais, and you'd be preaching to them nigger boys we seen on the magic lantern in Band of Hope, the ones that was sticking a pole up the elephant's behind."

"Trying to make 'im run, was they, Het?" her father laughed.

There was a knock on the front door. Morlais slipped down from the settle.

"There's a good boy; see who it is," his mother said.

He ran along the passage to the door.

"Give this to your sister, from Ben James," said the boy who was standing at the door. It was Dilwyn's buttie, the errand boy from James the grocer's. Dilwyn was probably with him, hiding in a doorway at a safe distance, no doubt. Morlais took the note without a word, shut the door and slipped upstairs.

Doris's door was half open, a blade of uncertain yellow light falling down the faded and tattered wallpaper. He pushed the door open and went softly in. She was sitting on the side of the bed, her head plunged in her hands, her elbows resting on her thighs. She looked round sharply, her face scared, and stared at him with her dark nervous eyes.

"For you, Dor," he said, diffidently holding out the dirty envelope to her. "From Ben James."

She took it slowly and ripped it open with hesitant fingers. He stood uncertainly by the bed rail, thinking he ought to go and yet staying, watching the silky gloss of her hair and the brooding of her painted mouth. She used to fill the house with her singing and swishing, making the air swirl with her impulsive laughter. The kitchen was always littered with lengths of calico and artificial silk, the table strewn with thimble and needle and thread and snippets of cloth. And such excitement in choosing patterns and holding the loosely cobbled dress against her to make sure of the length! And at last she was clad in the finished glory of her dream, pirouetting in the kitchen in the glow of their approval. It was like Christmas morning, Sunday School outing, Saturday matinees in the pictures, butterflies among the dahlias, this parade of frocks. But it wasn't the same now. When she laughed there was something unbalanced and raw-edged about it; most of the time she moved about restlessly, glancing through the paper and flinging it petulantly onto the floor, wandering from room to room till she got on her father's nerves, and on rainy afternoons brooding by the blurred window in the kitchen or the frigid parlour, looking out vacantly at the desolate street.

"Well, what do you want?" she snapped, looking at him and through him.

He started from his dark reverie to find her eyes dark and passionate upon him. That engrossed look of grown-ups, smouldering with thoughts too intricate and hidden to be shared, always swept him with confusion, making him feel unwanted and despicable. He shrank up like a hedgehog in some hostile presence.

"No, don't go, Morlais," she said impetuously as he turned to go. "Come and sit here a minute. Only a minute," she pleaded.

He came round the foot of the bed and sat down by her where she patted the counterpane. She put her hand on his shoulder, her arm lying like soft rose petals on his neck. She pulled his head against her side where he felt against his cheek the fluttering of her heart and the swelling of her breast.

"Ben James can't see me to-night," she said. "He'd rather go with his men pals, that's what it is." She was silent for a long time. He knew she didn't want him to say anything. Then she spoke again, a curious curl in her voice. "There's nobody I can talk to about this. The girls would only go telling everybody. And mam — she'd finish with me. It's all in the ten commandments with her. Dad hasn't looked kindly on me since I started going with Ben James. You're the only one I want to talk to, Morley porley." She pressed his head against her side.

"Come to the pitchers with me and Hetty?" he asked.

She let him go and stood up.

"Pictures?" she echoed, fixing a hair clip in front of the mirror. "No I don't want to go to the pictures to-night." She turned and looked at him, her face a grey wash, her hand clenched against her side. "Oh dear," she gasped. "I feel bad."

"Where?" he asked in alarm. "Where you hand is?"

"No, not that kind of bad," she said. "*Bad.* I feel bad, through and through, shameful." Then she flung her head back with a defiant toss of her thick tresses. "Well, go on down before mam comes up to fetch us."

She took him by the shoulders, turned him towards the door and marched him downstairs.

"Serve your faults for being so long in front of the glass," her mother said. "There's only a little widow left in the teapot and I'm not going to make a fresh pot for you. So there."

"I don't want any tea," Doris flung back, sitting carelessly in her chair, one knee over the other. "I think I'll go dancing to-night."

"Not till you've 'ad a talk with me first you won't," her father said steadily. He wiped his tobacco-stained moustache in the red handkerchief that he knotted round his neck when he went down the pit and looked at her with his grey severe eyes. She shrugged her shoulders and coloured, but dropped her eyes, the impudence beaten out of her.

"Here you are, Dor," Mrs. Jenkins said, making her a new cup of tea with the infuser, "'ave a square meal now like a sensible girl." Doris took the cup listlessly and stirred it slowly.

"And you two children put your coats and bonnets on and wrap your mufflers round your ears and get off to that old bug-house out of the way," she said. "You'd better put your gaiters on, Hetty. I don't want you in bed again for a bit."

Hetty hopped about excitedly while her mother buttoned on her coat, tucked in her scarf and hooked up her gaiters. Morlais didn't make a move to dress himself.

"Come on, Mor," Hetty said. "We'll miss the beginning if you don't watch."

He stood still uncomfortably, looking down at his shifting feet.

"Put your coat on, mun," his father said impatiently.

"You said I wasn't to go," Morlais answered dully.

"Did I? I didn't. Go on out the way with you."

"I don't want to go."

"A good shaking you want, my boy, with your tantrums all the time," Mr. Jenkins said, standing up and towering over Morlais. "Give them a penny each out of the milk jug, mam, and pack them off. D'you think we got time to bother with everything you want and don't want?"

Dumbly Morlais pulled on his coat and cap and took the coppers from his mother. She tidied him up, pulled his tie straight and pushed his hair back under his cap.

"There you are," she said, putting his hand in Hetty's. "Off with you and enjoy yourselves."

Morlais looked at Doris; she was leaning forward in her chair.

"I'll come with you, Mor," she said suddenly, starting up.

"No you won't," Mr. Jenkins said, putting his huge horny hand on her slender shoulder. "You sit still for a minute."

The next moment Morlais and Hetty were out in the dark drizzle of the windy night, picking their way through the puddles of the back lane, gripping hands tightly and not saying a word.

They were just in time to get in at children's prices. After five o'clock they would have had to pay sixpence, which was more than they had ever possessed. The cinema clock showed a minute to five.

"There's lucky," Morlais whispered, forgetting about Doris in the excitement of the moment.

There were no seats left and they had to stand in the gangway, right at the front. The figures on the screen were all distorted, as though seen in a concave mirror or a bedknob. What was worse, a tall boy stood plumb in front of Hetty and she could only see a corner of the screen.

"Tell me what's happening?" she begged, tugging at Morlais's coat.

"I can't see myself," he replied.

They were bitterly vexed, and when the children packed in the front rows roared with laughter Morlais clenched his fists with impotence and stamped his feet. But they stuck it out till the end of the show, standing there seeing nothing for two and a half hours. Then at last the lights came on and the audience made a noisy rush for the doors, shouting boys climbing over the seats while the pianist played the national anthem. Morlais held Hetty's hand tightly and pressed through the scramble. Having squeezed through the narrow door into the foyer he stopped a moment to let Hetty recover.

"I didn't like it much, did you?" he said.

She looked up at him timidly and smiled. She was thankful that he too had disliked it. They'd be able to grumble about it together now.

"Morlais," a little voice called.

A boy of about Hetty's size was excitedly pulling at Morlais with one hand and tugging a very elegant lady through the crowd with the other. He wore a tweed beret and well-cut grey-blue overcoat. And kid gloves. "Were you in there, Morlais?" he said breathlessly.

Morlaid nodded his head, too taken aback to answer. There was this tall lady standing over him, smiling behind a thin gauze veil with a grey fox fur over her dark costume.

"Is this one of your little friends, David?" she asked.

"Yes, of course," the boy replied. "This is Morlais."

He gave the name such importance that Morlais didn't know what to do. Especially as everybody was looking at them. He hung his head.

"Well, I'm very pleased to meet you, Morlais," she said. "Did you enjoy the picture? David insisted on taking me. Somebody'd been telling him there was an exciting serial on there."

"That *was* Morlais," David said in a scornful tone that implied that she should have known that already.

"I'm sorry, dear," she said. "You chatter so much that I can't remember everything, can I? Well, you *did* enjoy it then, Morlais."

Morlais nodded assent and looked up at her. Their eyes met and he too smiled. The smile came from deep down in him, and broke like a light wave, tingling along his limbs.

"Well, we must be off to get supper for David's daddy," she said. "Say goodnight to Morlais, David."

"Goodnight, Morlais," David said, turning his head to see him again as she led him down the steps and out into the darkness.

Slowly and thoughtfully Morlais followed, still holding Hetty's hand. When they had walked to the top of the hill in silence Hetty reminded him of her presence by asking, in an awed whisper, "Who was that, Mor?"

"David," he replied curtly.

"David what?" she insisted.

"His father's the manager of the pit our dad works in," he said.

"Was that lady his mummy?"

"I suppose so. Anything else you want to know?"

Hetty stopped asking questions abruptly. After a long silence she said, "She was a lady, wasn't she?"

Morlais thought this over.

"She's his mother anyway," he said at last.

They didn't say any more until they got home. As he pushed the back door open Morlais remembered something important. He took a fistful of Hetty's scarf.

"You go off to bed straight away, see?" he whispered.

"Why?" she asked, aggrieved and disappointed.

"It won't be nice staying down tonight," he said. "There's a row going to be."

"Oh, alright," she said, accepting his superior knowledge.

The kitchen was forbiddingly quiet. Doris was sitting on one side of the fire, her mother on the other. On the mantelpiece the scratched and battered alarm clock ticked loudly. Morlais heard it as soon as he went in. He took his cap off. His mother was watching him, but very quietly, in a preoccupied way. Doris didn't look up at all. She was gazing into the fire, her face troubled and moody. Hetty brushed past Morlais, sending the silence up the chimney like a puff of flame.

"Guess who we seen in the pitchers, mam?" she said, taking her mother's folded hands up and shaking them.

"Tell me quick and get up to bed," her mother said, indifferently.

"Mrs Reames," Hetty said dejectedly. There was no triumph after that rebuff.

"Did you kiss 'er feet?" Mrs Jenkins said shortly. "Cut the girl a piece of bread and jam, Doris. Do one for Morlais too."

Doris got up with the slow movements of a somnambulist, fetched a loaf and knife and jampot from the pantry and cut two thick slices for the children. Meanwhile Morlais had taken his school copybook and arithmetic primer from the table drawer and a penny bottle of ink from the window sill. He set his books out carefully on the end of the table, curled his leg underneath him because the chair he was sitting on was too low, and dipped his pen reflectively in the ink.

"You're not going to work now, surely to goodness," his mother said.

"Only two sums," he begged.

"Alright, then. But off you go this instant, Hetty. And you go, too, Morlais, as soon as Ben James and dad come in."

"Ben James?" Morlais said quickly. "Is he coming?"

"Get on with your sums," she said sharply. "Hetty!"

Hetty, who had been standing by the door, sucking the jam from her crust and looking longingly at the fire and lamplight, disappeared. Doris returned to her seat. Morlais sat over a blank page in his copy book, his pen abandoned in the ink bottle.

"Goodnight all," Hetty called from upstairs.

No-one answered. The clock ticked audibly, again, Morlais's finger keeping time with it. His leg grew numb and painful after a time but he was afraid to move it, to break the silence, to attract attention. His mother had stopped darning. Her hands were still. A dog barked outside, and whined. Then silence again.

It was almost a relief when the latch of the outer door at last clicked and heavy boots sounded on the flagstones. The women sighed, Morlais changed legs, the fire slumped down, a shower of red cinders falling into the grate. Mr Jenkins in his tweed cap and old raincoat came in, and after him Ben James.

When she saw him Doris sprang from her seat and put her hands on his arms.

"I couldn't help it, Ben," she said. "I had to tell them." Her eyes were warm and frantic.

"Yes, of course," he said softly. "That's alright, that's alright."

She looked at him a moment, full in the eyes. His handsome suave smile assured her. She let her hands fall.

"Take a chair, Ben James," Mr Jenkins said. "We'll only start shouting if we stand up."

"Shouting?" said Ben James, putting his head on one side and opening his palms. "You don't want to start quarreling with your son-in-law before the wedding even, do you?"

Doris gasped.

"You will — you will — ? Oh Ben," she hid her face against his natty overcoat, pulling herself close to him and shuddering. "I thought you wouldn't," she said brokenly.

"Darling," he said, "you know there's nothing I'd like more. Only — " he hesitated.

"Only what?" Mrs Jenkins said.

He shrugged his shoulders diffidently and smiled. He had the situation well in hand.

"Well, my mother isn't willing," he said. "And you know how old people are, you can't go across them."

"Better take a chair, Ben James," Mr Jenkins said.

"Alright," said Ben.

He sat on the settle and took out a packet of Churchman's.

"Mind if I smoke?" he asked.

"Now," said Mr Jenkins, still standing, "tell me jest what your old mother've got to say against my daughter."

Ben pulled the knot of his tie down from his Adam's apple and stretched his blue-shaven chin up.

"It's like this," he said carefully, holding out his hands as if to show there was nothing in them. They were fleshy hands, pink; two heavy gold rings sunk into his fat fingers. They seemed to cover the floor of the little kitchen. Unconsciously everybody looked at his hands. "She've got her little fads, you know, and one of them is for me to marry into a good family with money to put into the business."

Mr Jenkins laughed grimly.

"It would break 'er 'eart if she 'ad to pay seven and six a week for 'er son's pleasure," he said. "So you don't think our family is good enough, eh, Ben James?"

"Please don't misunderstand me," Ben said hurriedly, frightened by the brawny collier's step forward. "I think you're a very good family."

"And more confident of the Day of Judgment then yours, Ben

James," Mrs Jenkins said. "Nobody's never drunk 'imself into bankruptsy in this 'ouse the same as your old man did."

"Oh mam, stop it, for God's sake," Doris said, in anguish. "What's the use? Finish it, for God's sake."

She flexed and clenched her fingers, the firelight sharpening her taut features and shaking knuckles.

"You keep quiet," her father said. "You've done enough damage already. Sit still for a minute."

Doris gripped the arms of her chair and her lips became two thin lines. The skin under her eyes was dark blue and her cheeks a hard chalky white. Morlais forgot Ben James and the sick fascination he felt for him; instead he fixed his eyes on Doris, whose pain drew him as though into a whirlpool.

"Well, are you going to marry the girl or not?" Mr Jenkins said.

"Well, you see," Ben replied, "you can't rush into these things. My mother owns the business for one thing — my father made it over to her before he went bankrupt, see? And she only pays me thirty bob a week. I can't get married on that, can I?"

"I know a lot of young couples that started on less," Mr Jenkins said.

"Well it's not enough for me," Ben said. "Besides, if I married without her consent she might leave the business to one of her nephews. She threatened to."

"You can talk like a minister, Ben James," Mr Jenkins said. "Is it backing out you are?"

"No indeed," he replied. "I'm willing to pay my debts. But my mother said I shouldn't marry any girl that didn't bring two hundred pounds into the business with her. And that's flat."

Mr Jenkins grunted, breathing loudly. Ben watched him. So did the others. He paced about, putting his hands on things as if they wanted something strong to grip — the mantelpiece, the table's white surface where the wood had been scrubbed down to the grain, the varnished back of the settle. Doris turned and looked dully into the fire. Mrs Jenkins stood up and put her hand on her husband's worn sleeve.

"You've got to give it to him, William," she said. "You can't let our Doris be shamed before all the village."

"I know that, woman," he shouted, turning on her in fury. The tension broke. He slumped down onto the little chair and let his hand fall dead on the table.

"You can 'ave your two 'undred, Ben James," he said dully. He sighed. "It took me twenty years to save. I didn't reckon to throw it into the wind."

Doris was crying softly.

Ben James stood up.

"I'm glad we've been able to settle it, Mr Jenkins," he said lightly. "Of course, you understand it's my mother's fault. If she'd died last year when she went to Hospital this trouble wouldn't have arisen. I personally wouldn't have dreamed — "

Mr Jenkins silenced him with a hard grey look. He lost his composure.

"Well, I won't stay," he stammered. "I'll call up tomorrow to make arrangements for the wedding. In the Baptist's it will be, I suppose, Mrs Jenkins?"

"Yes," she said, half to herself. "That's where I was married."

"Well, goodnight all. Don't bother to show me out. 'Night, Doris," he said breezily, and taking up his velvety slouch hat in his unsteady hand he went out through the kitchen door.

"The twister," Mr Jenkins muttered, pressing his flattened palm on the table.

Doris jumped up, eyes flaring.

"Alright," she said, "alright, alright. I'm sorry you've lost your money. But never mind. You've not lost as much as me." Her breasts were heaving. "Don't worry. I won't darken your doorstep much longer."

"Doris," her mother called. "Don't take on, bach. It could be worse."

"Could it?" Doris flashed, and with a gasp ran from the room, along the passage and upstairs. Her bedroom door slammed.

Leaving his books open on the table Morlais slid down from his chair and softly followed her. His mother saw him, and yet said nothing. She looked washed out and grey, her face heavy, like suet. His father just sat, his shoulders like black buffs of rock, his legs sprawled out — old gardening trousers pitched and mended, thick woollen socks, great hob-nailed boots. When he was in the kitchen the children never told their mother any secrets. There wasn't any room.

Morlais tiptoed into his bedroom and climbed onto the bed in his clothes. He stared at the greenish light of the street lamp falling upon the cracked china bowl on the old tin box that was the only furniture of his poky attic. Dilwyn wasn't in yet. He could fill the whole room with his thoughts, not hide them away in the dark as he had to when Dilwyn lay restlessly beside him and pinched his behind. He lay for a long time watching the pale sick light until it rose in a ghostly wave and threw its clammy veils against him. He turned shuddering into the wall and pressed his hands over his eyes. And in the intense darkness of crushed eyelids and clenched hands pressing into them he heard Doris sobbing uncontrollably through the three-ply wooden partition. And he knew something terrible was happening inside her. Something had got into the house.

He woke in terror. The street lights were out. He felt for Dilwyn. He wasn't there. He was shivering and put his hands out to pull the blankets over him. He found he was clothed, and lying on top of the blankets. He began frantically to unknot his tie and undress. His fingers were cold and shaky. Then his boots, stockings, trousers, jersey, shirt. He just managed to slip his naked little body between the rough warmth of the blankets before the door opened and Dilwyn came in. He was snuffling, sobbing; he'd had a leathering for being out late, and for Hetty's teddy. Morlais didn't stir when he climbed into bed beside him. That was the last thing he remembered, that cold night.

Impasse

Gwyn could see nobody at all on the mountain; nothing but miles of heather and whin bounded by the curling hill crest whose marble line was rimmed with pellucid blue sky. So black and iron-sharp ws the ridge that it seemed to Gwyn that, if he but scaled the peak, he could look down from the world's end into the clear and infinite abyss of the falling sun.

Then he turned his back on the west and set off along the grass track for home, the greyhound loping along by his side on a slack leash.

"Feeling fit for the race to-night, my Beauty?" he said, and laughed. "I've been telling you every day for a week that you're in for the race of your life to-night; yet I don't think you know about it even now."

He bent down and slipped the leash.

"Come on, boy," he laughed, "let's see you move."

He sprinted forward and the dog immediately flashed past him. Twenty yards ahead it slackened again into its gambolling, loose-limbed trot.

"Snow-white you are, my Beauty," the boy said, breathlessly, clipping the leash on to its collar again, "like the winged horse we read about in the Council school, isn't it? And to-night they're matching you against Black Diamond. Never 'eard of 'im, I suppose? Well, 'e's the best dog in South Wales, so they all say. You won't 'ave a smell against 'im, they do say. But then, they don't know you like I do, Beauty, do they?"

He tugged the leash and began running again, laughing and leaping over the clumps of rushes along the wet path, until they reached the crest and began descending the zigzag track into the valley. Over the clustered houses the dusk lay like sloe dust, pricked out with street lights glowing like ineffectual stars.

At the foot of the hill the path widened into a lane which skirted the biggest house in the village. The manager of the colliery lived there. Gwyn walked slowly past the garden and peeped through the iron gates at the entrance to the drive. A girl was coming down the path, and when he saw her he hastily straightened his muffler, hitched up his baggy grey trousers and buttoned his coat.

"Hallo, Anne," he said.

She started and looked quickly at him; then, reassured, shrugged her shoulders in a way that was at once aloof and saucily inviting.

"Oh, it's you, is it?" she said, buttoning her coat up to her chin to hide the starched collar of a maid's uniform.

"I was hoping I'd see you, Anne," he said, his voice intense and subdued.

"Were you, really?" she laughed, climbing onto the pedestal his voice had made for her. "I'd nearly forgotten you existed." She let the words fall carelessly, like a bored child plucking the wings off a fly.

He wound the leash round his fingers and looked at his cracked shoes.

"Still taking that vulgar greyhound about with you?" she said.

"He's racing Black Diamond to-night," he said eagerly. "I wish you'd come and see the race."

"Me go to that lowdown race track?" she gasped. "Good gracious, what next I wonder."

"But he looks so — oh, Anne, if you saw 'im flash out of the trap and streak away under the arc lamps, you'd see then — "

She tossed her head. "Well, I think greyhounds are awful ugly, specially from the back," she said. "And if you like them, then you've got a funny idea of what's nice, that's all I say."

"Oh no, Anne — " he stopped his pleading and then said quietly, "I don't know what I'd do without the Beauty."

"Oh well, I can't stand here talking all night," she said in a huff. "And I really don't know *what* my mistress would say if she saw me with a grocer boy as goes dog racing."

"Oh, Anne," he said quivering.

"Oh Anne, no Anne," she mocked. "Can't you say something else for a change?"

"Yes," he said, striving to be articulate.

"What?" she asked, cocking her head to one side.

"I — I love you," he said, eyes brimming.

She laughed, a high glassy tinkle.

"Really?" she said. "More than your precious Beauty?"

"Yes," he said, bending his head to the ground.

"Well, sell the rotten thing then," she snapped.

"But I can't do that, Anne. You don't see — 'e's racing to-night and

— and 'e's *got* to win, see? Dad will be in a proper mess if 'e loses."

"Gambling, I suppose?" she said, distant and prudish.

"No, I don't gamble, Anne. I never touch it. You know that. It's Dad, see."

She turned through the gates and walked quickly up the drive.

"Oh Anne," he called urgently, "please come back. Oh please, Anne — "

The dusk washed her out of his sight. He turned and walked on to the village, stumbling down the uneven lane, the greyhound padding at his side. He went along the narrow street, past the shuttered shops and the blind parlour windows, turned the corner into the back lane, and entered his father's garden through the back door. A pale light fell from the kitchen window across the potatoes and asters at the top of the garden steps. He paused outside the kitchen door, rubbing his eyes vigorously with his sleeve, and with an effort stopped the trembling of his flesh.

"Where the 'ell 'ave you bin?" his father said, "giving me the wind-up like this. Don't you know the race starts in an hour?"

"'Course I know it," Gwyn said.

"Likely 'e'll forget, isn't it?" his mother said. "It's all 'e do think about, is that dog of 'is."

She was sitting by the fire in a straight-backed chair, her skinny fingers flashing deftly over the rag mat she was making. The greyhound rubbed its long slender flank against the table leg.

"I took the Beauty for a good stretch," Gwyn said. "We walked right over the mountain to the top of the Rhondda valley."

"And never mind about me keeping tea on the table all night, I suppose?" his mother snapped.

"Leave the boy be, gal," his father grunted. "If 'e can't go for a walk after early closing without you jumping down 'is throat, I'd like to know what."

"Trust you to stick up for 'im now," she said, "when it's you that's always down on 'im, not me. As long as 'e's doing something with that old dog it's all right, isn't it?"

Her fingers had stopped working and the tears stood in her eyes.

"Aw, for Christ's sake," his father said, "don't talk soft, mun."

"Soft?" she whipped back, her voice going hard. "The way 'e do dote on that dog, anybody'd think it was a magic carpet, not a whippet 'e won in a blooming raffle."

"Oh, what's wrong with you, Mam?" Gwyn said. "You're a fine dog, i'n't you, Beauty?"

"Aye, the Aga Khan wouldn't mind 'aving 'im, I can tell you," his father said.

"Well, take your old Aga Khan out of my kitchen 'fore 'e makes a mess on my carpet," she snapped. Her fingers returned to their work. "It's nothing but trouble that dog's brought to this 'ouse. 'E's turned you off your work and Gwyn the same."

"What's up with you, mun?" his father shouted. "Can't I go down the races now and again if I want to?"

"Oh yes. You can do what you like," she replied. "Spend your time with that fat bookie, and your money too, if you want to. You 'aven't cobbled a pair of shoes this week, I don't think."

"What's the good of me sitting in the shed all day with my mouth full of nails when everybody's taking their shoes to the Coop to be mended?" his father said surlily. "And as for Ben Lake, 'e may be a bookie, but 'e's none the worse for that."

"Oh all right," she said wearily. "It's only wasting my breath I am. But 'ow you'll pay all them bills on the window sill I don't know."

"Don't you worry about that," he said roughly. "I'll settle all them to-morrow, soon as the Beauty've won 'is race. Won't I, Gwyn?"

Gwyn shuffled uncomfortably.

"I don't know," he said. "I've got nothing to do with gambling. Nor the Beauty 'aven't, neither."

"Well, I can feel it in my bones," his mother said. "We've struggled for years now to keep tidy and respectable and be obliged to nobody, and now — " she bent her head over the mat and pulled a rag through the cord mesh, "it's the ruin of us now."

Gwyn put his hand gently on her high, narrow shoulders.

"Don't take on like that, Mam," he pleaded. "It's the cold weather that makes you upset. It's like a dog's nose outside the door."

There was a triple knock on the front door and his father clumped along the passage in his hob-nailed boots.

"If it's that Ben Lake calling again," his mother said, "I'm going out."

"Come on in, Ben, come and 'ave a warm," his father said, returning to the kitchen.

"Very welcome, too," Ben Lake said, looking at the fire and rubbing his flabby pink hands. His red puffed face was corded with purple veins; "Good evening to you, Mrs. Edwards."

"Good evening," she said, rolling up the mat and standing it in the corner. "You're getting quite a regular visitor, a'n't you?"

"Aye, indeed," he replied. "Only I always call when your 'usband's

in, so you can't call me a lodger yet, can you?" He laughed loudly.
"And 'ow's the Beauty, Gwyn? All set for the race?"

"Aye, 'e's champion," Gwyn said, taking the dog's fine tapering
head in his hands and putting his cheek against it.

"Proper courting couple, Ted, isn't they?" Lake laughed. "Going
out, is it, Mrs. Edwards?"

"Yes," she said, pinning her shiny black hat on her head, "I got to
get some vinegar and yeast from the shop."

She picked up her purse from the window sill and went out without
looking at any of them. When the door slammed behind her Lake burst
out laughing. "You look as if you'd just 'ad a smack on the chops,
Ted," he said.

"She's funny these days," Mr. Edwards answered, "You don't
know 'ow to take 'er."

"Oh well," Lake laughed, "safety in numbers where women are
concerned, that's my motto. Anyway, never mind about that now.
Look, 'ere's ten quid for you; put it on the Beauty just before the race
starts, see? They'll be laying three to one on Black Diamond, so we'll
pick up thirty quid if the Beauty wins."

"O.K., Ben," Mr. Edwards said, carefully folding away the crisp notes.

"I'll give you two quid commission on it," Lake said. "That'll mean
you'll owe me thirteen quid 'stead of fifteen."

"Fifteen quid, Dad?" Gwyn caught his father's arm. "That's not
right, Dad, is it? You don't owe 'im all that?"

"What's wrong boy?" Lake laughed. "What's fifteen quid amongst
friends? Anyway, that dog of yours is worth a fortune. Look 'ere. I tell
you what I'll do." He stuck his thumbs into the armpits of his waistcoat.
"I'll wipe the fifteen out and *give* you ten more if you'll sell me that dog."

"I'm not selling the Beauty," Gwyn said stubbornly. "And I'm not
racing 'im, neither, if — "

"Don't talk so daft, boy," Mr. Edwards said. "Come on, let's get
down the track."

He took Gwyn's cap from it's peg in the passage, put it on his head
and pushed him towards the door. Ben Lake followed them, leading
the greyhound by its leash . . . ..

"Well," said Ben Lake, beaming all over his face, "if you boys'll
come in to my little pub for ten minutes I'd like to make you a
proposition."

He lit a cigarette, cleared his throat, slapped Gwyn on the back and
smiled hugely.

"Bloody fine race, son, wasn't it?" he said. "I bet my granny turned in 'er grave when the Beauty slipped 'is 'ead in front of that Black Diamond. Right on the post, too, — oh my God."

He wiped his red face in a silk handkerchief.

"Aye, it was marv'lous," Gwyn said, flushed, transported. "But d'you mind if I don't come with you now, Mr. Lake? I've got to meet somebody."

"Women again, is it?" Lake laughed. "Garn, mun, let them wait. You come on with me and your dad now. It's about your future I want to talk."

He pushed the glazed door open and walked into the corridor. They had to elbow their way through the press of drinkers who crowded the corridor with their pint mugs. The thick blue tobacco smoke swirled as the door swung to after them, and the drinkers toasted them and the Beauty as they passed.

"Come round the back to my office, boys," Lake said. "Make way, gentlemen, please."

The office was a small room directly behind the Bar. A huge brewer's mirror stood over the empty fireplace and the walls were hung with large framed advertisements for beers and cocktails and cigarettes. Three one-legged tables, their rounded tops bearing the wet impress of beer mugs, filled the floor space. Two red plush seats were placed beside each table. Through an open doorway they could see the bar-room, full of vociferous race-goers and fuggy with smoke. Behind the counter Lake's new barmaid was bending over the sink, swilling glasses and filling them with draught beer. Mr. Edwards lit his pipe and Lake banged a bell on one of the tables.

"Sit down, boys," he said, "make yourselves at 'ome. Three pints of nut brown, Muriel, please."

She stood indolently in the doorway, smiling. Her blue silk blouse fitted so closely that her breasts seemed to press urgently against the stress of the silk. The thick brown waves of her hair glinted red and her eyes were cool and dark.

"O.K.," she said.

Gwyn followed her with his eyes, watching her smooth bare arms pull down the beer handles and her firm legs in flesh-coloured silk stockings stand slightly astride. When she brought the glasses in he leaned forward to take them off the tray.

"Thanks," she said, bending over him so that the scent and warmth of her body enveloped and dissolved him.

"Young Gwyn knows a lady when 'e sees one, eh Muriel?" Lake

said. Gwyn flushed and then looked up into her face. Her laughter filled him with eagerness.

"Is this your first glass of beer, boy?" Lake asked.

Gwyn nodded and laughed and set the empty glass down.

"Takes to it like a fish to water, don't 'e, Ned?" Lake said. "Same again, Muriel, please."

"Don't give 'im another, Ben," Mr. Edwards said. "'E's 'ad as much as 'e can carry already. And if 'is mother knew — "

"Garn, you old Jew," Lake said, "'e's enjoying 'imself, isn't 'e? Seeing *Life* for once, aren't you Gwyn?"

"Aye, that's right," Gwyn said. "It's great." His sweaty fingers slid through each other and he laughed, the laughter of his body. Lake laughed too and winked at Muriel.

"Pleasure before business, that's my motto," he said, taking a pull at his replenished pint.

"'Ow about the proposition you was going to make?" Mr. Edwards said, wiping the beer off his tobacco-stained moustache. His face was pale and worried.

"I was just coming to that now," Lake said. He drew up his chair and set his ham-like fists on the table. "Now look 'ere, boys. I've fixed up a return match with Black Diamond for next week at Merthyr, see?"

"'Ave you, by God?" said Mr. Edwards. "Why, that's money for jam, mun."

"Aye, the Beauty'll lick anything — anything you like," Gwyn shouted thickly.

"Aye, but look 'ere boys," Lake said, "you're forgetting one thing. The odds will be on Beauty next time. It won't be worth backing 'im from now on."

"Aye indeed, that's true enough," said Mr. Edwards, looking thoughtfully into his glass.

"So what I'm going to do is this," Lake said. "We'll put twenty quid on Black Diamond this time — at the last minute like, same as we did to-night."

Gwyn banged his glass on the table.

"What d'you want to do that for, mun?" he shouted.

"Steady on now, sonnie," Lake said viciously. "We'll back Black Diamond like I said, see? And the Beauty'll lose the race and we'll be quids in."

"'Ow can 'e lose, mun?" Gwyn shouted. "The Beauty'll beat anything."

"If we tie a hair under 'is paws 'e'll lose," Lake said.

Gwyn stood up, knocking his chair over and swaying on his feet.

"Not if I know it you won't," he said.

"Come on, mun, don't make a fool of yourself," Lake cajoled, standing up and taking him by the arm.

"Take your 'ands off me, you swine," Gwyn screamed. Lake tightened his grip, leaning over him.

"If you don't agree," he said, "I'll turn your whole bloody family into the street and sell your furniture up, too."

"Let go," Gwyn shouted. He picked up his glass and emptied it into Lake's face. His father caught him by the shoulder and he fought against the weight of the two men.

"Let me go," he shouted. The table toppled over and the men in the bar crowded round the counter, craning their necks.

"You bloody fool," Lake grunted, purple-faced and breathless with wrestling. Gwyn broke their grip and jumped away. He stood against the wall, his face working, his skin taut and sallow against his cheekbones. His features turned into a grotesque grin.

"You won't get me nor the Beauty," he said. "You'll never get us now." He laughed at the two waiting men.

A Salvation army woman walked into the saloon, handed them each a leaflet and quietly said, "God bless you all."

Gwyn watched her turn and go out through the swing doors and then broke into a high peal of laughter. Muriel took him by the arm.

"Come on, Gwyn," she said. "How about some fresh air, now?"

He trembled under her touch and stopped laughing.

"I'm going now," he said, and turning away he walked quietly out into the street.

"Better go after 'im, I reckon," Mr. Edwards said.

"Leave the little swine be," Lake said, wiping his face and sitting down heavily. "Let's get down to business . . . "

Gwyn walked unsteadily along the back lane. Once he stopped and leaned against the wall, pressing his face against the grimy stone. Then he went on until he reached the back door. There was a light in the kitchen, but no sound. His mother would be working at the mat, no doubt. He walked softly up the garden to the little outhouse where the Beauty was kennelled. The dog rattled its chain and whined at the sound of his step. He stopped for a minute, unable to go on. Then he suddenly breathed deeply, lifted his arms to the black sky and laughed. He took the padlock off the door, felt along the floor for a candle stump, found it and struck a match. The Beauty stood up, straining eagerly against the leash, clear and milk-white in the yellow, uncertain light.

Gwyn stood in the doorway, looking down at the dog — bright eyes, the panting mouth and slavering tongue, the fine narrow head.

"You know why I'm doing it, Beauty, don't you?" he said.

He knelt down beside the dog and put his arms round its neck. Its body was pulsing with life and the afterheat of the race.

Then he stood up and, lifting above his head the pickaxe that always lay in the corner, he brought it down cleanly between the dog's eyes.

'Enid didn't know what to do'

Enid didn't know what to do. She sat on the worn linoleum nailed over the table and dangled her legs and watched her feet cross and recross, and tried terribly hard to make up her mind immediately. Pictures? But she'd seen Gary Cooper twice in the last week and anyway she didn't *like* Gary Cooper. Nor the Plaza — your knees all bunched up and your bottom stiff and numb. Jane Palmer was nuts on him, kept his photograph under her pillow — silly fool. Go down Auntie's, then? Oh, dear, she didn't *want* to — she could go down Auntie's any night. She wanted something *different* to-night, seeing it was her fourteenth birthday. Fourteen — your body changes at fourteen; you want to do something different then, don't you? Not wash the dishes, and do your homework in between taking medicine up to your mother, and put the wireless on till Dad comes in with his old politics and Les with his billiards and his brilliantine. Not *that* all the time. You get *sick* of it, somehow.

She just couldn't decide. There wasn't anything to do. "Oh pot," she said in a temper. She felt ill with frustration. She turned the wireless on, fiddled with the knobs, listened impatiently to gipsy music, jazz, German, fat stock prices, fiddling with the knobs and perspiring because she *couldn't* decide. And then, quite suddenly the overheated little kitchen was washed clean out and her fevered mind rinsed and cooled — in the music of a violin and piano — music Miss Felton had played on the radiogram in music lesson that afternoon — lovely disembodied music, full of happiness. Miss Felton said the man who wrote it was called Mozart, and Enid *saw* him at once, a little boy of a man with beady eyes and a mottled coat like a thrush, and fine white hands you wanted to curtsey over and kiss only he wasn't looking at you. And here he was in the room, and Miss Felton too with her rustly silk dress and breathless swish of grace and rose water and the silver bangle on her wrist. Neither of them looking at her, though. She put her lips against the illuminated indicator on the wireless set and the music flowed right over her, like over a fish in a low-tide pool that's been waiting for the white salt swirl for so long.

"Shut the old row off, can't you?"

Just like his cheek. He never thought of you; there wasn't anybody else in the world except Les. Bang on the door, drop your tennis racket with a clatter into the zinc bath tub, switch the wireless over to Swingtime — that was Les all right.

"All right," she said, sucking her lips in and giving him a look.

"Pretending you like that snob music," he sneered.

She nearly screamed at him. She felt a hot impulse leap like a huge river bore into her throat and involuntarily she clenched her hands. For a moment she stood rigid, like a little tin soldier. Then she went limp, flaccid, dull.

"Go on out and do something," he said unctuously. "I want the kitchen for myself to-night. Annie's coming in now just."

She didn't know whether it was his voice or a voice inside her sulkily telling her to go. She obeyed passively; when she pulled her school-blue coat off the peg her arm ached with lifting it up. It wouldn't slip off the peg. She tugged. The tab broke. Tears filled her eyes.

"You'll 'ave it, busting your coat," Les warned.

"I don't care," she said. "Solong."

"Stop being in a temper," she said to herself as she walked down the road, rubbing her hand against the wall and kicking at the loose stones. Her other hand she kept in her pocket, clenching the shilling she'd been given by Auntie Morfydd for her birthday. It was such a lovely thing, a shilling; like those diamonds that seem to pulse, waxing and waning; like the sun on a very hot day. Thinking of the shilling made her feel better.

"I'll go and spend," she decided.

Now she knew where she was going. She was going to the shop windows. As she walked she skipped a little, now and again, and when she saw Jane Palmer going into the Plaza she stuck her tongue out and laughed at her and ran away laughing when Jane beckoned to her.

And outside the railway station was a big green bus, and a man standing beside it with a sandwich board saying, "MYSTERY TOUR JUST STARTING. PRICE ADULTS 2 SHILLINGS, CHILDREN ONE SHILLING."

And before she knew what she was doing Enid was sitting in the front seat of the bus, where she could watch the driver.

She felt sure they were all looking at her and thinking what a fool she must be, going on a mystery tour by herself. Hadn't she got any friends, they'd be saying to themselves. She folded her arms together and stuck her bony shoulder blades out and made herself so small that the people behind stopped seeing her and began talking about dole and sunday school outings and somebody having a baby, poor girl; very carefully, and with extreme difficulty, Enid breathed again, a deep, deep breath.

But a moment later something inside her took a great leap, making her all gooseflesh and dizzily excited. For Miss Felton, her music teacher, had come out of the cafe on the other side of the road and was crossing to the bus, smiling and saying something to the man who was with her. She was wearing her fawn summer coat and she had a flower in her thick yellow hair, like a gipsy. She looked cool and perfect, like cut glass. The man pointed to the bus and took her elbow and pushed her. She laughed with a shrug of her shoulders and Enid knew they'd decided to go on the mystery tour.

They came in and sat in the empty seat opposite her.

Enid tried not to look red and helpless when Miss Felton smiled at her.

"Hallo, Enid," Miss Felton said, "You're going on this adventure, too, are you?"

"Yes, miss," Enid said, as calmly as she could. She wanted to add that it was her birthday, a special day. Miss Felton would understand. If it had been Miss Foulkes, the Senior mistress, Enid would have had to explain about her birthday. "A girl from a poor home, having free milk and free dinners in school, wearing the same coat for four years, — poor, indeed. Mean, not poor. Saves her money to squander it on charabanc outings; I know them, they're all the same." That's what Miss Foulkes's look would have said, and Enid would have said abjectly "It's my birthday, miss." Oh, she was so glad it was Miss Felton. So glad.

"You can't get away from being a schoolma'am," the man whispered to Miss Felton, "not even on a mystery tour."

Enid shrivelled up inside her. Of course, Miss Felton was cross to see a school kid there. Under her smile she was cross.

Enid wanted to degrade herself completely, fall on her knees and bury her face in Miss Felton's skirt and sob out her apologies. And she wanted to take Miss Felton's shopping bag and hold it carefully and holily for her. And also she wanted to slap Miss Felton in the face.

"Well, there's lucky, *Enid.*"

Of course it was Bessie Eynon. Nobody else would shout a thing out in such a high soft voice. Flabby thing.

"Shift up, gal," Bessie said, flopping down beside her. "You going on this trip too? Well, well, fancy seeing you. 'S ages since I seen you last. I'm going out with a different boy now, too. Works in James the ironmonger's, dark hair, *rather* slim. Well, well, it's funny meeting you . . . ."

Enid could imagine what Miss Felton would be thinking. She didn't dare look to see her ironic high smile. She knew. She just sat rigid and everything was painful and hard, like dripping black granite closing in on her in a nightmare.

"Yes, 'e lives in our street, and I wasn't very attracted at first, — you don't *bother* to go with a boy if you know him well, like, do you? — but 'e's very good looking since 'e left school, and I thought to myself 'Why not, anyway?' — it's a proper affair now. Wonder you 'aven't seen us together . . . ."

Bessie went on and on in her high singsong voice. It was terrible. Enid hoped her boy would come soon. He said he might be late and Bessie was bouncing up and down in her seat with anxiety.

He didn't come.

The driver started the engine and the bus proprietor came in with a sealed envelope and everybody turned round and listened excitedly.

"Ladies and gents," he said. "This is the tenth of our popular mystery tours, and in this sealed letter is the instructions to the driver which he will open a mile out of town. Only then, ladies and gents, will you know where you are being taken. And I promise you your hopes and expectations will not be dashed. Pleasant journey to you."

He beamed on them, picking at a pimple on his chin and presenting the envelope to the driver as though it were a medal for life-saving.

"There's a nice man," Bessie said, momentarily forgetting her boy's desertion in the strong and pungent scent of another male.

The bus proprietor shook hands with the driver and waved to them all and returned to the pub from which he had emerged.

The mystery tour began.

"I never did think much of him. I was only going with him for the time being. Well, it's no good making excuses to *me* — if 'e goes on 'is knees till 'is face is blue I won't go out with 'im again . . . ." Bessie launched into a bitter denunciation of all men.

The jolting of the bus, the rattle of loose screws, the throb of the engine, the hot heady petrol smell, Bessie's loud and resentful voice . . . Miss Felton talking in an undertone and her man taking his pipe out of his mouth to reply and pointing with the wet stem at Bessie . . . . The fat woman pealing with laughter in the seat benind, the heat forming a mist on the closed windows and blurring the hedges and fields that swung away and behind them like spokes from a whirling hub . . . .

"Nice change, isn't it?" Bessie said, recovering her verve. "Takes you *out* of yourself, somehow, don't it?"

Bessie began looking at Miss Felton's man, trying to catch his eye. After a while she succeeded. She blushed and dropped her eyes demurely and nudged Enid secretly with her elbow.

"Smart chap," she said breathlessly, "I wouldn't mind being *her*. Who is she?"

Enid tried to say "Miss Felton, our music mistress." But something obstructed her, some thick lump in her lungs and throat. Her head was swimming.

She nodded her head.

"Don't know," she gasped.

And then, incredibly, so utterly had her misery converted her into a jolted part of the plush upholstery of the bus, the engine stopped boring through her and the driver pulled the bus into the side of the road.

"We 'ave now reached the famous beauty spot of the Welsh 'ighlands," he said automatically. "If you will pull down the window you will find a most wonderful view to admire. We are stopping thirty minutes by 'ere in order that our patrons may see for themselves the sights of Nature in these parts."

He dropped back into his seat and took a newspaper out of his pocket.

"Coming?" Enid said sickly.

"Me?" Bessie said, opening her eyes as wide as she could because Miss Felton's man was looking at her. "Catch me spoiling my shoes. The grass will be soaking and there's nothing there anyway. *You* go, though. Don't stay because of me, my dear."

"All right," said Enid listlessly, and unsteadily she walked down the aisle behind Miss Felton and her man. The fat woman behind her was sleeping with her mouth open.

The road felt strange under her soles. She felt like someone new born and bewildered and lost. The mountains rose in great masses of heathery rock, range after range, and the cloudy sky was as barren and unchartered as the land. She felt so small that it didn't matter about the panic inside her. It was just a pinpoint, a rotten little crab apple lying in the wet grass of a huge orchard. A plover swept over her and sailed down into the long bog-grass, crying to itself about nothing at all. She didn't mind now. She wasn't alone, or embarrassed about Miss Felton or mad with Bessie. She watched Miss Felton slip her hand into the crook of her man's elbow and set off across the moor to a clump of trees down in the combe. When they had gone a little way Enid set off quietly by herself, plucking tufts of cotton grass as she went and skimming the dewdrops off the long grasses.

When she came to the river bank she looked round, and there was nobody there to see her. Nobody. It was so lovely. She was by herself. Herself. She jumped into the air, flinging her hands up, and kissing the sky. And then, because action was spendthrift, she kneeled down by the rushes and looked at her face in the pool. It was herself. There was nobody else.

The river was dammed up for the sheep dipping by a board slipped into a cemented groove. A shute of smooth rock sloped down into the next pool. Little trickles of water slid under the board and spread into a little fan of smooth bubbles, keeping the moss dark green and slimy. Enid bent over to touch the moss with her fingers. Only then did she see the baby eels. There were *heaps* of them, tiny wriggling brown baby eels. They were trying to get up the slimy slope of rock into the next pool. They were wriggling all over each other, all over each other. It made her wriggle inside. She could feel them trying to get up the rock, wriggling against each other and against the dribble of water that washed them back and back and back. Their eyes were too small for her to see them, and they had such funny bodies, so thin and with no features, no hands or anything. They didn't seem real at all. They were the same all over. And yet they were *alive*, terribly alive, and they *wanted* to get up that slimy rock. It was so strange. She forgot about everything, bending over the baby eels.

When at last she did go she was thinking about them all the time, like a peasant returning home after seeing a miracle performed in the market place. Yes, it was *true*. And suddenly she felt happier than she had ever felt in her life. She hadn't felt happy watching the eels. They were all horrible in a way, being so different, and fighting with all they had, blindly, to climb the rock. But they had done something to her and now she was utterly happy. Disembodied. Her hands flung about in free, beautiful gestures and her feet tripped and ran. Her head tossed itself back and her voice came singing out of her mouth. She ran up the river bank and when she came to the first tree in the alder grove below the farm she flung her arms round it and rubbed her cheek against the mossed and flaky bark. There were little insects in the bark, hundreds of them, doing nothing except cling to rotting cracks and sleep. She released the tree as a light-hearted lover might push her beloved fondly away from her.

"No. No."

Enid froze with terror and stood stockstill.

"*No*, I say. *No.*"

It was terrible, the pain in her voice. Miss Felton's voice. They were only five yards away, by the side of the grey rock. She was half sitting up, her arms tight against her sides and her face drawn back taut from her body. He was kneeling, his hands on the ground, like a begging bear going back on all-fours. Enid couldn't see his face. She looked for his face, and couldn't see it, and felt glad for that much. She felt all that swiftly, jab jab jab, in the midst of the petrifying horror of staring at Miss Felton's face. It was white and frightened and ashamed, and twisted with wanting something hateful and unbearable. Her eyes had no home in her face. They stared and stared until they became as devoid of meaning as icicles. And the man whose face she couldn't see suddenly laughed. Enid saw the havoc the laugh made on Miss Felton's face. It shuddered and went blank. She let her head slump forward on her breast. Enid could only see her huddled body now, a poor lump of a thing without a face or a wish or a self. And the begging bear without a face, the thing from which the laughter had come so terribly, was as silent as she.

Enid turned with an immense effort away from them, away, and made her trembling legs carry her away. A rotten twig broke under her shoe. She heard the man catch his breath.

"Hoi," he shouted. And less loudly, "She's been pimping on us."

Enid didn't stop or turn round. Instead she broke into a mad run, racing across the marshy land, stumbling, panting, striving away from the watching man and woman as blindly as the baby eels had striven, the baby eels which would become for ever a bitter pain in her mind.

Alexander's Feast

At home they called her Lizzie. The girls in the shop used to call her Bet. All her girl friends called her Bet. When *he* asked her name she said "Elizabeth," very quietly, her face half turned away from him. He said "How lovely to have a name like that." And she had felt silly and hot all over and ridiculously self-conscious.

Indeed she was never at ease with him. Of course she'd only been with him twice — they'd hardly had time to get used to each other. But she doubted whether she'd ever get used to him, or to herself with him. He was so much better than she, for one thing. He spoke more nicely and had naturally polite ways when she had to be always thinking how to behave; he was *educated*. And more that all that was the constant memory of how she had got on to him — it was no good hiding it from herself, she *had* got on to him. She had never done it before, walked the streets like the other girls every evening. When the shop shut she used always to go straight home and knit or sew or help with the housework and the darning. She knew her own face. Before settling down in the kitchen after tea she used to stick her face in front of the watery mirror in her garret and make it smile. That row of yellowish teeth, how she hated them. And the bony white gum that her upper lip bared. And her skin, so blotchy and lifeless this last year or two. Imagine parading all that up and down town on the look-out!

But the girls had always been on to her about her domestic habit. They regaled her with their own exciting affairs, called her windy, shy, prudish. In the end she went with them; to be exact it was the day she was leaving the shop for good — the day, that is, after the doctor had examined her and told her it would be suicide if she continued standing behind the counter all day, day after day . . . .

Anyway, there it was. She hoped he'd come soon to end this horrible self-disgust and breathe such life into the present that the past would vanish underground. Everybody seemed to be looking at her as she stood outside the new super cinema, the white inhuman ferro-concrete palace. Boys going in looked her all over, coolly. Men glanced at her legs, her thin legs. Women looked right through her. It was like an obscene crucifixion; she felt like vermin.

Her heart gave a great leap when she saw him coming. She smiled with gladness, forgetting her gums.

He took her to the one-and-threepennies, upstairs, at the back. They had to step over the entwined legs of spooning couples to get to their seats. She was so glad when they settled down at last into the dark comfortable plush seats. The comfort and the darkness rose slowly through her body like sap, restoring her, like water flowing cleanly through her, like a healing anaesthetic, blessing her with anonymity. She closed her eyes for a minute, not bothering about the film, until a sudden gust of laughter from the audience startled her into attention. He put a packet of chocolates on her lap, his hand momentarily touching her thigh, making her body quiver, and then retiring into the warm impersonal darkness, leaving his offering on the altar of her lap. She kissed the first chocolate as she put it into her mouth.

The big picture ended five minutes after they entered. The audience stirred with expectation. The organ solo. The town was plastered with announcements of the personal appearance of Louis Burton, the world-famous organist, direct from his American tour, at the illuminated Mighty Wurlitzer. It rose from below the floor. The audience craned their necks. Elizabeth felt the excitement of the subdued buzz of voices.

Yes. Yes. It was rising out of the orchestra pit, the whole cinema trembling with the vibrant opening chords of his signature tune — "Happy days are here again and the sky above is" — the torrent of clapping drowning his triumphant exultant syncopation. He stood up and bowed, his black dinner jacket gleaming like silk in the blue spotlight that was fixed on him, poor moth. The proscenium glowed with exciting coloured lamps, mauve, magenta, crimson lake, sky blue, soft seeping green, — changing, waxing, waning till the blood beat a tattoo.

Louis Burton was playing again before she realised how — how *ugly* he was. Thin greased-back hair, red dome of a forehead, pointed sweaty face and hanging jowl; and as fat as he was tall. Oh, he was ugly. And he was playing so marvellously. The whole building was passionate with his playing. The deep bass chords burst inside her bowels, and when he chose to be sweet, it was like divine ambrosial honey in her mouth, sweet past bearing. He played Tiger Rag and her heart pulsed with daring, with oblivion to the consequences. He played the St. Louis Blues and the abandoned gutter-walking apathy of the theme melted her into an ecstasy of depraved morbid desires. And he was so ugly. His physical presence was a constant counterpoint to the music, drenching the tones and colours of it as lilac scents drench small gardens. It was revolting and irresistible, a foul fascination which brought the sweat out of her and made her body tense and sticky. And then, just then, as the fat stubby fingers made a single-minded Ophelia of her and compelled her body to lie willingly on the seductive smooth flow of the Blue Danube, just then she felt an arm come around her neck and move slowly, terribly slowly, and inevitably downwards, till the hand pressed over her breast. She closed her eyes, shuddering, and let her head fall sideways against his shoulder. When his finger tilted her head back her lips were waiting for him, half-parted. She thought she would die, so completely was her whole life caught up in that kiss. And inextricably fused with it was the image of that fat black-clothed figure, the padded shoulders moving up and down in obedience to the rhythm, the blue spotlight holding him relentlessy, like a fly pinned to a collector's card. She thought she would die. She *was* — yes, *dying* — she couldn't breathe. Oh God! She broke violently loose from the embrace and sat up, dizzy and sick and limp, lips sucking at the black stifling darkness for life. The audience were clapping, cheering; the organ sinkng below the stage, the fat greasy organist was bowing, smiling, as ugly as *sin*. She said, "Will you stay, please? I'm going home, out — I'm sick."

"No, of course, I'll come too," he whispered back.

She was too sick to argue or care. She squeezed blindly past the row of spooning couples, not knowing or minding whether he was following her or not, wanting nothing except to get out. *Out . . . .*

In bed at last, with a cold wet towel on her forehead, in her own friendly bed, she recovered herself slowly and difficultly. He had escorted her home, sitting by her in the bus, never speaking except to ask her how she was. At the door of the house he had left her; yes, without making a date. She had felt the resentment under his polite concern. What was it? The waste of half a crown? Well, he was gone for good. He'd never know now how much she cared for him. He'd forget about her. He was healthy, and young. But she, she wouldn't forget him. He'd be as real as life to her, till the bitter end. He'd never know that it was the first time she had been kissed, either. Would he know what that meant, supposing she *had* told him? Would he have felt the height and depth of it, the passionate fusion of all life and all death that had been in that kiss? Or would he have said to himself "Better late than never!'"? She turned onto her side and breathed quietly. How lovely it was, just to breathe. She kept the wet towel from slipping off her forehead by holding it with her tired hand. The towel wasn't cold now. Mother would change it when she came up with the milk and brandy. The doctor had said brandy was good for her. It tasted nice, anyway, tingling in her veins. She almost wished she *had* spoken, instead of just letting him go without a final effort. But her voice wouldn't come. Yes, she *had* tried. And failed. And it was just as well. It would have been asking too much, asking him to come and visit her when she had gone to the T.B. Sanatorium. It would have been bad manners, too . . . .

Her sister brought her milk and brandy up, changed the towel, and sat by her bed while she sipped the glass, and prattled to her about county school. Edith was full of life, and intelligent too. She was having an education.

Lizzie smiled faintly when Edith asked her about the pictures. *Was* he great, that Louis Burton they were advertising about in town? Lizzie said yes, he was marvellous. Edith must go on Friday night, or Saturday matinee. And then, as Edith tucked her into bed and took her empty glass away, she whispered in her thin voice "Be a sport, Edie, when you go to the pictures; get me his autograph will you? I dare you to get it, see?"